DEAD

LIES

DREAMING

CHARLES STROSS

orbitbooks.net

ORBIT

First published in Great Britain in 2020 by Orbit

1 3 5 7 9 10 8 6 4 2

Copyright © 2020 by Charles Stross

Excerpt from *Ink & Sigil* by Kevin Hearne
Copyright © 2020 by Kevin Hearne

The moral right of the author has been asserted.

A CIP catalogue record for this book
is available from the British Library.

ISBN 978-0-356-51380-5

Typeset in Sabon by M Rules
Printed and bound in Great Britain by Clays Ltd, Elcograf, S.p.A.

Papers used by Orbit are from well-managed forests
and other responsible sources.

Orbit
An imprint of
Little, Brown Book Group
Carmelite House
50 Victoria Embankment
London EC4Y 0DZ

An Hachette UK Company
www.hachette.co.uk

www.orbitbooks.net

In memory of Cecilie Stross
17 April 1929–8 September 2019

CRIMES AGAINST
MARKETING

Imp froze as he rounded the corner onto Regent Street, and saw four elven warriors shackling a Santa to a stainless-steel cross outside Hamleys Toy Shop.

"Now *that's* not something you see every day," Doc drawled shakily. His fake bravado didn't fool anyone.

Game Boy shook his head and blew a scummy pink bubble. When the *alfär* executioner held his heavy-duty electric screwdriver against Santa's wrist, the screams were audible over the rumble of passing buses. Game Boy's gum bubble burst; blood dripped from Santa's polyester sleeve. Numb-faced police officers blocked the pavement to either side, directing the flood of Christmas shoppers across the street, holding up the traffic.

This was the second public execution they'd run across this week, but it still had the power to shock. "What's this one in aid of?" Imp asked wearily, as Game Boy slurped his gum back in and gave him a guilty, sidelong glance: "That's disgusting, kid. Show some respect."

"Hold on, I'm reading." Doc squinted at one of the execution notices taped to the lamp posts. "Huh. He's an unregistered transhuman." Superpowered, in other words. *Like us* went without saying. "Identifies as, well, Santa. Guilty of breaking and entering, animal cruelty, flying under the influence, violating controlled airspace—" his eyebrows rose steadily—"human trafficking, slave labor, shoplifting toys, breaking rabies quarantine with reindeer." Which explained why he was being scragged outside the world's biggest toy shop. Under the old regime the worst he'd have gotten would have been a couple of years in the slammer, but the New Management had brought back the eighteenth-century Bloody Code, so named because it prescribed capital punishment for just about everything.

"Fuck." Deliverator turned her back on the scene, shoulders hunched—from anger, not fear, Imp figured.

Imp shook himself. "C'mon, guys." As their self-appointed leader, it was up to him to keep them moving. He detoured around the execution site and marched smartly into the toy shop. Game Boy drifted in his wake, followed (in his usual desultory manner) by Doc and, finally, Del, shivering and averting her eyes.

The New Management had taken over the British government some nine months ago, and Del wasn't handling the changes they'd wrought very well. Admittedly, life with an Elder God for Prime Minister was harsh, especially for the fringes of society. But to Imp's way of thinking, Del's perpetually seething low-key state of rage was a potentially lethal weakness. Imp expended considerable emotional labor on a daily basis, keeping his more vulnerable housemates from losing their shit, then they stumbled on something like *this* on their way to a job.

"Don't worry," he reassured her, "it's probably not real—a seasonal marketing stunt or something." He sent her a tiny mental *push* to solidify the supposition in her head, soothing the raw edges of her outrage. It was his talent: with a little mental muscle, he could convince anyone of absolutely *anything* by force of will alone—but only for a short while, and only face to face. Normally he tried not to use it on his friends, but prior consent be damned if it kept Del from making a scene and bringing the Black Pharaoh's wrath down on their heads. "By the time we've finished, Santa will be taking a tea break, yucking it up with his pointy-eared homies."

Doc was about to contradict him, but Game Boy elbowed him in the ribs sharply and gave him a wide-eyed look, and Doc held his tongue. *Time for a distraction*, Imp thought. He spread his arms as if in benediction and turned in place, in the glittering lobby of the largest and oldest toy shop in the world. "Behold!" he cried. "The place where dreams are made!" He nudged Del and added, "And by dreams, I mean supervillains."

The ground floor of Hamleys was decked out in green baize carpet and bleached pine. A gigantic Christmas tree loomed over elaborate Lego and Playmobil displays on every side. Imp led them towards a bank of escalators, passing between dueling toy franchises—a line of Disney Princess demonstrators facing off against a My Little Police Unicorn cavalry charge. The magic staircase lofted them into childhood heaven: model railways and Sylvanian Families, party costumes and wishes granted. A seasonal frosting of spray-on snow dusted every display surface like the icing sugar on a diabetic nightmare.

"What are we looking for again?" Doc asked.

"Three motorized turnouts, a bunch of track segments, an' a kicking second locomotive," said Game Boy.

Imp sighed. Game Boy was single-minded. "Priorities, kid: you've got to get your ducks in a row. We need the costumes first. Your model railroad will have to wait for another time."

"But, but, *shiny*!" Game Boy's face was pressed up against

a display cabinet almost as high as the top of his flaming orange crop-top, nostrils flaring twin plumes of condensation on the glass in front of a halogen-spotlit Class 23 Baby Deltic in 1970s British Rail livery.

"*Homie.*" Del laid a warning hand on Game Boy's scrawny upper arm.

"It's, like, only three hundred quid . . ."

"Dude. You can't afford it right now. Add it to your Amazon wish list and move on."

But Game Boy was in love. "If I was to, uh, make it fall into your messenger bag you could—"

Imp spoke out of the corner of his mouth: "Camera, ceiling, ten o'clock, range three meters. Camera, ceiling, your six o'clock, range eight meters. Store detective, my three o'clock, other side of the floor. And we still haven't got the costumes. Are you feeling lucky?"

The giant toy store's interior had been carefully designed by retail psychologists to engage the imagination. More recently, management had brought in a sorcerer to amplify it: everything felt bright and colorful and hyperreal, popping like the onset of an acid trip. But Imp instinctively knew that any trip he did here would go bad fast. Even the normally ebullient Game Boy was cowed by the possible consequences of what they were about to do. Imp, as ringleader, felt a sick sense of dread—like an apprehension of gangrene in toyland—that he was at pains to conceal from his crew.

The New Management had reintroduced the Bloody Code (the old eighteenth-century penal system that prescribed the death penalty for pretty much everything above the level of a parking ticket) during the Queen's Speech at the state opening of Parliament earlier this year. Sensible shoplifters were reconsidering their life choices. Not that shoplifting was *ever* a sensible career choice, but hanging was a brutally disproportionate response. Imp, despite his other character flaws, didn't want to see any of his crew executed. "*Are* you feeling lucky?" he repeated, backing it up with a gentle morale-boosting push.

Game Boy's shoulders slumped. "Pervert suits first," he mumbled.

"I'm a professional, I've got a store card and I know how to work it," Imp reminded them. "DeeDee, are you ready to motivate?"

Doc Depression could pass for a store detective himself, in his seedy Oxfam charity-case suit and skinny tie. "If necessary."

"Let's go, then."

Party costumes were on the third floor, and once they ran the gauntlet of pink tulle princess gowns and *alfär* warrior armor they came to an aisle of reasonably priced outfits for adult party hosts: clowns, mostly, but also pirates, princesses (subtype: grown-up), bank robbers (in questionable taste), escaped convicts (ditto), highwaymen (Imp wasn't going *anywhere* near *that* gibbet, thank you very much), and, finally, transhumans. Fictional cops like Judge Dredd and Judge Death (very edgy, very of the moment) vied with the Marvel and DC Comics franchises, then real-life capes like Officer Friendly, White Mask, and the other Home Office supes.

"You are *not* putting me in a dress!" Game Boy shrilled as Del menaced him with a frilly black and white maid's uniform.

"But you look better in a frock than I do——" Del pitched her tone low, trying for sultry and missing by a mile.

"Fuck off!" Game Boy recoiled as Del leaned over him, propping herself against a clothes rail.

"Children!" Imp stepped between them, a bundle of adult

cape-and-mask outfits draped over his arm. "Store detective, two o'clock, closing." He tipped Doc a nod and wink. "Showtime." To Del, he added, "Stop triggering Game Boy, *asshole*."

"Aw, you're no fun." Deliverator punched him lightly on the shoulder, then slid the maid's uniform back on the rail, defusing Game Boy's impending panic attack.

The store detective loomed over Imp like an overly polite brick wall. "Can I help you gentlemen and lady?" he asked, clearly winding up to eject them from the store.

"Yes, you absolutely can!" Imp smiled and *pushed*. "My sister just told me I'm hosting a surprise birthday party for my nephew, the theme is Capes and Villains, we're really short on time, and we all need grown-up costumes! Can you point me at the changing rooms?" He held up his zeroed-out John Lewis store card. "Amex Black," he added, and *pushed* again.

A minute later they were inside the changing room area. "Here, try this one," Imp said, handing Game Boy an outfit: Robin, from Wes Craven's *Arkham Asylum* remake. Game Boy's gasps were slowing, the nervous whoops coming under control. "Robin's about your build, isn't he? You won't have to femme up."

"Fuuu—thanks." Game Boy swallowed and ducked into a cubicle, limp with gratitude.

Imp turned to Del. "Just for *that* you're playing Princess Shuri." He shoved a bagged-up costume at her. "Serves you right for gaslighting the boy: you can be the odd one out in this rodeo."

"I'm more than my skin color, bitch." She lowered her brows and glared. For a moment Imp thought she was going to punch him, but then the tension left her shoulders and she chuckled darkly. "I'd rather be Harley Quinn. I could hit people with a baseball bat."

"Payback for GeeBee." He turned to Doc. "*You're* the Bat."

Doc's mouth turned down. "Gloomy and introspective, what kind of disguise do you call *that*?" He blinked at Imp. "Hey, who are you going to be?"

Imp took a step back in the direction of his own changing room. "I'm the Joker, of course!" he declared, beaming at Doc. "I've got a scheme, a crazy scheme, to take over Gotham City! But to bankroll it we've got to start by robbing a strong room. Suit up, everyone, Showtime starts in five."

While Santa's public execution was taking place on Regent Street, Evelyn Starkey was taking an hour-long break from work to browse the most exclusive kitchenware store in Mayfair. As Imp was declaring his nefarious goals, she was staring intently at a gleaming display of microplane graters.

"Beautiful," she murmured, visions of their uses dancing in her mind's eye. "Guard!"

"Miss?" Her new bodyguard, two meters of steroid-enhanced gammon in a black Hugo Boss suit, was unprepared. He clearly hadn't bothered to read the checklist Human Resources always included in the briefing pack for her new minions. "What is it, Miss?" He glanced around dimly, nostrils flaring as he searched for threats.

"Take a memo," she drawled. "Re: Rupert's request for possible performance improvement incentives. HR to investigate the use of microplane technology for epidermal degloving as a possible alternative to current Yakuza protocol. A/B testing to be applied after the next stack-ranking identifies suitable candidates for downsizing who need remedial motivation."

Rupert, her boss, had tasked Eve with finding a modern

replacement for the Bigge Organization's use of the Yakuza protocol for motivating underachievers; after all, pinkie fingers could be surgically reattached. But she hadn't expected to find a likely candidate in a kitchenware store. Her gaze slid along the aisle to a fetching display of long-handled Perspex and chrome grinders loaded with pink Himalayan rock salt. "Fetch me two of those, if you please. And one of every kind of microplane grater that's available from stock."

"Are yer buyin' a new kitchen, Miss?" asked the Gammon, grinning like a self-satisfied Rottweiler who didn't quite understand that his mistress required him to return the postman's hand to its owner without further ado. "I've got a mate in Logistics at IKEA 'oo can fix you up wiv—"

"You can stop talking now." She smiled sweetly up at the guard—he overtopped her in spite of her five-inch heels—until the color drained from his face. Then she showed him her teeth. "That's better. You will speak to me only when I address you directly, or to warn me of an immediate threat. Otherwise, company regulations require me to have your larynx surgically inerted. You would find that unpleasant, don't you agree?" He nodded frantically: obviously he'd at least listened to *that* part of his induction interview. The Bigge Organization paid astoundingly well, but its approach to discipline was draconian. "Jolly good! Remember, I want one of everything available from this display, and two of those *absolutely delightful* salt grinders." She let the threat hang in the air as she turned away from the assorted graters, zesters, and shavers, then strolled towards a display of meat tenderizers. Perhaps the Gammon suspected she was bluffing, but he wasn't stupid enough to test her: he simply trailed in her wake, silently cringing. *Gutless*, she thought. That would never do.

Eve's lunch hour was about to be interrupted. Being on

duty 24/7 had certain drawbacks, and the switchboard chose just that moment to redirect a priority caller to her personal phone. Her only warning was a double-beep from her earpiece. She answered instantly: "Mr. Bigge's secretary, how may I help you?" (That Eve was actually an executive assistant, had a degree in Business and Accountancy with an MBA on top, and was stock exchange certified and licensed to trade in her own right meant nothing to Rupert, who insisted she answer his calls this way.)

"Eve?" The privileged Home Counties drawl was tantalizingly familiar, but it took her a second to work out precisely which member of Rupert's inner circle was speaking. They all did their utmost to sound identically bored, rich, and disdainful, as if in the grip of some collective phobia of being seen to be busy, poor, and desperate.

"James! How delightful to hear from you. What can I do for you today?" James Wall was one of Rupert's fund managers.

"I'm well, how are you, I'm trying to get hold of Rupert to give him a sitrep on the Macao transfer and the funding call for the Dubai venture but he's not picking up his phone or answering his messages—is something wrong?" It came out as a torrent of finely tuned dealer desk bullshit and none of it had anything to do with the real reason for his call, but Evelyn knew exactly what it was about all the same. James was effective at his job, but high maintenance—something Rupert tolerated only because they'd been at Eton together, and the boss had a soft spot for his old school friend. As long as James continued to show a 6 percent or greater annual return on the £600M fund he managed, Rupert would keep him in Krug, Maseratis, and hookers—this was Eve's understanding—but James needed to hear his master's voice at least once a week or he got anxious, and Rupert had been busy with more important matters of late. Matters like pursuing good relations with the New Management.

"Why isn't he answering his private number? Is everything all right?" James asked anxiously.

"I'm sure everything is going *swimmingly*," Evelyn gushed, holding up a warning hand to keep her minion from misguidedly leaping to battle stations. "But I tell you what, James, I'll make a note to have Rupert call you *specially*, just to set your mind at ease, as soon as he's out of his meeting with"—she lowered her voice confidingly—"Number Eleven."

11 Downing Street was the official residence of the Chancellor of the Exchequer, the minister in charge of the British government's finances. As the old saying had it, if you owe the bank ten thousand pounds, you have a problem; if you owe the bank ten million pounds, the bank has a problem; and if you owe the bank ten billion pounds, the Chancellor has a problem. The New Management took a drastic approach to dealing with problems—they simply *went away*, as did the skeletons of the people who created them—so Rupert was always at pains to keep Number Eleven briefed, ideally well in advance, about his more adventurous money-making initiatives. "It's on the down-low, so please keep it to yourself," she purred.

"Oh, oh! Of course!" James sounded ecstatic. *Pants on fire*, she thought to herself. She'd just thrown him a juicy piece of gossip, *of course* he'd share it with the boys in the back room at his gentleman's club. She'd also implied that he had been trumped in Rupe's affections only by a Very Important Person Indeed, namely the Black Pharaoh's personal treasurer. James's ego duly stroked into turgidity, he sprayed gratitude like jizz in a skin flick, carrying on in a most distasteful manner until Eve maneuvered him into hanging up.

It left her feeling faintly unclean. Sometimes her job was a bit too much like being a phone sex line operator for comfort.

But Eve had always found it easy to lose herself in work, taking joy from the efficient discharge of her duties. Now her gaze fell upon a chromed-steel rack that dangled from the ceiling on a pulley-and-chain arrangement. It was currently festooned with tinsel and saucepans, but it was clearly destined for a higher purpose—one that involved overly needy merchant bankers who failed to live up to Rupert's exacting requirements.

"I'll have one of those, too," she declared. "And as many meat hooks as it'll take."

Meanwhile, in a sparsely furnished cubicle in a cheap office in Clapham, an operational asset known to senior management as ABLE ARCHER was reading her latest work assignment with increasing displeasure. "What the—" *fucking fuck,* she continued silently, biting her cheek in disgust, hyper-aware of her manager breathing stertorously as he leaned over the back of her chair—"*whatting what* is this about?" Her voice cracked and Bill retreated a half step. "I'm on a zero-hours contract and they seriously expect me to get by on two half-day shifts next week? What *is* this? Is it some kind of punishment for not brushing my teeth last Tuesday? I mean, what the hell?"

"Don't blame me, Darling, I don't hand out trial dates!" Bill's nasal whine rose to a tooth-grinding pitch. "There's not much call for escorts this month, that's all! Computer says you're blocked from doing foot work in preparation for some other job that hasn't come through, so I can't reassign you. Otherwise I could put you back on the stands for Saturday's Millwall friendly. So, eh, two mornings on prisoner transport between Wandsworth nick and the courts is all you're getting until the other job turns up."

"But that's—" Wendy did the numbers—"fuck, I'll be relying on Universal Credit." She shook her head in dismay. At £10 per hour the two half shifts would pay her a measly £100, about a quarter of the weekly rent on her bedsit. UC would kick in eventually, but the money would take at least six weeks to come through, and the rent was due in just over a fortnight. Never mind food, heat, her phone . . . "I need at least two whole days' extra work to make ends meet, otherwise I'm fucked."

"Language, *Darling*." Bill invariably had a fit of the vapors whenever a woman used strong language in his presence: just another of the ways he pissed Wendy off without even trying.

"You know that's not my fucking name!" Not that complaining yet again would make him stop. He only *Darling*'d her because he knew it annoyed, and he could get away with it. She bounced to her feet. "Fuck, I'd be better off turning tricks on the harborfront in Portsmouth." She unclipped her rentacop tie, loosened her collar, and turned on her heel. "If you've got no fucking work for me until Thursday I'm fucking out of here."

"Not so fast, Wendy Deere. Got a moment?"

Wendy froze. Bill recovered first: "Mister Gibson, sir? Sorry, I didn't see you."

Gibson actually wore the company uniform as if he meant it, unlike Bill, who occupied his uniform like a hermit crab living in an abandoned Coke can. Aside from the lack of police insignia, Gibson was the spitting image of Wendy's old Chief Inspector—which made her jaw muscles clench and her hands instinctively curl for other reasons. But that was unfair to Gibson. He'd never been a cop. He'd left the army to pursue a career in HiveCo Services management, and he ran her (and Bill's) division reasonably fairly, which was more than she could say for Chief Inspector Barrett.

"Of course you didn't see me," he agreed. He looked at Wendy. "Deere, Bill's missing your job because it came through to my desk. Come up to my office and we'll discuss it." To Bill, he added, "You'll need to find someone else for the prison transport. I'm pulling Wendy off your roster indefinitely."

"But there's a level three prisoner due up in front of the beak on Tuesday and Darling's my only certificated escort for level threes!" Bill whined. "Where am I going to—"

Gibson waved Wendy towards the door with something suspiciously close to a wink. She hot-footed it to the stairwell, despite the impulse to eavesdrop on Gibson, who seemed set to tear Bill a new one. Halfway up the stairs she remembered her clip-on tie. *This had better pay more than a tenner an hour*, she thought, ducking into the toilet to smarten up before she stepped into management country.

Her grandboss had an office with a door of its own, although his name card fitted neatly inside a slot as impersonal as the label on a filing cabinet. Wendy knocked just in case, then let herself in and sat in the visitor's chair, leaving the door ajar. A minute or so later Gibson entered. "Make yourself at home, why don't you," he said, sliding into the much nicer office chair behind the desk.

Wendy shrugged, thought of a sarcastic response, then reconsidered her position and asked, "What do you want?"

Gibson fixed her with a stare that probably terrified hungover second lieutenants, but bored Wendy. *More bloody male posturing.* "Bill gets away with it because he's a superannuated bouncer. What's *your* excuse, Detective Constable Deere?"

Wendy crossed her arms. "*Ex*-DC," she griped, "who does not play well with assholes. I've been having a *really bad month* so far. Can we get to the point so I can hand in my notice and go look for a real job—one that pays my rent on time?"

Gibson's brows furrowed. "Really?" he asked, mirroring her crossed arms. It was so transparent she nearly laughed.

"Yes, really. You heard Bill giving me ten hours this week? Last week it was fourteen, and I'm on a zero-hours contract, no side-hustles allowed. Seriously, I'm living on cat food and lentils—"

"—Would a raise change your mind about quitting? Say, to fifty an hour?"

Gibson's offer caught her by surprise. Wendy blinked. "Is that some kind of joke? Because it's not funny."

Gibson looked displeased. "It's not meant to be. Some-one fucked with your personnel file and assigned you the wrong—lower—grade. Your basic hourly rate—you've been getting a tenner an hour for rentabody work, haven't you? You should have been on twenty-two fifty. And because of the non-compete clause, you should have been getting ten-fifty an hour as a retainer while you're on-call for up to forty hours a week."

"But—" Utterly gobsmacked, Wendy stared across the ta-ble. "What's the catch?" she demanded, barely able to credit her own ears.

"The catch is, you're being regraded. You'll be reporting directly to me, as a Field Investigator (Transhuman). No more Bill. Your hours for detection and retrieval assignments booked through HiveCo Security will be paid at fifty an hour." He slid a contract towards her. "You need to sign here and here."

Wendy's eyes slitted as she stared at the paper. *Hang on a moment.* "You said they fucked up my contract," she muttered to herself. Louder: "So this is HR's fault. I want this backdated."

Gibson straightened. "I don't have the authority to backdate the regrading—it's a promotion," he pointed out. "I can recommend that they take it to payroll and do something about it, but—"

"That's perfectly all right." Wendy took the contract in hand and smiled, starting to stand. "You don't have to pay me and I don't have to work here any more."

Gibson surrendered. "All right! I'll see if I can shake something loose. I don't think I can make backdating the promotion fly, but you were supposed to be on a higher grade plus retainer all along, so you're due a bunch of hours you haven't been paid for . . ."

Wendy nodded. "Six months," she said. She sat down again, calculating rapidly. Twenty hours a week for six months at a tenner an hour for sitting around with her thumb up her ass added up to five large—enough to pay off her credit card and keep the student loan company from repossessing the furniture. And that was before taking into account her worked hours at nearly double her previous pay grade. "That's my minimum if you want me to stay. Not budging on that." She leaned forward and began to read the contract. "This is sweet." She read some more. "Still looking for the catch." She glanced up. "Where is it buried?"

Gibson watched her. "It depends on what you mean by a catch," he said slowly. "Really, it was probably just an HR cock-up—unless someone had the knives out for you. You were pegged as a level two transhuman and former trainee constable, hence the rentabody jobs and the prisoner transports. But you're not, are you? You graduated from Hendon Police College and made detective, in addition to being a level three-plus. Incidentally, why *did* you leave the force?"

"I had a polite disagreement with Chief Inspector Grabby Hands." Chief Inspector Barrett. "It was him or me, and he had rank. Do you need me to draw you a diagram?"

"No, that won't be necessary." Gibson nodded to himself, as if confirming a suspicion. He seemed indecently satisfied, but she was damned if she could see why. "Their loss, our gain, and incidentally you *may* have exposed an issue between HR and the Met which will have to be dealt with—but that's not your problem. Leave it to me. It'll make it easier to get your pay backdated, though," he added, almost as an afterthought.

"What exactly is it you want me to do?" Wendy leaned forward. "You said something about transhuman field investigations . . ."

"Well spotted." Gibson cracked a smile. "We're bidding for a Home Office contract to supply thief-taking services to the Bench. They're outsourcing stuff these days, as you've probably noticed, and this *is* a time of cuts. What are the Met down to—sixty percent of their 2010 budget in just five years? It's austerity inherited from the previous government, but the New Management sees no reason to reverse it. They're outsourcing certain tasks to the private sector—specialities where they lack a history of institutional coverage."

"By specialities you mean transhuman crime?" She sat up, small print forgotten.

"Yes, Deere, and you're both a detective *and* a transhuman. They've already brought back the Bloody Code, is it any surprise that they're bringing back the old thief-takers, too? But this time they're imposing modern management practices: nobody wants to see a Jonathan Wilde with superpowers."

She filed the name for later, planning a Wikipedia attack once she got her head around where this discussion was heading. "You're going to be billing them a lot more than fifty an hour for me," she stated.

Gibson nodded. "Yes. And they'll pay, too." He raised a finger. "But don't imagine you can get in on the business as a freelancer. They're only talking to big outsourcing agencies: G4S, Serco, and us. Still, fifty an hour plus twenty-one seventy when you're on standby is only a starting salary. Transhumans are all unique, and if you can deliver the goods I can recommend a raise in due course."

"Well . . ." At a loss for words, Wendy picked up the contract. The gear train of the dismal engine propelling her seemingly inexorable descent into poverty had seized: she was in a state of barely controlled shock. "I—I need to think about this."

"Take your time." He smiled at her. "Go home, read it carefully, and come back tomorrow morning. I'll talk you through it. There's a nondisclosure agreement and an exclusivity clause once you sign on, just so you know what to expect. I'll see if I can sort out your back pay in the meantime. How does that sound?"

"How long do you think it'll be before I'm needed?" she asked.

"No time at all, we've already got a contract pending. Starts tomorrow."

"Can you tell me anything about it?" She leaned forward. "The first forty-eight hours are golden . . ."

"Signature first, then nondisclosure agreement. I can't brief you ahead of time."

Wendy tried again. "Can you give me a clue what this is about? Just a silhouette, sir?"

"There's a transhuman thief. You're a transhuman thief-taker." He shrugged. "There may also be some stolen goods that need retrieving. That's what thief-takers traditionally did, wasn't it? That and dragging the perps down to the Old Bailey for sentencing before they danced the Tyburn Tango."

"I don't think they'd invented the tango in the eighteenth century, sir."

"Mm-hmm, possibly not. Anyway, that's all for tomorrow. My office, nine o'clock."

Three heroes and a famous fool marched out of the changing room in Hamleys, collected their unnaturally obliging escort from Store Security, and followed him through the keypad-locked door into the back offices.

"Does my butt look big in this?" Robin hissed through tightly pursed lips.

"Your cape covers your ass: I don't see what you're so upset about," grumped the Bat. "Look at me, I look like a latex fetish show model." He stumbled badly, catching his heel on the hem of his cape—it trailed along the floor behind him—and the store detective caught his elbow just in time to save him from a nasty tumble.

"Easy does it, sir."

"Thanks." The Bat drew himself up to his full one-eighty centimeters and draped the cape over one arm with exaggerated dignity, like a dowager managing the unwieldy train of her gown. "I'll take it from here."

Once behind the magic curtain they entered the wondrous water-stained world of retail management. Toys and color gave way to faded gray carpet tiles, noticeboards on white partition walls, and battered staff lockers.

Retail real estate on Regent Street was among the most expensive in Europe, far too costly to waste on stockrooms and non-essential offices that could be moved off-site. But some functions were business-critical and had to be housed above the sales floor. Among these was the strong room where locked cash drawers were taken and checked, then prepared for bank transfer via armored car. Over 90 percent of the store's receipts came by electronic payment these days, but that still left a million pounds in cash to process over the pre-Christmas season. On a busy Saturday like today, the strong room might have up to a hundred thousand pounds in notes and coin on hand by close of business—and soon, if Imp had his way, some of it would be in *his* hands.

A fine joke, he thought.

"Who's in charge of the strong room?" he asked the store detective, giving just a little extra push to loosen his tongue.

"One of the audit team leaders," their escort blabbed happily. "Probably Bob or Alice, but it's the weekend so it's anybody's guess who's on. They'll be watched by an assistant manager and two security guards as they count each trolley in, and the trolley team has two shop staff and two guards whenever they're out on the floor. It's quite labor-intensive, you can see why they're so eager to go fully contactless, it'll make my job easier, too—"

"Can you get past the guards if I shut down the managers?" the Bat asked Robin, hanging back behind Imp and his hapless victim.

"Sure, if I've got enough space to work in." Game Boy glowered at the Black Panther: "You up for a home run, Princess?"

"Abso-fucking-lutely," Del sneered back at him.

"Welp. Whatever I can grab, I grab, then it's over to you."

The Bat's frown deepened. "I thought the plan was for Dear Leader to sweet-talk us all the way down—"

"Yes, but you know what they say about plans: Always have a backup, right? And that goes double for one of Imp's capers."

They were out of time. Ahead of them, the store detective stopped at an almost aggressively anonymous door, distinguished from the others on this corridor by the presence of a mirrored glass window, a suspiciously robust frame, and another keypad. Their escort pressed a discreet buzzer, then paused. "Who are you again?" he asked, looking mildly puzzled.

"We're the cash collection team you were expecting from HiveCo," Imp said smoothly.

"Oh, right. It's cash collection," the detective spoke into an entryphone. "They're early today."

"We thought you might be near to your floor capacity," Imp explained.

A buzzer sounded and the reinforced door of the strong room swung open.

The room was fronted by a battered desk. One wall was covered by a row of filing cabinets, and at the back of the room stood an enormous safe. Camera bubbles protruded from every corner of the ceiling, electronic mushrooms dripping the mold spores of money. The air was heavy with the stale smell of recirculated bank notes battling it out with a nostril-stinging brew of cleaning fluids. A tired-looking woman sat at the front desk, feeding bundles of loose twenty-pound notes through a counting and binding machine. She looked up. "Hey, Ralph, what's with the fancy dress—"

"I'm not sure, Amy, they didn't—"

Imp flourished a corner-clipped Albanian passport at Amy: "We're your scheduled cash escort from HiveCo, ma'am." He pushed *hard*, radiating an oppressive aura of beneficence and sincerity. "We're dressed like members of staff from the DC and Marvel tie-in concessions instead of being in uniform because we had a tip-off. A gang are reported to be planning a robbery between here and the van, so we're using a new stealthy transport protocol." To the store detective: "You've done an excellent job! But you're overdue for your coffee break. Why don't you go and put your feet up for a while? You've certainly earned it!"

"Gosh." Amy, the audit manager, wilted visibly under the strain of reconciling Imp's narrative with her expectations. "Nobody told me . . . but I suppose . . ."

Her assistant's head nodded like a lucky cat, but the guard to the left of the vault began to stand. Unlike the others, he had some resistance to Imp's mind manipulation. "Hey—"

The Bat stepped up beside the Joker, nostrils flaring. "Don't you worry about anything," Doc intoned, frowning as he tamped his emotional state down into a concentrated bolus of apathy and shoved it at the troublemaker. "I've got it all covered." He laid a hand on the Joker's pin-striped shoulder as he continued: "You can relax. In fact, you *want* to relax. You're really tired, it's been a long day, and you slept badly last night. We've got your back, and you can rely on Robin and the Bat to take care of it from here."

Amy the auditor slumped, open-mouthed, drooling a little under the impact of Imp's assault. "Everything is totally under control!" he told her, hamming it up for the cameras in character as the Joker. "Nothing to see here!" He produced a heavy-duty refuse sack from his sleeve with a flourish and offered it to his victim. "Cash transfer now," he ordered. Amy nodded vacantly and swept an armful of bundled banknotes off the counting-desk, straight into the open bin liner.

Game Boy nonchalantly approached the vault. "*Niiiice,*" he remarked. The guard on the left ignored him, eyes closed by the burden of Doc Depression's projected exhaustion. Game Boy peered at the electronic keypad and tsked as he noticed the card reader for the first time. "Keys, please," he requested.

"You need to open the vault for the regular cash collection service," Imp told Amy. He moderated his force. He held her soul in the palm of his hand: it was a fragile thing of spun glass and imagination, and it was already warping beneath the weight of his self-confidence. Imp was, he smugly admitted, a bad man. But he took some satisfaction in not being a *terrible* man, and he didn't want to leave a trail of shattered minds in his wake. "The key, Amy," he emphasized.

"The key," Amy echoed. She stumbled towards the vault and produced a keycard which she palmed against the reader. She touched her index finger to a fingerprint scanner, then punched in a six-digit number. The door unlatched and swung open. "The cash transfer." She reached inside and withdrew a canvas satchel secured with padlocks. "I need you to sign for it," she said in a monotone as she presented Imp with the bag.

Then the Bat sneezed, and all hell broke loose.

Doc Depression's peculiar talent required steady concentration. The unbearable itch of old money tickled his sinuses, broke him out of his focus, and shattered his grip on the guards. The left guard, the middle-aged jobsworth who had held out longest against Imp's will-to-believe, jerked upright. "Hey!" he shouted. "Stop!" He slapped his hand against a big red button mounted on the wall. "Stop right there!"

His co-worker, a decade younger and skinnier, bounced to his feet, yanked a baton out of a loop on his utility belt, and waved it at Game Boy. "Yeah, not cool! Hold it right there!"

"I don't think so." Game Boy yanked the satchel away from Amy the auditor and threw it over his shoulder, not bothering to check where it fell. It landed neatly with its strap snug across the Wakandan princess's shoulder. Del jerked her chin once, then sped off with the eerie economy of motion that only she could achieve. Once she had her hands on the goods, nobody on Earth could catch her.

DEAD LIES DREAMING   29

Game Boy turned to leave just as the guards made an ill-judged attempt to stop him. The older guard grabbed; the younger one swept his baton around, evidently aiming for Game Boy, but caught his elder colleague in the face instead. Then the youngster tripped over his own bootlaces—which had inexplicably knotted themselves together—and toppled sideways. Meanwhile the older guard screamed as his nose sprayed blood, then he, too, tripped and fell. As he fell he threw out an arm for balance, but succeeded only in punching the younger guard in the crotch. Then his handcuffs spilled from his belt pouch and closed around his wrist and his colleague's ankle. The youngster flailed around for a few seconds before his cuffs fell out too, and mysteriously shackled his free wrist to the leg of Amy's desk.

Game Boy stepped over the fallen guards as if nothing untoward had happened: "I'm done here," he announced, then walked out the door. The Bat shook his head, then trailed after him. Elsewhere in the building, alarms were shrilling.

That just left Imp to tidy up. "You can go to sleep now," he told Amy, "everything is just copacetic!" He gave her a final psychic nudge and she slumped slowly forward across her desk. Behind her, the two guards were fitfully pawing at each other, trying to disentangle themselves from their inadvertent bondage scene. The assistant manager in the corner was facing the wall and giggling cheerfully. As Imp left, he tugged the door closed behind him. The silent alarm was also a lockdown trigger. The strong room crew wouldn't be getting out any time soon.

Imp turned and moonwalked down the corridor. He briefly paused to stuff two fat bundles of banknotes into his pockets, then dropped the bin bag, even though it was still half full. Then he ran after Robin and the Bat.

Back in the fitting room they ditched their disguises and

changed back into street clothes. The plan was to split up and make their separate ways home. Del, carrying her more valuable cargo, had her own special way of making an exit that none of the others could emulate. Imp intended to pause in Model Railways on his way out: just long enough to purchase a Baby Deltic to round out Game Boy's stocking, using the banknotes he'd stolen only minutes earlier. *Never say I don't look out for you, GeeBee,* he told himself. One Christmas present down, two to go. Del was easy—she'd had her eye on a new bike for ages—and that just left Doc Depression.

It's fun being a Secret Santa, Imp decided.

As long as you didn't get caught.

THE INTERIOR LIFE

Mr. Bigge maintained a modest mansion in Knightsbridge, stomping ground of tech billionaires and revolution-averse Middle-Eastern potentates: the only people wealthy enough to buy property in Central London in the twenty-first century.

(A few local families still occupied their inherited family homes. But their numbers were dwindling. Fear of losing big in the property casino gradually overcame their attachment to their roots. Then they shuffled wearily off to their suburban exile, weeping on the shoulders of their newly acquired personal wealth management advisors.)

Rupert was an anomaly. He'd inherited the family home but he fitted in well with the elite newcomers. He came from old money but his fortune had exploded over the past decade, and he'd invested heavily in his house, trying to keep up with the oligarchs. What had once been a three-story Georgian town house (with cellar) now featured a dormered attic and two new subbasement levels. It had a cinema, swimming pool, boardroom, library, prayer room, panic room, owner's den, staff offices, and the usual Grave of the Unknown Komatsu Mini-Excavator.[1] It was, in short, a typical billionaire supervillain's London town house.

---

1 The only direction in which to expand in Knightsbridge being straight down, this decade *all* the hip billionaires were excavating grotesque megabasements beneath their mansions. And once having dug, it was cheaper to

This was not Rupert's only residence—he had suites in Tokyo, Manhattan, and Vancouver, a mansion in Madrid, a chateau in Normandy, and for the pièce de résistance a medieval castle on the small Channel Island where he was feudal lord—but the Knightsbridge house was his base in London.

Miss Starkey dwelt in the attic like a business-suited Miss Havisham, sleeping in the once-upon-a-Victorian-housekeeper's bedroom. Admittedly, this was a step up from the senior domestics, who had bunk beds in the dormer attic. (Never mind the kitchen and cellar maids who slept on bedrolls in the laundry, and paid for the privilege.) But it underlined the uncomfortable reality that in the House of Bigge, if you were not the master, you could only be a servant.

Not that Eve spent much time in her room. Sleep was a privilege reserved for the rich, and as Rupert's extremely busy executive assistant she could be called into action at any time of day or night to fight fires in her employer's global empire. Eve had no family life: her father was dead, her brother estranged, and her mother indisposed. She had neither the time nor the inclination to nurture friendships. But in exchange for total devotion to her job, Eve had gained the privilege of power.

Rupert might insist that she introduce herself to callers as his secretary, but she was effectively a corporate vice-president—lacking only the title, the pay, and the stock options. She oversaw operations on behalf of Rupert when he was unavailable. Her decrees carried the weight of her master's voice, and she exercised his power vicariously, a power

---

inter the digger in the basement than to remove it, like pharaonic pyramids where the skeletons of its builders were sealed into the foundations. Today, an estimated three thousand mini-diggers are entombed below London, leaving a plethora of sacrificial sites to confuse the hell out of future archaeologists.

that she'd become addicted to. Her borrowed agency made an acceptable substitute for family life for now, and with enough money even cloning and surrogacy would be within reach—the only way she'd ever dare have children. Having a life of her own could wait until she was something more than Rupert's semi-detached shadow. So it was towards this eventual emancipation, and in pursuit of her own long-term goals, that Eve bent every sinew and dedicated every waking moment of her life in the service of Rupert de Montfort Bigge.

This week Rupert was off on a jaunt to Cyprus, hobnobbing with his tax exile Russian friends and a sketchy Turkish arms dealer or two. Maybe he had already concluded his business and was plotting his next campaign from the fastness of his island castle; or perhaps he was living it up in Monaco. Either way, in his absence Eve reigned in Knightsbridge. So when she got home, she sent the Gammon down to the sub-subbasement with the kitchenware acquisitions and a work order for Sweeney the Handyman—the rack would be absolutely *perfect* there, as long as it was securely bolted to the ceiling—then she settled down at her desk in the office just outside Rupert's den. There were emails to answer, memos to approve, and a press release to sign off on—all useful distractions with which to work off her nervous energy. But work was a game she played in boss mode, and all too soon she had caught up with her to-do list and was left staring at her empty inbox with a nagging sense of dissatisfaction.

She phoned the kitchen for lunch and ordered her usual: a salad of mixed greens topped with a modest slab of bluefin tuna and a thimbleful of λ olive oil from Speiron. (Cook had said they were running low, so she dashed off a reminder to Rupert's valet to pick up another case: at $14,600 a pop it was a steal.) While she ate at her desk, she idly priced her options for blepharoplasty, then checked her rogues' gallery of Top 100 Richest Female Entrepreneurs for signs of unannounced plastic surgery again.

Closing in on the big three-zero had made Eve acutely aware that her options for leveraging her appearance were narrowing, and it was time to start upgrading her outward presentation before it became too obvious. She'd realized early on that there was an eigenface towards which all female CEOs converged, a strikingly standardized Boardroom Barbie look that those who made it to the top table generally shared. She had actual proof of this: she'd had Rupert's quants run the algorithms, and they'd spit out the precise ratio of nose length to lip fullness, hips to chest.

The numbers didn't lie. To make it to the top it wasn't necessary or even desirable to be supermodel-beautiful—stereotypes could bite you, unless you were a pop star or came from serious inherited wealth—but if you didn't have the good fortune to start out mind-buggeringly rich, you *absolutely* had to have the Look that coded for female executive authority. Eve intended to become the ultimate executive. She had already jettisoned any shred of her personal life that threatened to hold her back; her ears and breasts and cheekbones were just more skin in the game she was playing. Now she spent her surplus income on plastic surgery. Her objective: to become the face that launched a thousand investment vehicles.

She wouldn't be Rupert's amanuensis forever.

The desk phone rang while she was collating reviews of superstar plastic surgeons. Focus shattered, she glared at it for a moment: but switchboard had a little list of people who could handle level 2 through 4 calls while she was unavailable, which meant that it must be a level 1, which basically boiled down to Rupert or the Prince of Wales or someone of equivalent stature. She twitched her headset mic back into position. "Afternoon, Boss!" she chirped brightly. "What can I do for you?"

Rupe chuckled glutinously. "I want you to talk dirty to me," he said. Oh, it was one of *those* calls. "Where were we?"

Eve's brow furrowed minutely as she leaned back in her Aeron: "Let's see, I'm working my jaw and licking my lips as I kneel in front of you, Master. My! Aren't you hard!" (Rupe, she knew, was a marshmallow in the absence of chemical assistance.) "I can feel your pulse through your trousers as I unbutton your fly . . ."

"Yes, but what are you wearing?"

Eve closed her eyes. "My olive-green Armani suit, sheer black hold-ups, the black Jimmy Choos, and my black Rigby & Peller corset." (Which was *not* what she was wearing right now, Jimmy Choos excepted, but that was the whole point.) "And the stainless steel number-three butt plug."

"No panties?"

"I waxed yesterday, thinking about you, Master. I don't want to wear panties, they'd only get soaked when I run my tongue down the underside of your throbbing man-tool . . ."

Rupe's demand for telephone sex was tiresome but predictable, and he engaged in it like a dog marking its territory by pissing: *You belong to me*, he was reminding her, *even though I'm three thousand kilometers away*. He probably did it just to remind himself that, for all her deadly efficiency, he was still the boss of her.

Rupert de Montfort Bigge was a creature of hierarchy and privilege. He'd have been perfectly at home in the House of Commons, wagging his willy at the Leader of the Opposition during Prime Minister's Question Time; but his political career came to a sticky end almost before it got started.

If only those unfortunate photos from the secret university dining society hadn't come out just as he was up for approval by the candidate selection committee! The photos of his throbbing man-tool getting along splendidly with a roast hog's face, *in* a roast hog's face, with applesauce spurting out of the hog's eye sockets in viscous gouts as he pumped away with verve and enthusiasm, had certainly captured Party HQ's attention.

It was, in all, a bit of a career-killing move, even for a high-flyer like Rupert who was born and bred to inherit a safe Conservative seat. Because the question the committee had to consider was, if all this is coming out *now*, what's going to come out *later*?

(If only they'd known . . .)

After his political career crashed and burned at the end of the runway, Rupert threw himself single-mindedly into a life of dissolution and vice. His reputation became such that pedigreed parents warned their debutante daughters away from him despite his near-billionaire status. (Marrying for money was all very well, but not if it meant marrying an overdose flying in loose formation with several strains of sexually transmitted diseases hitherto unknown to science.) So extreme was his drug use that the injections of cocaine threatened to rot the arteries in his cock, and his personal bodyguard required special training in administering opiate antidotes. But Rupert came to his senses just short of a mid-thirties heart attack and turned his voracious appetites away from sex and drugs, towards a single-minded pursuit of money and power. With enough money it became possible to pursue political power by proxy, and with enough political power all enemies could be vanquished. So Rupert upped his game and focussed obsessively on the business of money and power. He used his own legitimate trading activities as cover for darker transactions, which he carefully delegated to his minions so that his own hands remained clean. Meanwhile, he amused himself with acts of petty sadism—the less consensual the better. Buying up and asset-stripping nursing home chains, looting employee pension funds, drowning kittens, and hunting giant pandas: it was all balm to his soul. Best of all, as a captain of industry he didn't even have to hide his vices from the voting public.

It amused Rupert to demand telephone sex from Eve, whose outer shell of puritanical frigidity he found vexing. In his clubbable old-boys world view women were wives, whores, or servants. Eve certainly didn't have the pedigree to be a society wife, although her effectiveness as a business subordinate (never dare to say partner) was unquestionable; so he alternated between door two and door three, never realizing that there was a fourth door behind which was chained a man-eating tiger, held in check only by a fraying rope of ruthlessly deferred gratification.

The phone sex had a secondary purpose of course. It bored the crap out of the intelligence officers who were undoubtedly listening in on his mobile phone conversations: for Rupert was a Person of Interest to numerous stock exchanges, futures markets, and financial fraud investigative agencies. Crypto might be hacked (Rupe didn't trust scramblers: what one boffin could make, another could break), but a bored officer who'd stopped listening after wanking himself silly was liable to miss the significance of the post-coital pillow talk.

"I'll be home tomorrow night, my dear, and I was thinking I'd like you to obtain a book for me. It's a little something for the weekend I heard about on my travels: everyone's talking about it in Nicosia. I'd like to read it with you when I get back. Do you think you could find it for me?"

"A book, Master?" Eve sat up and uncapped the fountain

pen she'd been twirling idly for creative inspiration, notepad at the ready.

"A *banned* book, Eve, a very naughty, wicked book indeed! Positively filthy, I should say." He chuckled lasciviously. "Absolutely one of a kind, and we'll have so much fun with it!"

"Does it have pictures?" she asked, staying in character.

"It's not *that* kind of book, I'm afraid, but yes, it does have pictures. It's a concordance of a lost manuscript, mentioned in the secret annex to the Index Librorum Prohibitorum—the Vatican index of books deemed heretical or contrary to morality. It was never printed, and the original was held under lock and key in the vaults of the Sacred Congregation of the Index until it disappeared in 1871, probably stolen. Someone tried to auction it in 1888, and it crops up a couple of times in various historical accounts—I've had it on my Amazon wish list forever—but no joy. Anyway, I want you to talk to Bernard, tell him it's up for auction again right on our doorstep, in London! A little bird whispered in my ear." (One of Rupe's oligarch buddies had gone long on the nose candy and bragged about it, in other words.) "He'll know exactly which book I mean and how to bid on it. I want you to expedite it for me. Can you do that?"

"Of course." Eve diligently took notes in an arcane shorthand of her own invention. If the boss was worried about eavesdroppers, this was serious. All this beating-off banter by way of beating around the bush was just cover for the real message. But . . . *a book*? "I'll tell Bernard to look up your wish list. Do you have a price in mind, Boss?"

"Whatever it costs," he said flatly.

Eve felt a cold sweat wash over her. "*Whatever* it costs?" she echoed, seeking confirmation.

"Whatever." He dismissed the topic as casually as if he

was discussing the weather, rather than giving her carte blanche to spill blood or money like water. "I'll be back next week. You might as well take it easy until then. Except for the book, of course."

"Yes, Boss." She stared hungrily at her notes, then double-underlined a squiggly glyph that in her own internal notation signified more work for the Komatsu in the subbasement, more quick-setting cement to fill the shallow graves, more money to silence those who could be bought and to buy the permanent silence of those who couldn't. "I'm on it."

He hung up on her, and Eve fanned herself. Her skin suddenly felt a size too small and prickled with a sullen heat. *Whatever it costs* was Rupert-code for *do whatever it takes to win*. A controlling interest in a software company, a shiny new Gulfstream, a stolen Michelangelo, an assassination, a kilo of weapons-grade plutonium from North Korea: whatever he wanted, whatever the cost.

As a rule, Rupe negotiated his less savory acquisitions carefully, confining himself to ambiguous verbal agreements, then delegating execution to someone else. Someone like Miss Evelyn Starkey, executive assistant extraordinaire. She was the one who worked the long hours, buried the bones, and painted over the cracks in Rupert's veneer of legality. She was under no illusions about why he worked this way: if he ever got caught it was his intention that she, not Rupert, would take the fall. But beggars couldn't be choosers, and Rupe had got the drop on her.

As a condition for hiring her on special terms (which included paying off her student debt and providing gold-plated family medical insurance), he'd imposed a geas on her, a magical binding to enforce the non-compete clause in her contract. Eve had thought it amusingly weak, so pathetic she'd never bothered to break it. And the work he gave her was interesting, if morally dubious and intermittently illegal. But when, after a couple of months, he showed her the file he'd been keeping on her, she realized it was a snare. The very weakness of the geas meant that it wouldn't stand scrutiny as a mitigating factor if she was ever charged with any crimes—crimes she'd committed at his direction, but which she appeared to have initiated. Every time he pulled this trick on her the file got fatter, like a cursed magical tome feeding on the life energy of the sorcerer who thought *he* was using *it,* not vice versa. The geas was irrelevant: if she didn't want to be subjected to the full might and majesty of the law, she'd continue to fetch and carry and suck like a dead pig's face— until he slipped, of course.

She only needed to get lucky once.

Eve sat in silence for a while, pondering. *A concordance?* The Inquisition banned it even though it was just an index to another book, then hid it in a secret appendix to the list of banned books so nobody would even know it existed? *And Rupert is willing to sanction wet work to get his hands on it?* She shook her head. Rupert did not sanction murder trivially, not unless at least eight digits of profit were in play. It was a purely pragmatic risk/benefit trade-off: Rupert was ruthless but not rash. The index had to be *immensely* valuable in the right hands. And he'd heard about it in Cyprus, from one or other of his dodgy oligarch business partners.

After taking a minute to compose herself, Eve put through a call to Bernard Harris, an overpriced and eccentric antiquarian book dealer with whom the boss was oddly thick.

"Mr. Harris? Hi, it's Evelyn Starkey. The boss just told me about a rare book he's heard is up for auction somewhere in London this week, and I was wondering if you could look into it and get back to me? Handwriting only, yes please, courier it over ASAP if you don't mind; yes, yes, something from his, ah, *Amazon wish list*, last up in 1888, Vatican-prohibited, a concordance, one of a kind. Yes? Absolutely! That sounds like it. Mr. Bigge wants it, yes, definitely, he says price is no object. Will you let me know? Splendid! Ciao."

Good things come to those who wait, Eve told herself, and turned back to her PC's screen with a secretive smile.

Once Bernard put out feelers and identified the item that was up for auction, she'd authorize him to place a bid on Rupert's behalf and set up the necessary machinery to transfer the (undoubtedly enormous) sum of laundered funds from one of the black accounts. And if there were rival bidders who wanted to play hardball, maybe go outside the rules? She'd be ready for them, too.

Meanwhile, there were plastic surgeons to evaluate for their potential to give her the chilly face of corporate perfection. The face she'd wear once she completed her takeover of the Bigge Organization. The last face her enemies would ever see.

Imp strolled past the overgrown hedges and boarded up windows of Billionaire's Row, ignoring the leaking roofs and snarling-dog security signs as he headed towards the high stone wall at the back of Kensington Palace. He was going home, for some debatable value of home.

Once upon a time this had been a street of well-to-do family houses, the town residences of straitlaced minor gentry nestling in the shade of a second-tier palace (now serving as a state-subsidized dorm for minor royalty). A century ago, Imp's great-grandparents had bought one of these houses with the proceeds of an early silent movie fortune. His grandparents had lived here and his father had grown up hearing tales of it, but it had been sold off to cover death duties in the sixties along with the rest of the homes on this street, as the London property market inflated out of reach of mere mortals.

Today the average plot on Kensington Palace Gardens passed hands for roughly two hundred million pounds. Yet they all stood empty and derelict, roofs leaking, carpets mildewed, woodwork decaying, and wallpaper peeling. The sovereign wealth funds that bought the houses as investment vehicles were remote from mundane affairs like tenants and rent, never mind domestic maintenance. If the roof caved in, what did a million in reconstruction costs matter, when the title deed was appreciating by twenty million a year? Why bother with repairs when nobody lived there; and nobody could be permitted to live there lest they acquire some vestigial tenancy rights in law and encumber the liquidity of the asset.

Imp's ancestral pile was fronted by a rusting chain-link fence secured with padlocks, monitored by cameras on poles. He unlocked the gate and slouched up the driveway. He'd started by hacksawing the original lock, replacing it with one of his own. The cameras had been a little harder, but there were blind spots. Then Game Boy had hacked them. He'd found their unsecured logins on Shodan and tweaked their settings. The security company so proudly boasting of 24-hour monitoring on their warning signs was in fact watching the hell out of a house just down the street that shared the same long-dead architect.

Imp marched up the front steps and rapped smartly on the door frame. "Hi, homeys, I'm honey!" he trilled, puffing out his chest as he opened the door. It squealed noisily across the floor tiles. The rain had warped it so that it tended to jam. Inside the seemingly derelict house, the porch was swept clean of debris and the inner door was sturdy despite a fresh coat of graffiti. Del was working on another of her murals, a street scene of heroic bike couriers racing to dodge shark-like cars and police with piranha heads. Muffled dance music was pounding away upstairs. Imp slung his rain-damped trench coat on a hook, wiped his feet on the doormat, removed his boots, and entered the hall.

The front hall was lined with oak wainscoting almost to the ceiling, and floored in black and white marble. It was as snobby a lobby as any snooty butler could hope for. Imp thought it a shame that he lacked an Alfred to take the piss out of Doc's Bat-persona. He opened a door to the left of the hall and flipped on the drawing room lights.

To maintain the pretense of abandonment, he and Doc had installed slanted plywood cutouts just behind the bay windows, a stage backdrop painted in an Ames room illusion. From the outside, the flats provided a forced-perspective illusion of empty rooms, peeling wallpaper, and filthy floors. But the backdrops were barely a meter deep. Behind them the rest of the house was fully inhabited, albeit not in a manner of which the owners would approve.

"Anyone in?" he called, glancing round the squat. The big-ass TV was on, blocking out the disgusting mess in the Adam fireplace with a photorealistic display of dancing flames. Immediately behind the backdrop to the windows at the front of the room was a row of bland office desks, covered to a considerable depth in assorted semi-functional e-waste. Game Boy's rig perched beside it, three giant monitors on arms angled inwards to focus on his joystick-and-keyboard-encrusted bucket seat. At the back of the room, a dress rack bowed under the weight of costumes, fronted by a snowdrift of discarded underwear. But the centerpiece of the room was a brown leather sofa of roughly the same dimensions as Jabba the Hutt. This was Imp's pride and joy, and it was currently unoccupied. "Ahoy there, children! Any sign of—"

A lithe arm snaked around his shoulders and clamped a palm over his mouth. "Shut it," Del hissed in his ear. "No pirates here, only me."

"Ay, my little Tiger Lily!"

"Fuck you, pay me." She let go and shoved him in the small of his back, sending him reeling until he collapsed theatrically atop the giant sofa. He flopped on his back with arms spreadeagled as she tossed the canvas bank bag at him.

"Hey, not nice!" He managed to keep the bag from whacking him in the face with its heavy padlock, which swung open. "This tagged?"

"Not any more: I disarmed the dye packs."

Imp struggled towards a sitting position—the sofa was almost as big as a double bed—and looked inside.

"Money, money, money, it's a rich—"

"Fuck you, pay me." Deliverator grinned, easing the sting of her demand slightly. She was, Imp decided, extremely cute when she smiled: but despite being extremely cute she was the least likely of all his housemates to put out, as he'd established to his regret. She was totally immune to all attempts to charm her out of her skintight Lycra pants: a gold star lesbian, he figured. "Pay me now."

"Can I pay you in kisses?" he asked hopefully, and gave her mind a little *push*. "Will you do it for exposure? I can make you a star—"

She pushed back, *hard* (pushing was always iffy if the pushee was another transhuman). "Try that again and I'll introduce your kneecaps to my baseball bat." Her grin turned menacing.

"Only kidding! I was hoping you'd cut me a discount."

"Asshole. No, and just for that shit, I want an extra ten

percent. And it'll double if you ever do that again," she warned. "Double or baseball bat: your call, mister."

"Ouch." Imp massaged his forehead ruefully, then rooted around in the bag for a bit, before giving up and emptying it on the floor nearby. Bundles of bound banknotes fell out, fives and tens and twenties—nobody except dealers and gangsters used fifty pound notes. He picked up a centimeter-thick bundle. "A thousand quid—this one's your fine: catch." He bowled it at her. Del caught it, her mood lightening instantly. It was true: money couldn't buy love, but it made one hell of an apology. Another: "Thousand quid." And another. Del began to giggle.

"Cut that out!" She jumped over the end of the sofa, pulled up his shirt-tails, and started to tickle.

"Thousand—help! Uncle! Aunt! A kingdom for my horse! Have pity, have pity belle dame sans merci, oh the humanity!"

She stopped. "Does anybody *really* say that?" she demanded.

"Probably. Santa. As they were cru—" He trailed off, shocked sober by his tongue's treachery in reminding him of things better forgotten. "Listen, we agreed your cut was five large—"

"—Six now."

"—Okay, six. Let me up and I'll give it to you. Here. Remember to wear gloves and count them in the kitchen sink, just in case you missed any packs."

"Can't count *anything* in the kitchen sink until you do the washing-up. I swear the beer glasses are campaigning for the vote."

"It's not my turn to—"

"I'm sure the botulism doesn't care whether it's your turn or Doc's to boil it to death in a stream of detergent; *man up* and get your big boy Marigolds on or I'm inviting *everyone* to the next tickle party."

"Slave driver!"

"Bitch." She grinned as he rolled to his feet and shuffled towards the kitchen. "Barefoot in the kitchen, that's how I like my men."

"Not pregnant as well?"

"Don't test me, I've got a friend who'd lend me an ovipositor sex toy—"

Working together made the washing up go significantly faster, although Imp kept up a steady stream of complaints as he dried dishes. Del ignored them pointedly. They both ignored the overflowing ashtrays on the window ledge: judging by the smell of stale skunk there was nothing of tobacco in them, which meant they were Game Boy's. The highly regrettable remnants of several Cornish pasties, in contrast, were obviously Doc's. He had a weakness for the things, but for some reason never ate the crescent section of the crust, leaving little half-moons of abandoned pastry rind lying around the place.

After Imp bagged up the empty beer cans and Del dumped the bottles in a crate for recycling, she stepped back and produced a roll-up out of thin air. "We need to talk."

Crap, Imp thought. Striking a pose against the worktop with a broken cupboard door, he declaimed:

> "'The time has come,' the Walrus said,
>   'To talk of many things:
>   of shoes—and ships—and sealing-wax—'"

"—I'll give you sealing-wax!" Del snarled at him with a promise of physical injury if he continued, which only caused Imp to raise his voice to auditorium-filling levels—

"'Of cabbages—and kings—
And why the sea is boiling hot—
and whether pigs have wings.'

Ahem. You were saying?"

"Fuck it." Del flicked her fingers, summoning a blue flare of light that danced around the tip of her spliff before vanishing with a giggle: "Thanks, Tink." She drew in a long, slow lungful and held it for a couple of seconds before allowing it to trickle from her nostrils. Imp grabbed at the joint but, swift as an angry bee, Del snatched it out of reach and held it above his head. "You are *pissing me off* with these improv stunts," she complained, relaxing only very slightly as the joint began to hit her. "It's all fun and games until someone loses a fucking eye, Imp, they nearly grabbed GeeBee! Are you *insane?*"

Imp forced himself not to wilt under the glowering weight of her regard. "I'm insane on Tuesdays, Thursdays, and days with a Q in their name. Otherwise I'm totally in touch with reality, thankee kindly. And thankee kindly for putting Gee-Bee off his game, really, what was *that* about, you utter toad-plucker? Were you *trying* to trigger him?"

"Hmm. Yeah, nope, I didn't think I was—no, I just didn't think. None of us is fault-free. I'll apologize later." Del took another toke then reached a decision. She offered him the joint, then when he accepted it, grabbed his right ear and marched him briskly towards the drawing room. Imp staggered after her, inhaling wheezily, pursued by a faint giggling and the chiming of tiny bells. "Sit," she commanded, shoving him down atop a hideously stained futon. "What I want to say is, there will be no more half-cocked schemes which you make up on the spur of the moment and where we get scragged if anyone stumbles. Is that understood?"

"You're no fun when you're like this, Becca." Imp whined,

but at least he was listening. "If you only wanted to talk why did we have to do the dishes?"

"Dishes weren't going to do themselves, fool." Del—known to her parents and the court system as Rebecca—frowned, then plucked the joint from his lips and took another furious puff. "Quit the act. You're plotting mayhem and chaos. Confess."

He twitched. "I, uh, may have updated the spreadsheet. Again."

Del rolled her eyes. "You and your fucking spreadsheet. What's it say this time?"

"We made sixty, sixty-two thou today. That leaves thirty in the kitty after I pay you, him, and other-him your salaries for the next month. But the overheads just went through the roof, so it's going to take a couple more jobs before we're ready to start shooting, if we stick to the schedule."

"Oh for—" Del abruptly sat beside him. "Can't you improvise?"

"It's the tech," Imp complained, "4K and 8K cameras are no longer available for hire without criminal background checks. The Home Office just classified them as munitions! Sobek alone knows why they did it, but I can't just borrow a Red One and a couple of lenses any more, they're all stored in bank vaults under armed guard." He grimaced. "Film cameras are another matter—yeah, *as if.* There's a six-month waiting list to get your hands on a Super 16 and then you've got to pay for the film and development, which is going to come in at around a tenner a second if you do it on the cheap, and *then* you've got to get a license from the Ministry of Propaganda before they'll let you digitize it."

"What the ever-loving fuck?"

"They're afraid of demons crawling out of the HDTV screens and eating people." Imp took a slow, moody drag on the butt of the joint, then stubbed it out on the sole of his boot and glowered at the dustsheet-draped baby grand piano. "Clunge-licking magic." There was a jangling discord of tiny bells: "No offense," he added hastily.

"So you need more money because now you have to pay for film and development costs on top of everything else?"

"Yeah, that's about the size of it."

"Well." Del side-eyed him. "This film had better be fucking worth it in the end, mister big-shot director." Standing, she added: "No more improv capers, understand?" He nodded. "Next time, you give us a script *first* and we all kick the tires." He nodded unenthusiastically. "And it's a *team* effort. And there is no *I* in team, are you with me? We're doing this *together*. I'm not your sidekick, dude, we're all equals here. Partners in crime." Imp managed to nod and hold his tongue. "Good." The echo of a frightening smile danced at the corners of her mouth. "Now let's go and tell the boys, shall we?"

Wendy Deere caught the bus home to Lewisham, where she lived in one of half a dozen bedsits in a converted 1930s family house. It was cramped, damp, and inconveniently close to the diesel fumes and noise of the high street, but it was all she could afford. As she walked the last couple hundred meters the gray overcast finally began to drizzle. It had been a clear, cold day when she'd left for work. Coatless, she was now exposed to the kind of irritatingly persistent rain that lingered like a drunk in a pub doorway.

Annoyed, she raised her left hand tentatively and willed the handle of an umbrella into existence in her palm. She knew she shouldn't, but . . . Hard, knobbly plastic slid from imagination into reality, tugging in the intermittent gusts as raindrops pattered across it. Head bowed and brolly lowered to cover her hair, she sped up, dodging dog turds and uncollected refuse, resisting the uncanny tugging on her mind which always came with such manifestations. (The papers were full of scare stories about Metahuman-Associated Dementia and saying it was connected to overuse of talents: well maybe, but then again, most smokers didn't die of lung cancer, did they?) She crossed the street and fumbled for her front door keys; while she was distracted the umbrella returned from whence it came, leaving her bare neck exposed to the icy droplets.

Shitgoblins, she swore silently, *and fucksticks*. She closed the door and flicked the light switch to no avail. Of course the card meter had run out of credit while she was at work, because the landlord-supplied fridge-freezer kept icing up. The door wouldn't close properly and it kept trying to freeze the entire living space. (Her so-called kitchen was an illegally windowless nook with about a square meter of floor space, separated from the main room by a doorless doorway. Before the house had been turned into bedsits it had probably been an airing closet.)

Wendy changed out of her work uniform into her parkour gear (combat pants and a hoodie), pulled her DMs back on, stuffed her phone, keys, and purse into trouser pockets, then grabbed the electricity meter keycard and went out to buy a top-up.

Poverty was expensive, and electricity on the card plan cost nearly twice as much as a regular tariff. As with her mobile phone bill, and the gas. Wendy lived week to week on top-ups, buying a little extra when she got enough work to cover it. At least today she could afford to turn the lights on again (and bloody had to, before the food in the laughably small freezer compartment defrosted and went off). If Gibson came through—

There was a note taped to the inside of the shared front

door in the lobby. She hadn't noticed it on her way in, too intent on getting to her own bedsit, but now she read it.

"Fuck," she swore aloud.

NOTICE TO ALL TENANTS:
THE FREEHOLD ON THIS BUILDING
IS BEING SOLD TO—

There goes the neighborhood. Gentrification was a cruel predator, pricing real people out of homes, regardless of their circumstances, however long they'd lived there. In retrospect, the signs had been obvious for months. Houses up and down the road were boarding up their windows, long-term residents draining away like an outgoing tide. A developer was moving in, determined to buy all the old semis and replace them with an estate of luxury apartments with valet parking and a residents' health club, single bedroom flats starting at only £900,000, truly a bargain, snap yours up now—

They can't kick us all out immediately, Wendy reasoned. Assured shorthold tenancies had to expire first. Something would come up, and if it didn't, at least on her new contract she'd be earning enough to move somewhere better. (She hoped.)

Gearing up to a brisk walk, Wendy headed towards the post office in the shopping center a half mile away. The rain had let up, dwindling to an intermittent spatter of small droplets. She turned the corner onto another residential street, to see more signs outside boarded-up ground-floor windows reading THIS SITE PROTECTED BY HIVECO HOME SECURITY. *As if.* Wendy snorted. Sure, HiveCo would take the property owner's money in return for a cardboard sign out front and a weekly drive-by; but *protected* implied something more and different. *Protected* meant active security, cameras monitored 24/7, maybe a human body on-site, dogs, lights, fences. Derelict homes awaiting demolition weren't—

"Huh." Wendy slowed, then stopped. The hasp on the padlock securing the front door of the house she'd just passed was hanging loose, and when she looked she saw that the door was ajar. Not open, just not properly shut. "Well, then." Taking a closer look couldn't hurt, could it?

The police are the public and the public are the police had been drilled into Wendy during her Hendon days, back when she was training to be a copper. She could recite the Peelian principles in her sleep: the police were just members of the public who were paid to give full-time attention to duties every citizen should support. *But I'm not a cop any more*, Wendy reminded herself, and anyway the current government didn't have much time for empowered citizenship. Trespassing and squatting had only been made criminal offenses in the current millennium, but the New Management had tightened up the penalties for almost everything, as if they thought the threat of sadistic and unusual punishments would distract the voters from noticing cuts to police numbers. *But it's my beat because I live here and nobody else is taking responsibility . . . Shit.*

Wendy eyed the broken doorway apprehensively. Maybe it was kids, maybe it was homeless people, maybe it was crackheads or a neighborhood dealer: these were not exclusive sets. There were other possibilities, too, less obviously criminal ones. But whoever they were, they ought to know better, and Wendy hadn't *quite* had all the community spirit beaten out of her. She felt responsible, although any gods that knew why remained silent on the matter when she cried, *Why does it have to be me?* And in the absence of any sworn officers to remind the squatters of the law (and also to check that they weren't dying of neglect), it was a duty that fell to her. Peelian principles in action.

Breathing deeply, she glanced up and down the road to ensure she was unobserved, then hopped over the rotting wooden fence that surrounded the house. The tiny garden was overgrown, knee-deep in dirty grass concealing trip hazards and discarded refuse. A wooden hut with broken windows that gaped emptily stood between two dying trees and an overgrown hedge at the back. No wonder they'd picked this one, whoever they were. The rear aspect was concealed, and there were numerous escape routes across neighboring gardens. *Good for them.* The windows on the upper floor at the back weren't boarded up: light shone from one of the bedrooms, a peculiar flickering blue like an electric arc—and suddenly, by the prickling in her fingers, Wendy *knew* that she had to check this out, just in case. She'd seen this kind of thing before, after all.

"Right, let's do this," Wendy muttered, nerving herself. She checked for watchers again, then willed a crowbar into existence as she approached the back door. Like the front, this too had been secured with a shiny aluminum latch and a padlock. It was cheaper than changing the original locks on a house destined for demolition and it signalled vacant possession, but the latch was only stapled to the doorframe. Wendy hefted the pry bar and with a practiced flick ripped the latch away. She pushed inside, then paused to listen while she let her eyes grow accustomed to the twilight within.

Unlike her own home, this house hadn't been turned into an HMO or subdivided into cramped bedsits. In fact, it looked to have been left untouched since the 1970s. Peeling wallpaper still trapped the eye in endless paisley-print swirls of brown and orange. Wood-veneered kitchen cupboards flanked an ancient electric cooker with coiled heating elements on top. The lino was almost worn away in front of the fridge and the stainless steel sink. Beneath the latter a twin-tub washing machine had once been tucked for safe keeping. A strange smell pervaded the room, like a combination of malodorous socks, rotten vegetables, and chlorinated swimming pools.

Wendy inhaled slowly, arms and shoulders tense. Something was *wrong*. Responding to her unease, her crowbar transformed into a friction-lock ASP baton, the model she'd carried on duty. A muffled voice drifted from the darkened hallway, muttering imprecations, and then, amidst a sudden burst of hissing and crackling, a triumphant howl: "It *lives*! Ahahaha! *Science!*"

Wendy relaxed instantly. *Of course it would be* him. *It's like a tradition, or an old charter, or something.* She strode through the darkened house, boots squelching softly on the soaking remains of the hall carpet. Reaching the staircase, she rapped on the wall with her baton. "Professor? It's Wendy; I'm coming upstairs."

"I told them they'd be sorry, the fools! But I—*Wendy?*" Prof's voice abruptly dropped out of his Mad Science falsetto into something only a stone's throw away from sanity. "Oh good, is it visiting time already? Wait, what are you doing? No, don't eat her! She's our *friend*—"

Wendy heard an overloud scuttling noise then a chirr of mandibles, cut off sharply. A bedroom door opened, spilling light across the landing. She sighed, exasperated. "You can't keep wandering off like this, Prof!"

"Really?" Professor Skullface blinked at her in confusion. "Why ever not?"

"You *know* why! People will talk. Are you going to invite me in or—"

"Of course! Come in, come in, I'm forgetting my manners, would you care for a tube of tea?"

"Maybe," she said doubtfully. She followed Prof as he retreated back inside his lair, tugging his grimy lab coat tight around his shoulders. He wore it with panache over striped pajamas and felt slipper-boots. One of them still sported a price tag. He'd refurbished the master bedroom, fitting it out with all the homely comforts of a mad scientist's lab. (Or perhaps that should be MAD scientist: Prof could have been a poster model for Metahuman-Associated Dementia.) Benches with bubbling stills and retorts burbled cheerfully alongside the walls; in the middle of the room a pair of Jacob's ladders flanked an operating table, atop which was strapped a supine form.

"Mine's an Earl Grey, milk, one sugar, please." She tried to ignore the jump leads connected to the body on the slab. There was no point worrying: anyway, it was probably a shop dummy. Most of Prof's workplace was just set dressing.

"They called me—milk, one sugar—a madman, but I showed them!" Prof scooped dark powder into an Erlenmeyer flask full of liquid, then swirled it over a Bunsen burner, gripping it with a pair of tongs. She couldn't help noticing that the hand tremors had gotten worse. Leaping gaslight flared reflections off his wire-rimmed spectacles. "And I make a mean tube of tea while I do it, if I say so myself."

"Prof. Prof." Wendy found herself smiling despite herself. "How long have you been liv—uh, working here?"

"You know, I couldn't say," he said vaguely. The flask of tea was beginning to boil from the bottom up. He lifted it out of the flame and placed it on a heatproof tile to steep. "The lease was up on the castle, and the villagers kept threatening me, so I sent Igor out to find a new lair, and he brought me here." Igor *chirred* emphatically from under the operating table. Wendy took a cautious step backwards. Igor was a construct Prof had manifested, much like Wendy's baton; but while she was limited to simple mechanical tools, Prof could make minions. Igor resembled a giant robotic scorpion with hands instead of claws, forking into ever tinier hands at each fingertip, branching endlessly down into a rainbow fuzz of light-diffracting nanoscale digits. Igor wasn't aggressive or evil, but Igor *was* dangerous the way a badly programmed industrial robot was dangerous—or a construct animated by a transhuman with the Mad Science delusion who had come into his powers at the same time the Metahuman-Associated Dementia took hold. (And don't even start on the transhuman/metahuman terminology wars: more than one lexicographer had been driven to a nervous breakdown by the flame wars over what to call the people the public still insisted on referring to as caped freaks.)

Wendy accepted Prof's offering of tea and sipped it in silence, considering her options. She allowed her telescoping baton to dissolve back into the shadows. She used to visit Prof regularly as part of her caseload back when she was with the Old Bill, along with a handful of other transhumans who required an occasional steady hand. This was the third time he'd wandered away from a care home or forgotten his way back, or been turned out on the street. The causes might vary but the progression was always the same. Prof inevitably told Igor to find him a lab, and Igor would do exactly as he was told. So Prof would hole up somewhere wildly inappropriate (a shuttered petrol station, a house scheduled for demolition), and settle into a life of genteel squalor and mad science. Igor raided the bins behind supermarkets and fast food outlets to feed the master, while Prof whipped up gizmos for his lair—a turbogenerator powered by the water mains to provide electricity, the grow-lamps from an urban cannabis farm repurposed as a mind-control laser. Or, on one memorable occasion (*thank fuck* Prof had been working in a cellar at the time), a working muon-catalyzed cold fusion reactor.

Prof and Igor were mostly harmless, really more a danger to themselves than others—Prof's instinct to retreat into a mad science lair when disturbed meant that he tended to avoid situations where he might frighten his neighbors into forming a pitchfork-wielding mob—but he was still not safe on his own. If a stroke left him paralyzed Igor would go in search of help, which might mean dismantling and stealing an air ambulance. Or it might progress to kidnapping a trainee nurse and demanding brain surgery through the medium of interpretative dance. That was the problem with mad scientists who succumbed to MAD: as they went downhill the constructs they animated became dangerously unpredictable, not to say prone to episodes of gratuitous bugfuckery. And for some reason, if he was going to turn up on anybody's doorstep, it would be Wendy's. She had this to look forward to if she overused her own ability: it was almost enough to make her swear off crime fighting for life.

"Do you remember who you were staying with?" She tried again, between sips of tea. "What the home was called?"

"I'm not quite sure." For a moment Prof looked puzzled. "The Golden Farm Residential Care Community, perhaps?" He scratched his head. Privately, Wendy despaired. Golden Farm Residential had kicked Prof out two years ago when the private equity firm that had purchased the care home chain finished looting their pension scheme and forced them into bankruptcy. But as he raised his arm Wendy saw a band looped around his scrawny wrist: a Tyvek label with a bar code and some writing on it. "Itches," he said indistinctly, worrying at it with his teeth.

"Let me help you with that?" she offered, and slowly leaned in close. PROF. ARTHUR P. MACANDLESS, ST. BRIDE'S CATHOLIC CARE HOME, it read. CONTACT PHONE ... *Gotcha*, she thought. Before the New Management, about 80 percent of modern police work had been indistinguishable from social work: domestic violence mediation, getting drunks home safely on a Saturday night, rounding up dementia patients who'd wandered away with only their lab coats and killer robots to look after them. "I'll just take this down to the kitchen and wash it," she said, showing him the empty Erlenmeyer flask. Then she sidled out of the doorway and trotted down the stairs to make a quiet phone call without agitating the patient. While the New Management had cranked all the judicial penalties up to 11, the law still operated much the same as previously—and as a dementia sufferer Prof was clearly not competent to stand trial. But the house was unfit for human habitation, and probably unsafe as well. She still had the social work department's front desk number in her phone. They could take it from here.

However, the path to neighborly virtue was paved with stumbling blocks. In this case, they took the form of successive government cuts that had pared public services to the bone. Bounced from extension to extension, it took Wendy most of an hour to get through to Prof's case worker, who agreed to come straight over—as soon as she'd visited her next two extremely urgent patients and contacted St. Bride's to confirm that they hadn't reallocated the mad scientist's bed. In the event, it took three and a half hours for Mavis from Social Services to get to the condemned house. By which time it was raining steadily, Wendy was out of fucks to give, Professor Skullface had run out of tea—and the Post Office had shut for the day.

While Evelyn Starkey was being subjected to sordid telephone sex by her boss, Del and Imp bickered in the drawing
room, and Wendy Deere struggled to sort out a care home
bed for a mad scientist, Game Boy and Doc Depression were
discussing breaking and entering on the top floor.

"It doesn't make sense," Game Boy complained, bouncing
on the balls of his feet. "It shouldn't be there!"

"And yet, it is." Doc leaned against the wall, detachment
personified, and watched as Game Boy got more and more
excited about a painted-over closet door.

The top floor of the town house had once housed servants
beneath the steeply pitched roof. Four bedrooms opened off
a central landing at the top of the stairs. Each had a dormer
window projecting out through the sloping roof, so that it
was possible to stand upright in the middle of the rooms. (The
roofline sloped down to eaves only a meter beyond the outer
wall of each bedroom, so that there was barely space to sit
up in bed if the bed abutted that wall.) Doc and Game Boy
had moved into the attic, stripping out the ancient carpets
and slapping a coat of landlord magnolia paint over the
walls and ceilings in an effort to render them habitable. Doc
had claimed one of the rooms as his own, and Game Boy
was building a model railway layout in another (though he
preferred to sleep downstairs on a roll-up futon beside his
gaming rig).

But there was one more door on the landing. It stood opposite the top of the attic staircase. It had been nailed shut
and painted over long ago, its keyhole blocked with putty
as if some previous occupant had been determined to bar-

ricade it against all intruders. And Game Boy had observed that it shouldn't exist. When he'd brought a tape measure to check, he'd found a gap of only fifteen centimeters between the interior walls of the two back rooms: the thickness of an internal load-bearing wall. The painted-shut door was positioned right between the two bedroom doors, and by rights there should be no room for anything behind it—not even a cupboard.

"I say we open it," said Game Boy.

Doc yawned. "You can if you want; I'm going to take a nap."

Game Boy pouted. "No fun!"

"Raid tonight," Doc reminded him. "Got to get my beauty sleep in first or you'll have me falling asleep on you."

"Fuuu . . ." Game Boy trailed off. "Really?"

"Yeah." Doc yawned again. "I pushed it too hard this afternoon. Got a headache. *Fucking* Imp." He grimaced. "I had to hold five of them down at the same time back there: *five*. Why did there have to be five?"

"Hey, you're not the one the guards tried to get physical with!" Game Boy puffed his chest out: "Did you see the way I left them? Did you?"

"Yes, yes I did," Doc said gravely. Game Boy preened. "You did great back there." Doc's shoulders slumped. "Good thing too," he added faintly. "It could have gone bad so easily."

"Yeah, Deliverator—" Game Boy's voice caught, and his fragile bravado turned brittle as he looked at Doc for approval.

"Becca should know better," Doc agreed. He opened his arms and straightened up. "Hugs?"

"Hugs." Game Boy leaned his head against Doc's shoulder

and shivered like he was cold. Doc held him tight until the shudders subsided.

"She should know it triggers you by now," Doc murmured. "I'll have a word with her."

"Please don't, I mean, you don't have to get involved . . ."

"She can be an asshole at times. Like, she just doesn't think. No excuses."

Doc knew—they all knew—what Game Boy's parents had put him through before he ran away: the conversion therapy and the pray-away-the-gay sessions intended to turn him into the obedient teenaged daughter they expected. Del—Rebecca—was out and proud, ferociously so: she took no shit from anyone, ever, and couldn't quite get her head around Game Boy's lack of resilience. She had no feel for how his marginal identity could be so much more tenuous than her own. He'd had it half beaten out of him by his family with their oppressive conformity and their capital-E Expectations, a background quite unlike her own experience of benign neglect. When Del came out to her mother at sixteen, her mother had said, "That's nice, dear," and continued painting her nails. When Game Boy announced he was trans at fourteen, his parents made him undergo compulsory desistence "therapy" at a clinic with a 30 percent suicide rate.

"Doc, she didn't mean—"

Doc let go of Game Boy. "You're doing it again? The apologizing thing? Remember what I told you about it last time?"

"*Crap.* Yes." Game Boy glanced at him furtively. "I know I shouldn't, but it just comes out."

Time to change the subject, Doc decided. "Listen, I'd help you with the cupboard, but like I said, I've got a headache and something tells me there's going to be a lot of hammering."

"Nope, I've got a better idea." Game Boy's smile crept out

again, briefly. "I was going to use paint stripper and a heat gun on the hinges and the frame. Then see if it's actually locked, before I start with the crowbar. How 'bout you take a painkiller and crash out for a bit? I'll wake you when I need help."

It was, Doc thought, not a terrible plan. He decided Game Boy needed encouragement: "No hammering, but if you can get it open I'll lend a hand. Wake me up, okay? But bring bin bags! It's probably full of crap." Likely it was just a closet, shelves piled high with yellowing newspapers and cans of lead-laced paint curdled with age. Likely they'd just mismeasured the interior dimensions of the bedrooms. *But*: "You never know, there might be some buried treasure . . ."

Game Boy gave a perfunctory nod, then scurried off to his hobby room. Doc glanced after him, just once, and sighed. *And I thought I had problems?* Everyone who lived in Chateau Impresario was at least a little bit fucked-up, but Game Boy was the worst by a mile. He wasn't quite eighteen and he was desperate but couldn't even get on the waiting list at a gender clinic without parental approval for another five months. He was a lot better now he was on black market hormone supplements and out from under his folks' roof, but he was still fragile. Doc felt as if he had to tiptoe around Game Boy: if he ever got angry and lashed out Doc could easily break him. It would be as easy as dropping an egg from the top of a skyscraper. *With great power comes great responsibility* he reminded himself, and snorted. Then he went into his bedroom, closed the door, and lay down.

It felt as if only seconds passed but it must have been a lot longer when Doc awakened to find Game Boy leaning over him. "Doc? Doc!"

"What." Doc yawned. He'd been lying on his back, mouth

open, and now it felt gluey and his throat was dry. But his headache had receded. "What is it?"

"You told me to wake you if I found something! And I found all the things!" Game Boy was back to what passed for normal again, ebullient and excited.

It was so contagious that Doc found himself smiling back at him. "What did you uncover?"

"The door wasn't locked and it's not a closet! You've got to see this! We've got a bathroom!"

It took Doc a few seconds to set his brain in motion. He sat up, yawning, and pulled his shoes on. "A bathroom? Where?"

"Off the corridor behind the door! It's not a closet, it's more like the wardrobe in *The Lion, the Witch, and*—"

Doc bit his tongue before he could say the first—stupid, negative—thing that slipped into his head: *You've been raiding Imp's special stash, haven't you?* He settled for an ambiguous "This I have got to see," as he followed Game Boy out onto the landing.

Game Boy had been busy. He'd heaped a pile of crap—rags, paint scrapings, tools—atop an old newspaper at one side of the landing, then attacked the frame and hinges. The door, previously a grubby white expanse of gloss paint, was now a mess, scraped all the way down to bare wood in places. The brass knucklebones of hinges peeped around the frame. It stood ajar, and now Doc could see why Game Boy was excited. He wouldn't have credited it otherwise.

"There's a corridor," he said stupidly.

"Yes! And look, doors!"

It wasn't a particularly pretty passageway. The carpet was the sort of muddy brown weave beloved by landlords in decades past. It was wallpapered in woodchip-textured light brown, and it stank of dust and a dank note of mold that made Doc's sinuses clench like fists. There were no windows, but a naked filament bulb, so dim that Doc could almost look at it directly, hung overhead. It cast a questionable light on two closed doors to either side, and another at the end of the corridor. Doors which, quite obviously, couldn't possibly exist.

"Right, that's it." Doc turned, about to march downstairs to have it out with Imp (who had clearly been a bit too generous with the hallucinogens lately) when something Game Boy had said, in combination with the state of his post-nap bladder, made him pause. "Hey. You said there's a bathroom?"

"First door on the left. Check it out!"

I'm going to regret this, Doc thought, and opened the first door on the left.

The bathroom was quite unexceptional—for a room furnished in the 1970s with the sort of fixtures and fittings that had been commonplace when Doc's parents were growing up. The suite was a peculiar shade of bilious green—optimistically dubbed "avocado" by marketers—with plastic taps and a showerhead that promised to spray a lukewarm dribble of water all over the bathroom floor if one dared to use it. There was a frosted-glass window, and a bathroom cabinet with mirror-fronted doors. A radiant heater bolted high up on one wall and controlled via a pull-cord threatened a charmingly domestic electrocution to anyone who used it. It was all completely mundane and normal, except that it couldn't possibly exist because it occupied the same space as the back bedroom on the left.

"Okay, then." Doc shut the bathroom door behind him and raised the toilet lid. He sniffed. *Water.* He wished he hadn't: it was quite appallingly stagnant. He pushed down on the old-style handle and it flushed, almost as if it was real. There was even a roll of toilet paper on a wall-mounted holder beside it. Sighing, he lowered the toilet seat, and then his trousers, and gingerly lowered himself until he felt the seat rim—quite solid—under his buttocks. "Fucking hell."

After flushing again, he stumbled back onto the landing at the top of the stairs and shook his head. He looked doubtfully back at the door, then went inside the back bedroom on the left and looked around. Nobody had broken into their house and installed an avocado suite while they'd been robbing Hamleys, that much was clear. Increasingly worried, he checked the other back bedroom, with similar results. *This makes no sense.* "Game Boy?" he called, then looked down the corridor again.

"Here!" A flaming orange haircut popped out of the door opposite the bathroom.

"What have you found?" *What now?*

"It's a bedroom! I mean, there's a bed and a chest of drawers and a wardrobe but everything's really old, there's a thing that I think is a stereo? It's got a vinyl record player and a radio and one of those old cassette things, all in one box with lots of dials and knobs on it, like my grandparents had? But it doesn't work!" Game Boy paused, drew breath, and gave vent to an elephantine sneeze. "It's so dusty! It's like nobody's been up here for years and years and years!"

Afterwards Doc was never quite sure from whence it came, but a deep sense of foreboding settled over him. "This is—" he took a deep breath—"it shouldn't *be* here. It *can't* be here. Or *we* shouldn't be here. It's somewhere that shouldn't exist. That's some fucked-up Narnia-grade shit right there."

"Yeah! Great, isn't it?"

"I think we should tell Imp," he said, then reluctantly added, "and Del." *See if Imp knows something he wasn't tell-*

ing us. Anything at all. The house had been in his family for generations, up until the late 1960s. *We've wandered into a fucking TARDIS: What if there are Daleks?* An urgent impulse prompted him to add: "Whatever you do, don't split up!"

"Yeah, I've seen the slasher flicks too . . ."

"I'm going to get Imp." *And Del.* "Don't go any deeper until I get back?"

"Okay! I'll just fetch my phone. I can't wait to Instagram the hell out of it!"

After he hung up on Miss Starkey, Rupert de Montfort Bigge sighed happily, slipped his phone inside the breast pocket of his suit, and strolled onto the balcony to survey his estate. The flagstones were warm beneath the afternoon sun, and heat rose from the steep streets on the hillside below. Waves broke on the pebbled foreshore a quarter of a kilometer away, singing the never-ending song of the wild seas. *All of this is mine* he reminded himself, and if a man's heart could burst from the joy of gloating over his possessions, he could not think of a better way to go at just that moment.

This was not, admittedly, as large a demesne as a fellow like Rupert might wish for. The territorial rights that had come with the title of Seigneur of Skaro—a steal for the asking price of a mere £48.2M—only covered the 2.8 square kilometers of Skaro itself, plus the surrounding fisheries out to the internationally agreed territorial limit. He barely had the right to levy taxes on the population of 462 souls, and he owed feudal dues to the Duke of Normandy by way of the Lieutenant Governor in Guernsey, dammit, so strike out the dream of a seat at the United Nations General Assembly. (At least for now.) But he was nevertheless the undisputed Lord of Skaro, and it was a *start*, and that was the main thing: he had an island base with minions, a castle, a luxury helicopter, and a multibillion-pound hedge fund to manage.

What more could a man ask for?

(Quite a lot, actually.)

It was early afternoon, and far to the west the dealer floor on Wall Street would be open for business. But business could wait on his attention for just a little longer. Rupert's calling was more esoteric than the simple-minded worship of Mammon he was identified with in the public eye. He searched the horizon, gazing into the distance as if looking for signs of trouble in his private paradise: but his attention was directed inwards.

Footsteps approached him from behind, then stopped on the threshold of the balcony.

"Mr. Bond," he said.

The name was Rupert's little joke. A succession of men had played this role for him, their faces changing with the years (and seldom for any reason as benign as cosmetic surgery). They all answered in turn to the same code name. Indeed, Rupert was at pains never to learn their actual identity, to preserve a fig leaf of deniability. This one, being a twenty-first-century Bond, had a neatly groomed beard and moustache, wore his dress shirt with an open collar, and softened his hard-edged appearance with spectacles (albeit with non-corrective lenses). But despite the overhaul, he was still a Bond—the bludgeon-wielding counterpart to Miss Starkey's poisoned stiletto.

"You asked for me, sir?"

"Yes, I did," he said vaguely, then fell silent.

"The usual, sir?"

"With variations." Rupert glanced at him. "I have recently tasked Miss Starkey with an extremely sensitive procurement job. I believe she will perform her assignment with her usual efficiency."

"Sir." The Bond's eyebrows furrowed minutely, but otherwise his face displayed all the expressiveness of a brick wall. The faint twang of a Midwestern accent and the bulky musculature of a former US Navy SEAL were all that betrayed his background. (Rupert supposed he could have hired some former SBS muscle, but he liked to keep the Bonds just slightly alienated; in Rupert's experience, British mercenaries tended to lack the deference towards nobility that he expected of his servants.)

"There may be loose ends," Rupert continued. "Miss Starkey will tie off any that she notices, but the nature of the assignment is such that there *will* be competition, and it will leave a trail. So your job is to mop up after her."

The Bond nodded, almost imperceptibly, then spoke: "Is Miss Starkey herself to be considered a loose end?"

Rupert turned the idea over in his mind, imagining Eve's luscious lips turning blue and cyanotic, her purpling tongue protruding between them, eyes wide and innocent. It was almost enough to make him hard again: *but no.* "Not unless you find clear proof of treachery, which I don't expect." *She's not stupid: she knows the consequences of disloyalty.*

Once again, he savored the memory of her shock and anger when he revealed his opening hand in their little game. Her submission had been grudgingly given at first, then resigned, finally willing—eager, even, once she grasped the advantages of his patronage. The lengthy, enjoyable training program he'd subjected her to had tested her loyalty: but she'd never quite reached breaking point, requiring him to fully reveal his power over her. She clearly didn't realize how much further his control went than the petty little geas he'd imposed at the start via her employment contract. He sincerely hoped it wouldn't be necessary to liquidate her: it would take him a *very* long time to replace Eve if she turned rotten, even without taking into account her unique birthright. "She knows I'm watching. The panopticon sees all, what?"

"Very good, sir." The Bond actually clicked his heels. "Will there be anything else, sir?"

"On your way out, tell Anthony to lay out my vestments in the dressing room, I'll be conducting the midnight rites tonight. That's all for now. You may take the helicopter as far as London, but send it back once you arrive."

"Sir." The Bond was waiting for something.

"Dismissed, Mr. Bond."

Rupert ignored the Bond until he went away. Then he returned to his office. The bulletproof French windows whirred shut behind him as he sat at his desk, opened the humidor, and selected a cigar. It was one of the few vices he still permitted himself, and that in moderation: doctor's orders lest he die before the Great Working was complete. He prepared and lit it, then leaned back in his chair for a few minutes of peaceful meditation. It was his last window of solitude until after tonight's communion service: partaking of the blood and body of the innocent, reading their entrails, juggling their giblets, and conducting the divination to learn which trades to place when the markets opened in the Far East tomorrow.

No rest for the wicked, he thought, and chuckled to himself. It would be another sleepless night but in the morning he would be the richer for it, and the Great Working would be one step closer to fruition.

BOOKISH LORE

Game Boy went exploring while Doc went to fetch Imp and Del.

This wasn't deliberate perversity on Game Boy's part; it was just that he hated being bossed around, even by Doc, who he liked, a lot. He'd always had an itchy impulse towards activity, but when he'd been a kid he'd been drowned in parental expectations of passivity and feminine behavior, which were now tangled up inextricably in his sense of identity. Telling Game Boy not to do something was a surefire way to make him do it, even despite his own better judgment. So while Doc went downstairs, Game Boy began opening doors to see where they led.

Fragments from Game Boy's photo stream:

Bathroom: First door on the left. Avocado suite with corner bath, bidet, pedestal washbasin. Mirror-fronted bathroom cabinet above washbasin. Floored in cork tiles, walls in green and white ceramic up to one meter, painted white up to ceiling. Wall-mounted filament bulbs behind splash-proof covers. Radiant electric heater on wall above small, single-glazed sash window with frosted glass lower pane. Vintage: late 1970s.

Bedroom 1: First door on the right, opposite bathroom. 3.5 meters by 2.5 meters. Double bed with sprung mattress and down pillows, duvet, and plain white sheets, covered by dustsheet. Wardrobe in corner, chest of drawers (one meter high) at foot of bed, one bedside table with ceramic bedside lamp. 1970s Hitachi music center (stereo radio/cassette/record player) on top of chest of drawers, not plugged in, speakers on floor to either side. Wallpaper: dark orange and red abstract pattern. Carpet: plum woolen shag, medium pile. Curtains: brown, concealing sash window overlooking garden to rear of house. Mains socket: single BS 1363 socket with a 2-way adapter for the lamp, one receptacle free.

Bedroom wardrobe (door open): There are jeans and slacks with flares, lots of flares. A Biba maxi-dress; a couple of Laura Ashley frocks, plus blouses and skirts: all 1970s vintage.

View along corridor, outside bedroom door: There are two more doors to right and left. At the end of the corridor, four steps lead down to another corridor, turning right.

Bedroom 2: Second door on the left. Similar to Bedroom 1, but the bed is a single-width, and instead of a wardrobe there's a schoolroom desk. Dusty Airfix models of Spitfires and Heinkels, carefully painted in Second World War camouflage, dangle on cotton threads from the ceiling. A creased promotional poster for the original *Star Wars* movie is sellotaped to one wall. It faces off against an Eagle Transporter from *Space: 1999* and a photograph of Arsenal's 1973 first eleven on the pitch at Wembley.

Bedroom 3: As Bedroom 1, but no clothes or personal effects—set up as a guest room.

View from top of stairs along short corridor to right: Corridor opens into rectangular hallway, 5 meters by 3.5 meters. High ceiling (3 meters) with fluorescent lighting tube: original plaster cornicework in place, painted white. Wooden floor, sanded and sealed, with rectangular woven rug in center. Five doors open off this space: one opposite the corridor, and two to either side. Indirect natural illumination provided via rectangular windowpanes above four doors.

Kitchen 1: First door on left from corridor: 6 meters by 4 meters, cream linoleum floor, cream and pale blue paint. Center of opposite wall: AGA three-oven, oil-fired cooking range with two insulated hot plates on top (currently inoperative and cold). Floor-to-ceiling shelves to left of AGA filled with crockery, silverware, cooking utensils, 1950s vintage Kenwood mixer and accessories. Worktop to right of AGA, with window opening over garden. Left wall: two stainless steel sinks with spigot over cabinets. Right wall: floor and wall cabinets, worktop, refrigerator. Center of room: oak rustic kitchen table with extending flaps, three wooden chairs (assorted).

Bathroom 2: White ceramic bathtub, toilet, and washbasin on pedestal. No carpet, linoleum floor. Window hinges outwards, gauze curtain. Mirror on wall above washbasin, floor-standing wooden cupboard. Fittings: 1940s?

Laundry Room 1: Rectangular, 3 meters by 3.5 meters. Window hinges outwards, gauze curtain. White ceramic sluice basin, drain. Top-loading, twin-tub washing machine with drain and fill tubes plumbed into wall-mounted taps beside wooden worktop/draining board. Clothes airer suspended from ceiling by pulley: clothes rack opposite. Shelves with white cotton sheets, towels. Late 1940s?

Pantry 1: 2 meters by 1.5 meters. Stone cold slab, icebox, wooden cupboards, shelves above cold slab. Vintage: predates domestic refrigeration and electric lighting.

Library: Rectangular, 4 meters by 8 meters, bookshelves on all available wall surfaces . . .

*

Normally, Rupert's habit of handing her a drop-everything-do-this-right-now black op annoyed the hell out of Evelyn. But just for once, everything was under control. Rupe was out from underfoot, the various business deals in progress were wrapping up or winding down for the annual holiday shutdown, and Eve was able to offload all her lesser bullshit jobs onto lower-level executive staff.

Rupert wasn't one for recreational reading—not when he could be indulging in more physical, not to mention less cerebrally demanding, pursuits—but over the years he had acquired a collection of rare editions and manuscripts. In Eve's opinion it was mostly esoteric junk, but if the boss wanted to collect eighteenth-century anatomies bound in the skin of the hanged felon whose autopsy they documented, that was his lookout—it certainly wasn't the most offensive of his hobbies. Over the years he'd cultivated a connection with an antiquarian book broker, Bernard Harris, who had traded out of an attic on Charing Cross Road since the 1970s.

The bookshops of Charing Cross Road were barely a shadow of their former glory (rent rises and rapacious property developers had seen to that), but Bernard's specialty didn't require lots of retail floor space. Rather than holding stock, Bernard maintained a database and brokered private sales: occasionally he acted as an acquisitions agent on behalf of well-heeled buyers. A copy of *The Lord of the Rings*—the original Allen & Unwin hardcover, first impression, mint condition with unfoxed dust covers and flat-signed by the author—would have been about the cheapest item on his list.

Not holding stock of his own had numerous advantages for Bernard. He could operate out of his home apartment without paying business rates—a discreet form of tax avoidance. There was no insurance premium due on rare books he didn't hold, no need for security to protect his business premises, no working capital tied up in stock. And it meant no dusting. Just a comfortably furnished third-floor flat, crammed with floor-to-ceiling bookcases on every available wall.[1] He'd converted the second bedroom into an office straight out of the early 1990s, complete with rotary dial telephones, a 286 PC with a tube monitor (its case the yellow of old ivory due to age), filing cabinets, and a modem with blinking red LEDs to bring it bang up to date. It was very atmospheric: a snapshot of a bygone age taped between the leaves of a photo album, taken just before the internet became a thing.

Eve put her research into plastic surgery on hold, ordered the switchboard to hold or divert *all* her non-emergency calls, and told the Gammon to bring the Bentley round to the front door. It was time to visit the master's favorite book dealer.

Bernard's apartment was on a stairwell hidden behind a metal door in an alleyway just round the corner from Charing Cross Road. It was one of several well-hidden flats occupied by stubborn revenants of the book trade, clinging on despite the multimillion pound valuations attached to even a cramped, dark, damp-stained tenement this close to the heart of London. Eve left the Gammon to find somewhere to stash Rupert's wheels and climbed the stairs.

Bernard waited with ill-concealed impatience behind his front door, which was just barely ajar. He tried to present as a parody sixty-something book dealer, from the scuffed tips of his oxfords to his corduroy elbow patches, but somehow

---

1 For his personal collection. Bernard was, like most rare book dealers, a bibliophile and a hoarder.

managed to make it creepy. "Ah, Miss Starkey, hello, hello! Do please come in!" he oozed.

Eve smiled automatically as she stepped across the threshold. Bookshelves lined the walls from floor to ceiling, so close that she could reach out to touch both sides of the passage. The carpet, gray with grime and threadbare in patches, was trapped beneath the wooden galleys. "I'm so glad I was able to catch you," she gushed—laying it on a little thick since Bernard was a notorious agoraphobe who ventured outside only with the greatest reluctance. "You always seem to be so awfully busy." She glanced back at the door.

"Oh, excuse me . . ." Bernard slithered past her and chained the door, then slid an insane number of deadbolts into place on both sides of the heavily reinforced frame. "That's better! Now we don't need to worry about interruptions. Would you care for a cup of tea?" he asked. He led her to the sitting room, which featured a bay window with a fetching view of the back wall of a Uniqlo store. This room, too, seemed to be furnished principally with floor-to-ceiling bookcases, not to mention piles of books on the carpet that had accumulated like stalagmites, products of a steady drip of publication. "How do you take yours again?"

"Milk, no sugar," Eve replied automatically. *Why am I even* saying *that*, she wondered briefly, then nerved herself to drink what passed for Bernard's brew and pretend to like it. Eve was a coffee person, but if it took drinking his tea to convince Bernard he shared a rapport with her, she'd suck it up.

"Excellent!" Bernard bustled off to the tiny galley kitchen at the other end of the flat, monologuing about some sort of rare books trade show he wished he could attend in Antwerp while the kettle boiled. Eve perched on the edge of one of his ancient wing-back armchairs, the arms stained and grubby from use. Eventually Bernard returned from the kitchen, bearing a tray with two chipped and steaming mugs of orange-brown liquid. "Your tea, my lady. Now, what can I do for you?"

"The book Mr. de Montfort Bigge caught wind of," Eve said carefully. "What have you been able to learn about it?"

"It's absolutely fascinating!" Bernard settled into the other armchair. "The book—yes, it's on Rupert's wish list, but at first I thought it was a joke." As with all Bernard's customers, Rupert had left a hit file of targets for acquisition with the dealer. "To my certain knowledge, at least seventeen different pastiches purporting to be the *Necronomicon* were published in the last century. Most of them are novelty items or ephemera, targeting fans of the works of H. P. Lovecraft. The book itself is widely considered to be a fictional construct Lovecraft concocted, supposedly a fount of blasphemous wisdom relating to the so-called 'Elder Gods' and their—"

Eve's smile became fixed. In a momentary lapse of attention she actually raised her mug and took a sip. To her credit, she managed not to spit it out again. She licked her lips: "I hardly think Rupert would be interested in a practical joke, do you?"

"Of course not." Bernard's eyes almost crossed as he took a scalding mouthful of his brew. "To cut a long story short: like all the best stories, there is a nugget of truth buried beneath a continent of lies."

"Do go on." Eve nodded encouragingly. "Please?"

Bernard needed little or no encouragement to mansplain. "The title of *Necronomicon*, or *Book of Dead Names*, has been assigned to at least three different manuscripts that circulated in Europe between the late thirteenth and early eighteenth centuries. One—the most likely candidate—originated as an Andalusian work of scholarship titled *Al Azif*, which found its way into the custody of the Dominican order in the 1590s—its existence may have been part of the impetus for the creation of the Spanish Inquisition—at any rate, it has a most foul reputation. There's a copy in the obscene manuscripts collection of the Bodleian Library, but it's been sealed since 1945. Apparently the three most recent readers committed suicide after working on the damned book."

"Really?"

"Yes, really. There were reports of delusions—hearing strange voices, paranoia, a conviction that certain dead things were controlling their limbs while they slept—the usual. One of the scholars was so upset he sought an exorcism; afterwards, the priest had a nervous breakdown. Another of them shot his mistress then hanged himself, leaving a suicide note that said she was pregnant with the anti-Christ. But the *real* clue that this might be the actual book is that it isn't in the Bod's sealed collection any more."

"What happened?" Eve had noticed the tendency of Bernard's gaze to track towards her chest, and adjusted her posture accordingly, leaning forward to present him with a better view.

"It was *borrowed*," Bernard confided, with evident relish, "by the Prime Minister."

"But the Bodleian doesn't lend—" Eve bit her tongue before she could say too much. "*Right*."

"Right." He nodded emphatically. "So, that's Rare Manuscript AW-312.4, the Third Candidate. There are two other known copies: one's in the Vatican archives, the other is in the royal library in Riyadh, although it disappeared after the Salafi ascendancy in the 1980s. But that's not what's for sale. Oh no." He took another mouthful, then put his mug down on the carpet, slopping tea, and leaned closer. "This is even rarer. It's the concordance!"

"A concordance?" Eve forced a puzzled smile onto her face.

"Indeed." Bernard gazed into her eyes. "If simply *reading* AW-312.4 is bad for you, how damaging would it be to try and index the thing? To read it and to comprehend the significance of *every word*, to study the interrelation of concepts and interplay of references within the manuscript, and then to map every single occurrence of every term?" His smile was bright, fey, and not entirely sane.

"Who was responsible?" Eve asked. If Bernard noticed the slight tension in her voice, he pretended not to.

"Various friars and monks, during the seventeenth century." Bernard sat back and waved his hand dismissively. "It always ended in tears before bedtime. Well, there were also a couple of autos-da-fé and burnings at the stake as well, but what else would you expect of the Spanish Inquisition? At least, that's how they usually ended. There was a final attempt in 1833 and *that* was successful."

"How?"

"Technology and . . . determination? A fortuitous combination. After the Napoleonic Wars, the Vatican copy came into the custody of a librarian, an Archbishop Rodriguez, whose ambition was to index *everything*. After all, what use is a territory without a map? He had heard of AW-312.4 and the disastrous attempts to index it, and he decided he was going to finish the job, once and for all, so that future clergy might be vigilant for even the most fragmentary sign of these unholy scriptures. And he had access to three things that no previous indexer had been blessed with: an entire scriptorium of Dominican monks; the scholarly letters and published patents of Sir Charles Babbage; and an early punched-card-controlled jacquard weaving machine."

Eve blinked. "Let me guess. One page per scribe, one punched card per index word, and he was familiar with Babbage's difference engine? Perhaps how it might be used to drive a printer? Division of labor?"

"Not exactly. The monks all wore an eyepatch, so they still had one working eyeball after they finished their assigned page. And they didn't build a Babbage printer like the one in the Science Museum: they just wove a, a *demonic tapestry*. Afterwards they burned the Jacquard loom and the card deck in a last, secret auto-da-fé. Then Archbishop Rodriguez went into seclusion for six months, fasting and praying as he un-stitched the embroidered cloth encoding the concordance and transcribed it by hand onto pages blessed by the Pope himself." Bernard leaned forward again, and touched her right knee: "It didn't save him, of course; the poor bastard gouged his eyes out and died raving about a month later. But at least he finished the job."

Fascinating, Eve thought, resisting the impulse to break his fingers, one by one. "So what happened to the manuscript?"

"Oh, the usual. They made a couple of attempts to print copies for Inquisition use, but something always went wrong, so eventually they decided to stop killing editors and proofreaders. This was back before it was practical to ship it to China for typesetting, where the workers, being unable to read the manuscript, would be immune to its effects. AW-312.4 vanished back into the archives and the concordance was locked in a closet for a few decades. It's rumored that the concordance is warded, powerfully—an anti-theft sigil. You're safe if somebody gives you the book, but if you try to steal it, oh dear *no*. Anyway, some time later it *was* stolen. Which ended badly for the thief, but at that point it was free for the taking by anyone who stumbled across it. And they did. It crops up again in Paris in 1872, then again in London in 1888, in a secret auction brokered by a barrister in chambers in Middle Temple who died within six months of its conclusion. And then the trail goes cold. The concordance vanishes from history—the chambers' records were bombed during the Blitz—until about a week ago."

Eve nodded again. "What's the story?"

"Well." Bernard squinted. "I can't attest that it's definitely the real thing, you understand, although the prospectus is *quite*—" he shuddered and finally removed his hand— "convincing. Ah, I will need to invoice you for expenses incurred, by the way." She nodded encouragement. "They included a fragment of a book cover allegedly containing human DNA, as evidence of anthropodermic bibliopegy. There was also a scan of a single sheet that *quite* made my eyes water, even though their laser printer crashed a quarter of the way down the page. Ah-hem. *Anyway.* The prospectus and sample, along with bidding instructions, are in my bank deposit box—I couldn't sleep with that thing in the house— and if you give me a ceiling I'll submit a sealed bid. The seller wants ten percent, non-refundable, in advance to cover auction expenses, and the rest held in escrow—they're retaining one law firm to disburse funds and another to receive bids, both offshore, it's all a bit complicated. The winning bidder will receive instructions to retrieve the manuscript from secure storage. So, ah, how much is it worth to Rupert? And you?"

Eve stared at him for a minute as she pulled her scattered thoughts together. Thoughts like, *Another goddamn cursed magic tome,* really? And, *Sealed bids? We* definitely *have competitors?* And, *Is this a come-on?* She swallowed. "I'm not the purchaser you need to satisfy," she finally told him. "Are there any other concordances of this . . . this book?"

"Not that I know of." Bernard paused. "There *is* a rumor."

"A rumor."

"The Bod's copy. Right before Number Ten grabbed it, some civil service bunch got their greasy paws on it. Something to do with training a deep learning neural network to recognize the script in AW-312.4 and generate a concordance automatically."

"And did it?"

Bernard kept a poker face. "Rumor has it they discovered six ways—hitherto unknown to computer science—to drive a neural network insane."

"So." She leaned forward again, deliberately giving him an eyeful. "Let me get back to you with Rupert's bid?" She smiled. "You won't be talking about this to anybody, will you?"

Bernard swallowed. "Of course not, my dear."

"That's sweet of you." She rose. "If you should happen to overhear the names of any rival bidders I'm sure you could find a way to let me know?"

"Absolutely! But the vendor is being very secretive. Between you and me, I think they're probably afraid of the Russian element." Followers of Chernobog, or worse. He stood hastily. "My commission—"

"Will be the usual." She smiled: "But if you hear any names, there might be a bonus in it." Bernard's usual was 3 percent plus expenses, but 3 percent of upwards of ten million was nothing to sneeze at. "And ten percent plus a half million bonus if you can identify the seller before it goes to auction. I'm eager to make them an offer to preempt."

"Jolly good then, I'll get digging right away—"

"I'm sure you will! And Bernard? One more thing?"

"Yes?"

"Really don't tell anyone else about this; it wouldn't do for the wrong people to get the idea that they could get a leg up by gazumping Rupert in an auction. Rupert finds that sort of thing *intensely* irritating." Rupert's preferred treatment for irritants was an unmarked grave. "And he can be *very* possessive."

"I'm sure—" Bernard's face flushed as he got the message: *good, so he knows about Rupe's temper*—"that won't be a problem!"

"Of course not," Eve said graciously as she let herself out. "Be seeing you!"

"This is nuts," Doc said when he caught up with Game Boy, in lieu of telling him off—he was still in a fragile state, Doc guessed. "A *library*?"

"Wouldn't you want one in your house if you could have one?" Game Boy enthused.

"I don't see what's so special about a load of old books," said Del, blowing a plume of dust off a tome as fat as an old-timey computer manual. The book was bound in green cloth, the spine bleached by sunlight. She flipped it open and recited the title: "*A Boy's Compendium of Lore and Legend: Valiant Legends from before the British Empire*. Yeah, *right*." She dropped it on the floor: Game Boy winced but didn't bend to pick it up.

"Some of these are probably worth something second-hand," said Imp, his eyes alight with avarice. He'd heard stories about places like this in his infancy, fairy tales Dad told him at bedtime, but he could hardly credit the reality of it. Mind scrabbling for traction, he latched onto its most mundane utility first.

"Good luck figuring out which," Doc opined dourly. "Have you checked your phone signal?"

Imp squinted at his phone. "You got no signal either? That sucks."

"There's no signal anywhere once you get past the steps at

the end of the first corridor," Game Boy volunteered. "I tried to Instagram it, but . . ." He shrugged adorably and Doc had to fight the impulse to pick him up and carry him to safety, away from this confusing spatiotemporal maze of rooms. There was something disturbing about the idea of being cut off from modern communications even though they were so close to the throbbing heart of a capital city—especially as his phone had plenty of data out on the landing, just beyond the door Game Boy had opened.

"What the fuck *is* this place anyway?" complained Del. "I counted paces. We should be next door by now!"

Imp was poking around the lower shelves, replete and bulging with leatherbound hardbacks. "Look what I found." He bent down and, with a grunt of effort, heaved a book out of a row of identically bound volumes. He laid it on the leather-topped reading desk in the middle of the room, directly beneath the warm beam of sunlight that filtered in through the skylight. Dust rose as he leafed through it. He took an uncharacteristic degree of care. "*Encyclopaedia Britannica* . . . *tenth edition?* That's, uh—" he puzzled over the roman numerals for a bit—"published in 1902. My great-grandparents could have owned this." He looked up. Rebecca was staring at him. "What?"

"I thought you only read graphic novels these days?" She sounded as if she felt personally betrayed.

"I can read if I want to! I used to read lots!"

"*Children,*" Doc intervened, "what we have here is a puzzle and a problem and can I suggest we discuss it downstairs, maybe over a can of beer?" He side-eyed the two closed doors at the far end of the library. Doors that he'd noticed Game Boy eyeing with a worrying degree of curiosity. They were a peril and a provocation. "It would be really easy to get lost in here," he explained. The thought of Game Boy haring off into who-knew-what liminal spaces made him sweat.

"That's an excellent idea!" Imp wasn't far behind the curve of his thoughts: "We need a strategy, and a plan for exploration, and a map and a key and a ball of string to find our way back if we get lost! I shall work on an exploration plan forthwith! But I really think we jolly well ought to go downstairs *right now*."

"There are no games up here." Rebecca turned to Game Boy. "Can you even survive?"

"There'll be something," he said confidently. "There'll be a games room, you'll see! And it'll be full of 1970s games consoles and pinball machines!" But he still followed Imp back down the hallway and up the staircase and past the avocado suite of mundane contemporanea.

Doc didn't have the heart to point out the other thing he'd noticed down on the skirting board, the thing that Imp had also clocked. The electricity sockets in this room all had round holes, rather than the more normal rectangular cross-section ones. He'd seen round-pin sockets in a documentary about home life during the Great War. They'd gone out of use in the 1940s. There was no phone signal here. Nor were there LED and halogen lights, automatic machinery, or (beyond the first few rooms) modern electrical appliances. Where might it all end—with gaslight and coal fires, or all the way back to Roman hypocausts?

Eve found the whole idea of a cursed concordance of a book of spells fascinating. But not as fascinating as the fact that Rupert had gotten wind of it and was willing to trust her— her!—with its acquisition.

Rupert had kept Eve on a tight rein for years, ever since

the day he'd laid his cards before her and told her how things were going to be. That day he'd taught her that in order to win at the high-stakes games of the elite, it was not enough to be right: you had to be powerful and ruthless enough not to have to play by someone else's rules. This had been a hard lesson to stomach. True, over the years since then he'd given her progressively more autonomy. But the rope around her neck was still a rope, whether it was woven from hemp or silk. The benefits of every project she masterminded accrued to Rupert, while the penalties for failure were hers alone to bear.

As part of her penance these past five years, Eve had single-mindedly studied Rupert for weaknesses she could exploit. If she tried to escape him prematurely, he could make a single phone call that would condemn her to life as a fugitive or even, these days, have her executed: his real hold was not any kind of geas or spellwork, but a dossier of cold, hard crimes she had committed in his service. But knowing he held one end of her noose had made him complacent. Rupert had come to rely on her for too many services, minor and major. In the process, she'd become intimately aware of certain aspects of his business that he should not have trusted to anybody, let alone to one who served out of fear rather than love.

It was Eve who had commissioned the architectural drawings and managed the planning process and hired the contractors who dug out the second subbasement beneath the Knightsbridge apartment. It was Eve who, working with the head of security, had arranged for the secret tunnel with the pits and the quick-drying cement. It was Eve who had helped Rupert's strange co-religionists—never say cult—convert the old home theater room into a shrine with an altar that required drainage and running water. And it was Eve who carried out his acquisition, over a multi-year period, of a collection of texts on the subject of witchcraft and magic that started with the swivel-eyed lunacy of the *Malleus Maleficarum*, worked through the bloodthirsty magnificence of the *Codex Yoalli Ehēcatl*, and included not less than six pretenders to the title of *Al Azif*, the *Book of Dead Names*.

Frankly, it had come as no surprise whatsoever to Eve to learn that her employer was an ecclesiast in the Cult of the Mute Poet—an esoteric religious order that, because of the sanguinary nature of its devotions, had a pronounced tendency towards secrecy. These days cultists were crawling out of the woodwork like cockroaches. Under the New Management, membership of such dark churches was hardly a career-killing move, as long as they did not challenge the supremacy of the Mad God of Downing Street. And enough money could buy a worrying amount of selective blindness on the part of the authorities. Rupert had *connections*, Bullingdon Club connections, Piers Gaveston Society connections. Rupert had probably been inducted into the cult by Count Gottfried von Bismarck himself. Rupert could get away with shit that would have any normal person gazing eyelessly down from the glass and chrome skull rack at Marble Arch before you could blink.

But that was okay, because Eve didn't plan to tackle Rupert head-on. She wasn't going to denounce him to the secular authorities, or leak about him to the press.

Information wants to be free: but information also wants to cost the Earth. Eve was acutely aware of this. Eve was also aware that, over the past few years, certain strange things had crept across the threshold of possibility, slithering out of the shadows to caper in the daylight, openly mocking the age of rationality and reason that had prevailed for the past several centuries. Superheroes flying overhead, the charismatic narcissism of a reborn god in pinstripes sitting in Parliament, *magic* that *worked*—Eve was hardly an innocent, and she knew enough about the contents of Rupert's locked and alarmed cabinet of curiosities to know that the concordance of AW-312.4 was a most desirable asset.

Rupert had complacently told her to obtain it by any means necessary, putting her in charge of the process of procurement. It hadn't occurred to him to ask why he'd been allowed to hear about the auction in the first place, or just how broadly Eve might interpret her remit.

Eve intended to do exactly as she'd been told, and take custody of the manuscript.

And then she intended to give it to Rupert.

Give it good and hard.

Safely downstairs, once the door to Neverland on the top floor was wedged shut with wadded-up newspapers to stop the history from leaking out, Imp celebrated their deliverance by opening a half-gallon jug of Old Rosie. He sloshed generous libations into four mugs and then handed them out as Rebecca passed around a never-ending spliff provisioned from Imp's stash.

"We need gridded paper and pencils," said Doc.

Game Boy nodded along to a beat only he could hear through imaginary headphones. "Used to do paper-and-pencil dungeon crawls with all that stuff."

"You won't get the angles right." Rebecca waved her joint around by way of punctuation. "Need to measure everything."

"No." Imp glared around the room, slightly red-eyed from the smoke. "That's not necessary. We know the angles don't add up to three hundred and sixty degrees up there! The distances don't sum, the spaces overlap. What we need are the, the *connections*. Like a tube map, where the lines are nothing to do with the actual distance between stations. This way we won't get lost even if the measurements say we've doubled back on ourselves." He leaned backward precariously, sinking into the carnivorous brown sofa until he nearly toppled sideways onto Doc. "Huh. I could totally use that shit in the script—an infinite house! Somewhere."

"If it keeps getting older the further back we go, eventually we'll hit the Victorian period," Game Boy said. "Could you use it for filming the set for the Darlings' house?"

"Yes!" Imp sat up excitedly, nearly spilling the dregs of a mug of scrumpy across his lap: Doc caught it in time and gently took it away from him. "The Darling household! That totally works! We'll need lights, which means power, but did you notice there wasn't any traffic noise up there? It'll work for all the indoor scenes!" Then his smile sagged. "I'll still need to sneak into a soundstage for the motion capture bits aboard the asteroid base and pirate ship, though. Hmm." Doc pulled him closer and rubbed his hand in small circles on the small of Imp's back.

"So it all comes back to the great work, huh?" Rebecca blew a lazy smoke ring at the ceiling.

"*Everything* converges on the great work," Imp confirmed. He took his mug back from Doc, then frowned at the lack of contents. "Top me up, boy," he demanded, waving it languorously.

His pose was so theatrically exaggerated that for a moment Doc expected him to add something tasteless—a thoughtlessly racist *chop-chop*, perhaps—but Imp wasn't quite that wasted, or was finally beginning to get a clue. Or maybe Game Boy was just in a good mood and chose to ignore it. Either way it summed to zero. Game Boy shook the jug of scrumpy, then threw it in the air, lidless: as it fell back into his hands it sprayed cloudy hard cider that somehow all ended up in Imp's mug. Oblivious, Imp raised a toast: "Here's to the great work!"

Mugs, or joints, or both, were raised all around as the Lost Boys drank, or toked, or both, to Imp's projected fifteen minutes of fame.

Imp was mercurial, charismatic, and theatrical by disposition. He was also full of himself. Since the age of seven and three-quarters he had held an unshakable conviction that he was destined to be London's twenty-first-century answer to Pittsburgh's Andrew Warhola (if Andy Warhol had grown up with computer graphics, a Peter Pan fixation, and a willingness to fund his art by robbing toy shops rather than painting soup cans). Imp's magnum opus, the project upon which he had lavished the majority of his creative energies for years, was to be the definitive video (and now classic, old-school, film-camera movie) experience of *Peter and Wendy*—the stage play by J. M. Barrie. He'd gotten hooked on it as an infant, when his father read it to him at bedtime. It was a family tradition, Dad had insisted. You read *Peter and Wendy* to your children when it's your turn to have them. Imp had no intention of ever having children—in fact, he found the prospect existentially terrifying—but the book still had a profound influence on him.

Imp intended to channel the spirit of the original author's intent, not the twee rubbish pandered by the Disney Corporation. Peter Pan was an inspiration to Imp in every way imaginable: a chillingly grandiloquent and narcissistic serial killer, detached even from his own shadow. Even in adulthood Imp found himself unaccountably irritated by his inability to fly.[2]

However there were obstacles on Imp's path to greatness. For starters, the bank of Mum and Dad wasn't around any

2 Imp could only emulate the power of flight when he got stoned enough to jump up and down on the trampoline in the back garden, which never ended well.

more. He had a not-terribly-large trust fund, but most of the checks went to keeping the Student Loans Company off his back for his time at art school. Then there was the vexatious issue of copyright law. *Peter and Wendy* was in perpetual copyright—a copyright granted by Act of Parliament to Great Ormond Street Hospital. All recordings and derivative works were liable to pay royalties, and a pirate production would be perceived by the public as a sin as dastardly as any of Hook's escapades. Stealing money from sick kids never played well with the tabloids unless you were a billionaire. (Billionaires, in Imp's world view, could do *anything*. They could—and many did—play the villain in their very own live-action Bond movies.)

So Imp's goal involved egregious and lamentable copyright violation as a precondition, followed by folding, spindling, and rendering nightmarish a children's fantasy beloved by the millions who had been brainwashed by the evil Wizard of Walt. (*Never forgive, never forget*—Imp had committed to memory an impassioned half-hour peroration on the evils of the Rodent Corporation, just in case he was ever called upon to monologue, or even soliloquize, in the dock at the Old Bailey.)

And finally there was the matter of the ever-evolving script, which in Imp's view required alterations to render it palatable to a modern audience.

Imp's version of *Peter and Wendy* featured dead kids being downloaded from cyberspace and resurrected by the hacker Peter, a maniac with a detachable shadow who led the Lost Boys. Peter was a ruthless gang leader locked in eternal struggle with a lawless cyborg ravager, the Dread Space Pirate Hook, with whom he shared a mutual homoerotic love-death relationship. (Imp *totally* shipped Peter and Hook. In fact, Imp was bent on starring in his own movie as Peter, with Doc playing opposite him as Hook.)

A psychopathic murderer and child kidnapper, Peter slew without remorse or affection, and demanded absolute unquestioning obedience of his followers on pain of being *thinned out.* (This bit was totally faithful to the original.) He had a malign ghostly AI servant that ran through the tunnels and structures of the abandoned asteroid colony where they lived. She had a crush on Peter—Peter was nothing if not pansexual—and tinkled maliciously as she vented the air from the sleeping capsules of any Lost Boys who dared grow up. But that didn't happen often because Peter kept them trapped in an eternally delayed pre-pubertal state using a cocktail of hormone suppressors (Game Boy had given him a list), for to grow up was the ultimate betrayal of the principles of the Neotenous Underground.

Other aspects of Imp's script were distinctly heterodox. (That is: they took liberties with the source material's intent.) His Wendy was in no respect a maternal figure—Rebecca would have kicked Imp's ass all the way around Camden Market if he tried to write her into any kind of mothering role. She was a lethal bounty hunter, modelled on Grace Jones's character in Luc Besson's *The Sixth Element.* Imp's Wendy had been sent to the asteroid to infiltrate Peter's cell of nihilistic terror-children and assassinate their leader, but she was destined to fall in love with him and, after his heart was cut out by Hook, she was to graft his head onto the side of her own neck while his body regenerated. Finally there was the alien, the ticking lizard-monster in the ventilation ducts, that lived only to lay its eggs inside their bodies. And there was also going to be a blue, six-legged, brain-upgraded, psychopomp cyberdog called Nana that would win the boss fight with the crocodalien, just because it was awesome.

("Steal from the best" was Imp's watchword, as was "steal from more than one source and remix them so nobody spots what you're doing." (This last assertion was, Doc insisted, highly questionable.) And so was "try to make sure your sources are dead: if they're still worth stealing, they've stood the test of time." *Alien* wasn't dead yet, but since the Disney takeover the Alien Queen was technically a Disney Princess. So it was all a moot point in Imp's opinion; and anyway, revenge was sweet.)

In the two years he'd been working full-time on *Peter and Wendy: A Cyberpunk Dystopia in Space*, Imp had completed eleven drafts of the script. He had also figured out how to get unemployed actors to work for him "for the exposure" (it helped that Imp could convince rain that it was dry and night it was day); how to walk into an Apple Store and blag his way into being given a sweet Mac Pro loaded with video editing software; how to talk his way into endless free training courses in film editing, and even a one-on-one workshop session with Robert McKee; how to cozen his dealer into giving him a 70 percent discount on blow; and how to carry out foolproof bank robberies.

He hadn't actually filmed anything yet, although that was going to change real soon now.

"We start shooting at the beginning of next month, and that's final," he announced, staring up at the smoke dragons circling lazily under the ceiling lights. "Before we can do that, we need another job, to pay for the film and the lab time. But don't worry, I'm sure something will come up . . ."

The day after she rescued Professor Skullface, Wendy returned to work. Her first destination was the staff canteen for a coffee that hadn't been festering in its jug for hours, and her second call was Gibson's office.

"I'll take the job," she said. A cold night in the dark with no electricity had made up her mind for her.

"Great, first I need you to sign this—" He slid a sheet of paper titled *Nondisclosure Agreement* across the desk— "then I'll talk you through this—" a much fatter document titled *Employment Contract: Transhuman Investigations Division*. "It'll take a while. Then I can brief you on the job."

It did not escape her attention that the NDA came first: but she signed it anyway. It was pretty much what she expected. All the obligations for secrecy were on her, and all the benefits went to HiveCo. The employment contract was a little better. It guaranteed an hourly rate plus a higher pay band when on jobs, plus actual sick pay and annual leave— "This looks like I'm on salary?" she asked.

"Next clause."

"One month probationary period, then I'm permanent, subject to *three months'* notice if I want to leave?"

"Unless we fire you for gross misconduct." Gibson's expression was unreadable, but Wendy got the message loud and clear. *We need you.* Which also meant, she realized, *we're getting you cheap while we can.* But with no experience in this higher-level role she had no bargaining leverage—

"This non-compete." She put her finger on the next clause. "You know that shit is legally unenforceable in the UK?"

Gibson smiled. "That is the current law, yes."

"Doesn't matter, I'm not having it." She crossed her arms and glowered.

In the end they compromised: three months' notice with three months' non-compete, and a no-headhunting agreement on top, rather than the two years' non-compete the contract started out with. HR had given Gibson some wiggle room for negotiating. Then they signed both copies, after which Gibson shook her hand across the desk and said, "Welcome to Investigations! I knew we'd come to an arrangement. Now you've got an appointment in Secure Briefing C for your first assignment."

"Wait." Wendy stood. "Don't I get the usual HR dog and pony show? Induction, code of conduct, training in procedures, uniform kit?"

"You get all of that except a uniform," Gibson said as he walked around his desk, "but we'll fit it in when you've got some dead time—there's an urgent job waiting for you, and I want you to hit the ground running. Right after lunch, if not before."

Secure Briefing C was in a part of the building Wendy hadn't visited previously. That wing was secured with a smart badge reader that her ID now had permission to open. Other than that, it looked much like any other HiveCo site office until Gibson waved his own badge at a reader outside an unmarked door and ushered her into something out of an X-Men movie. Exposed ductwork and cables lined a hollow concrete cube that contained a transparent-walled room suspended from hooks in the ceiling. Even the furniture in the glass room was transparent—off-the-shelf Louis Ghost chairs and a matching transparent table. The only opaque artifact it contained was a Microsoft Surface tablet sitting on the table.

"What *is* this?" Wendy asked, looking around as Gibson shut the outer door and turned a handle. Her ears popped and the hiss of air conditioning dampened.

"Anti-eavesdropping precautions. We're suspended inside a Faraday cage with a pressure-controlled, filtered air supply. There are no hiding places for drones or bugs." Someone had doodled a pentacle from a seventies Hammer Horror movie on the bare cement below the transparent floor. Now it lit up, glowing an eerie green like a poisonous deep-sea creature warning off its predators. "Ah, good, grid's up. Have a seat, Deere."

"What kind of eavesdropping needs this, sir?"

"Demons." Gibson said it matter-of-factly. "Also vampires." He gestured at the ceiling where a couple of LED lights reflected violet highlights off the Perspex roof. "The UV spots are to deal with them." Above the dangling overhead lights, another pentacle-in-a-circle diagram pulsed red. "Not to mention gates into the dreamlands. You can't be too careful these days."

Wendy took a couple of seconds to catch up. "I thought we were in the business of apprehending criminals, sir."

"Yes, but there are criminals and there are *criminals*."

"All this—" her gesture swept the room—"you're talking about magical shit? I thought we were dealing with transhumans . . ."

"Same thing," he said dismissively. "Any sufficiently advanced magic is indistinguishable from technology. Where do you think your power comes from, anyway?" Before she could answer he tapped the computer screen, then plugged a small USB key into one port. "It's a physical authentication token," he told her. "We don't just rely on passwords for this stuff." He stabbed the ball of his thumb with a sterile needle, then smeared a trace of blood onto a glass window in the USB stick. "Soul lock confirmed." The Windows login screen vanished to reveal a PowerPoint project and a green-screen window that, after a moment, Wendy recognized as a terminal emulator connected to the Police National Computer system. (And how that worked inside a shielded room was anybody's guess.) "Okay, here we go. First, I want to show you the security camera feed from a robbery at a Pennine Bank branch on Kensington High Street three weeks ago.

Then we'll get to the really interesting stuff—what the perps said in the interview suite."

If you caught the robbers why are you showing me this? Wendy wondered. But she was on the clock at her new working pay grade, so she nodded and went with the flow.

The video side of the presentation divided the screen into quadrants, each showing the view from a different camera covering the interior of a bank branch. The bank was laid out old-style, with three counters separating the clerks from the members of the public queuing in the lobby. A couple of ATMs had been installed along one wall. To one side of the counters there was an armored door with a mirror-glass window, and there were open-plan desks out in front for staff dealing with customer transactions that didn't involve cash. It was clearly a busy time of day—12:54 according to the clock in one of the CCTV windows, peak lunchtime rush hour—and ten customers were queueing for the clerks at the two staffed windows.

"Old-school bank at lunchtime. Now watch this," Gibson said.

Three figures wearing masks and body-stockings rushed the front door. Wendy leaned forward. They weren't obviously armed, but—*transhumans*, she figured—the body language was aggressive and the leader was shouting orders, telling the customers to get on the ground. The elderly video cameras didn't deliver enough pixels to lip-read from, and there was no audio track.

"He's saying, 'This is a stick-up, you are all hostages, open the door to the back or we start shooting people.'"

Wendy drew breath sharply. In her thankfully limited experience, sane robbers didn't *do* that: robbery was bad enough, but with just one sentence the leader had added kidnapping and aggravated assault charges on top. Which, under the new laws promulgated by the New Management, pretty much guaranteed a short drop with a sudden stop at the end.

The bank clerks weren't stupid: they jumped up and fled. But a couple of seconds later the security door sprang open. Someone in a control center elsewhere, intent on avoiding a massacre, had hit the big red button. (The liability payout if a customer lost their life would be far larger than any amount of cash held in the branch safe.) Two of the robbers rushed through the door into the back office, while the one waiting out front with the hostages struck a pose.

The camera views switched. In the back room, the villains shoveled the contents of the cash drawers into laundry bags. The staff had all made a clean escape. Desks cleared out, one of the robbers turned and asked the other a question. He shrugged.

"He asked if the vault was open, if they were supposed to open it and take the contents," Gibson explained. "*He* said he didn't know, it wasn't in the script." Wendy squinted, suddenly getting an inkling that this wasn't business as usual. "Now watch the next bit."

The two supervillains stalked out of the back room and lined up beside their colleague. Then, to Wendy's astonishment, they high-fived and bowed to the hostages.

"He said, 'That's a wrap.'" Gibson narrated. "Quote, 'We nailed the shoot.'"

Half the customers stood up and scattered, rushing for the exit. The other half mobbed the supervillains. For a few seconds it was chaos in the bank, then two cops stormed through the door and tased the robbers. "*Count them,*" Gibson hissed. "Count *everybody.*"

"Pause it for me?" Wendy grabbed the Surface and began to scrub back and forth through the video. "Ten customers at first, four when it ends, plus two cops—no, wait, what am I looking for?"

"The money bags. Where did they go?"

It took Wendy just a minute to retrace the sequence. "Holy shit. *Holy shit.*"

"Did you see that customer's face?" Gibson demanded.

"Nuh-no . . ." Wendy blinked in surprise. "He didn't show his face to *any* of the cameras, not at *any* time." In admiration. "That was slick. Tell me about the marks?"

"Three wannabe actors." Gibson huffed like a frustrated dog after a snatched-away snack. "They answered an ad on Facebook offering work on an amateur video project. Cinema verité, heard of it? The pitch was that the director had rented an old bank building and had replaced the CCTV cameras with the kit they needed to film his movie. The customers and clerks were all extras. The wannabes were given a script and told to make it look good. They thought it was entirely legal and they were doing it for the exposure."

"Except it was a real bank and the real robber was waiting to snatch the cash and do a dash while they provided a distraction?"

"Pretty much." Gibson scowled.

"And the transhuman angle?"

"The marks all met the director. He pitched them in person, script and all, gave them an audition and screen test, and promised them a good day's pay for a good day's work. You'd think they could tell us who the guy that hired them was, wouldn't you? Or that they'd have asked some questions?"

"They didn't ask—" Wendy had a suspicious mind at the best of times, and now her inner alarm bells were ringing. "*Riiight.*"

"They were tampered with." Gibson's scowl deepened. "The loss adjusters hired a forensic psychiatrist to examine them. They were acting under a high-level geas. If it ever goes to trial they'll probably be found not guilty on grounds of diminished responsibility. The, uh, *director* has supernatural powers of conviction: people believe whatever he tells them. The bag man is impossible to grab, he's as slippery as an eel, and the getaway driver—just don't go there. This isn't the only job the gang has pulled in the past two months, Deere, or even the first job that's hit one of our customers."

"You want the director and his associates, not the fall-guy actors."

"Yes! But it's not going to be easy. Most bank robbers have a simple MO, which is how we eventually catch them. That, or they talk to someone and we get a tip. These guys are different. Not only do they have transhuman characteristics, but they do a variety of jobs—not just banks. They're really good at not showing up on videos, and they mix it up creatively." Gibson pulled the Surface over to his side of the desk. "So let's talk about their most recent job, when they hit the cash room at Hamleys Toy Shop . . ."

Bernard wasn't answering his phone, so Eve decided to pay him a visit.

She stood on his doorstep, waiting impatiently for him to answer the entryphone. After a minute, she pushed the button again.

"Dammit, Harris," she swore quietly. She'd expected him to report back this morning—the commission she'd dangled in front of him should have seen to that. She pulled out her phone—a Caviar-modded iPhone 6S with a 24-carat gold body—and called his landline again. There was no reply, and Harris's antique tape-based answering machine didn't cut in.

She turned to make eye contact with the replacement

Gammon. (The old one had proven inadequate; the new one was ex-military and *vastly* more effective.) He came to attention. "Open it," she ordered.

"Yes, ma'am." He cleared his throat. "If you'd care to stand back . . ."

Eve stepped away from the door as the Gammon undid the button on his suit jacket, shrugged to loosen his shoulders, then pivoted and slammed a size thirteen boot into the lock.

The door crashed open and rebounded. The Gammon caught it before it slammed shut and held it for her: "Ma'am."

Eve stepped past him without comment. *This one's an improvement*, she noted. *Maybe he's a keeper.*

She took the stairs to the flat at a measured pace, not hurrying—it wouldn't do to arrive out of breath—but not dawdling, either. Something was clearly wrong. Bernard never forgot to switch on the answering machine on the rare occasions when he went out.

Eve paused on the top-floor landing. The Gammon arrived behind her, not even huffing. "Ma'am?"

"One moment." Eve reached towards the door handle, then paused. "Hmm."

"Want me to open it, ma'am?"

Preoccupied, Eve forgot to bite his head off. (He was, in any case, trailing her own line of thought, albeit a few steps behind.) "Not yet."

She clasped her hands behind her back as she reached for the door handle again, this time by force of will alone. *Mind over matter*, she chanted to herself, quivering with effort. A prickly perspiration broke out across her forehead. Eve had a knack for telekinesis, but to her total disgust, she could bench-press greater weights using her arm muscles alone. Her other abilities were all so risibly feeble that a less determined woman would have given up on them. But Eve had persisted, exploring her limits and learning how to use her powers in combination and to best effect. Precision and perception could, if deployed correctly, compensate for a lack of raw power. So although her mind could barely hold a twenty-kilogram weight against gravity, she could reach behind a keyhole and feel for hidden tumblers. And it took much less than twenty kilos of force to spring a Yale lock.

There was a click: then the doorknob rotated, and the door swung softly inwards.

"Ma'am?"

She pointed: "That's a steel door frame, and the door's re-inforced. You'd have broken your ankle." *And a broken front door and an unlocked inner door will tell a misleading story if the police come calling.* "You go first."

The Gammon had already snapped on a pair of blue surgi-cal gloves. He bulled through the door and swept along Ber-nard's narrow hallway, one hand concealed under his jacket. He cast left, covering the hall closet and the bathroom, then right, checking out the living room. "Clear," he called softly. On into the rear of the flat: the compact kitchen, the bed-room. "Clear, clear—" At the end of the hall, the office door stood shut. The Gammon froze beside it, drew his pistol, then looked to Eve for direction.

"Allow me." Eve stepped into the bedroom doorway, then reached out with her mind. The door handle turned and the Gammon crouched as he followed the door in, covering the room.

"Clear," he said, then paused. "Ma'am, you're not going to like this."

"How long has he been dead?" she asked, stepping out from behind her cover.

The Gammon knelt beside Bernard's body. His death had not been dignified. The sleazy book spiv lay face down on the office floor, his head half-covered by a wool cardigan that had fallen on top of him. The feet splayed out behind him were shod in bedroom slippers, their leather soles worn to a high gloss. He was, she observed, still wearing his pajama bottoms. There was a significant amount of blood, but blood loss wasn't what had killed him.

"No rigor, ma'am." The Gammon touched the back of the victim's neck. "He hasn't been dead long enough to go cold. I'd say less than six hours, maybe less than four."

Eve glanced around the room. The computer's monitor stared darkly back at her. Its usual hum was absent, and there was a gaping rectangular hole in the front of the system unit where a hard drive would normally be. The desk drawers were open, their contents disturbed.

"Well." She composed herself, took a deep breath, and mustered up a smile: "Well! This is a setback." *Stop babbling in front of the help*, she admonished herself sternly. *Stiff upper lip.* "Obviously somebody was *extremely* eager to pre-empt the auction." She toed the corpse distastefully with the tip of one Manolo Blahnik. "Turn him over."

"Ma'am? Preserving the crime scene—"

"Is not our concern," she said crisply.

"Yes, ma'am." He gripped the body by one shoulder and heaved.

Eve pulled on a pair of gloves and crouched beside him. "Right. Right." She touched the back of Bernard's head, through the matted, bloody hair. Bone grated mushily under her fingertips. "A blow to the occipital bone, showing signs of extreme force. Probably sent splinters into the foramen magnum, tearing the medulla oblongata. The hemorrhaging is from the posterior spinal artery: there isn't much because cardiac arrest was nearly instantaneous." She stood and contemplated Bernard's mortal remains for almost a minute. Her hands itched for a scalpel.

"Ma'am? What should I do?"

"Go and close the front door, then stand guard. If anyone you don't know tries to enter, kill them."

"Very good, ma'am." For such a large man he could move surprisingly quietly.

Once he was gone, Evelyn closed the office door, then pulled out her phone and dialed. "Julian, this is Eve," she said without preamble. "I want a cleanup team round at Bernard Harris's flat. Crash priority, open checkbook. Prime the pig farm to expect a consignment for disposal. I need the contents of the office here bagging and tagging, and a full forensic teardown of Mr. Harris's PC, although it looks like the hard drive's been removed. He's old school, so you'll need to search for paper records, notebooks, diaries, that sort of thing. Oh, and there's an old-fashioned printer—not an inkjet or laser, the kind with a ribbon. I want you to look into lifting an impression of the last document he printed on it."

Eve hung up. She knew better than to turn on the PC and meddle. Bernard probably didn't keep anything valuable on it anyway, and if he did there'd be passwords and maybe booby traps for the unwary. Whoever had killed him and taken the hard drive was pursuing a fool's errand.

She glanced at the filing cabinet. The top drawer was ajar. Papers had been pulled out, but she saw a scattering of rectangular plastic containers like wombat turds in the bottom. They were diskette boxes: when she'd been growing up, the cash-starved comprehensive school she'd attended had still used PCs with floppy disks, even though they were long-obsolete in business.

Eve smiled to herself. The killer was not only impulsive and slapdash: they were young or expensively educated or both. And Eve, who was neither of those things, now had the beginnings of a profile of her enemy.

Bernard's antiquarian PC might have lost its hard drive, but it gave up its secrets with barely a fight.

Eve's first stop on her arrival back at Chateau de Montfort Bigge was the IT Department. IT, in keeping with Rupe's disdain for boffins, were confined to a sad, windowless gerbil hutch under the main staircase that had once served as a cloakroom. There was always at least one semi-interchangeable minion on duty. "You!" she barked at the nearest gerbil—or possibly the least able to scramble for cover when she slammed through the door. "What's your name?"

"M-Marcus, Miss?" Marcus was bald, bearded, and gnomishly middle-aged. He wrung his hands as he looked up at her through horn-rimmed glasses with pebble-thick lenses. "Can I help you?"

"I should think so." She reached into her Louis Vuitton handbag and produced three boxes of floppies. "These are backup disks from a PC. I want them imaged, cracked, and a copy of the original files restored."

Marcus froze, then focussed on the boxes, oddly intent. "May I, Miss?" he asked eagerly. She tipped the boxes into his cupped hands: he stared at them as if they were a particularly delectable treat. "Ooh, I haven't seen these in a while!" He carefully popped the lid on one box and peered inside. "High density, 1.44 jobs. Definitely an old PC, not a Mac?"

"A beige boxy thing from the late 1980s. It didn't have a mouse, if that's any help. The hard disk is missing, and this is the only material that could be salvaged. I'm relying on you," she said.

His eyes glazed as he dreamily stroked the exterior of the box. "I may need to get hold of some specialized kit, I don't think we've got anything that can read floppies any more, but having said that—"

"Buy anything you need; just keep the receipts. I expect a full work-up within twenty-four hours."

"Uh-uh-yes, Miss." Marcus snapped back to terrified obedience. "Right away, Miss."

Eve stalked back to her lair, brooding. Someone had killed Bernard and taken the hard disk. The timing strongly implied that his murder was connected to the auction. So it suggested that the item was worth considerably more on the market than Rupe had indicated. *Interesting.* The killer was now one jump ahead of her, unless they were incompetent and had killed Bernard by mistake before weaseling the auction details out of him. In which case (an unpalatable thought) they might have irremediably fucked up the entire job for everybody and she'd have to start again from scratch, this time using an unfamiliar book dealer. Either way, Eve was clear on the steps she needed to take.

It occurred to Eve that she'd need a thief. And for a job like this, there was only one person she could turn to.

Eve didn't need much sleep, and the promise of the coming treasure hunt kept her awake as effectively as a pint of espresso. She spent the early evening making use of the gym in the basement, then moved on to the firing range, where she flung ball bearings at pistol targets by force of will alone until her head ached. Returning to the office, she handled issues arising in the American subsidiaries. For dinner she ordered up a cold collation from the kitchen, which she ate at her desk. At eleven, she rose, restless, and returned to the shooting gallery, where she amused herself with a bag of marbles that shattered satisfactorily when they slammed into their targets. By two in the morning she was drained, but she was no closer to sleep than she had been at eight the night before: the febrile anticipation of action had her in its grip.

Finally she could no longer contain herself. She returned to her lair, restored her appearance—hair secured in a scalp-tugging bun, lips and mascara retouched, suit straightened—then marched on IT. "Well?" she demanded.

Marcus was still at work, but clearly flagging. He jolted upright at her voice: "Yes Miss!" he blurted. "It's done and dusted!"

"What *precisely* is done and dusted?"

"You were right about it being an antique, Miss! Norton Backup, vintage 1992, from a 40Mb hard disk on a 286. The disks weren't corrupt but the backup was encrypted, so I had to copy the images and spin up a few thousand VM instances on EC2—" Eve narrowed her eyes at him and he gulped— "erm, I cracked the password and there's a VirtualBox with a bootable copy of the hard drive *right here*." His hands fluttered above the keyboard of his workstation. "What do you want me to do to it?"

"Get out and leave me to it," she told him. Marcus bolted from his chair as if she was a cheetah. Eve took his place at the desk and found herself doing a double-take.

Bernard's PC had run MS-DOS—nothing as sophisticated and slickly modern as Windows 3.1—but he'd had an email client, a text-mode monstrosity that collected mail from some weird modem-connected lacuna of the internet that hadn't yet discovered fire, let alone the World Wide Web. After some swearing she got it working and fumbled her way into his mailbox. (It was refreshingly free of spam, for some reason.) Running on modern hardware, virtually everything happened instantaneously, including text searches. It took her barely ten minutes to find what she was looking for in his inbox. *That's interesting*, she thought, then smiled to herself. It was all here: the anonymized email address of the auctioneer, Bernard's banking details, Rupert's wish list. It took her another couple of minutes to shut down the VM and upload a copy to her personal area on the office file storage, then delete the original from Marcus's machine. The disk boxes were sitting beside it, next to a very shiny-looking floppy disk drive, and she took the lot.

Marcus was waiting outside the office door, knees knocking. "Excellent job," she reassured him generously: "I'll be sure to let HR know. I'm taking these," she added. "You didn't look at the contents of the disks, did you?"

"No, no, Miss!" The poor little rodent was eager to return to his cage.

"Excellent. You won't speak of this to anyone. You can go home now—wherever you go when you're not here, that is."

Marcus was still babbling his thanks as she stalked back to the elevator. *He's good, but he's much too talkative for comfort*, she realized. *I'll have to reassign him.* Once back at her desk with her office door locked, she checked that the disk image was bootable. Then she shredded the floppy disks and drafted a memo to Human Resources, asking them to put him on the next flight out to the British Antarctic Survey's Halley Research Station. Let him blab to the penguins: the birds weren't about to bid on the book.

Eve smiled again. Then she picked up her phone and called her thief.

Imp and the gang stayed up late into the night, wasted on a never-ending roll-up and a periodically emptying jug of scrumpy (followed by Del's distressingly crap stockpile of lager when the good stuff ran out). Eventually Game Boy staggered off to the games room, where he could cuddle up close to his PC and obsessively play KOF until he fell asleep. Some time later, Del announced she was going to the bathroom and never came back. That left Imp and Doc passing the guttering embers of a joint with which they exchanged sloppy blowbacks, too wasted to get properly amorous. "I'm drunk and you're ugly," Doc slurred, "but in the morning I'll be hungover and you'll still be ugly." He leaned sideways and kissed Imp deeply, his mouth smoky. But before Imp could get anything more than his hopes up, Doc stumbled to his feet and wandered towards the staircase.

"Don't let the door hit you on the way out!" Imp called from his pit on the sofa. He yawned resentfully. "I dunno. Some people. Lightweights." The room pancaked and wobbled around his head. Doc had a point, he had to admit, and whistled a few out-of-key bars of "Too Drunk to Fuck" by way of self-deprecatory comment. Then he lay on his back alone, his mind empty for once.

Then, for the first time in over a week, his phone rang.

"What the—*what*—fuck—" Imp sat bolt upright and flung out a hand in the direction of the device. It was thundering out the bass line of "Making Plans for Nigel" at audible-over-traffic volume, even though it was three in the bloody morning.

"*He has his future in a British Steel*—hello, who the fuck is this do you know what time it oh *hello*, sis, long time no see, really, you're calling *now*? Who died and made you pope?"

"Are you drunk?" his sister accused.

He chuckled: "Maybe a little?"

"Listen carefully," Imp's sister said, enunciating each word with obsidian precision, sharp enough to slash his eardrums. "This is *very important*."

Instant sobriety: "It's not Mum, is it? Has she died?"

"No, she's not dead. You'd know if you bothered to visit her."

Imp bit back his instinctive response. "What is it, then?"

"I need a favor."

Imp blinked at the ceiling, perplexed, and took stock of his surroundings. Nope, he hadn't suddenly been transported to Neverland. He was lying on his back, holding his phone in one hand—it *was* his phone, it hadn't magically metamorphosed into a rainbow chameleon baby while his attention was elsewhere—and yes, he was still lying in the carnivorous living room sofa, surrounded by discarded beer cans and overflowing ashtrays. He took stock. There was a chill of dampness in the air despite the oil-filled radiator running off the stolen electricity supply. It was December 2015, and he was drunk *and* stoned, and his sister, of all people, wanted a favor.

"You're mad," he said, and waited for the explosion.

There was no big sister detonation. Instead, something much more disturbing happened. She chuckled. Imp cringed: he knew that laugh, had known it since before he learned to walk, and it meant nothing good. She didn't use it very often, but when she did . . . It was a laugh worthy of a young Shakespearian witch, a laugh destined to grow up to be a cackle of malice. Mischief was afoot. *Oh fuck*, he thought fuzzily. Stoned and drunk, Imp was no match for his big sister. He'd rather face a police raid or Game Boy's tiger parents in full hue and corrupting-our-daughter cry. He'd even undergo a Work Capability Assessment, if it meant never again hearing that horrible ululation.

"Stop," he implored, "please, just *stop*. It's three in the fucking morning!"

"If I knew all I had to do was *laugh* at you I'd have phoned years ago." She tittered briefly, sending chills scurrying up and down his spine. At three in the morning his sister could titter like a ghoul. "But I'm serious, Jeremy. I want you to do me a favor."

"What's in it for me?" he asked automatically, before his tongue caught up: "Don't call me that!"

"I think I can make it worth your while." Pause. "I know where you live." Another pause. "I know who you live *with*. And I know it can't be easy or cheap."

"No need to rub it in." Big sis had always had a knack for getting under his skin.

"If the shoplifting and petty larceny aren't cutting it, you could always put your artistic projects on hold. Get a real job. The trustees would even pay for you to go back to university, as long as you study something employable this time." A bitter tone crept into her voice.

Skin crawling, Imp had to work hard to resist the urge to tell his sister to fuck off. Like him, she'd chosen her own path and pursued it with terrifying tenacity. He felt it was almost his duty to counterbalance her workaholism by slacking. "Would I have to wear a suit and tie?" he asked idly. "Because that'd be a hard *no*."

"Oh you." She chuckled again, almost indulgently. "Never change."

His vision doubled, blurring as she whipsawed him from love to hate and back again. You could build your own family through choice, but you couldn't erase the one you were born with, even if you chose to avoid them. With a supreme effort of will he gathered his wits. "Listen, it's three in the fucking morning and you want a favor and it can't wait, which means it's pretty fucking big, so why are we pissing around the bush like this? What do you *want*?"

"I'd like to hire you," she said, "to do a job."

"No." It came out instantly, without having to think. "You can't make me work for you." *Or see you*.

"You misunderstand: this is a one-off, not a permanent position. And it pays *very* well . . ."

"Doesn't matter: I'm still not going to work for you."

"Not even freelance? On your own terms?"

"Huh." Imp stared at his phone for a moment, wondering if he was dreaming, or maybe nightmaring. "Good try, but the answer is still no."

"I just want you to get hold of a book for me. There's eighty large in it for you, no questions asked."

"*Eighty*—" Imp remembered who he was talking to at the last instant and body-swerved—"no."

"I can make your dyke biker chick's Yardie neighbors leave her mom alone. I can get you what you need to make your boyfriend with the attitude problem happy. I can get the Chinese kid's parents off his back. I can even hook him up with SexChange."

"SexChange is a myth," Imp said automatically. Game Boy had spent ages chasing after the mirage in question, whose power was the ability to put the trans into transhuman.

"SexChange is real." Her voice dropped an octave: "And I can get *you* the use of a RED Dragon and all the lenses you need, and a slot on the number four sound stage at Millennium Studios in Elstree whenever you're ready for it."

"I—" Imp's larynx froze. This was a nightmare scenario: Big Sis was back in his life, wanted *him* back in *her* life, and knew how to pull his strings—"cunt!"

"I'll take that as a yes, shall I?" She sounded idly amused, and far too awake for the time of night.

"Fucknuggets. Yes, all right, but can we talk about it in the morning when I'm sober?"

"Of course. My office, backside of n—no, ten o'clock, I know what you're like before breakfast. Yes, come to my office at ten o'clock and I'll fill you in." She rattled off an address. It was, Imp realized with dismay, a mere fifteen-minute walk from the squat. "Security will be expecting you. Be there or stay poor, Jeremy! *Ciao!*"

Jeremy—Imp—lay back on the sofa and groaned softly, clutching his head. *She's found me*, he thought dismally. By the sound of it she'd been watching him from afar for some time. *Typical.* Five years of avoiding her and suddenly it turned out she'd known where he was all along. *Just please god don't tell me it's for Mum.* The less he had to do with his family, the better for everyone. *Jesus fuck.*

But he had to, however unwillingly, face the facts. It was three o'clock in the morning, an hour when nightmares came true; and his sister was willing to pay eighty thousand pounds and a bounty of dreams in return for a rare book. She hadn't *actually* threatened Del, Doc, or Game Boy, at least not explicitly. As for why: if anyone knew what Imp was capable of, it'd be his big sister. And it would be her sleazebag boss's money she was spending. Even so, eighty grand was a lot to pay for a book.

There was no alternative: tomorrow morning he'd go round to her office and find out what Eve wanted.

FOUL PAPERS

The next morning Imp forced himself to shave, brush his teeth, and dress for a business meeting. Which was to say, he wore the morning suit he'd acquired from the back of an Oxfam shop some years ago for Court Appearances and similar occasions. (He'd been caught with an ounce of grass at sixth form college and the barrister had insisted he wear a suit when he came up before the magistrate. Imp had taken to heart the maxim that you can never be underdressed for a formal occasion, and went large, or as large as he could while being broke.) Because it looked dangerously similar to a real suit, he'd accessorized it with a wing-collared shirt and a cravat that was auditioning for a future role as a dishcloth.

Imp emerged, yawning and blinking at the unaccustomed sight of London before noon, and strolled towards the de Montfort Bigge household. He clasped his hands behind his back and tilted his head forward, like a particularly hungover pigeon. The address his sister had sent him was a few streets over from the squat, in a significantly cheaper part of the borough—one where mere multimillionaires could still afford to live, behind high stone walls surveilled by CCTV cameras.

The front door of Chez Bigge opened directly onto the pavement. From the outside it resembled any other Georgian house of a certain vintage, although the windows to either side were blocked by Venetian blinds. A featureless stone wall extending on either side of the house enclosed the grounds, broken only by a garage door. It was so unwelcoming that Imp put a deliberate spring in his step as he bounced up to the front step and mashed his thumb on the doorbell. He eased up only when someone finally came to open it. "Yes?" demanded the impeccably groomed butler.

Imp grinned cheekily. "I have an appointment with Evelyn Starkey."

He thrust out a hand. The butler ignored it. "Who should I say is calling?"

"Ebeneezer Goode—nah, it's her brother Jeremy, and *we're* good, mate."

At the word *brother* the butler's face turned an intriguing shade of gray. "I'll see if she's available, sir," he muttered, backing into the hallway. He maintained a wary eye contact while he retreated, as if he feared Imp might attack if he turned his back.

The interior was decorated pretty much as Imp expected of one of the snooty residences in this neck of the woods: boringly valuable antique furniture, a vestibule for a modern office at one side of the entrance (in what had clearly been a morning room, once upon a time), a security checkpoint and alarm panel opening off the other side. Someone with more money than taste had shoehorned a cramped elevator into the wall beside a closed door—at a guess, the former drawing room had been truncated to provide access to one of the subterranean minotaur-labyrinths where the oligarchs stored their treasure chests. Imp loved it to bits: *I could totally use this as a set for Bad Guy Central*, he thought, discreetly studying the decor as the butler conferred with the ornamental blonde at the receptionist's workstation.

The receptionist nodded at him, the rigidity of her posture

telegraphing apprehension; then she tapped a button on her desk phone. Imp didn't need to be a lip-reader to figure out her words. "Miss Starkey, your brother is in the lobby." *Please get him out of here.*

A few seconds later, the butler strolled towards him. "Follow me, sir." Imp nodded, deliberately ignoring the whine of motors as the front door eased shut behind him. The butler ushered him directly to the elevator. "In here, please," he said, as the doors slid open to reveal a small mirror-walled cubicle floored in Italian marble. "Your sister will meet you below."

It did not escape Imp's attention that the lift had three different security cameras and no visible control panel.

The lift slowly descended. When it stopped, the doors revealed a bland corporate lobby area. Only the decorative cornices distinguished it from a modern office building.

"Hello, Jeremy. Appropriately attired as ever. It's been, what, two and a half years?"

"Closer to four," Imp corrected. "You've changed," he said, staring stupidly at his sister.

"Follow me." Eve turned and clicked away on sky-high stilettos, Imp trailing behind.

"I like what you've done with your hair," he snarked. It was very blonde and pinned in a tight bun. *You had pink dreads and wore flower-printed DMs and hippie dresses when I was a kid.*

"Come in," she said as the door opened for her. She walked around a gigantic desk, then sat, very primly, in a huge and complicated office chair. She stared at him as the door hissed shut. There were no windows, just cameras in every corner, discreetly embedded in the cornices and skirting boards. "Sit down," she suggested. Imp sat. "The doors are all remote-controlled. The building security computer monitors visitor movements. Face recognition technology, you know."

Imp couldn't stop himself. "What happens to non-approved visitors?"

Evelyn's smile was warm enough to boil liquid nitrogen. "If I had a stroke right now, you could starve to death in here."

"Then please don't die? You're the only sister I've got." *Arguably*, he added silently. This polished, hard-shell version of his sister was unpleasantly distant, almost a stranger to him. "What do you do here?"

"Oh, this and that." She lost the false smile. Without the mask she almost looked human, like the Evie he'd grown up with. Five years his elder, she'd always been the responsible one, somewhere between an elder sister and a younger aunt when he was a child. Now he studied her and realized something was wrong with her face: some aspect of her cheekbones, or maybe it was her chin or her nose, didn't look quite right. It was almost as if she'd undergone a face transplant, leaving the underlying bone structure intact but blending her features with those of another woman. "I work for Mr. de Montfort Bigge, Jeremy. This is his London residence, and I'm his executive assistant."

"Lovely." Imp flung one knee across the other, leaned back, and forced himself to beam at her. *A secretary*, he thought disappointedly. *For all her dedication she's just a secretary?* "What does Mr. Bigge do, exactly?"

"Oh, a bit of this and that. Investments and imports and exports, that sort of thing." Her eyes narrowed.

"And what happened to you?" Imp looked at her. "This is hardcore, Eve. You've changed so much." *Too much.*

"Now is not the time." She sounded more irritated than offended.

"Really?" He stared. "What happened?"

"Reality happened. School of hard knocks, I suppose."

She gleamed like a Photoshop-retouched version of herself, flawless and glossy and inhumanly perfect. Her silk blouse probably cost more than Del's entire wardrobe. She'd had dental work, evidently taken care of by the kind of orthodontist who serviced Hollywood stars and corporate sharks. "Or maybe I just had to grow up. It's different for boys, I don't expect you to understand." She looked down her long, perfectly flawless nose at him.

Imp refused to be intimidated. "Don't push it, sis. Anyway, you've only got five years on me."

"True. But I still know how to deal with you, just like old times." She smiled alarmingly and burst into rhyme, shocking Imp with half-forgotten memories: "*Speak roughly to your little boy, and beat him when he sneezes; he only does it to annoy—*"

"—*Because he knows it teases*, yes, yes, I get it, sis, no need to rub it in!" Lewis Carroll had been a shared love of theirs, and evidently she hadn't quite forgotten. "What's this all about then?"

"It'll take a bit of explaining. Do you still take your coffee the same way?"

"Um." Rattled, Imp tried hard to get a grip, but ultimately failed. "Maybe?"

"No problem." Eve glanced towards the sideboard that took up the far wall of her office. There was a jug of water there, a couple of mugs, and a small built-in fridge. "Allow me to serve you." A stream of water snaked up and out of the jug, looped across to one of the mugs and dived in. Then the lid rose from a jar. The odor of roast coffee filled the room as a gritty cloud of grounds rose to join the water.

Imp watched Eve closely. Her face was a mask of tension as she wrestled with her materials by force of will alone. "There's no need to—"

"Yes there is," she grated, then ignored him. The mug began to steam. The airbrushed perfection of her forehead was very slightly shiny: *Is that sweat?* he wondered. Fine bubbles began to surface in the mug. "Ninety degrees is the correct temperature for fresh brewed coffee," she noted. "Boiling water scalds the grounds."

"You *really* don't have to—"

Imp trailed off. A dripping mass of brown sludge rose from the mug and drifted towards the small rubbish bin on the sideboard. Next, the fridge door opened. The rising stream of milk didn't surprise Imp now: he was, however, impressed despite himself when the mug of freshly brewed coffee rose from the sideboard and floated towards him.

"Take it," Eve gasped.

Imp grabbed the mug out of the air. "Thank you," he said, raising it in toast to her, his mind spinning. "I didn't know you could do—" his eyes tracked to the sideboard—"that." *Making coffee as a superpower?* He wondered: *Am I meant to be impressed?* Then he worked through the exact sequence of actions his sister had just carried out by force of will alone, and his mouth dried up.

"I'm *so* glad we understand one another." She smiled winningly as he took a sip; on the sideboard, a second mug was underway. It was, Imp decided, a very good cup of coffee. And a warning. A very pointed warning. He swallowed carelessly and burned the roof of his mouth.

"Good coffee. Technically impressive. Much precision, very superpower, wow."

"The family aptitude for esoterica apparently extends to more than . . . you know." Her smile vanished. "I only discovered I could do this a couple of years ago. The reemergence of magic has made all sorts of things possible for people like us."

"You say opportunity, I say threat: the family tragedy re-dux." Imp, now brooding, put his mug down on the edge of her desk. "How did you find me?"

"My position gives me certain privileges. I've had people watching you for a while."

Somehow Imp did not find this revelation in any way surprising—or reassuring. "Why?"

She shrugged, but the gesture was swallowed by her jack-et's tailoring. "In case I ever needed you. In case you ever needed me."

"Come to the Dark Side, Luke . . ." Imp took another sip. "Have you seen Mum recently?"

The mug of coffee steeping on the sideboard shattered, leaving a boiling brown jellyfish hanging in the air above the French-polished walnut. Eve scowled. "You did *not* just say that!" Her discarded drink extended a liquid pseudopod towards the mouth of the bin.

"I've been visiting her whenever I could." Imp slid the knife in. "How about you?"

"I visit the nursing home regularly." Eve narrowed her eyes at him: "I've got a very important job. Lots of people depend on me. I'm very busy."

"I'm sure you are. You're so busy you ignore your brother for four years." It was an unfair accusation, intended to hurt: in truth *he'd* been avoiding *her* for four years, they had good reason for avoiding one another. But he wanted her to give some sign that she shared his pain. A bolus of coffee bulged along the tentacle and dripped into the waste. "But it's okay because you have people to monitor your relatives for you."

Eve's face went mannequin-still, and for a gut-curdling second Imp thought he'd pushed her too far. But somewhere beneath the glossy, lacquered surface, there still beat the shrivelled remains of his sister's heart. "Yes, I do," she said very softly, "because I *am* very busy. I'm not a nice person these days; ten-years-ago-me would have been horrified if she could see nowadays-me. No question about it. But the people I have to do business with are much, much worse than you can possibly imagine. The distance I maintain is for your own safety: I cut you out of my life because I care about you, not just because of the family curse."

Imp put his mug down. He folded his hands to stop them shaking. "Is it really that bad?" *Can't you leave?* he wanted to ask.

"Oh, you have *no* idea." Her cheek twitched, the glaze cracking for a moment. "I didn't want to drag you into this. But I've been given a job—ordinarily, a straightforward job—with a tight deadline, and I'm afraid I need your and your team's skills. I have to get my hands on a rare book that's up for auction, but unfortunately my acquisitions agent, the only person I know who knows how to contact the seller, has been murdered—" she rolled over Imp's startle reflex implacably—"and I'm concerned that there might be a leak within the organization. Some of the very bad people I alluded to may also be after the book. So I need your help. I'm willing to pay whatever it takes. Not just money. I can make your problems go away. I can get you whatever resources you need to make your film. I just need you to get me the book."

Imp leaned forward in his chair. "I want you to stop threatening my friends," he said, in a semblance of a calm voice.

"Of course." She gave him a slight moue of amusement. "They're your *friends*. If I actually did anything to damage them, you'd never forgive me."

He sighed. "You're not going to make this easy, are you?"

A flicker of a smile. "Why would I?"

"Because—" Imp met her gaze, and gently *pushed*. "Tell me what's going on? What's the catch?"

Something was wrong and he barely noticed at first, but then his sister beamed at him, blood-red lips pulling back from polished ivory teeth like fangs, and there was a buzzing in his ears and a tingling in his hands and feet as everything went very far away for a few seconds. "Ah, some fighting spirit at last!" Her smile broadened. "I'm warded," she explained. "Good try, but don't do it again—you'll hurt yourself."

Imp gasped and dropped the connection. The relief came as instantly as letting go of a live wire. "*Damn* that's a sharp one."

"We have the best of everything here. Best coffee, best cars, best occult defenses." She smirked as he shook his head roughly. "At least as good as the toys the New Management hands out to its favored minions."

He gulped. "Are you—"

"No! I work for Mr. Bigge, not the Prime Minister. But," she side-eyed the surveillance cameras, "unanticipated State Level Actors are popping out of the woodwork everywhere. New ones, and not-so-new: Advanced Persistent Threats, the security people call them. Like your little found family of waifs and strays, for instance."

"What? We're not a—"

"*Don't* underestimate yourself, Jeremy, false modesty is unbecoming. Also, don't underestimate your team: the whole is greater than the sum, et cetera. So great, in fact, that it's just your *damn good luck* that the first Very Important Person you've come to the attention of is your ever-loving elder sister, rather than, say, the Baroness Sanguinary, or the Thief-Taker General."

Imp's skin crawled. "You're threatening me again."

"No I'm not. I'd happily leave your friends alone. But if you want to protect them from the Black Pharaoh's agents, you'll need to do a lot more." She hesitated. "Do this one thing for me and I'll teach you how to protect yourselves. Not just you, I mean *all* of you. How not to attract the things that hide in shadows. I hope I'm not going to regret this offer," she added with evident foreboding.

This reticence did more to convince Imp that she was on the up-and-up than all her previous offers combined. That, and the blood they shared: all the heartache and resentment and loss that only a family's shared experiences could inflict. "Tell me what you need and when you need it by," he said. "I can't promise anything until I've had a chance to talk to the gang." Eve reached into her drawer and withdrew a slim envelope. She slid it across the desktop and Imp took it. Going by feel, it contained something small and hard. "A memory stick?"

She nodded. "And some other stuff: a bank card, some paperwork. There's an explanation in the README."

Imp tucked it into his breast pocket. "Okay. And how long have we got?"

She squared her shoulders. "Five days."

"What—"

"That's when the boss gets home. He'll expect results, and he gets annoyed when he's thwarted."

Imp drained his coffee mug, and rose. "I'd better get going, hadn't I?"

Eve nodded, then stood and walked over to the door, which opened at her approach. "Follow me." She led him back to the lobby. The butler and receptionist cringed at her approach, as if she were royalty, or at least minor nobility. *Secretary, indeed.* Imp smiled at them in passing and they flinched, avoiding eye contact.

"Good luck," Eve said as they parted company on the

doorstep. But he couldn't help noticing that at no point in the encounter did she try to hug him.

Game Boy had slept badly, tossing and turning in his sleeping bag on the floor of the games room, his feet warmed by the toasty exhaust from his PC, and his head chilled by the draft from the sash windows behind the cardboard Ames room cutouts. He suffered from claustrophobia dreams, albeit less frequently since he'd moved in with Doc and Imp.

The commonest, least malignant version resonated with their explorations the day before. He opened a room in a new home, one his parents had just moved into, and discovered rooms and rooms and more endless rooms, an infinite manifold of branching spaces populated with charity-shop furniture and secondhand G Plan suites, windows opening onto impossible light wells between tight-packed buildings. The dream echoed stories his grandmother had told him of life in Hong Kong before reunification with the motherland. It was like a bizarre procedural animation, an infinite dungeon generator populated with 1960s castoffs, Dwarf Fortress in the grip of a hostile takeover by the Gnomes of IKEA.

The dreams themselves weren't unpleasant, but waking from them on an acquaintance's sofa, or in a hostel bunk—or, worse, in his cramped bedroom in his parents' house—invariably crushed him.

(Less frequently, but more distressingly, Game Boy dreamed of being claustrophobically crammed into feminine mode, tucked and laced into an outgrown little girl's identity, deadnamed and shamed and shouted at for wanting to live as himself. And the worst dreams were the ones where he was back in the Church-run gender boot camp his parents had sent him to—they called it a cure for trans kids, not talking about the ones who killed themselves—lost in a maze of ever-branching, ever-narrower corridors, unable to escape the suffocating burden of his parents' rigid expectations.)

What he'd dreamed of this night perplexed him, but left him with an edgy and unusual sense of agoraphobia. He'd been upstairs, exploring the new space they'd found, getting increasingly uneasy because it *wasn't the same dream*. His recurring nocturnal real estate visitation was temporally and spatially consistent, unlike this one. He wasn't accustomed to drilling down into the twilight of history, through layers of furnishings at first quaint and then antique, with doors that opened onto giant rooms that paid no heed to the floor plan. The further in he went the wronger it felt, wrongness piling atop mind-warping geometry. He'd been lost. He'd unwisely ignored Doc's advice about string and markers, wandering ever-deeper until he realized he'd lost count of the twists and turns and had no idea how to get back to lived reality. He cast around, opening doors, never finding familiar ground; and whenever he glanced at a mirror from the corner of his eye, he saw a female mirror-image staring back at him in horrified dismay. Breaking into a run, he chased through endless rooms and passages until he came to an austere institutional kitchen lit by high, steel-barred windows, like the one in the camp. The wan daylight illuminated a row of refrigerators lined up against one wall like a display of coffins in a showroom. And if he opened them he'd find her inside—

Game Boy awakened with a shuddery jolt and found his neck was sore. He'd been clenching his jaw in his sleep. His hands curled into fists involuntarily as he gasped for air, breathless in the wake of the not-quite-a-nightmare intensity of his dream. When he unfisted them he grabbed at the threadbare neck of his sleeping bag: *"Waaaa-urgh,"* he groaned, then worked his jaws and swallowed. Unlike his nightmares of the second type, where awakening brought relief, this one clamped down hard. He closed his eyes and focussed on deep, slow breathing, intent on thwarting an impending panic attack. *What's happening to me?* he wondered. He didn't have to ask *what brought this on*—that much was obvious.

"Yo, Boy?"

He triangulated on Doc's voice. It came from the kitchen. He wormed his way out of the sleeping bag, aching and stiff. He'd gotten so stoned that he'd slept in his binder again: top surgery, already on his priority list, climbed another couple of notches. (Not that he could sign up for it before his eighteenth birthday without his parents' consent, which would never be forthcoming.) He ran fingers across his scalp, checking: *Is my hair getting long again?* was part of his morning ritual.

"Doc?" he called.

"Need coffee?"

"Yeah." It was a pointless question, little more than a network latency check, meaningless as an early morning *how are you?* Still, it served to warn Doc that he was inbound. He slouched out into the hallway, then through the kitchen door, and did a double-take as he saw Doc leaning against the fridge-freezer—which, to his infinite relief, looked nothing like the ones in his dream.

"We're fresh out of cow juice," Doc grumped. "Imp must have guzzled it all with his Weetabix."

"Where is he?"

"Went out."

"Move over—" Doc moved and Game Boy opened the freezer compartment. He pulled out a frozen cardboard carton of milk, its waxed sides bulging. "Lemme run this under the cold tap."

"Ugly, Boy, *ugly*."

Game Boy flashed him a grin from the sinkside: "It works, doesn't it?" Soon there was a frozen carton of milk bobbing in a saucepan full of water, slowly thawing. Doc pulled out a mug as the filter machine coughed asthmatically and shut off. "Thanks," Game Boy said, accepting his coffee.

"Plans?" Doc was monosyllabic in the morning.

"*Brr*," Game Boy shivered, both because of the morning chill and the memory of a near-nightmare. "Gotta work out, you know? Drink this, then train." *Training* meant three hours of straight Dota 2 in All Random mode with his teammates, practicing for flexibility.

"What about going upstairs?" Doc unerringly put his thumb on the pressure sore.

"What about it?"

Doc looked puzzled. "Yesterday you were shit hot to go exploring. . . ."

"Yeah, but that was yesterday." Game Boy flapped his free hand irritably. Coffee slopped on the worn kitchen lino. "This morning it creeps me out. All that *history* hanging around up there." He was gripped by an unaccountable fear of refrigerators in kitchens. "Maybe there's something horrible just waiting for us to stumble into it."

Doc gave Game Boy a disbelieving look. "Are. You. Chicken?"

"Am not!" Game Boy straightened and puffed his chest out, a bantam rooster defending his base. Then his eyes narrowed. "Hey, no fair. You cheat!"

"I cheat?" Doc raised an eyebrow.

"Stop pushing me!" His voice broke into an adolescent squeak. "I hate it when you do that!"

"Busted."

"Fuck you!" Game Boy stormed out, gripping his mug as if he meant to throw it.

Doc's *"hee hee hee . . ."* haunted Game Boy all the way back to the games room, like an irritating mosquito whine. Fuming, he drained the scalding coffee mug, then grabbed Imp's dumbbells and worked out his anger through an overly abrupt warmup set.

Over the course of the morning, work took the edge off Game Boy's irritation. Doc's attempt to push some curiosity into his head had been so totally transparent it was almost pathetic. Doc was terrible at projecting positive and abstract emotions—he worked best with things like hatred, despair, and fatigue. So when Doc brought him lunch (a bowl of Szechuan noodles and two microwaved Greggs sausage rolls) he decided to accept the peace offering in return for conditional forgiveness. "You wanna go upstairs?" he demanded, slurping noisily with his mouth open because it totally annoyed Doc.

"Stop that, you'll catch flies—" Doc shook his head. "I walked into that. Upstairs?"

"Yeah." Game Boy kicked at the edge of his desk and his chair spun around lazily. "I was thinking we'll need to hit a stationers for supplies first, though."

Supplies were procured from a high street Ryman, where Doc made sure that the somnolent store detectives ignored the Dalek-like shrieks of rage from the automated checkout when Game Boy pretended to scan his loot. They made their way home uneventfully and unpacked the spoils of shoplifting: dry powder markers, spray paint, school stationery kits, a pad of graph paper, and a clipboard. Then they huffed their way to the top floor, shouldered their exploration kits, nodded at one another in a spirit of intrepid dungeon-crawling brotherhood, and said as one, "Let's do this."

And that they did, for the next hour and fifty-two minutes.

They quickly fell into a routine. Doc would open a door, give a terse description, then recite distances and bearings to the next portal. Boy would add lines and descriptions to the tube map, pausing only when it was time to start a new page. Like: "Terminus, bathroom"; "Corridor, two meters, doors left and right, four meters, door opposite"; "Full-size swimming pool, changing room door left, twenty-five meters, changing room door right, opposite emergency exit—what the hell, Game Boy?"

"At least it's not Olympic size. Hey, do you suppose it's heated?"

"Fuck if I want to find out, looks like nobody's cleaned it since the First World War. Okay, let's back up a room and try the first door on the right."

One hour and fifty-three minutes—and five densely scribed sheets of A4 graph paper—into their mapping run, Game Boy cried uncle. "Listen, I gotta go bad." (They had just opened a door onto a water closet. The splendid white ceramic throne perched beneath an overhead cistern bearing the monogram of Thos. Crapper. The walls were dusty painted brickwork, illuminated by a small glass skylight above the entrance. Vintage: late Victorian, servants, for the use of.)

"Okay, I guess." Doc leaned against the wall while Game Boy went inside and pulled the door almost all the way shut, leaving a crack to allow for conversation.

"This is fucking crazytown," Game Boy complained as he did his business. "We've done what, two hundred rooms?"

"One hundred and eighty-four rooms, thirty-nine corridors, twelve staircases, four swimming pools, nine garages, five coal cellars, three empty lift shafts, and the maze."

"Yeah, the maze. What the fuck was up with *that*, Doc?"

"I have no idea what was up with that, Boy." Game Boy

frowned furiously as he pinched a loaf. Doc winced at the splash: "I did not need to hear that."

"Sorry not sorry. Who builds a giant glassed-over conservatory on the roof of their house and puts a hedge maze in it? With memorial headstones? Then leaves the hedge to die?"

"Did you notice how old they were?"

"What, the hedge—"

"—The memorial stones: they were all for kids or teenagers . . ." Doc trailed off. "Are you going to be much longer? My feet hurt and I think we skipped lunch."

"No, I'm nearly done here." Too late, Game Boy saw to his dismay that the toilet paper was weird and shiny-surfaced stuff. "Oh yuck."

Doc sighed. "Let's head back, I think I'm done exploring for now."

Game Boy finished up hastily, stood, and restored his attire to a semblance of order. When he pulled the chain the cistern groaned ominously, then vomited a torrent of red-brown water into the toilet bowl. *It's probably rust*, he consoled himself.

"I want to check one of the ground-level exits before we go home," Game Boy mused. "They worry me. How do we know nothing can sneak in and find their way through the hedge maze and the library and murder us in our sleep if we don't check that they're locked? Also, where do they come out?"

Doc began to say something, then swallowed his tongue. He tried again. "Yeah, smart thinking. Let's open the door to some place that shouldn't exist in our universe and see if there's something horrible on the other side."

"Yes, let's!" Game Boy snarked.

Retreating through the manifold was faster than breaking new ground, although they had a couple of nasty moments when Game Boy screwed up his left and right turns. "I'm really getting a workout," Doc wheezed as they finally made it back onto the first sheet of graph paper.

"You should get out more." Game Boy paused to consult the map. "If we take the next left, then the second right, go down the gallery to the end, through the kitchen, and take the next left onto the landing, there's a servants' staircase. It's not far off our route. Wanna do it?"

"Yes. Let me just catch my breath first? I'm not cut out for this Lara Croft shit."

"Come on, it's not far! We've only walked—" Game Boy chunked average room sizes in his head—"about three kilometers!" He giggled, a high, silly chime of pure delight. "And we haven't met any wandering monsters yet! Not even a gelatinous cube!"

They entered the servants' staircase via a doorway from an old-fashioned kitchen that was, thankfully, refrigerator-free. It was severe and narrow, its walls plain, the stone treads of the steep steps worn from use. They descended five floors, until Doc was sweating and complaining. Game Boy hastily pencilled in the landings and doors. Finally they bottomed out on another landing with three doors. One of them clearly opened outside.

"If we go out—" Doc hesitated—"we need to wedge it firmly. There's no telling . . . just a quick look?"

"Yes, yes! A quick look!" Despite his hunger, Game Boy bounced up and down on his toes. "I just want to know!"

"How does this open—" Doc peered at the door. There was an old-fashioned keyhole below the doorknob, and very sturdy cast-iron bolts at top and bottom. He slid back the bolts, then reached an impasse. "How do we unlock it?"

"With one of these?" Game Boy excitedly flourished a bunch of slightly rusty keys bound with garden twine. They'd been hanging on a nail hammered into the side of the stairs, where Doc had missed it.

"Okay, let's do this." Doc reached for the keys.

"No! Mine!" Game Boy darted in and shoved the biggest key at the hole. By luck or something else, it turned. "Leee-roy—"

"Hush." Doc twisted the doorknob and pulled, then froze, blocking the doorway. An odd noise came from beyond him: a distant ululation, rising and falling like the mating call of zeppelins.

"What's that noise—"

"Fuck!" Doc stepped back, sending Game Boy stumbling against the stairs as he slammed the door. "Sorry." He took a deep breath. "I only ever heard them in old movies, should have recognized them sooner."

"Not cool, dude! What the fuck got in you?"

"Those were air raid sirens," said Doc. He stared at Game Boy in silence. "Do you still want to go out?" he asked.

Game Boy shook his head sullenly. "Want lunch."

"I think . . . that would be for the best."

Wendy had a bunch of paperwork to go over, but Gibson agreed to shelve it, and instead sent her packing with an admonition to get to work, and the promise of an advance against her wages by the end of the day. One piece of admin-istrivia that he did impose on her: HiveCo thief-takers were expected to dress like professional detectives, rather than minimum wage security drones. Luckily for her, Wendy had hung onto her old work clobber—wishful thinking in case she ever landed an office job. So when she hit the streets after lunch, she was wearing sensible shoes and a sturdy suit that was less than half a decade out of fashion. Despite the faint smell of mothballs, it felt like coming home.

By three o'clock coming home was getting old. She had a crick in her neck, a sore back, and a much lower opinion of office jobs—especially if they came with chairs like the orthopedic disaster she'd ended up with in the Hamleys camera room.

"Walk me through it again," she said, leaning subtly away from Jeanine from HR, who occupied the middle seat, and who in turn was discreetly avoiding Sydney from Security's mouse-elbow.

Sydney expectorated glutinously, then croaked: "Yerss, mam." With a degree of dainty fingertip precision that belied every other aspect of his appearance, he scrubbed the mouse cursor back along the camera feed timeline. "'Ere's where our perps walked in."

The cameras in Hamleys' lobby area recorded in full-color HD plus infrared. They were a far cry from the usual grainy corner-shop crap Wendy was used to. Nevertheless, she had a hard job identifying the figures Sydney was intent on tracking—there was just too much foot traffic. Finally she got a handle on them when Sydney paused and moused over their faces.

"Huh. Give me a second." She jotted down notes. Perp 1: tall white male, lightly built, clean-shaven, gray or check coat, dark trousers, white open-necked shirt, hair covered by a narrow-brimmed hat. Perp 2: average height white male, average build, dark hair and eyes, clean-shaven, wearing a suit so deplorable it might have been in its owner's family since his grandfather was demobbed from national service in the fifties. "Hm, not exactly your average toy shoppers." Perp 3: Black female in fleece windbreaker, exercise leggings or . . . "Cycling kit?" She had her hair tied back in dreadlocks, and wore no jewelry (or at least nothing visible on video). Perp 4: shorter-than-average East Asian or Chinese male, black hoodie with hood raised, jeans, trainers—the only one who carried an obvious shoplifter vibe, which meant he was a decoy, except—"There's something off about this one." She tapped the screen. "Something about the way he walks."

"I dun't see't," Sydney grumped.

"The hips." Jeanine from HR said suddenly. "He swaggers. He's putting too much effort into it. Like he's . . ."

"Tryin' ter 'tract attention," Sydney agglutinated.

Wendy winced, hoping he couldn't see her. "He swaggers like he doesn't care where he's going, but he doesn't bump into anything," she said. "Or any*one*."

The perps took the escalator up to the first floor. Wendy watched as Short Hoodie bounced up to Hat Guy and exchanged words in Model Railways. Hands pressed up against a gleaming display cabinet, beseeching. "Did you dust that for prints?"

"Too late," Jeanine said apologetically. "The front of store display cases get polished every time there's a lull in business. Nobody linked it with the robbery until the police ran the tapes a couple of hours later."

A couple of hours? Wendy stifled a groan. Either somebody senior had lost the plot, or the cuts to Metropolitan Police funding were worse than she'd realized—armed/transhuman robbery of a cash room ought to rate an emergency response. "Did you get anything?"

"Mebbe." Sydney scrubbed forward. The cameras jerked and jumped, following the foursome through Party Costumes and as far as the changing room. "Look." He froze the stream, then stepped frame by frame through an altercation: Black Biker Babe shoving a bishoujo maid's frock at

Short Hoodie, who reacted as if it were kryptonite, recoiling and falling back against a rail of costumes. "Maybe we'll lift some prints there." He zoomed the image in closer. There being no CSI-style *enhance* button in the real world, all this gave her was an eyeful of blurry block pixels. But she got to see Black Biker Babe's hand wrap around a chromed rail as she leaned close to her homie.

"Did you check that?" Wendy demanded.

"No, no we didn't!" Jeanine sat up. "And they don't polish the clothes rails anything like often enough! Good catch, Sid!"

The video stream played on. Wendy watched as Hat Guy, who was apparently the ringleader or instigator, thrust superhero costumes at his posse. They changed, picked up their zombified store detective escort, and headed into the back.

"The store detective—what happened to him?" she asked.

"Oh, we fired his sorry ass."

Wendy resisted the urge to grind her teeth. "I mean, what did *they* do to him? Was he an inside man, or—"

"Oh no, the raiders messed with everybody's head! The bloke with the hat, you know, the Joker? He has some kind of mind control power. Ralph barely remembered anything from the moment he intercepted them until after they left."

So why did you bloody sack *him?* Wendy kept her trap shut. *Ours not to wonder why.* Mistakes were made, management needed a scapegoat, same old story. "Next."

She watched in silence as the heist went down in the strong room. Then she watched it again in slo-mo, slack-jawed, as Chinese Hoodie Dude—now dressed as Robin—executed the most amazingly slick slapstick routine she'd ever seen carried out in a single shoot, without a stunt double in sight. "Now *that's* something else." She peered at the screen. "What happened to the guards?"

"They fell over," Sydney opined.

"It looks like they tried to hit Robin, missed him and hit each other, then accidentally handcuffed themselves to the furniture upside-down and back-to-front."

"Yeah. We fired them, too," Jeanine observed.

"Do you lot do anything *but* fire people?" Wendy demanded. "You realize I'm going to have to track them down and interview them, and you just ensured that'll take, like, about ten times as long? And you're being billed by the hour?"

"I don't see what you're complaining about, then," Jeanine sniffed.

"But *why*?"

"Because when the shareholders ask how we lost a hundred thousand in cash takings and demand to know what we did about it, we can point to it and say that we did something. Don't sweat it, I'm sure they'll get new jobs eventually."

"I suppose you're right," Wendy lied, mentally smacking herself in penance. "I'll need their home addresses and any relevant contact details you have on file. All right, the disguises, what happened to them?"

"The robbers dumped them back in the changing rooms when they reclaimed their streetwear. The police got a couple of poor-quality prints off the cubicle door latches, and took the costumes as evidence. I've got a crime report number for you, if you want to ask for the details?"

"That'll do nicely. And you've got close-ups of the robbers' faces, I hope? Any stills I can take? Both face and full-body, preferably next to a display cabinet of known height so I can work up some vital stats?"

"Yuh, c'n do that," Sydney sniffed, then emitted a dreadful snorkeling sound, as if his nasal cavities were filling up with quick-drying cement. Jeanine gave Wendy a glance of shared misery: evidently having a sinus infection was the one thing that wasn't a sacking offense in this place.

Wendy stood up. "I need those stills now," she said. "I've got to visit the police next, then I'll make the rounds of the witnesses." *Who you helpfully sacked.* "After that, we'll see."

"Do you think you'll find them?" Jeanine asked eagerly. "Will there be tickets to the hanging?"

Wendy smiled wearily, then resumed her professional demeanor: "I can't promise anything, ma'am, but I'll ask," she lied. "Now, about those stills . . ."

One set of prints, several bewildered brain-controlled witnesses to interview, and some blurry photos. It didn't sound like much to go on, but Wendy'd been handed worse cases. Her biggest concern was that the golden forty-eight hours had long since ticked over into penalty time, and if the cops had cracked the case Gibson wouldn't have handed it to her. After that, her second-biggest worry was the weather. Actually confronting and arresting a gang of transhuman robbers with mind control mojo was way down the list.

Still. A cold case, at fifty quid an hour? She could put up with a *lot* of rain for that.

Imp was deep in thought as he trudged home from his meeting with Big Sis. When he got there everybody else was out, so he ditched his suit in favor of something less likely to attract attention and headed out in search of lunch. There were a couple of all-you-can-eat buffets not far away. It was easy to fool the waiter into thinking he'd already paid, so long as he ate during the lunchtime rush and never hit them twice in the same week. So his stomach was groaning with roast beef, chicken, and mashed potato as he ambled home in midafternoon. Where he discovered a freaked-out Doc, a glum Game

Boy in need of comfort hugs, and—of course—no sign of their Deliverator.

"Where's Becca?" he asked. "I had a *very interesting* meeting this morning!" He steepled his fingers, then proceeded to tug them, one by one, until his knuckles clicked.

"Fuck knows," Game Boy muttered despondently. "Are you going to nail it shut or am I, Doc?"

"Nail what shut?" Imp asked, momentarily distracted.

"The door into 1940." Doc shuddered dramatically. "At least I *hope* it was 1940."

"It coulda been 1983," Game Boy moaned. "*Threads* for real."

Imp stared: "What the baculum-gobbling shite are you talking about?"

Doc stopped trying to give Game Boy a back rub—Game Boy was still hunched in on himself, but there were no tears—and glared at Imp. "The doorway to the end of the world upstairs. We went exploring . . ."

Ten minutes and a little bit of clarification later, Imp paused the spiel, raced to the kitchen, and returned with an unlabelled brown bottle and three paper cups. "This calls for a little something to settle your nerves." He poured and then passed the cups around. "Do carry on, dear fellow."

Doc took a sip from his cup, went straight into a volcanic blast of coughing, wiped his lips, and took another sip. "What *is* this?" he asked hoarsely.

"Fell off the back of a lorry bound for the Scotch Malt Whisky Society. Cask strength, of course. You were saying?"

(Game Boy lowered his face to his cup and huffed.)

"There is *stuff* up there," Doc said portentously. "And it is up-gefucked."

(Game Boy risked a tentative sip, like a cat testing an unfamiliar water bowl for potability.)

"So it's kind of wild." Imp shrugged. "No biggie, we've been living here for months—" a couple of years, in his case—"without anything breaking loose. So?"

"We opened the door!" Game Boy's voice, if he had raised it further, could reasonably have been described as a shriek: "Anything could happen!"

"Nonsense," Imp said firmly. He pushed gently. "Nothing can possibly come through. And if it did, it would almost certainly wander off at random, get lost, and starve to death in the maze. Or drown in the swimming pool. We're perfectly safe down here, it's safe as houses."

"I'm afraid of refrigerators," Game Boy admitted under his breath. He took a full sip of his whisky and gasped as it hit his throat.

"Where's Del?" Imp asked again.

"Hi, homies, how've you been?" Rebecca bounced in, the front door slamming in her wake. "I had a *great* morning!"

"Oh good, gang's all here." Doc peered into his paper cup, clearly wishing it would magically refill itself.

"Excellent!" Imp stood. "You can sit down then and have a drink. We have a job to get started on."

"A—" Rebecca peeled her cycling gloves off as she sat— "what kind of job?"

"The best kind, a treasure hunt!"

"What?" Rebecca peered at him, then sniffed her cup. "Hey, there's booze in this, I can't drink it, what if I'm pulled over?"

Doc shook his head. "On your bike? Never happen—"

"See what's parked out front." She grinned smugly.

"If you get pulled over driving a stolen van, you've got bigger things to worry about than a breathalyzer—"

"'S not a van, what do you take me for?" She crossed her arms and feigned disdain.

"Go ahead," Imp said wearily, "check it out, give her a round of applause."

"I'll go." Game Boy stood and trudged towards the front door. Paused, then returned: "Why the ever-loving fuck did you boost a Chelsea tractor, Del?"

Rebecca smirked. "That, my friend, is not just *any* Chelsea tractor: it's a 2010-model Porsche Cayenne Turbo S. With disabled anti-theft and tracking, and a—" she held up a remote keyfob—"*working* ignition. More than five hundred horsepower and enough torque to tow a jumbo jet. Just right for this neighborhood."

Game Boy reddened. "Are you *trying* to bring the—"

"Relax, GeeBee," Imp commanded: "I said *relax*, Boy." He touched Game Boy's shoulder. "I'm sure Del has a plan for avoiding the gentlemen of the law, right? Rebecca?" He put a slight hard edge on her name, casting her a warning look.

"The bloke who sold it to me put cloned plates on it first. They match a real one registered in Clapham, so it's all legit, see? I thought I'd park it round in the long grass at the back."

"Just so we're all keeping busy, children," Imp grinned, "practicing our skills, yes? So: while you were driving without insurance or whatever, Game Boy and Doc went exploring upstairs, and I've been catching up with fam and getting us a job."

"Yeah, about this job—" Game Boy began.

"I will explain everything in due course!" Imp struck a pose.

"What's it worth?" the Deliverator asked with barely concealed avarice.

"Lots." Imp side-eyed the corners of the room. "Eighty large in cash, *plus extras*. Cameras, lenses, lights, a sound stage. And some payments in kind as well."

"The fuck! What do we have to do, hand over our kidneys?"

"It's quite simple. A rare book came up for auction this week. Trouble is, the book dealer who had the details has been murdered—yes, it's that valuable. He kept the contact details for the seller in a safe deposit box. My customer hired him to bid in the auction, but one of the rival bidders has gotten a bit overenthusiastic, so she's asked me to try and get hold of the book first." He narrowed his eyes and frowned at Del's keyfob. "It's really no riskier than being in possession of *that*."

Doc beat the others to the punch: "Who's the customer? Why the fuck would they pay that much for a book? This stinks, are we being set up?"

Imp smiled thinly. "The customer is my sister. Or rather, her boss is paying and she's organizing everything. I very much doubt she's going to double-cross me."

"Your sis—" Game Boy's eyes widened—"you've got *a sister*?" From the way he shrank back into the sofa, he found the idea of a family of Imps terrifying.

"Obviously he got parents, Boy, where's your head at?"

"I've got a sister," Imp acknowledged with the haughty dignity of one who'd been caught out and now felt compelled to bluff his way to the bitter end. "She's not an overachiever like me, but she occasionally has her uses."

"A book." Doc leaned forward. "Tell us about this hundred thousand pound book."

"I thought you'd never ask." Imp relaxed. He reached for a plastic document wallet, and began leafing through the pages he'd printed out. "What we're after in the first place is not the actual book itself, nobody's got *that*. We don't even know who's selling it yet, or rather, selling the treasure map—directions to where the book is hidden. Once we've got *that*, we've got to get hold of the book before anyone else, and then it's finders keepers. The book itself is a unique manuscript, and the last legal keeper was the Vatican Library, where it was stashed in the Vatican secret archive. It was stolen during the Napoleonic Wars and went missing in London in the 1880s . . ."

"The book dealer," Game Boy raised a finger, "he was killed by someone else who wants the book, do I have it right?"

"Yes." Imp looked slightly abashed. "A rival buyer who's not terribly concerned with legal niceties seems to be after it, and it looks like they're a jump ahead of us. So we've got to get hold of the deposit box with the auction details in it toot sweet. But that's going to be a bit of a problem, you see."

"Why?" Imp wondered if Doc and Game Boy were tag-teaming him.

"Well, you know the branch of Pennine Bank that we, uh, *filmed in* last month?"

"Oh fuck off," said Del, her eyes widening, "it's in a deposit box *there*?"

"Yes." Imp nodded.

"You want us to rob the same bank *twice in a month*?" Del's voice rose.

"It'll be a piece of cake! You see, I've got a plan . . ."

The Bond was having a bad day.

"What do you mean, you can't get any data off it?" he hissed over the counter.

"It's ancient, sir." The technician gave him a company-approved cheerful smile. "I mean, it's a 40-megabyte SCSI disk—that's short for Small Computer Serial Intelligence— they don't make them any more? You said the PC was a 1988 model? You might be able to read it on a Mac like the one my gran still uses, as long as it was made before 1995, but PCs won't work with them without a special card. Are you *sure* it came out of a PC?"

"For the third time, yes, it came out of a PC. Big beige box, amber screen, one of those printers that shrieks like it's having its toenails torn out with pliers. Can you get the data off it for me?"

"Um . . . to be perfectly honest, I don't think so, sir. But it's not as if there can be anything important on it, they haven't made these things for more than twenty years and it's less than a tenth the capacity of a single CD-ROM, there isn't even room for a five-minute YouTube clip on it. I'll just put it in the recycling box here and we can sort you out with a nice new Packard Bell laptop instead; I can throw in a free Office 365 subscription if you sign up for our extended—"

The Bond reached across the counter and grabbed the technician's tie. "Give. It. Back," he grated.

The technician's eyes went wide and he began to gabble: "Sir, here at HiveMart Digital we have a strict zero-tolerance policy for employee abuse I am going to have to call security and kindly ask you to leave the store also your actions are being recorded by surveillance cameras and we *always* prosecute—"

"Disk. Now." The Bond snapped the fingers of his free hand, and let go of the technician. "*Give me back my disk.*" He didn't bother to finish the sentence with *if you want to live*: the technician seemed to understand instinctively.

"Right you are sir!" He shoved the piece of delicate machinery at the Bond, letting go of it without warning. The Bond caught it effortlessly, and glared at the technician as he gabbled his way through the rest of his script in a cold-sweat panic: "Thank you for shopping at HiveMart Digital we hope you are happy with your purchase and or technical support please call again soon."

The Bond turned and strode towards the exit, ignoring the store security guards who dawdled towards him at the most leisurely pace they could manage without obviously shirking.

Standards had dropped since HiveMart took over Radio Shack, he reflected grimly. He needed a real IT specialist. But his usual go-to geek was doing time in a Federal penitentiary—he'd been running some kind of Bitcoin extortion ring targeting Darknet users—and he didn't want to use up Rupert's people. The boss would not be happy to find bloodstains on his office parquet when he got home. Meanwhile, the high street chains that advertised the expertise of while-you-wait data migration experts turned out to be unable to migrate any data older than a time-expired carton of yoghurt. They mostly seemed to want to up-sell him a gaming laptop with a seven-year parts and labor warranty and a "free" color inkjet printer with a monthly subscription for print cartridges.

The Bond was not technologically illiterate, but he knew his limits. Trying to excavate the contents of a hard disk that was older than he was lay outside them. Walking across the car park, he blipped the button on the keyfob until the DB9 flashed its lights at him.[1] *Technical support*, he mused. *I need technical support*. And suddenly he knew exactly where to go.

He was almost at the North Circular, following the satnav directions to the computer museum at Bletchley Park, when his phone rang. "Mike—Mister Bond speaking." The caller failed to catch the slip. *Damn it*, the Bond thought. There

1 It amused Rupert to give his Bonds the use of his Aston Martin when they were running errands on his behalf: it was better than leaving it to gather dust in a secure parking garage while he was out of the country.

were serious drawbacks to working for a narcissistic fanta-sist, unlimited budget be damned. *Must remember I answer to James this week*. "What can I do for you today, sir?"

"Did you take care of business?" Rupert barked.

"Yes sir. The dealer is closed but I got the hard drive with the data on it."

"Yes, about that." Rupert's voice sharpened. "Miss Star-key reports that someone got to Bernard before she did. And his computer was gutted."

"Yes sir. It was absolutely necessary to ensure there were no loose ends, so I'm in physical custody of the drive right now. Ev-erything is under control and I will notify Miss Starkey where to find the target in due course, through regular channels."

"I see. So I suppose you have a read out?"

The Bond drew a deep breath, then regretted it as he stared at the rear end of a dump truck. They were stationary at traffic lights and the climate control was struggling. "It's in progress, sir." Admittedly it was very stop-go progress right now, but progress of a kind. "It's in a rather unusual format. I'm taking it to a specialist facility."

"See that they don't retain any copies. Eyes only."

"Yes sir."

"Is there any chance—*any chance at all*—that Bernard disclosed anything to a rival bidder before you terminated the auction?"

The Bond chose his next words carefully. "Nothing is cer-tain in war, sir. What I can say is that I acquired the drive with his email folders. He won't be talking to anyone who comes calling—" never again—"and without the email fold-ers the target can't be acquired. I will anonymously provide Miss Starkey with the data she requires, minimizing the risk of a leak, and deal with whoever she assigns to the immedi-ate pick-up."

The Bond carefully didn't mention that he'd found Bernard dead when he broke into the apartment and stole the hard disk. Nor did he speculate about who might have killed him and why—a rival bidder seemed most likely—or what he might have told them before he died, or why they didn't bother taking the PC. It was, in the Bond's experience, usually a bad idea to keep his employers overinformed about his activities—especially an employer with a tendency to micromanage, and a mission that had gone off the rails before the starting gun was fired.

There were clearly one or more adversaries in the loop. But with the email records on the hard disk, he could probably work out who they were and how they'd been alerted by Bernard's enquiries. Then he could take them out, clearing the path for Miss Starkey who, unaware of his involvement, would collect the item. Once he knew what had Rupert so engaged, he could decide what to do about it: whether to let Miss Starkey hand it over, or to take possession for himself.

That was the trouble with "big picture" types like Rupert, after all. They relied on little people to handle the details for them, and it never seemed to occur to them that the little people might have agendas of their own.

OVERDRAWN AT THE PENNINE BANK

The very next day, Wendy wrote up her preliminary notes on the Hamleys cash room job and her interviews with the fired security staff. Then she went to the bank.

She was already familiar with the front-of-shop layout thanks to Gibson's briefing and videos, but no amount of poor quality CCTV could convey the ambiance of a site. Nor could a report substitute for interviews with witnesses. It wasn't what they wanted to tell you that was important—human memory could be disastrously misleading—but what they revealed in response to questioning, the insights they let slip without even noticing. Not that she suspected an inside job, but something about this crew of robbers raised her hackles. She had an uneasy sense that there was more to them than met the eye.

"Hello, I'm Wendy from HiveCo Security. I have an appointment with Mr. Granger."

The combination of her shiny new HiveCo Security badge and an appointment brokered via the bank's insurance underwriters got her whisked straight through the armored door without even a pat-down. There was nothing on-site worth dying for, after all: it was only money, and precious little of it at that in banking terms. (Retail branches were in any case insured against robbery.) Professional bank robbers knew this, and in recent decades almost never got violent. It wasn't worth an extra-heavy sentence. Meanwhile, the mirror-glass and riveted door frames and very visible safe in the back room reassured the customers that their paychecks were safe. It was, in short, security theater rather than effective security.

The smiling clerk (Alicia, according to her badge) led Wendy past an open plan area to the manager's office. "Nigel's in this morning and you're in luck, he was on duty during the incident the other week," she confided. Pausing at the door she called, "Nigel? Nigel?" (A muffled grunt came in reply.) "I have a Miss Deere from HiveCo Investigations to see you? It's about the incident."

Wendy slipped past her and twisted the door handle. "You'll find there's an appointment in your Outlook," she called, then pushed the door open. "Mr. Granger, I presume?"

A second grunt, louder this time, clearly originated from the bald-headed man behind the desk. Wendy pushed past Alicia, who gave a startled squeak: she clearly wasn't accustomed to being sidelined so easily. *Babes in the woods*, Wendy thought. Three toddlers armed with paper clips could raid this place. As she cleared the doorway Wendy saw the reason for the wordless grunts. *Did nobody teach you not to chew with your mouth open?* She smiled tightly at the manager as he hastily swallowed, then placed the uneaten half of his baguette on his mouse mat.

"Ahrm. Hem. Mrs. Darling, HiveCo? Is this about the incident?"

"If by *incident* you are referring to the armed robbery on the fourteenth, then yes, I'm here to follow up on the investigation. I have some questions that the police report didn't answer." Her long glance took in Alicia; the clerk hovered in the hallway, staring at her wide-eyed. If this was her idea of excitement, she'd clearly led a very sheltered life. Wendy pulled out her badge and held it up for the surveillance cameras: "Let me introduce myself properly. Wendy Deere, consulting detective, HiveCo Security. HiveCo has been commissioned by the Ministry of Justice to provide domain-specific support for investigations into transhuman crimes such as your recent incident, and I'm your case officer."

Mr. Granger cleared his throat. "The MOJ? I thought the Home Office were in charge of policing?"

Wendy smiled. "You might think that, but the New Management disagrees. I have common-law powers of arrest, and a warrant to remand the perpetrators for trial at the Old Bailey, bypassing the Home Office and Met Police bureaucracy. In fact, I used to be with the Met before this role was outsourced." Misleading, but technically true. "HiveCo Security are paid on commission and we get results. Marketing call it Agile Incident Management, but we're really just old-fashioned thief-takers." Her smile widened. "Are you a thief, Mr. Granger?" To his sudden and exaggerated head-shaking, she nodded: "Then you've got nothing to be afraid of."

Without waiting to be invited, she took a seat before his desk. "Now." She held up a USB key loaded with the CCTV video files. "I've got a copy of your video recordings from the day in question, and I'd like you to talk me through them."

Granger looked at her USB stick as if it was a poisonous centipede. "I suppose so?" He glanced at Alicia, then back at Wendy: "Tea or coffee?"

"Tea, please. Milk, no sugar." She placed the USB stick in front of him.

"We're not allowed to plug personal electronic devices into company computers," he said with ill-feigned regret.

"Well then." Wendy had come prepared. She opened her briefcase and pulled out a tablet: "We can watch it on this, but I'd still like to record your commentary as we go through it."

Granger frowned unhappily but nodded, clearly not enthused at having to sacrifice his lunch break. *Tough*, Wendy thought to herself; *if your security was worth a bucket of warm spit, we wouldn't be having this conversation.* "First, let's look at the camera behind the tellers' windows. Would you mind talking me through what's going on? In your own words, please . . ."

"Sure. On the left, that's Marie. On the right, John's handling the premier account and forex desk. The middle would be Alicia, but she was on an early break that day so there's an empty position. The usual SIA Level 2 certified warm body from G4S is on door duty, can't remember his name but I can look him up if you want. Off-screen to the left are the two in-house ATMs and the two check deposit terminals. Queue for machines on the left, counter service on the right, and Eric is walking the floor looking for personal banking walk-ins and loan appointments. It's early in the lunchtime rush so the queue isn't too—"

But Wendy was no longer listening. Because she'd spotted something very interesting indeed on the second screen on Granger's desk—the one streaming the live camera feed from the branch interior, where two now-familiar figures had just walked in the door. "Fuck me," she breathed, "they couldn't *possibly* be that stupid." Could they?

At precisely the moment that Wendy Deere was sitting down to review CCTV files with Mr. Granger, Eve pushed the button and smiled at the entryphone camera of a very different institution. It was a false smile, a brittle layer of ice covering the black waters beneath—waters in which she was drowning. But she kept coming back out of a sense of duty: filial piety, if you wanted a euphemism, although guilt was closer to the mark.

The buzzer sounded. Eve stepped into the lobby, then signed the guest book, starting her twice-a-month routine. The lobby was well lit, with padded armchairs and a touching floral display on a side-table—a memorial to a former resident, recently departed. The manager's office was empty, as it was most of the time over the weekend, but the CCTV monitor showed views of the main corridors. Eve turned left from the lobby, entered the PIN to unlock the door, and walked past a dining room (currently empty, the tables set for dinner) towards her mother's bedroom.

Pay no attention to the TVs blaring through open doorways, the occasional repetitive chime of a call button. Ignore the bad-tempered bitching from Room 11's resident, who shouted every five minutes for her long-dead mummy and daddy to take her home to a house she'd moved on from two-thirds of a century ago. This was a *good* home. One of the signs of a good home was that it didn't reek of piss and shit. Her mother's nursing home passed this test: the carpets were clean, the paintwork bright, the orderlies friendly and patient and just a little bit dull. Dull was good, dull didn't get bored or abusive or take liberties. The regular nurses were middle-aged and experienced, sensible and on the ball, although at the weekend there tended to be fresh faces, agency staff covering gaps in the rota.

Nursing homes were expensive, and most people stayed out of them as long as possible. Consequently there was a lot of churn, a lot of residents in the late stages of dementia or infirmity who checked in for the last few months until the end, with a leavening of bedbound and chairbound folks with longer-term prognoses. Mum was unusual: she was long-term stable but profoundly disabled, bedbound and fed through a gastric tube, clutching repetitively at the side of her hospital bed. Helplessly dependent, in other words. The Bigge Organization paid the bills as long as Eve worked for Rupert. It was another of the barbed hooks he'd caught her on, so that she must dance whenever he pulled her puppet strings.

Eve hated nursing home visits, and not just because of her guilt and shame over Mum. She hated them because they were a reminder that no torment she could possibly inflict compared to the artistry of dementia, the king of torturers.

Rupert had once made her slowly skin an arms dealer alive, over nearly three days. The arms dealer had stiffed Rupe over a consignment of lewisite—second-generation mustard gas—for the Syrian government. Not only did the dealer have to pay, he had to be seen to have paid by his replacement. Rupert made her wear a torturer's mask and fetish gear—a leather corset and thigh-high stiletto boots—and recorded the vivisection in full HD video.[1] But the delicate *Mona Lisa* brushwork of Alzheimer's disease beat any pain she could inflict as thoroughly as Leonardo's masterpiece outshone a toddler's finger painting.

Mrs. Morris in room 18 was a Holocaust survivor. The electric chair couldn't hold a candle to the incandescent terror she experienced whenever they showered her, for her past had imploded into the present: this was her eternal Auschwitz, and her kindly but slightly dull carers were

[1] Rupert told her afterwards that a copy of the recording would be delivered to the police if she ever turned on him, but it wasn't as if he didn't already have enough leverage on her. What pissed her off about the incident was the way her calves had ached for a week afterwards—all because Rupe had to combine pleasure with business.

camp guards who'd escaped from her nightmares. Eve had once tried to settle her, grounding her in the present—but five minutes later she'd forgotten again, and was sucked right back into her private final solution.

Eve did not—could not—believe in a loving God because she visited Hell every second Sunday of the month to take tea with the damned. No loving God could possibly allow a place like this to exist. Hell came with beige carpets, en suite bedrooms, and satellite TV. But through every open bedroom door the screaming of souls in torment could be heard. And the worst thing about it was that there was no reason for it. There were no capering demons with pitchforks to enumerate the sins of the damned, no mercy for the virtuous, and no justice for anyone. Just endless suffering for all, trapped in the swirling mists of the eternal present.

The nursing office door was ajar. Eve knocked, then smiled stiffly at the occupant. Marcia was a middle-aged professional, one of the regular staff nurses. She held up a finger for a moment as she finished writing in a fat lever-arch file, then closed it and returned it to a lockable file cabinet. Eventually she met Eve's gaze and nodded, acknowledging her. "Miss Starkey? Have you seen your mother yet?"

Miss Starkey. She knew her name. Eve was a regular here.

Eve shook her head. "I just arrived and saw you were in," she said. "How is she this month? How's her weight?"

"I'll just check for you." Marcia pulled her mother's file from the cabinet. "Let's see . . . hmm. Down five hundred grams since your last visit? Oh dear. I need to look at the feeding records, we may need to add another supplement dose to her meals."

Eve's smile froze over. "I thought the nutritionist was booked to see her last Tuesday?"

"Hmm, let's see—you're quite right, of course. As usual.

Looks like Linda dropped the ball—I'll action it at the staff meeting on Monday and book another appointment."

"That would be good, yes." Eve's smile warmed slightly. "I'll go and see her now. I don't suppose there've been any changes?"

Marcia's expression melted into sympathy. "I'm sorry, love."

Eve nodded, then turned and stalked up the corridor to her biweekly bedside appointment with the hollowed-out shell of her mother, who wailed continuously in the grip of a terror from which no respite was possible.

"Hello sir, how may I help you?"

The junior manager in the grass-green suit smiled up at Doc, slightly glassy-eyed but keeping a game professional face on.

Imp smiled back at her, then discreetly poked Doc in the ribs. Doc startled.

"Uh," he said.

"The box," Imp reminded him. Doc cast him an aggrieved look and Imp chilled. They were well inside the lobby and there were three short queues forming.

"Getting there." Doc glowered at him, then turned back to the woman, who was fighting off an embryonic frown. "I have a safe deposit box," Doc told her. "I need to check the contents: there's a bearer bond that may have expired and the bloody computer's eaten my scan—"

"Yes sir, if you'd care to take a seat over there?" She gestured at an unoccupied desk. "Someone will be with you shortly. And your—"

"Husband," Doc said with a straight face.

"Please."

Imp smiled at her, tucked Doc's hand under his arm, and led him to the waiting area.

"What was that about?" Imp murmured between motion-less lips as he sat down.

"Overloading her with meaningless trivia—" Doc patted him on the back of the wrist—"dear."

"Really." Imp paused. "You remembered to bring the account details and the ID, didn't you?"

"Of course."

They'd agreed that Doc, with his penchant for highly regret-table suits, would be better at masquerading as the Bernard bloke. Imp could camp it up as his usual flamboyantly louche self, and provide top cover for Doc if it became necessary to bullshit their way out of a sticky wicket. The forged driving license and wallet padding—Bernard's bank card, PIN, in-side leg measurement, and other details—had come via Imp's sister.

Imp's plan was quite simple: they weren't going to rob the bank *at all*. They needed to go through the contents of the deposit box and photograph the paper contents, but if the se-curity drones wanted to cavity-search them at any point in the process then that was totes copacetic, at least as far as Imp was concerned. (Doc's opinion of cavity searches had not been solicited during the formulation of this plan. In Imp's opinion, it was best not to invite a negative reaction.)

Both of them had smartphones. Del, lurking nearby in her posh ride, was on speed dial. Either of them could sweet-talk their way out of any trouble short of a shoot-out with a bit of skull sweat. The plan didn't call for any risk-taking at all: What could possibly go wrong?

Fuck fuck fuck . . . "Look!" Wendy stared at the CCTV feed, transfixed.

"What?" Mr. Granger frowned at her. "What is it?"

"Look! It's them!" She stabbed her finger at the desktop monitor, then pointed back at the tablet, freezing the replay on it.

"I don't see—"

Wendy had pored over the footage of the original robbery enough times that the faces leapt out at her. "It's them!" Hat Guy and Bad Suit, as large as life and twice as ugly, holding hands and sitting at a desk in the open-plan area. They made a surprisingly cute couple, she thought. "It's them!" She bounced up and down unconsciously. "They're two of the transhumans behind the robbery, right there!" She pulled out her phone and began to text Gibson immediately: *Suspects returned to SOC, send backup stat.*

"They're not in costume—"

"No, of course not! These are the planners, the brains behind it! They're probably casing you for a follow-up job right now!"

Mr. Granger's Adam's apple bobbed up and down as he narrowly avoided swallowing his tongue. "I should call the—"

"No, stop and listen, this is *very important*." Wendy turned her best officer-of-the-law expression on him: "We have a chance to catch them red-handed *right now*, but we need to separate them from their accomplices, who won't be far away *at all*. We also need evidence of what they're up to. CCTV on its own won't be quite enough to convict them—neither of them laid a finger on the proceeds of the robbery: they could legitimately claim to just be bystanders and it's all a coincidence. So I want you to find out what they want, and give it to them, while *I* sit here and watch.

Once we know what they're doing, we can either grab them or set up a sting later. It's all perfectly safe. Just remember: I'll be watching you from back here. If you think there's trouble and you want me to drop the hammer, tug your left ear, like this." Wendy demonstrated.

Granger's face turned a very interesting shade of green. "But, but, what if you're wrong and they're armed? You can't protect me on your own!"

Wendy grinned like a maniac. "Did you ever see that movie, *Kill Bill: Volume One*?" she asked. Granger looked confused. "I can do *this*," she said, pulling her riot baton out of thin air with a flourish and pointing it at the camera, "and if they're packing heat, I can do *this*." The baton vanished, replaced by something sharper. "And that's just for starters . . ."

Imp was bored enough to already be fidgeting and plotting mischief when a door at the back of the bank finally opened. A middle-aged, balding bloke in a suit with a tie in the bank's colors came out and made eye contact with Doc. His approach to the desk was almost furtive: Imp would have been genuinely concerned that they might have been rumbled if the guy didn't have the pinch-faced demeanor of a complete prat.

The manager extended a hand and Doc rose to shake it: "Good morning, I'm Mr. Granger. You are . . . ?"

"Bernard Harris," Doc said easily, pumping the Granger dude's hand. Granger twitched it away and wiped it on his leg as he sat down. Imp instantly took a dislike to him. Something about Granger struck him as being as phoney as a thirteen-pound note. "I'd like to check my deposit box," Doc said before Imp could intervene.

Granger nodded. "That can be arranged. Do you have any ID with you, sir?"

Doc handed over his faked driving license and the stolen cash card Eve had provided. There was a bit of to-ing and fro-ing with a PINsentry reader and a computer screen, then Granger asked some obvious security questions that they'd both been briefed on—date of birth, postal code, nothing remotely challenging. Then Granger unwound infinitesimally. "You just want to check your safe deposit box?" he asked.

"Yes. There are some papers in it and I'm afraid my computer ate its hard disk last week, so I just need to copy down some numbers, otherwise my accountant will shout at me." Doc leaned back, mirroring Granger's posture.

"You just want to . . ." Granger mumbled under his breath. "Yes, well, that sounds entirely normal. You'll need to come into the back office," he added, so studiously offhand that Imp instantly flipped into paranoid alertness: *It's a trap, Admiral!* "Follow me, please?" Granger stood and Doc copied him. Against his better judgment, Imp rose.

"After you," Doc murmured.

Granger led them into a corridor running into the back of the building. Offices with interior windows and doors opened off it to either side. (The security door and the tellers' counters appeared not to be so easily accessible from this side of the building.) He ushered them into one of the offices. "If you wait here, I'll have Miss Deere bring you your safe deposit box," he said. His moustache writhed in an approximation of a smile. "Don't go anywhere," he muttered rapidly. He ducked out into the corridor, pulling the door shut.

"I've got a feeling—" Imp started, before Doc elbowed him in the ribs and side-eyed a corner of the room. Imp followed Doc's line of sight—*"a feeling deep inside,"* he continued in a squeaky falsetto, as badly out of tune as a grand

piano with a buckled frame—"must be lunchtime," he concluded. "Laibach, in case you were wondering."

"Really? I thought it was the Beatles."

Doc was twitching his cheeks in what was probably a
Morse code of his own invention.

"I really need to go urgently," Imp said, bouncing up and
down in his chair, "to the loo."

"Just hold it." Doc looked irritated. "We'll be done in ten
minutes."

Imp took a deep breath and held it. *That's what I'm afraid
of.* Someone was coming. He hated this part, the rising tension as a job came to life. *Get a grip,* he told himself. The
door handle turned and the door opened to admit a woman
in a dark trouser suit. "Which of you two gentlemen is Mr.
Harris?" she asked, glancing at them: "I'm Ms. Deere." Before either of them could move, she nudged the door shut: it
latched with an ominous click.

Ring ring, Imp thought, *you're a ringer.* Something about
her bearing told him she was no more a bank manager than
he was. It took him a moment to register what was wrong: she
was wearing black Doc Martens shoes, not office-appropriate
heels. She had an ID badge on a lanyard, but it was back-to-
front and tucked behind one jacket lapel, rendering it unreadable. *Floor security,* he figured. But she was carrying Bernard's
bank deposit box, so there was still a chance they could bluff
their way through and out the other side, so *stay cool, Imp*—

"He's just here to look inside the box," Imp told her, giving
a little nudge, a push in the direction of plausibility. An instant stab of pain told him that Deere was warded. It wasn't
as strong as the one Eve had been wearing, but it still hurt
like biting down on an olive pit.

"I'll handle this," Doc said, sparing Imp an irritated look.
Deere didn't seem to have noticed the nudge. She placed

the box on the table. *Locked.* "Can I see some ID?" she asked, rolling out a totally fake smile: "For both of you."

"Certainly," said Doc, reaching for his wallet, just as Imp patted his front pocket and said, "Shit." His eyes widened as he conjured up the mind-set of a man who'd just discovered he'd lost his wallet on the underground: "Shit! I've left my—"

"There, there, dear." Doc patted his arm. "You probably put it in the wrong pocket again."

While Imp made a show of checking his jacket and trouser pockets, Ms. Deere scrutinized Doc's driving license and card minutely. Finally she admitted, "This appears to be in order, Mr. Harris." She returned his card, then reached into her jacket pocket for a bunch of keys—*Wait, what kind of woman's suit jacket has pockets?* Imp worried—and unlocked the strong box.

"Voila." Ms. Deere stepped out of the way, leaving the contents of the box to Doc and Imp. It did not escape Imp's notice that she had taken up a position between them and the door. Nor did he fail to notice that she was balanced on the balls of her feet, arms held loosely by her sides, almost like some kind of martial arts enthusiast waiting for trouble to kick off. Or that she'd noticed him noticing her watching him.

Doc reached towards the box and slowly turned it so that the contents were visible. There were a couple of plastic boxes inside, like cigarette packets only three or four times as thick. *Are those diskettes?* Imp wondered. There were also some papers and an envelope. Doc pulled out the envelope and looked at the name on it: Evelyn Starkey. *So that's what she's calling herself these days.* "Huh. I think I need to update this," Doc grunted.

"Who is Evelyn Starkey?" asked Ms. Deere.

"My sister—" Imp bit his tongue so hard he nearly drew blood. *What did I just say?* The alarm bells in his head were ringing deafeningly loud, now; bank guards were emphatically *not* paid to ask customers questions like that.

"Just asking," she said guardedly. "You going to be long?"

"I hope not," Doc muttered. He pulled out the sheet of paper from inside the envelope and laid it on the table. "Would you mind photographing this? I'll write up a fresh copy when I get home," he told Imp, who was already reaching for his Samsung. "Or," Doc continued, "I don't suppose you have a copier here?" he asked Ms. Deere: "I could amend and sign it right now, and then there'd be no need for anyone to make a second trip to the strong room—"

"There should be some paper in the printer," Ms. Deere said, pointing to the laser printer beside the desk. "Why don't you—"

She was interrupted by a burst of gunfire from the front of the bank.

Game Boy was chilling on the street in front of the Pennine Bank, idly flattening the oppo in a capture the flag game on his phone, when he got the first intimation that something hinky was going on.

In truth he was bored, though as he was supposed to be running surveillance on the target this should have been a good thing. He had his Bluetooth headset on and dialed in on a live conference call with Rebecca, who was cruising the block in her posh wheels. Doc and Imp were on the inside. His job was to call Del for a pickup, then dive indoors and create a diversion if one of them made the dumb phone in his pocket vibrate, signalling that the job was off. But nothing had gone wrong so far, nothing was going to go wrong, nothing *could* go wrong—

Right up until a black Ford Transit screeched up onto the

curb outside the bank, the rear doors opened, and four guys in Reservoir Dogs cosplay outfits piled out and charged in the front door, bellowing hoarse commands to get on the fucking ground *now* as they waved their motherfucking AK-47s around.

"What the shitstained wank?" Game Boy gaped, then hit the speed dial on his burner to ping Imp and Doc's phones.

"Wassat, Boy?" The Deliverator sounded distracted.

"Bad company, gonna need pickup! *Fuuuu*—" He tried not to swallow his tongue as he vibrated with fear—"this bunch of white guys with assault rifles just ran in—"

"Stop making shit up, Boy, this is London, that kind of thing doesn't happen here—"

A thunderous hammering like a chorus of road drills from hell made Game Boy wince and drop to the ground. "Shooting," he gasped. Getting a grip, he rose to a crouch and moved towards the front door. "I'm going hot."

Rebecca's voice flattened. "On my way. I hit traffic, expect pickup round the back within two minutes."

They'd played a closely related scenario in a hacked-for-purpose level of *Grand Theft Auto* so many times it was almost instinctive: what to do if a Police Armed Response Unit turned up in the middle of a job. Guys in dark suits with AK-47s were not so different—fewer handcuffs, maybe. But it was much scarier in real life than any simulation.

Game Boy pushed through the doors, dodging half a dozen terrified customers scurrying to get out. There was another burst of gunfire, so tooth-rattlingly loud he could feel it in his stomach. A rain of plaster dust fell from the ceiling: *"Everybody get on the fucking floor the next motherfucker to move dies this is not a fucking Quentin Tarantino movie—"* The boss gunman had lost his porkpie, revealing a pink and shiny dome above his contorted face, eyes concealed behind Ray-

Bans. "You *fucking eat carpet you fucking carpetshagger—*"
he screamed at Game Boy, spittle flying as his three thuggish
helpers swung round to cover the room.

Game Boy raised his hands, then dived for the carpet, interrupting his descent with a duck-and-roll that somehow
spun him behind a desk, tugging a computer cable to send a
monitor flying sharp-corner-first into the ankles of one of the
armed robbers. The robber stumbled, stitching a neat row
of bullet holes across the outside wall of the bank just as the
front door opened again to admit a neatly bearded man in
a much more expensive suit, terrifyingly accessorized with
an AA-12 assault shotgun. "Cease fire!" he bellowed. "Drop
your weapons!"

Game Boy scuttled for cover behind the next desk along,
heedless of the arms and legs he was crawling across, despite
a quiet squawk of protest from one of the bank clerks. He
was just in time: moments later the bald-headed robber lit up
the newcomer with his Kalashnikov.

CRASH. Plaster and blood sprayed everywhere. *CRASH.*
What the fuck? Game Boy gibbered silently. The rifles left
his ears ringing, but he could feel the assault shotgun in his
bowels. Automatic fire hammered across the room as the
newcomer (and the first wave of gunmen) took cover.

"We're in an office off the back corridor," Imp shouted in
Game Boy's earbud, "what's going on out there?"

Game Boy got to his knees behind the desk, feeling for the
zone: an itching in the back of his neck and a tension in his
thighs told him *time to dance* as he sprang forward.

"Hey! Get him—"

Game Boy lunged towards the door to the back offices as
one of the AK-toting goons took aim from behind the pho-
tocopier. Satan's drum machine beat a rapid tattoo as the
gunman's heel slid out from under him and he toppled over

backwards, bringing down another, more substantial chunk of ceiling. Shotgun Dude joined the bass line with a slammingly percussive gun solo. Game Boy's leg twisted as he jinked sideways, dodging another robber's fire—this one was smart enough to squeeze off aimed shots rather than wasting ammo—then he crashed through the open door and slammed it shut with one heel. Bullets punched holes in the wall above his head as he scrambled towards the office at the end of the corridor. "Open up, Imp, I'm coming in," he gasped. Behind him, the gunmen were kicking at the door: a freak ricochet had jammed the latch in its reinforced strike plate.

The man who Wendy was absolutely certain wasn't Bernard Harris exchanged a wide-eyed look with his maybe-not husband: "What the ferret-legging hell?" he demanded, ducking instinctively at a second burst of automatic gunfire.

It was a sentiment that Wendy fervently shared, but right now she had another priority: "Two bank robberies at once is a bit of a coincidence isn't it, gentlemen? You're under arrest."

"You don't want to do this." Not-his-husband focussed on her, and the ward she wore under her collar grew hot.

"Stop that shit if you want to get out of here alive," she said evenly as she raised her hands and summoned her katana into existence. "What are you after?" Not-husband—the movie impresario, bloke-in-a-hat—flinched. Not-Harris gave the game away by glancing guiltily at the letter on the desk. "That? Right, I'm impounding it as evidence." She grabbed the letter left-handed, shoving it inside her jacket. "It's probably what our tooled up playmates are after so how about we—"

The door opened and she turned. "*No!*" screamed Imp as her sword began to move.

She froze with her blade hanging over the neck of a frightened Chinese kid, who crouched on his hands and knees across the threshold.

"Del's bringing the car round," gasped the kid, ignoring her: "ninety seconds." Another gasp, then, "They'll kill us if they find us—"

Her arrestees were unarmed, unlike the gang of heavies shooting up the front of the branch. She made a snap decision. "Follow me," she said, and stepped outside just in time to hear a hollow boom as the door at the front end of the corridor sprang open. (Evidently the shotgun-toting heavy had given up on subtlety and loaded a breaching round.)

Wendy let go of her sword—it evaporated, barely a wisp of vapor surviving to reach the floor—and raised her arms into a new position. She summoned, drew, and let fly an arrow in one smooth motion. She took a long step backwards, away from the front door, drawing and loosing again and again. The compound bow she'd trained herself to summon and shoot was compact but packed a punch: her arrows evaporated after a second, but that was plenty long enough to put a hole in the torso of anyone stupid enough to get in her way. Wendy had studied the Russian *kinzhalnaya* technique—very rapid fire using a short bow at close range—and could manifest a fresh arrow between her fingertips as fast as she could draw. And she could draw forty times in a minute, if she didn't mind wearing her arm in a sling the next day.

Fire: step back: fire: step back. The gunman (or gunmen) wasn't stupid—Wendy had at best seconds before he (or they) emptied a magazine down the passage—but the storm of arrows hissing past the broken door would give them pause. *Fire: step backwards.* She felt something cold and hard against her spine and shoved herself against the fire bar.

The alarm screeched as the door swung open and Wendy

tumbled onto the grimy tarmac in the alleyway, rolling out of the line of fire just as a shooter unloaded his magazine down the corridor. The shots stopped abruptly. Wendy cast around for cover, but the exit from the alleyway was at least ten meters away. Surely the raiders would have backup watching the escape route—

The sound of footsteps coming towards her was partially muffled by the ringing in her ears. She rolled onto her back, bow drawn and aiming between her toes, but it was just her two perps and their teenage sidekick. They walked like cats on black ice, tiptoeing backwards away from the fire exit as if they had to maintain eye contact with the gunmen in the bank.

"—Will he stay down?" not-husband asked not-Bernard.

"Depends if he decides to suck off his own AK instead of signing up for CBT. I hit him with all the fear and loathing in Islington. He'll be in therapy for years—"

"Where's Del?"

"She should be—hey!"

The kid had half-turned and spotted Wendy. She gave him a feral grin as she sat up and took aim at his chest. "Hello again! Hands up, no sudden movements."

Sirens rose and fell in the near distance, bouncing between the brick walls. Wendy's pulse hammered a manic counterpoint. The kid narrowed his eyes at her, somehow managing to look utterly freaked out and supremely bored simultaneously. "Nope, not playing that game."

What? Wendy glared. The kid was the stunt artist, wasn't he? The one who'd played Robin in the Hamleys heist, neutralizing the guards with their own gear. "Neither am I," she told him. "I know what you are and I've got what you want." She scrambled to her feet. *Step back. Step back.* The end of the alley was just a short sprint away.

A big black SUV turned the corner and roared towards her, then rocked to a sharp standstill just as she tensed for the moment of impact. Doors popped open: "All aboard!" shouted the gorgeous black woman behind the wheel. "Last train to trancentral leaving now!" She smirked at Wendy from behind her windscreen: "Aww, isn't she cute?"

Wendy evaporated her arrow just long enough to give Getaway Woman a two-fingered salute, the traditional insult started by the English archers at Agincourt. In an argument between an SUV and a shortbow, the one with the two-ton pedestrian masher was inevitably going to win; but once she moved . . . "I've got what you want," she taunted as the three miscreants trotted past her. "How about we go somewhere quiet and talk about how you're going to surrender?"

"Yeah nope—" The impresario scampered past her. "She's warded," he called to someone just out of sight.

"On it," said a voice behind her back.

Wendy let go of her bow as she turned, bringing her riot baton to the ready, but something tugged at her collar and then a bleak tide of depression washed over her. It felt like she'd jumped in a river of regrets, her pockets stuffed with cobblestones. It came to her distantly that she could barely muster the energy to breathe—in fact, begrudged herself every successive moment of mindlessly prolonged life. The kid slithered behind her, clutching her ward in his hand, its broken cord trailing. He leaned close and she couldn't quite bring herself to care about his hand groping past her breast to grab the crumpled note.

The big V8 howled as Getaway Woman threw it into reverse. "Justified and ancient!" she sang through the open window, as she backed up the alley under Wendy's despairing gaze. "Let them eat ice cream!"

What. The. Fuck?

Wendy shook herself as the big black Cayenne reversed rapidly into the street. She took a hesitant step forward. The weight of the world's woes gradually slid from her shoulders; her feet buoyed, and she ran after the car just as the fire door cracked open again and a gun banged.

They're getting away, she realized angrily. Nothing else mattered, not the sick sense of fury at her suspects slipping through her fingers, not even the bullets cracking past her head. *Gotta get my wheels on!* Wendy drew a deep breath as she stepped up on one foot, then up again on the other, wobbling slightly as she swapped her shoes for speed skates.

She kicked herself up to speed and jump-turned sharply onto the right-hand pavement at the end of the alleyway, narrowly avoiding an elderly shopper towing a wheelie-bag. The getaway Porsche screeched into a right turn outside a Waitrose, then braked sharply to avoid the back of a crawling Number 9 bus. Wendy grimaced and bared her teeth, panting as she jinked and wove her way between pedestrians, trying to catch up with the SUV on the other side of the road. It was a ridiculously one-sided race: the Porsche was theoretically capable of hitting two hundred and fifty kilometers per hour, but London traffic today travelled at the same crawl as it had in the 1880s. Meanwhile Wendy with her skates on could use pavement and road with equal aplomb, as long as she didn't mind the risk of being squished by a left-turning truck or caught in a bus's blind spot. She was gaining ground within a minute, even though the traffic was moving. But as she tried to second-guess Getaway Woman's likely route in order to cut her off, the phone rang.

What the fuck—Wendy hit the "accept call" button. "Kind of busy," she panted.

"Were you there?" demanded Gibson.

"Yes, I'm in hot pursuit—"

"Break it off!" Gibson sounded alarmed.

"They're unarmed—"

"The hell they are! I can't afford for you to get shot, our cleanup metrics will go to hell—"

"This bunch are unarmed!" she shouted. Getaway Woman had spotted a gap in the oncoming traffic and gunned the big Porsche, screeching out to nip smartly around the bus and accelerate down the wrong side of the street, pulling ahead again. "There were two gangs! Repeat, two gangs! I'm after our original targets—they're getting away—"

She glimpsed the edge of Holland Park between the buildings on the right, then had to take emergency evasive action to avoid a feral cycle courier hurtling out of Earls Court Road without looking. *Live action Frogger, fuck my life*, she thought. "Suspects are on Kensington High Street driving a black mark two Porsche Cayenne Turbo, plates Papa Hotel Ten Foxtrot Yankee India, going right right right onto Abbotsbury Road northbound—"

"Break off!" Gibson told her. "I'll run the plates, but for the love of god *back off now*!"

"Fuck." Wendy went into a drift along the pavement, slowing as the Porsche pulled away from her. It drove past the park before screeching into an unsignalled right turn and disappearing from view. "Why?"

"Need you back at the bank," Gibson said heavily. "The Met first responders are declaring a major incident and they have questions for you. It's a murder scene now. I thought our suspects were nonviolent, we're dropping the case if they're—"

"I can confirm the gang we're after are unarmed. I was in the process of arresting two of them when the shooting started outside. Their getaway team showed up and they were unarmed, too, I nearly *had* them, what the fuck happened?" *They have transhuman mind control voodoo, that's what happened*, she thought, but she wasn't about to say that to her boss until she could account for exactly how they'd used it to blindside her. *That* rankled.

"I don't know and I don't like it," said Gibson. "But you'd better return to Pennine Bank right away. I'll meet you there with our duty solicitor, and after we've got you out of the frame and scheduled the police interviews we can discuss what to do next."

The Bond paused at the end of the alleyway to adjust his suit jacket and straighten his tie before he stepped out onto the main road and walked away.

Next time, he promised himself grimly.

Behind him, the abandoned assault shotgun cooled slowly in one of the recycling bins just inside the end of the alley.

BIDDING WAR

It took hours for Wendy to disentangle herself from the investigation, even with a Home Office thief-taker ID card and the HiveCo lawyer's assistance. One of the bank employees and four civilians had been wounded, two of them seriously enough they might not survive. Two of the AK-toting thugs had died at the scene, shredded by the shotgun-wielding maniac. The police were collectively furious and confused, and Wendy *had* contributed to the fracas in a small way, peppering the inner door and walls of the bank with arrow holes. Luckily everything had been caught on camera and the duty solicitor's pointed comments about self-defense and the relative lethality of fully automatic weapons versus an imaginary bow and arrow finally got through to the Inspector in charge. Wendy was released under caution after four hours of questioning, with a stern admonition not to leave the country and to present herself at the local nick within forty-eight hours for a full deposition.

(That she had until two years earlier been one of the Met's own was not a point Wendy brought up: it might have led to uncomfortable questions about why she was no longer on the force, not to mention *what the blithering hell* was she doing engaging in a firefight with suspected terrorists. Best let sleeping dogs—and past careers—lie.)

"Let me get this straight," Mary, the duty solicitor, said,

"you were on the scene to interview the bank manager about a previous robbery, when you spotted the bank robbers on the CCTV feed from the front of the branch. Let's call them Group A."

"Yes." Wendy nodded encouragingly.

Mary nibbled the end of her propelling pencil. "You asked Mr. Granger to lure Group A into an office, and were in the process of arresting them when a different group of robbers—armed ones, let's call them Group B—showed up."

"Exactly. I was waiting for Group A to reveal what they were after before I arrested them."

"And then—" Gibson began.

"I made a risk assessment, that four thugs with automatic weapons—they were shooting by this point—were a far greater danger to the public than the two unarmed suspects I was with, so I temporarily confiscated the item that Group A were interested in, then attempted to get them out of the bank so I could arrest them without fear of Group B intervening."

"But there was a third party. Let's call him Individual C."

Wendy cringed. She'd never actually *seen* Individual C, but she'd heard the ear-bleeding crash of his shotgun, even over the roar of Group B's guns. "He made his presence known."

"What happened next?" Mary scribbled shorthand notes on her pad as she waited for Wendy to continue.

"Individual C shot out the lock on the corridor door. I assessed that Individual C—or members of Group B, if any survived—would be entering the corridor shortly, and they wouldn't be looking for tea and sympathy. So I shot first, not aiming at people, just suppressive fire."

Mary waited, but when Wendy didn't fill the silence, she moved on to the next question. "According to the police you were unarmed when they apprehended you. What happened to your gun?"

"Oh, I don't need a *gun* to shoot people . . ."

Mary sighed and massaged her forehead. "Run that by me again?"

Gibson cleared his throat. "Ms. Deere is a transhuman, class three, one of our augmented Field Investigators. Her ability is what we call a somatic illusionist."

"I can make imaginary things," Wendy tried to help.

"She creates illusions," Gibson clarified. "Illusions that are tangible enough you can weigh them or hit somebody over the head with them. They don't last very long if she loses physical contact with them—a couple of seconds—and she can't make anything complicated or very big, but she's never unarmed."

"Side-arm baton." Wendy raised her right hand and produced her nightstick with a flourish. "Or, in this case, a lightweight compound bow and as many arrows as I can shoot before my arm falls off."

The solicitor froze. "You went up against armed robbers with *a bow and arrow*?"

Wendy shook her head. "Not exactly—I just fired enough arrows down the corridor to make the robbers think twice about storming it while I evacuated everyone through the fire exit."

"I think I see why the police are having a hard time working out the sequence of events." Mary was keeping it professional but Wendy could tell that the solicitor was having a hard time believing her story. "What happened next?"

"The bank should have the CCTV recordings from the interior? I'm pretty sure they also had a couple of cameras overlooking the fire exits and the back alleyway. Um." Wendy glanced at her boss for confirmation.

Gibson nodded. "We're getting access," he said. "Continue."

Wendy took them through the sequence with the weird and abrupt wave of existential nausea that had swamped her, the teenage kid's uncanny ability to pick the pocket of an armed and alert thief-taker, then their escape in the getaway car and her abortive pursuit on imaginary rollerblades. "Did you run the plates—"

"Yes. Cloned," Gibson announced.

"Well *fuck*." Wendy was abruptly out of self-restraint. "After all that effort—"

"First things first." Gibson laid a restraining hand on her forearm. "What's the legal picture looking like?"

"Well." Mary the duty solicitor smiled like a rodent preparing to sink its teeth into the ball of an unsuspecting human's thumb. "Let's tackle the worst case analysis first. The police can charge you with carrying an offensive weapon. They can also charge you with reckless endangerment. Theft or handling stolen goods would be a bit of a reach—"

"*Excuse* me?" snarled Wendy.

"—Did you or did you not take an item from a safe deposit box that had been procured under false pretenses?" Mary shrugged: "I'm just playing devil's advocate here, channeling my inner Crown Prosecution Service jobsworth in search of an easy conviction. For what it's worth, I don't think that one would fly because you were given custody of the box by someone in a position of lawful supervision—Mr. Granger—and took the item for temporary safe-keeping in the presence of known criminals, with the intent of returning it. The offensive weapon charge I'd defend by taking the position that, as a transhuman, it's a manifestation of your person, and you can't reasonably set it aside any more than an Aikido black belt could reasonably be expected to refrain from using their skills in self-defense when attacked. The outcome . . . I'd say it depends on how good a barrister we could get for you, and whether the judge got up on the wrong side of the bed that morning. A toss-up, in other words. The hard bit is the reckless endangerment, *but* it's all on CCTV, and as you weren't aiming at anyone in particular . . . ?"

"Who, me? Nope, never."

"Good, then we have at least a mitigating factor to set beside the thugs with highly illegal automatic weapons who were shooting at you. No, Ms. Deere, the police are highly unlikely to charge you—not unless they have some reason to hold a grudge against you." She put her pen down on her notepad for emphasis, and smiled brightly.

Wendy offered her a strained smile in return. "We'll just have to see, won't we. Sir?"

"I suppose so." Gibson didn't sound happy. "I can't afford to have you off the job because some randos with heavy artillery took a dump in our punch bowl. This pilot program is too important." He glanced at Mary: "You don't need to hear this."

"Don't worry, I know when I'm not wanted." Mary stood as she gathered her papers. "I'll get this written up and you can call me if anything comes up. Be seeing you, I'm sure." She closed the door carefully behind her.

"Pilot program." Wendy gave Gibson a hard stare. "How many other transhuman investigators do you have, sir? I mean, surely you must have more than—"

"—How many transhumans do you think there are who've done full police training, worked the beat, and passed their detective exams?"

She was about to say *scores, surely*? But something gave her pause. "How many?"

"Two years ago, when the Home Office set up the TPCF and set this whole ball rolling, they started with *one*. You might have heard of him: Officer Friendly. Six months down the line, when TPCF was rolled into the Met, they were up to eight. But three of them were borrowed spooks, and the other four were still probationers. I gather they've only been full constables for a few months. You'd already left the force, otherwise you'd have been up for the world's fastest promotion to detective inspector."

She stared at him. "What you're saying is, I should have held out for more money."

To his credit, Gibson looked abashed. "It's a pilot program. We had to start somewhere, so we started with you. Management assigned you the codename ABLE ARCHER: that you're a named asset should tell you something. Once we can recruit some more transhumans, and once you're past your probationary term, you'll be in line for promotion. We'll need someone to take charge of training and draw up professional standards in conjunction with HR. As all that stuff is management-level, I'll be able to push through a re-grading, then shake the money tree again—if you're willing to rise to the challenge. But right now, while you're doing a gumshoe job, you get gumshoe wages. Is that clear?"

"Clear enough." She shrugged. "It was worth a try." *Gumshoe wages don't pay enough to put up with gangsters unloading Kalashnikovs at me*, she added silently.

"So." Gibson tilted his office chair back. "Any questions?"

"Let's see. Do we have any leads on Group A, after you made me abandon the pursuit?"

"Maybe." Gibson twitched the mouse on his computer, squinting at something on the screen. "Incidentally, engaging in an unsupported solo pursuit of a gang of escaping bank robbers may be brave, but another word for brave is foolhardy. You're not in the Met any more, you're not a sworn officer of the law, you're not protecting the public, and I will be *really annoyed* if you put yourself in hospital for six months by engaging in unauthorized heroics. Like inviting some thug to run you over with an SUV." Gibson's tone was even and he didn't raise his voice, but Wendy sat up straight as a flush of embarrassment stained her cheeks.

"Sorry sir. Won't happen again." She paused. "If I'm not protecting the public and upholding the law, what am I doing?"

"You're here to take in thieves we're contracted to arrest, Deere; it's a business. You're a fancy version of what our trans-Atlantic cousins call a bounty hunter. You are not paid to put your neck on the line. If you want to play at being a superhero, do it on your own time and don't come crying to me when it all goes horribly wrong." His cheek twitched. "So. What exactly was it about the safe deposit box that attracted our targets' interest?"

"A letter, sir." Wendy gave him a slow look. "I didn't get to read much of it, but it was addressed to an Eve Starkey, and it seemed to be an invitation to participate in an auction. Something about sealed bids and a rare manuscript. I, uh, got a number and a description, but no title or author? The letter referred to it as the AW-312.4 concordance."

Gibson leaned towards his computer and started rapid-fire typing. "AW-312.4? Okay, I'm actioning a search." He paused, then glanced at her. "This is major. More than one group wants that thing and they're willing to spray bullets around to get it. We may be pulled off the case—depends how Management assess the risk level. Remember, we're not cops and you're too valuable to put your life on the line. It's just a job. There are some sources I can consult and I'll get back to you if anything shakes loose, but that's all."

"Sources *you*—"

"Not police, not Home Office. You aren't cleared for those contacts, at least not yet."

"Oh. Then what should I do now?"

Gibson blinked. "I don't know—why don't you go and write up today's events while they're still fresh in your mind? Then . . . yes, take the rest of today off, and tomorrow as well—I'll write it up as sick leave. It can't have been any fun getting caught up in all that. If you need a referral for counseling—"

"That won't be necessary, sir," Wendy said hastily. "So, uh. I'll go write stuff up, then go home. See you the day after tomorrow, I guess?"

"Yes. Dismissed." Gibson's eyes were focussing on his computer as she stood. Already forgotten, she headed for the cubicle she'd been assigned for desk work. *You are not to put your neck on the line on company time.* Message received, loud and clear. But Gibson had overlooked something very important when he told her not to take risks.

This thing with the transhuman gang, the impresario and his not-husband and their teenage sidekick and dreadlock-rocking getaway driver, wasn't a job; it was personal. It had turned personal the moment they broke her ward, slammed her with mind control mojo, and stole the bid letter out of her inside pocket. Right after she got them out from under the guns of Group B and Automatic Shotgun Dude.

And Gibson was smart enough to notice and devious enough to want some baked-in deniability when she threw down with them. Otherwise, why else would he have given her the day off?

"I can't believe we did that! *Fuuuuuuuu . . . !*"

"Chill out, kid. We escaped, didn't we?"

"Did you *see* her on those blades? Where the shitting hell did she get them from anyway? She was chasing us like the fucking T-Rex from the first *Jurassic Park*—"

"She saved our lives." Imp tiredly cracked the ring-pull on one of Doc's cans of highly regrettable lager. "Sure, she was trying to arrest us, but she wasn't trying to shoot us."

"She saw our faces," said Doc. "*Fuck*. Who am I kidding?" He ran shaky fingers through his hair. "It was a trap and she was waiting for us and we sprang it. She probably knew what was in the deposit box all along."

"I need to talk to Eve—" Imp cleared his throat—"our employer. No way did she set this up, but there might be a leak in her organization." She'd told him as much, he just hadn't felt the need to share it with his family. He was looking out for them, he rationalized: Why worry them needlessly? Now he was regretting it as three pairs of eyes swivelled his way. He took a swig of beer. "What?" he asked.

"There were *guns*, Jeremy!" Game Boy's voice rose to a squeak: "Fucking guns!"

"Yeah." Del was uncharacteristically repressed. "I didn't sign up for guns, man."

"Neither did I," Imp pointed out, but nobody was listening to him.

"We should ditch this job," Doc proposed. "You can't make movies if you're dead, can you? Remember rule number one? *Don't die.* If you break rule one, you automatically lose at everything. Don't do it, Jeremy, it's not worth it."

Imp sighed. "Yeah, I guess." He took another mouthful of regrettable beer. "Um. This." He brandished the letter they'd found in the deposit box. "It's probably worth something to Eve anyway, so I should maybe go and haggle with her. See if she'll pay extra for it. But you're right, this shit isn't worth what she's paying us."

Del's sharp-eyed gaze tracked to the letter. "So what's it say?"

"Bear with me . . ." Imp smoothed the crumpled paper

out. "It's pretty much what I was expecting: an invitation to submit bids for a map leading to the location of a lost manuscript. There's some crap about a Darknet marketplace—"

"Let me see that." Game Boy grabbed at it and the paper somehow slid through Imp's fingers. "Huh. Good luck tracing this, it's almost definitely offshore. Bids with a deposit paid in US dollars to a numbered bank account in the Cayman Islands, to be held in crow—no, *es*crow, whatever the fuck that is—"

"It means the bank holds the money and releases it to the—"

"Enough already." Imp flapped his beer-unencumbered hand: "I hear you. We don't like the guns, we can't go any further without spending a metric fuckton of money that we don't have, so we're out of the game, yes? Are we all agreed? So all that remains is for me to sell this to Eve for as much extra dosh as I can guilt-trip out of her. Yes?"

"Yes!" Game Boy shouted at him excitedly.

"Great." Imp necked the rest of his can, then chucked it atop the overflowing pile in the far corner of the room. "I'm going out. Give me that," he added, taking the letter back from Game Boy. "Don't wait up."

Eve was not happy to be summoned by her brother. She was even less pleased by his choice of meeting place, even though it was within easy walking distance. "You did *not* bring me here for the coffee," she hissed. "It's terrible!"

"It's Costa." Imp shrugged. "Would you prefer Starbucks?"

Eve's gaze flickered briefly to the Gammon she was testdriving today. He stood close to the entrance, furtively sipping the spiced vanilla chai latte she'd inflicted on him, as if he was scared it would cost him his man card. (*He'll never do*, she decided, *what if an assassin ambushes me in the fitting rooms at Dolci Follie?*) "You did this to punish me for something," she guessed, projecting wildly.

"Busted." Imp smiled crookedly. Today he wore his normal art-student-gone-to-seed costume: a beautifully tailored wool coat that featured oil stains and a Frankensteinian line of stitches across the shoulders, paint-spattered jeans, and a once-smart dress shirt.

"So what is it?" she demanded. "Did you get the book?"

"Nope." He reached inside his jacket pocket and pulled out a creased envelope which he placed in front of her, oblivious to the Gammon frantically scrambling for his concealed pistol. "This is the bid letter you wanted me to retrieve. They want funds to be placed in escrow. I can't proceed any further."

Eve smiled. "Leave it to me." Behind Imp, the Gammon began to relax.

"No, I don't think you understand. *I can't proceed any further.*" Imp glowered at her. "We were *made*, Eve, we nearly got caught! A bunch of thugs with guns hit the bank while we were in the back, they were clearly after the same thing, and there was an undercover cop waiting to arrest us. Explosions! Machine guns! Car chases! Not my cup of orange pekoe *at all.*" He gesticulated dramatically, nearly spilling his espresso.

It all sounded a bit overblown to Eve. "Are you exaggerating?" she asked, raising one perfectly threaded eyebrow at him.

"Am I—" He recoiled indignantly, the picture of aggrieved innocence.

"It's just that you have a history of, shall we say, creative confabulation. Remember the hijacking incident?"

"I was *eight.*"

"You cleared out an entire airport terminal! And you kept doing it. There was that time when we went to the zoo and you gave lollipops made from energy drinks to the chimpanzees—"

"It was hot! I didn't like to see them suffer. And I was drunk." He crossed his arms defensively. "Right now I'm sober. The bank was full of lunatics with assault rifles, sis. I don't like it when bad men point big guns at me," he said plaintively. "I should have listened to—"

"Wait." She laid a slim, cold hand on his wrist. "It's going to be all right. Just give me a second to process this."

Eve picked up the letter and read it carefully. "This looks . . . useful, yes. I can deal with the money side of things, you don't need to worry about it." She reached into her handbag and pulled out her phone, photographed the letter, and emailed it to her duty assistant, along with brief instructions. "Bear with me." If her kid brother was *not* exaggerating for effect, then there was indeed an adversary at work, which meant she needed to get a handle on the book fast. The BBC news app had a story about—her eyes widened before she managed to freeze her face. A hot, shivery feeling rippled up her back, prickling sweat springing out under her blouse. *Three dead in bank bloodbath.* "Okay, I can see why you might be a little upset."

"*Upset*—"

Eve flashed him a sympathetic smile. "If I had *any* idea this was going to happen I wouldn't have sent you," she said, putting every microgram of sincerity she could muster into her reassurance. "But it's done now. I was going to authorize 20K for getting hold of this note, but in view of unforeseen circumstances I'm going to double that. Forty thousand pounds, okay? Where do you want me to send it?"

"We agreed eighty thousand."

"Eighty thousand for the entire job—for getting the book. This was just the first step, but, fair do's, it turns out it was a pretty big step: bigger than I expected." Eve allowed her cut-glass diction to slip back into the more relaxed dialect of their shared childhood, feeling a hateful pride in her ability to manipulate Jeremy so easily despite the passage of time. Nevertheless, a pang of conscience stabbed at her for endangering him. "Forty thousand puts you not too far off your funding goal, doesn't it? If you want to dump me and bail on the job, I'm not stopping you."

Imp shook his head. "Look, it's not just me, sis. I've got to think about my homies. They're really upset. If it was just me, and if you could take care of the troublesome details—" he brushed imaginary lint from his sleeve—"I could see my way to helping you out. But we've got a thief-taker on our tail now, know what I mean? We work as a team. I can't do this job on my own, and they're going to flat-out refuse if there are guns involved. Or thief-takers. Have you ever *seen* a public hanging? I mean for real, not on TV?"

"Good point." Eve chewed her lower lip pensively, quite forgetting her demeanor. "But I think the thief-taker may turn out to be good news. If it was real cops we might have a problem, but thief-takers—it should be easy enough to pay them off. They're all private sector contractors. Did you get a name? As for the gunmen—leave them to me." A thought struck her and she tittered quietly, then stopped when she saw her brother's expression. "What?"

"You scare me when you laugh like that."

She smiled. "I just thought, my boss owns a couple of private security companies. After I buy out the thief-taker who's looking for you, I can have them sort out you and your friends' criminal background checks and actually *hire* you—on payroll, as thief-takers in your own right—to hunt down the gang of transhumans that hit Hamleys toy shop. Wouldn't that be priceless?"

Imp's face was such a picture that she couldn't hold back another giggle.

"You don't have to do that," she told him when she regained control, "but the best way to short-circuit an investigation is to take it over and investigate yourself, don't you think? Anyway, I'll deal with the thief-taker. Then I'll bid on the treasure map. Meanwhile, I want you to sell your playmates on the idea that they're going to get paid extra and nobody is going to shoot at them—I'll provide security if there's even the *slightest* whiff of trouble. Will you do that for your sister? Special favor, Jerm? Pretty please?"

"Stop batting your eyelashes at me, it's not even remotely convincing . . . And yes, dammit, I'll try, seeing it's you who's asking. I'm not promising anything, though. Right now they're feeling burned."

School was out but, as Wendy was learning, being Head Prefect in ABLE ARCHER class gave her special privileges—like being able to raid the classroom supplies cupboard for her own projects.

Under the watchful eyes of the New Management coalition, the previous government's bonfire of red tape had been replaced by a blast furnace, principally fueled by any regulations that got in the way of big money doing whatever the hell it pleased. Loopholes in gun control laws for licensed security guards were the least of it. Data protection and privacy regulations had gone the same way as planning permission and habeas corpus, and HiveCo Security could tap into all sorts of interesting databases . . . such as the ANPR system used to levy a congestion charge on traffic entering the controlled zone around London, the Highways Agency traffic cameras monitoring major junctions, and even some weird-ass camera network called SCORPION STARE that seemed to have nodes *everywhere*. Shodan said it ran on IP addresses owned by the Ministry of Defense, but that was obvious bullshit. *I ought to get a poster for the office wall*, she mused: *Judge Dredd: I am the Law*.

Speaking of Shodan, HiveCo had a horrifyingly expensive corporate account on the internet-of-things search engine, and once Wendy discovered it, she was fascinated. Baby monitors, color-cycling light bulbs, shop CCTV systems, HD television sets with unpatched operating systems and unchanged administrator passwords: they were all there, leaking secrets incontinently on the public internet if you knew where to point your web browser. The HiveCo corporate feed could search by geographical location, and there was a plugin for Google Maps. Wendy could drill into London using Street View, ask for unsecured cameras in the neighborhood she was investigating, then window-peep to her heart's content.

It was probably still illegal, but who was going to call her on it in this time of 40 percent cuts to local government—and policing—budgets? If a free and frank exchange of ballistic projectiles in a bank robbery/bloodbath wasn't enough to get her a charge sheet, then she was unlikely to catch any shit for snooping on smart toilets.

Wendy wrote up her report in a blazing hurry then hung around her cubicle for a long time, snooping on camera feeds. Eventually she found a view of the back of her own head, disappearing down an alleyway (the view inconveniently barricaded by a row of overflowing bins). She picked up the trail in the high street, where a black Porsche SUV glided along in monochrome silence, pursued by an angry woman on rollerblades. She glimpsed herself weaving in and out of oblivious pedestrians, jumping into the street to avoid a pram, leaping back onto the pavement to dodge a delivery van. The SUV turned right across traffic to dodge down a street running past a park. Right on cue, the woman on skates dismounted, stumbling to a panting halt on the pavement as the order to break off pursuit reached her.

Wendy skipped from camera to camera, swearing whenever she hit a blank spot or a gap in the record—too many systems still only recorded in low-def, or even spooled to tape—but she kept following the getaway car as it cruised past Kensington Park and slowed. She froze a frame in which a door swung open, scrubbed forward a couple of seconds and counted fewer indistinct heads, then backed up.

There. Him. She spotted the teenager in the hoodie crossing the road behind the SUV, heading into the park. She bookmarked and carefully saved the stream, then moved on. No more flung-open door footage, but one fewer head: the flare of a coat, a familiar figure glimpsed from behind, walking along the pavement behind the car. She followed him to a zebra crossing, then a footpath. London's parks were heavily instrumented, a legacy of IRA bombing campaigns during the early 1990s. The municipal cameras were crap but they let her track Not-Bernard-Harris and Kid-in-Hoodie halfway across the park, in the direction of the mews behind Kensington Palace. Then she hit a blind spot. There was a dead zone where none of the cameras were working and nobody had fixed them because it was all outsourced these days, including monitoring the outsourcing agency's performance and deliverables, so why bother when you can spend your maintenance budget on comfy office chairs and a C-suite pay raise? Or maybe there was something more sinister than everyday corruption and negligence at work. *Hmm.*

Fuming, Wendy dropped a bunch of pins around the target area on the street map. Then she went back to tracking the cute getaway woman with the dreads and the infuriatingly insouciant attitude as she drove away from the park. Just a kilometer further away she parallel-parked the Cayenne neatly, then got out and walked a hundred meters and entered a tube station. Which would have been *great* for further surveillance if only the cameras in the lobby of that particular station had been working, but somehow Getaway Girl managed to vanish inside during a very precise six-minute interval when there was no monitoring because the computer that controlled the station's cameras was installing a Windows update and rebooting.

It was almost as if her target had known.

Wendy pushed her chair back from the desk and stretched to ease the crick in her neck. She blinked furiously, eyes watering from a couple of hours staring at a too-cheap monitor, and checked the time on her phone: it was nearly half past six. At least she had tomorrow off work, thanks to Gibson not being a total tool after she'd nearly gotten her ass shot off. She'd go home and cook herself dinner, maybe catch up on the washing, and have an early night. Then tomorrow she'd go for a walk in the park and see what she could find.

Back in her subterranean den Eve allowed herself a private Two Minute Hate—at Chez Bigge, one screamed silently in the privacy of one's own head if one knew what was good for one: *all* the walls had ears, not to mention eyes and speech stress analyzers—then, with every outward appearance of calm, she placed the bid letter on her desk and tried to stare it into submission. When that failed she busied herself with make-work, directing one of the less unreliable members of her staff to identify the thief-taker at the bank—best to buy off the pursuit, as long as they were clueless about the manuscript. But finally she ran out of delaying tactics. So she took a deep breath, moistened her lips, adjusted her telephone headset, and made the unavoidable call.

Rupert answered the phone unusually quickly. "Yes?" He sounded irritable.

"My Lord." He liked *My Lord* as a title, almost as much as he liked *Master* or *Boss*. "It's about the rare manuscript. The acquisition is still in progress, but I've encountered some pushback, and I need clarification on how to proceed. Is this a convenient time?"

"Not terribly, no." Rupert sounded distracted. "Don't stop, get on with it," she heard him tell someone else. "Ah, good." A shuddering gasp. "Talk to me, Eve."

Oh God, he's with a rent boy again, she realized, *or maybe a call girl, or*—Rupert spread his affections widely, and wasn't terribly happy to be interrupted in the act—"Yes, My Lord," she said, re-centering herself. "A rival firm is bidding high and there's already a body count—they tried to preempt with extreme prejudice. They smell of *siloviki* to me, but it might be a double-blind. Anyway, I've acquired the tender but I think it's time-critical and I'd like your permission to throw money at the problem."

"Yes, I already heard about it from Dmitry in Smyrna; it makes sense that there would be competition from that direction. Ahh, ahh—yes, how much money?" He sounded slightly breathless. "Keep going," he added.

"Twenty-five million should get their attention: Permission to escalate if it doesn't? Of course we'll repossess most of that when we terminate the acquisition process," she added; "I'll put Andrei on it."

"Yes yes, that's great, do it, do it—I'm talking to you, Eve, not you there. I mean here. By the way, Eve, what are you wearing?"

She squeezed her eyes shut. "I'm in my purple leather bodysuit," she began, "and the thigh-high boots you bought me in Cannes." She extemporized on the fly, narrating a fictional fetish session for her master while he pleasured himself upon his boy, girl, or bondage goat. He eventually climaxed with a glutinous ululation that made her skin crawl, then hung up on her.

Eve stared at the ceiling blindly. *I'd like to wrap you up tight in cling film*, she thought viciously, trying on a fantasy of her own for size. It wasn't particularly sexy, but—*I'd hang you from a meat hook in the dungeon until you're ripe and buzzing with flies.* Or maybe not. She closed her eyes and waited for the flames of rage and shame to subside. Right now Rupert was a long way away, and he almost certainly wasn't spying on her through the cameras in her office, since he hadn't commanded her to undress or masturbate for him. He didn't respect his chattels' personal boundaries, and for the time being that category included her. *We'll see what you say when the table is turned,* she promised herself, and jotted down a brief reminder for her future self: add *observe subordinates' personal boundaries (where reasonable)* to her list of policies when she seized control. Then she spent a soothing five minutes on the internet, pricing up elastrator devices for Rupert.

Next she took a deep breath and placed another call. This one used a Darknet voice server to connect to her personal concierge at a market-oriented Advanced Persistent Threat headquartered in Transnistria: a criminal enterprise so dangerous that the FBI had offered a multimillion-dollar bounty for anyone who could take them down.

"Hello, Andrei? This is Eve, Mr. Bigge's executive assistant.

How are you today? I need the services of an escrow agent with a sideline in post-acquisition repossessions . . ."

When in doubt, follow the detectives.

The Bond had obeyed this rubric on other track-and-trace jobs and found it to be worthwhile. This time it was turning out to be problematic.

After overcoming the minor obstacle posed by the unreadably ancient hard drive—the lab technician he'd procured from the National Museum of Computing at Bletchley Park had been pathetically eager to cooperate after the second fingernail—he'd been able to establish the details of Bernard's banking arrangements. *No loose ends:* he dutifully buried both body and hard drive platters (after giving the latter a good scrubbing with steel wool and denting them with a hammer) before tooling up and driving to Kensington High Street, whereupon he encountered another minor obstacle in the shape of an armed robbery in progress. The oppo had form and enthusiasm but precious little technique. He *tsked* silently to himself as he garotted the sentry in the back alley, shoved the corpse in a recycling bin, and cut the data cables to the bank. Then he adjusted his tie, straightened his lapels, and nipped round the front to make his appearance.

The *Reservoir Dogs* re-enactment society went down hard. The Bond wasn't self-indulgent enough to hang around for Mexican stand-offs and long expletive-filled soliloquies. His plan was simple: grab the document, go full Terminator on any witnesses, and get out. But the plan went off the rails immediately after he unloaded a breaching round into the door to the back offices. Some assclown wanted to play Robin of Sherwood. Normally this wouldn't have been a problem, but Robin was rocking it like he was snorting bath salts: he seemed to have an inexhaustible supply of arrows and they flew thick and fast.

The Bond, not being suicidally inclined, declined to storm a narrow corridor under beaten fire. But now he encountered a snag. Not being sartorially challenged, he hadn't thought to pad out his pockets with flash-bangs: they ruined the hang of his jacket. So he had to wait for a lull in the re-enactment of Agincourt before he stuck his Atchisson AA-12 around the corner and sent half a magazine of HEFA rounds downrange. And it turned out he'd waited just a second too long. The rain of baby fragmentation grenades stripped the wallpaper very efficiently—the bank's shopfitters could thank him later—but they failed to flay the flesh from the bones of his enemy because Robin Hood evidently moonlighted as the Scarlet Pimpernel.

By the time he'd searched the offices and made it to the back alleyway the alleyway was empty. He swore bitterly and tossed the assault shotgun in the paper recycling bin. Then he marched out onto the high street, pondering his options.

"Fucking *amateurs*," he huffed in disgust as he banged out an update to the boss via secure email. Then he stalked off in high dudgeon to a five-star hotel in Knightsbridge, where he'd drink a dry martini or two, pick up a MILF in search of some rough, and await an update on the identity of Eve's little helpers.

The following morning he rose before dawn, showered and dressed alone—the shag had staggered away at some point in the early hours, her scorecard updated—and checked in with HQ. Apparently Ms. Starkey had subcontracted the job of acquiring the manuscript to her brother, and it was he who had been in the back at the bank the day before. The Bond was intrigued to learn that Starkeys didn't reproduce by laying their eggs in paralyzed estate agents. It made the *leave no loose ends* directive somewhat iffy, to say the least. On the other hand he now had a name for his Robin Hood: a HiveCo Security thief-taker codenamed ABLE ARCHER. Well, well, *well*. ABLE ARCHER was clearly extremely motivated to locate Ms. Starkey's brother and his playmates. And so was the Bond. Starkey Jr. was very much off the grid, not showing up on the electoral register, the telephone directory, or any regular utility bills: his public footprint was so smudged that he might as well be sleeping under Waterloo Bridge. But he was in possession of the note, and absent authorization to go interrogate the ice queen the Bond was going to have to locate Jeremy Starkey himself.

A plan came together in his head. Obtaining ABLE ARCHER's phone number was easily accomplished through channels at HiveCo—all it took was an enquiry from the Bigge Organization about her availability for hire. Once he had her mobile number it was trivially easy to submit a location services disclosure order through one of the Bigge Organization's security subsidiaries, and with the LSDO in hand to start stalking her phone. Presently the Bond was back in the DB9, crawling towards Kensington Park. Where he was pretty sure ABLE ARCHER would attempt to pick up the trail come morning.

Meanwhile, Eve's escrow fixer had been busy overnight.

"Ms. Starkey? This is Andrei. I have news for you—yes, yes, your offer to preempt is accepted by the vendor. I keeped the offer to fifty million dollars US, this is acceptable, yes? The vendor requires completion within eighteen hours. The deposit wire transfer to VX Bank (BVI) Limited in Tortola for five million, I email you the account SWIFT and IBAN details now—"

"Excellent!" Eve smiled and nodded, even though there was no way Andrei could see her. She paused her review of options for improving her zygomatic arch and checked her Outlook inbox. Sure enough, the email appeared as she watched. "I'll review this and issue payment immediately. How is fulfillment to proceed?"

"The vendor will email me the collection instructions once the bank confirms the deposit is in their suspense account. I have local subcontractors on-site in the British Virgin Islands: you don't need to be aware of the details. Title deeds to appropriate properties to the value of forty-five million, held by the usual vehicles. We transfer ownership as usual: wire me my fee and I take care of repossession of assets once you confirm goods are correct." He chuckled drily. After a second or two, Eve joined him. "Do you ever get the feeling that you're living in a sixties crime caper movie?" he asked.

"I'm sorry, I can't say that I do," she said indulgently. Her cheek twitched. "But don't let me keep you! I have funds to transfer."

It took a little more than twenty minutes for Eve to dole out the payments—even with her stratospheric degree of access, Finance required confirmation that Rupert had authorized her to transfer millions of pounds to an anonymous numbered bank account in a tax haven, and to spend another few dozen million buying title to certain opaque investment vehicles that owned luxury properties and transferring them to a law firm in another tax haven—but by nine o'clock (eleven hundred hours in Dubăsari) the money had hit the vendor's offshore account, and Andrei phoned her back to confirm that the payment was confirmed.

"They have the deeds, many gracious thank-yous, Ms. Starkey, and I am forwarding you the encrypted email they sent me under your public key. When you have opened it you need to reply to the address in it to confirm receipt, is that acceptable?"

"I'll do that," Eve said. Outlook binged for attention, and she glanced at her screen again. "Aha, this looks like it." The message was quite large, and decrypting the attachments took almost a minute, but at last she could see them: a Word document and a PDF file, evidently a scan of some sort. "Excellent, I have decrypted them. I'll be back in touch shortly to confirm stage two."

Eve opened the covering letter first. The manuscript, it seemed, was bound inside the cover of another book, and misfiled on the wrong shelf in a private library somewhere in London. The directions to retrieve it could be found in the attached PDF, a scan of a hand-drawn treasure map of some antiquity. The handwriting was the beautiful copperplate cursive that clerks had used before typewriters, its authorship anonymous. She frowned as she looked at the scan. Weird: it wasn't a normal map, one with an absolute frame of reference and a compass rose. Rather, it was a series of waypoints on a treasure hunt. The starting point was an oddly familiar address on Kensington Palace Gardens. And then—

She swore softly to herself. *It's a set-up. Got to be.* There was absolutely no possible way that it could be a coincidence.

"Meet me at the same cafe as last time," she told her brother, then copied the map onto a memory stick and deleted the unencrypted copy from her PC. "Make sure nobody follows you. And leave your phone at home."

Half an hour later Imp sat down across the table from her in the branch of Costa. "Morning," he grumped. "This had better be good."

"Had a bad night? What did your crew say?"

"They said thanks for the forty large, now fuck off." He rubbed his forehead. "I really don't think it's going to work."

"Well, maybe I can change your mind." Eve waited patiently while he stirred three sachets of sugar into his coffee. "While you were lying in, I sorted out the map. You don't have to worry about anybody else coming after it—the auction is closed. And it turns out the manuscript is right on our doorstep. How well do you know—" And she told him the address.

"How well do I—" Imp froze—"the old family home?" he said, with studied disinterest. "Never been there, why?"

"It's interesting that you should say that." She smirked, and took a sip of her drink. "It turns out that's where the directions to retrieve the manuscript start. It's a schematic, a kind of diagram rather than a traditional map, and it says you need to start on the top floor—the third floor—of the ancestral pile, where there's a secret door. Do you know anything about that?"

"A secret door on the third floor?" His indignation was clearly feigned: "What rot!"

Eve just smiled tightly until he caught on, at which point he flushed silently and glanced aside.

"Ball, court, your side of the net." She slid the USB stick across the table towards him. After a moment he palmed it. "I don't know when you broke in there or why, I probably don't *want* to know, but that's where the treasure hunt starts."

"This stinks," he warned her.

She nodded. "It reminds me of Father. 'In magic, there are no coincidences.'" Her smile slipped. "Tell your crew, I can guarantee no pursuit—the other bids have been terminated, the trail dead-ends here. No thugs with guns will come after you, but I *do* need that manuscript, and there's another sixty thousand in it for you." Eve paused. "No, fuck that shit. He's not watching and you're fam, right? Get me the manuscript and I'll round it up to a quarter million, total. I'm pretty sure I can fly it under the radar. If necessary I'll hit my own savings. But do yourself a favor and do not *under any circumstances* look past the title page, 'kay? Or even handle the book yourself. Treat it like radioactive waste and let someone else pick up the lethal dose. Because it's the kind of book that Dad taught us *about*, rather than the kind he taught us *from*: it's the kind that eats people."

When Imp got home he found Doc and Game Boy in the back engaged in a *Warcraft* nostalgia tour, but no sign of the Deliverator. A miasma of burned toast filled the kitchen. Charcoal briquettes that had once been crumpets sat forgotten atop the overflowing compost bin.

"I've been to see my sister again," he announced to the backs of their heads, "and she upped her offer. She also said the guys with guns are out of the picture. But I still think we should turn her down." Then he chucked the USB stick at the back of Game Boy's head.

Game Boy reached out and snagged it without looking, then brought his hand back down to the keyboard in time to do something unspeakable to a green-haired minotaur with unfeasibly large jubblies who was wielding a glowing purple labrys the size of the Empire State Building. Moments later he slid the stick into a spare port on his gaming rig. "Get the healer," he chanted in the voice of Elmer Fudd.

Imp winced: "Dude, that's not how you sing Wagner," he began, then something explosively pyrotechnic lit up the battlefield that spanned the row of monitors.

Doc waved his fists in the air, and disconnected. "You distracted me!" he accused.

"Then you're too easily distracted."

Imp watched Game Boy play on for a few minutes.

"What's she offering now?" Doc asked cautiously.

"A quarter million if we complete the job." Imp shoved his hands in his pockets. "But I don't like it."

Game Boy broke off his song to ask, "What of?" just as Doc said, "You're right, that's too fucking much. There's something wrong with it."

Imp took a deep breath and nodded. "Evie got hold of the map. Guess where it starts?" His index finger circled in the air, pointed inexorably towards the ceiling.

"Well *fuuuuu . . .*"

Doc's frustration finally got Game Boy's undivided attention. He logged out, then spun his chair around. "How much money did you say again?"

"A quarter of a million, minus the forty thou we already got paid." A tinkling of tiny bells rattled through the room, tinny as the one-bit sound chip in a novelty greeting card. Imp shrugged. "But the map starts on the top floor, at the door to nowhere. And it's *old*. Like, old enough it probably dates to when my family lived here. Do I have to tell you how scary that is? I don't believe in coincidences, GeeBee. And Eve, she said don't, whatever you do, try to *read* the book."

"Why ever not?" asked Doc.

"Because it's a fucking *spell book*," Imp finally snapped. "I know one when I smell one, I learned that much from my dad." He paused. "It's why I don't have a family."

"What about your sister—"

But Imp was already shaking his head. "Evie is—" He hesitated to say *dead inside*, but the more he thought about it the more it felt right. He wasn't sure the sister he remembered growing up with was even in there any more, screaming wordlessly behind the glossy lacquered mask she wore all the time now. Eve had been all right when she was young, but after things went bad she'd turned hard. Not just hard: she'd turned to stone, made of herself a ferocious engine of destruction warped in widdershins coils opposed to Imp's clockwise rebellion. Their paths might cross twice in a turn but their directions couldn't be more different. "She went wrong," he said, then stopped, leaving the final words unspoken: *after Mum*.

"Not seeing it," said Doc, even as Game Boy burst out with "A spell book! Cool!"

Oh Jesus, Imp thought, rolling his eyes, *spare me*. "It's *not* cool," he snapped. "If you think it's cool you have no fucking idea what you're talking about. If you mess with it you will die in agony, slowly. It's the sort of thing that puts *ideas* into your head, ideas like corpse-worms and glowing phosphorescent hagfish, chewing their way through your dreams as they core out your soul."

"Is that why you were looking at all those old tomes in the library?" Game Boy asked cheekily.

"Oh for—" Imp sat down heavily. "It wasn't in the library," he said. "I'd have *felt* it. Spell books, there's a kind of *weight* to them, like you're reading your own execution notice, or a dead god's last will and testament." Books bound in human skin and written in a formal propositional calculus where each axiom was a closure wrapped around eternal damnation. "Big sis's boss is paying for a retrieval, and he's paying large, which means it's rare and dangerous."

Which meant it wasn't a fake-out, like the 99 percent of soi-disant spell books which eventually turned out to be a joke, a diary of a psychotic breakdown, or a farrago of myths and legends. Maybe one time in a hundred a spell book turned out to be that rarest of rare things—a necromantic laboratory workbook, a dream quest protocol, a distillation of true knowledge so compact that it burned like a beacon in the black void, attracting the attention of things that fed behind the walls of the world.

He continued to think aloud: "Eve won't get it herself, but is willing to more than triple her offer to us. She's worried. She knows—she believes in us—that we can do it, but it's dangerous." He met Doc's transfixed gaze. "So I'm selfish!" He burst out: "I don't want you to die and leave me alone."

"But a quarter of a million! You could make the movie! I could be a star!"

"You could die inside and something else would be walking around wearing your body like a cheap suit," Imp cautioned. "Would it be worth it then?"

"But it's somewhere upstairs," Doc pointed out. "Which means nobody else is going to get to it without us knowing. And your sister says the guys with the guns aren't going to bother us. How about we discuss it when Del gets here?"

"Huh. About that. Where is she?" asked Imp.

Doc looked at Game Boy: Game Boy looked at Doc. And suddenly it was apparent that neither of them knew where she'd gone.

Del walked across the park, her hoodie raised to cover her hair, heading for the side-street where she'd dumped her hot wheels the day before.

Successful career criminals have several rules of thumb to live by. *Don't shit in your own backyard* is one; *three people can keep a secret if two of them are dead* is another; and for a third, *never return to the scene of a successful caper.* However, Del was not a successful career criminal. Rebecca was the Deliverator—ironic nod to a fictional hero, the protagonist of a cyberpunk epic about ninjutsu, linguistics, and extreme pizza delivery—and she broke the rules in all innocence.

Del mostly didn't drive: she didn't have a license for one thing, and she couldn't be arsed jumping through the flaming hoops of the test process for another. She was happy with her bike, thank you very much. She could get just about anywhere in London on her bike faster than anything with a motor, flowing through crevices and pedestrianized zones like water. She could take it on the tube for the occasional excursion out as far as Zone Six, but her bike had its limits: and one *hard* limit was that you couldn't take your crew with you.

Hence Imp's insistence on teaching her to drive. Which, she had to admit, had been a ton of fun, from the process of stealthily casing her ride, sneaking in and springing the door lock, faking out the anti-theft immobilizer, and hot-wiring the ignition; to the raw physical power rush of putting metal and mass and explosive fuel in motion and taking to the highway. Driving held her attention. And driving spoke to her. Not in the same language as cycling, of course, but driving was like learning a second tongue, one that expanded and illuminated her view of the world. Being trapped inside a padded box and forced to interface with the road through a complicated series of linkages and gears and motors was claustrophobic after the fumes-in-her-face freedom of riding her bike, but some of her mojo came across nonetheless. She could ace the North Circular in a jacked Toyota Tercel faster than Sabine Schmitz could lap the Nürburgring in a Transit van, and the only times the plod had got on her tail she'd left them, well, plodding.

But modern cars were increasingly hard to steal. It wasn't just the chips and the remote unlocking and the LoJack trackers and the secret policeman in the engine management software. These days you had to worry about the pentacle scribed in goat blood under the driver's seat, the black tallow candle and the curse-stained ivory gear knob, the nightmares that would follow you home, dreams of your car-smashed carcass in a continuous stream of creative and agonizing exsanguinations whenever you closed your eyes. They'd keep it up until your throat was raw from screaming and throwing up. They'd keep it up until you turned yourself in to the insurance underwriters for exorcism and punishment, or aspirated and drowned on your own vomit without ever waking up.

So the 2010 Cayenne had been something of a sweet find for Del. It was old enough to predate in-car electronics sophisticated enough to support curseware, new enough to be seriously hot, and best of all, once equipped with the right cloned plates it was the identical twin to a wholly respectable Mom's Taxi in Chelmsford, owned by an investment banker's wife from the Home Counties who stayed the hell out of the congestion charge zone and used her five hundred horsepower turbocharged teutonic battle wagon to bus Emily and Callum to school and back every day, with a shopping sidequest to Waitrose twice a week.

Even though the Porsche was now dirty—Imp had warned her the bank had cameras out back, so they'd made the cloned plates—Del couldn't quite bring herself to abandon it for good without at least a token attempt to keep it. *I could get new plates*, she bluffed herself, *if it hasn't been towed*. Because that would be easier than finding a replacement, for sure.

Hence the early morning walk.

Gotcha.

Del swung round the corner and spotted the row of parked cars. The Cayenne was still shoehorned between a BMW and a Fiat, but some arsewipe private security company had stuck a boot on one wheel. Glowing green runes warned of appalling consequences for unauthorized removal. Also, a squirrel had shat on the windscreen. Del fumed silently as she turned away, barely caring if anybody saw her, barely noticing until warm fingers closed around her right wrist, shockingly intimate, followed by a sudden *snik* of cold metal.

"Not *exactly* an ice-cream van, is it?" chirped a voice as her arm was yanked up behind her shoulder. "Let's you and me go somewhere and talk, KLF girl."

"What—" Del grimaced—"the *fuck* are you on, woman?"

"Justified and Ancient! I'm not stupid, I know how to work Lyric Finder, even though the band split before either of us were born."

A metallic chinking and the drag of leg irons told Del that she was well and truly in the shit. The bottom dropped out of her stomach as if a trapdoor had sprung open beneath her feet. Fear threatened to choke her. She tried to swing her left hand but there was a manacle on that wrist too, and it twisted behind her back abruptly and then there were chains *everywhere*, locking her down and leashing her to the Cayenne's door handle.

The woman walked round in front of her. She had pale skin and spiky chestnut hair and eyes like a police recruiting poster, and if Del had met her in Ruby Tuesday over a couple of beers she might have thought she was cute, but there was nothing cute about this sickening sense of dread, about the chains, about the telescoping baton that kept flickering in and out of visibility in the woman's hand like a bad special effect. "I dunno what this is about, woman, you've got the wrong person, lemme *go*—"

"Chill." The woman reached out and tugged Del's hood back, then as she recoiled tapped her gently on the forehead with one index finger. "We know who you are: Rebecca McKee, age 21, no fixed abode but we know where your mum lives, we know where your dog goes to school, no fixed abode but you're a demon on two wheels and you're also the getaway driver for the gang that turfed Hamleys the other week."

Del flip-flopped like a gaffed fish for a few seconds, then yanked at the leash as hard as she could. With a scream of abused metal the Porsche's passenger door handle bent and she began to sidestep away, but the chain between her ankles somehow turned into a rigid bar. She began to face-plant and ended up with her nose tucked into the cleft between the cop's neck and shoulder. The woman smelled of lavender; Del wrinkled her nose and opened her mouth to bite, then felt strong arms circling her. "Will you just *stop freaking out* for a moment and listen to me?"

Del drew a shuddering breath: "Chains—"

The chains were gone, but the woman held her in a bear hug that trapped Del's arms. "Take a deep breath. And another. That better?" She peered into Del's blown pupils. "Still freaking. What are you afraid of? Are you on—"

"*Don't kill me—*"

"I'm not going to! Will you chill the hell out? I just want to talk, for Christ's sake!"

The adrenaline spike began to subside, the waves of chagrin, embarrassment, and grief finally washing Del up on the shore of acceptance. "What the fuck you want, then?"

"I'm Wendy, and there's an ice-cream parlor on the other side of the park: Is yours a 99?" A flashing smile lit up Del's face and she felt the knot of tension in her chest twist into hopeful incredulity.

"I'll—" she took a deep breath—"what?"

"If I let go of you, will you come with me and let me buy

you an ice cream and explain things? I'll let you go afterwards, I promise."

Del managed a shaky nod. Wendy still didn't let go, but the arms wrapped around Del no longer felt like handcuffs. "You're not going to arrest me?"

Wendy rolled her eyes. "I'm not a cop, and I'm not on the clock, so no, I'm not—I can't—do that."

"But Imp said you were—" She realized her mistake and shut her mouth before she could leak any more secrets.

"Imp is your theatrical friend with the shit fashion sense?" Wendy smirked at her expression. "Yes, I might have told him I was a cop. I might also have been kind of lying: whatever it takes to get the job done. I'm a private sector thief-taker, it's not my job to enforce the law. And like I said, I'm not working today." She opened her arms and took a step back, baffling Del. Suddenly she could feel the cold again, up and down her front. "Are you coming for that ice cream?"

Del shook herself. "Woman, it's fucking *December*." She stared at her, openly perplexed. "What?"

Wendy rubbed two fingers together. "My treat."

"I don't believe this," Del muttered, but Wendy held out a hand. She stared at it for a few seconds before she took it. Wendy drew her closer, placed Del's hand on her arm, then led them back into the park, towards the kiosk.

The Bond sat on a park bench, staring at his phone in faux-idleness. *Fucking dykes*, he thought, clutching resentment close to the shrivelled cockles of his heart. The burring hum of a quadrotor drone drifted overhead like a nightmare hornet. He squinted at the phone screen, lips curled judgmentally. The feed from the drone's stabilized imaging platform showed him the sway of the getaway driver's bundled dreads, the thief-taker's slyly stolen glances, the slight quirk of her lips. She held her target's arm too close. *Bet they'll be in bed within twenty-four hours. Assuming they last that long.* His imagination leered lasciviously.

Oblivious to the drone, Wendy steered Del towards the coffee and refreshments kiosk. Once they were indoors, the Bond recalled his remote-controlled minion. He opened the aluminum briefcase and packed the drone away to recharge. Then he picked it up and followed his targets over to the kiosk, to rent a seat for the price of a coffee.

The Bond had come to appreciate the benefits of wearing a well-cut business suit and conservative tie. It made you anonymous, at least if you were a clean-shaven white male like him. It was the civilian equivalent of the camouflage BDUs he'd worn to work before he took Rupert's shilling. Go low, people thought you were the Money; go high, they thought you worked for the Money. And the Money came with a license.

The Bond wasn't quite boring enough to be a Gray Man—a totally average guy, the perfect street-level tail—he was too tall and muscular. But with his suit and briefcase nobody would spare him a second glance. Nobody dreamed it contained a drone with an optional grenade launcher and thermobaric rounds, nobody imagined the suppressed Glock 17 Gen4 and its spare magazines, the duct tape and the gag and the row of foam-wrapped syringes loaded with flunitrazepam and suxamethonium. All the paraphernalia of what those in the trade euphemistically termed "wet work."

There was no equivalent anonymity for women or anyone else who didn't code as white and male. Both the thief-taker and the thief were distinctive and easy to track: the butch ex-cop in her combat pants and paratroop boots, the dark-skinned bike courier with her dreads and skintight leggings.

Put them in a boardroom or a ballroom and they'd stand out. Put them in cocktail dresses or skirt suits and drop them in a drafty warehouse or a bus terminus and they'd *still* stand out.

After giving them time to get settled, the Bond entered the kiosk and settled into a corner seat, where he pretended to look at his phone as he sipped his coffee. Smartphones had been another major innovation in tradecraft: everybody carried one, you could use them to track owners who were clueless about SIGINT, *and* you could hide your gaze behind a screen more easily than a newspaper. So he waited, and while he waited he eavesdropped.

"It's my day off and I was stood down from the job," the thief-taker was explaining, "so not only do I not have to arrest you, legally I *can't.* Unlike a police officer I don't have any particular powers of arrest, except when I'm on the clock and executing a warrant. Even then, I'm supposed to wait for the force to show up and do their job. I mean, the common law power of citizen's arrest—section 24A of the Police and Criminal Evidence Act (1984)—only works if I catch y—er, someone—in the act of committing a crime, and it has to be something serious, like assault or theft. At any other time I'd be committing a crime myself—unlawful detention."

The car thief narrowed her eyes suspiciously: "But you cuffed me!"

"Yep." The thief-taker briefly looked abashed. "You were having a panic attack. I thought you might hurt yourself. Also—" she side-eyed the car thief—"don't you think it was a little bit hot?"

"Fucking give me a safeword next time!" Del glared at her. "And ask, don't grab!"

"Consent is kind of difficult to get when you're freaking out." Wendy paused. "But next time, just so you know—if there *is* a next time—if you *want* me to chain you up, all you have to do is—"

Mount Deliverator blasted out a pyroclastic flow: *"No!"* She subsided, glowering. "We are *not* having this conversation in public!"

"You're so easy!" Wendy taunted: "You're so far in the closet you can see snowflakes falling in the street light!"

"You're going to get us chucked out! And I haven't had my ice cream yet!"

And so on and on and back and forth, verbal fencing moderating into heavy flirting for almost half an hour as the coffee cooled and the ice cream melted and the thief-taker worked—very effectively, the Bond thought—at building a rapport with her mark. Her snitch. Her informant.

Grooming, they called this, when conducted for unlawful ends. Not that the Bond cared one way or the other about legality—the only lawful authority that rocked his world was the privilege of money—but it was interesting to watch Wendy work her target over with words rather than weapons. It was apparent that they had a rapport, and not just the polarity of predator and prey, the cop and the robber, or even the black lead and the red lead clamped to the terminals of the car battery in the basement. The Bond had heard about the easy intimacy that the very best interrogators used to make their subjects spill their guts out of a misplaced desire to be *helpful*, but he'd scarcely credited its existence before now. His interrogations were messy affairs involving pliers and screaming. They usually ended up in a shallow grave in the forest: not in an ice cream parlor, feeding the other participant spoonfuls of frozen yoghurt while gazing wistfully into their eyes.

After a while Rebecca was sprawled at ease in her chair, not even trying to flee when Wendy went to order more refreshments. Instead, her gaze lingered on the other woman's ass. Then when Wendy returned, Rebecca's hand shyly crept across the table to touch her arm. (*Disgusting*, thought the Bond, salivating slightly as he leaned forward.)

"Admit it, you wanted me," Del said. "I mean, something *from*—"

"I know what you mean." Wendy smiled. "And yes. But what I want, and what my boss wants, and what his customer wants, are all different things, and my boss and the customer get zip while I'm off the clock. So this is *me* time, or maybe *us* time."

"Is there an *us*? You're moving kind of fast."

"Would you rather I moved slow?"

". . . Not really. So what *do* you want?"

"I thought maybe we could hang out together? Go for a drive in the country or something."

Del snorted. "Fat chance." Of a sudden, her expression clamped down, guarded and remote.

Wendy slowly reached inside her hoodie's pouch. "I can get your ride un-clamped. What do you think?"

"You know that's not—" Del licked her lips.

"Not your car, right? Doesn't matter, I'll do it anyway. Then we'll go for a drive together." She produced her phone with a flourish, then raised one eyebrow. "If you like?"

"You can't just . . ."

"Watch me." Wendy dialed a number. (The Bond waited patiently as the illegal picocell in his briefcase snatched her call from the aether, decrypted and recorded it, then forwarded it to its destination.) "Hey, boss? Yeah, it's Wendy. Listen, can you do me a favor? There's a car parked—yeah, that one, yeah, listen, some chancer's stuck a wheel clamp on it, yeah, can you get it removed? Really? Okay, that'd be great." Wendy paused. "Hang on, they what?" Her voice rose. "Can they even *do* that? Well, fuck!" She ended the call, then noticed Rebecca staring at her. "What?"

"What's happening?"

"I do *not* believe this." Wendy shook her head. "Shit was a lot simpler when I was a cop." She noticed Rebecca's sudden tension: "Oh, it's not about you, you can relax. Boss man says the boot's coming off your car within the hour." She shrugged. "The bad news for me is, I've been pulled off your case *completely*. So my employer doesn't get paid. Boo hoo, some other job will come up. The good news *for you* is someone coughed up more money than Hamleys insurance underwriters to buy out the investigation, and because we're HiveCo Security—not law enforcement—money talks. You have friends in high places, it seems. *Do* you have friends in high places?"

Rebecca boggled. "I don't get it."

"Well that's okay because that makes two of us. But it *does* make life a little easier, doesn't it? Now I'm not being paid to haul you in, but my boss *is* going to want to talk to you: he's actively trying to hire transhumans for this program I'm part of, and as there's always been a revolving door between thief-taking and smarter crim—" Her phone vibrated—"job done, boot's off. Listen, that's a sweet ride. How about we head for the M40, then once we hit the M25 you show me how fast you can lap London?"[1]

1 At 117 miles or 188 kilometers, the M25, London's orbital motorway, is accurately described as the world's biggest car park—if car parks had ten lanes, variable speed limits, and speed enforcement cameras. The fastest unofficial lap time is believed to be just over forty minutes.

CANNONBALL RUN
ON THE M25

In the end, the hammer blow that finally cracked the crystal shell around Eve's conscience was a phone call that interrupted her while preparing a request for tender.

The Komatsu buried in the sub-subbasement had been annoying Eve for some months now, if only by implication. They'd run out of room for further downwards excavation, which meant some creative outside-the-box thinking was required to deal with the mansion's persistent sanitation problem. The ground beneath central London was principally composed of sedimentary rocks: clay, chalk, and mudstone. If you dug too deep, then you were going to undermine your own foundations unless you were willing to be obvious about it (and sinking reinforced concrete pillars twenty meters underground was nothing if not obvious). Extend too far to either side and the neighboring billionaires would take offense and tie you up in court for years.

The Komatsu mini-digger was where it was because it was impossible to go any deeper, and the tunnel of shallow trenches behind it was slowly filling up, patches of shiny, fresh-poured cement betraying the final resting places of Rupe's victims.

An in-house crematorium being impractical, Eve had been

searching for a better solution to the problem of corpse disposal. But just as she thought she'd found a solution—just as she was drafting a serious requirements document and bill of materials for her very own *Eiserne Jungfrau*—the fucking phone rang.

"Yes?" she barked, quite forgetting herself for a moment—but only a moment, because then her eyes tracked to the caller ID and she gulped before continuing in a very different tone of voice: "Sorry sir, I wasn't expecting you, how may I be of service?"

"Am I interrupting something good?" Rupert sounded amused rather than outraged. *Phew.* Eve dabbed at her forehead.

"I'm *really* sorry, sir, I was working on a final solution to the packing density problem in the sub-subbasement—" she glanced sideways at the dog-eared paperback lying facedown on her desk, copiously annotated: *Stiff: The Curious Lives of Human Cadavers*, by Mary Roach—"and I may have become slightly distracted."

"Well jolly good, carry on then, nice to hear you're keeping busy!" Rupert whiffled on in this mode for a minute, during which Eve gradually felt more and more uneasy. Rupe didn't believe in soft-soaping his minions, especially her. Something was *very* wrong here. *Is it (a) something I've done, or (b) something I haven't done, or (c) something he wants me to do?* she wondered. "How soon can you have it up and running?" he demanded.

What—she stared at her notepad. She had sketched her idea with pencil and paper. Her computer was, of course, keylogged six ways from Sunday, but—*Oh, he must have upgraded the cameras again.* "I'm not sure, sir." It was going to require some complicated custom fabrications, unusual metalwork that wouldn't be embrittled by exposure to liquid nitrogen coolant. Actual rocket science. "There's apparently a cemetery in Canada that has a pilot plant that operates like this, but it's a bit new and experimental."

The fourteenth-century Iron Maiden of Nuremberg was a myth concocted in the Victorian era to titillate the proto-moderns and reinforce their sense of superiority over their benighted ancestors. According to the story, victims were forced inside the sarcophagus-shaped device and it was clamped shut around them, then spikes were screwed into their flesh. When the screams stopped and the blood slowed to a trickle, the spikes were withdrawn and what was left was dropped into a deep ravine through a hole in the bottom. It was bullshit, but it was prime grand guignol bullshit, the sort of thing guaranteed to keep the boss off her back for a while—especially once her twenty-first-century improvements were up and running.

"Set up a shell company and run the accounts through it," Rupert instructed her. "Index it under hobby projects. Before they start bending metal I'd like to see the schematics." This was typical Rupe behavior. Rupe loved snuff. One of his hobby subsidiaries existed solely to provide employment for a sick fuck of a former slaughterhouse technician in Somerset who turned standard-size shipping containers into mobile gallows. He was selling them by mail-order to the more sanity-challenged corners of the globe. (The less said about the concealed webcams Rupe had insisted on adding, the better; but the small print buried in the sales contract granted him exclusive copyright over their feeds. Rupe's true claim to genius lay in his expertise with buried small print.) "How does it work, exactly?" he asked eagerly.

For the next ten minutes Eve did her best to explain. Human bodies are notoriously hard to dispose of, but one promising approach is to compost them. First, the corpse needed to be chilled with liquid nitrogen. (For that purpose, her iron maiden would be lined with cold fingers fed from an LNG tank.) Once frozen, the body would be dropped into a modified industrial shredder—one with special blades, tempered to survive ultra-low temperatures—to reduce it to mulch. It would be piped into a fermentation vessel, where bacterial cultures would be injected, causing decomposition, breaking down the subject's DNA and generating heat for the mansion. Finally, the residual slurry would be flushed away through the sewer system. The Canadian cemetery also composted bodies, but the intent was to provide a dignified, environmentally approved final exit. Eve's approach was efficient, logical, but—

Her vision blurred and doubled as she stared at the sketch on her drawing pad. *Why the hell am I doing this?* she wondered, skewered on the cusp of acute cognitive dissonance.

She'd started this morning with a fantasy of slamming the iron maiden's lid on Rupert's grinning face (for once, set in a rictus of terror rather than gloating). She would listen to the scream of boiling liquid nitrogen escaping from around his rapidly cooling corpse, then push the button to drop him into the flashing blades of the shredder that would flush him into the septic tank for composting. Then she'd turn on her heel and ascend to take her place at the head of the boardroom table. The blame sat squarely on Rupert's shoulders: if he hadn't shackled her to him she could have simply left—

But now her fantasy was sharpening and coming into close-up focus, bright and clear beneath the voyeuristic cameras Rupe had scattered through her life, and it wasn't Rupe's face in the iron maiden: it was her brother's.

She realized with a sick sense of despair that she might

never be free of Rupert. Over the years he'd molded her into the perfect assistant, polished to a state of gleaming perfection to carry out his will. She could destroy his body, but he'd installed a little sliver of his soul inside her.

"I'm sorry?" she asked, acutely aware that she'd zoned out and missed a possibly critical question or two.

"—Said, if it looks good, I'll want you to file for patent rights and look into setting it up for limited batch-scale manufacturing? I'm sure the Home Office will be interested in buying it. Maybe you could give it glass walls so they can auction tickets to the executions?"

"Of course," she said automatically, and crabbed a tiny footnote on her pad. "I'll see to it, sir."

"Great!" Rupert sounded ever so jolly when she stroked his turgid ego. "Now, about that manuscript. How's the acquisition coming along? I see you retained Andrei's people to handle reclamation of the escrow funds and that's good, but there's a quarter of a million earmarked for non-recoverable expenses? And an ex-gratia payment to HiveCo Security?"

"Yes, yes, exactly so, My Lord." She swallowed. Had she really promised her kid brother a quarter of a big one? She must have been mad: it was well above her normal discretionary spending, which meant it would be flagged for Rupert's attention. She hoped like hell that she'd drawn up the title deeds properly and the mortgage was in order. If she'd screwed up, she and Imp were both dead. "The agents I retained ran into competition—the kind with very large guns, I'm afraid. It spooked them, so I upped their retainer rather than trying to recruit another team. Trying to keep the operation as small as possible, you see. We also had a problem with a HiveCo thief-taker but they were trivially easy to buy off, and meanwhile my team's back on the job. More importantly, I'm confident the opposition don't have any more leads. So there's that."

"Excellent! I look forward to reading it when I get home. Which, by the way, should be the day after tomorrow now—I had some unavoidable meetings in Panama, but I'm clearing them tomorrow and then I'm about eight hours away as the Gulfstream flies. Anyway, you don't need to worry about the oppo bidders getting back in the game, I've put my man on their case and—" He carried on for a few seconds before she could get a word in edgewise.

"—Wait," she said, scrabbling for traction, "you sent the Bond after them?"

"Yes! So I'm afraid you're stuck driving the Bentley or the Lambo for the next week—the DB9's fully booked. But you should have smooth sailing just as soon as he's tracked down all the loose ends and tidied them away."

"I'm sure you're right," she said, her voice just slightly strangled. The Bond—any of Rupert's Mr. Bonds—was always a son-of-a-bitch. The job demanded it, and Rupert worked them hard. As with Fleming's fictional 00-agents, their life expectancy was less than twenty-four months. However, the current incumbent was even worse than his predecessors: a stone-cold psychopath, death on two legs. "That's good to know." *Just keep him the hell away from me.* Eve had met the current Bond only twice and was not a fan. If she was ever trapped in a stuck lift with him only one of them was going to make it out alive, and she was determined it would be her. "Is the Bond going to get in my way?"

"Not unless something goes wrong!" Rupe said brightly. "But that's not happening. So." Expectant pause, then: "Tell me, what color is your thong?"

"I'm wearing the black lace Bordelle one you bought

me—" Her gaze sharpened. "Hey, don't you have a camera under my desk?"

"Good idea! Not yet, I'll get one put in once I'm home. When did you last wax?"

Eve put her pen down, set her shoulders back, plumped her lips out, and faked a lascivious grin. *Good thing I wore a trouser suit.* "Last night, before my bath, thinking about you, sir," she lied, simulating arousal in her bleak office cell under the gaze of Rupert's cameras. It was unusually easy to fake it while she talked dirty to him today. At some point in the past ten minutes a dam had burst. She'd known for years that she'd eventually have a final reckoning with Rupert, but now she knew it couldn't wait any longer. Imp was in the frame: if she didn't want to lose her brother for good—the last remaining connection to her old life, before she started down this darkling path—she'd have to deal with the Bond, and if she dealt with the Bond she'd have to deal with his master, which meant—

She grew increasingly turned on as she delivered the submissive spiel Rupert expected: tension winding tighter and higher, the blueprint on her blotter breathless with the promise of final release, imagining him choking and gagging and finally convulsing. After Rupert ended the call she sat motionless for a minute, pulse pounding, thinking about masturbating. That was one act for which telekinesis was a game-changer; but she couldn't bring herself to do it here, not under the gaze of Rupert's cameras. Especially not if it meant admitting to herself how much she'd grown to resemble her master's dark fixations.

Either way, this has to end soon, she thought, *and by soon, I mean before the boss gets home.*

"Whoo! That was fucking awesome!"

Del turned off the ignition. Wendy leaned across the transmission tunnel and tried to kiss her on the cheek, just as Del was turning to face her: their lips collided. Speech became difficult for a time; when they separated, Del was breathing fast. "You're telling me. Gonna need new plates."

"So sue me." Wendy checked her phone again. The lap timer on her clock app was frozen at 46 minutes and 27 seconds. "That makes an average of—holy fuck. And you did that in daylight hours, not at four in the morning!"

"Yup." Del looked smug. The engine pinged as it cooled. "Going to need a garage though, the tires are unhappy." (Somewhere in the trackless suburban wastes of London, a blameless banker's wife who had the misfortune to drive a similar bus was going to get a nasty surprise in the mail. She'd later claim an alibi, courtesy of the traffic cameras around her daughter's school gate.)

"Holy . . ." Wendy unlatched the passenger door and climbed out, shaky from the adrenaline crash. She took a deep breath. "I didn't scream." She took another breath. Nor had she thrown up when they passed the camera gantry with the display of skulls at Junction 24. Highways England could only stick you up there if they caught you, after all, and by then she was pretty confident that wasn't going to happen. "Next time I try to race with you, remind me to indent for a helicopter pursuit in advance."

"I'm faster than helicopters," Del said smugly as she stepped down from the SUV. The central locking chirped. She bent at the front and rear bumpers, pausing to peel a layer of laminate off the plates, which she then wadded up and shoved in a pocket. "So." She watched Wendy expectantly. "You going to bust me for dangerous driving, Officer? Or what was that *really* about?"

Wendy shook her head. "I just—" She shook her head again. "We were being watched, back in the cafe. Bloke in a suit tailed us when we left. But I'm pretty sure you lost him."

"Oh. Not one of your co-workers?"

"*Deffo* not one of mine." And that had Wendy well rattled. "Do you know what your mates were trying to st— liberate from the safe deposit box at the bank? The one that attracted all the unwelcome attention?"

"I dunno, some letter I think. I wasn't paying attention, you know? Too busy trying not to get stuck in traffic." She tapped the side of her forehead: "Better than satnav, but I don't have much room for anything else while I'm cogitating." Del was indeed better than satnav: it was her special genius to figure out perfect routes.[1] "Anyway, Imp took it to his sister. She's who hired us," Del added.

"Well." Wendy kicked the curb. "Looks like I need to talk to your friends. Can you hook me up?"

Del cocked her head to one side. "How about . . . nope?"

"Well." Wendy sniffed. "It's for their own good, you know? I think you're in danger."

"How about we go wherever it is you want to take me and then give me a reason why I should trust you?" Del jabbed back. Out of her armored cyborg shell she was thin-skinned and sensitive. "It better not be a cop shop, *Officer*."

"I keep telling you, I'm off the force." Wendy tugged her gently along the cracked pavement, stepping over dogshit and dandelions sprouting in the cracks, passing boarded-up win-

---

[1] And it was a special genius indeed, albeit one with alarming implications she was blessedly ignorant of. Google or IBM would have paid billions for ideal solutions to the Travelling Salesman problem or the Blind Knapsack problem, if they had known about it. The Pentagon would have paid, too, even if they had to strap Del into a chair and staple her eyelids open to use her.

dows until they came to an anonymous door in sun-bleached red paint. "This is where I live. It's not much, but I call it home."

Taking Rebecca home with her was her way of showing trust: a calculated risk, and not much of one at that. Wendy had already demonstrated she had the upper hand, proven that she could be useful to Del, held her hand . . . accidentally kissed her. Del wasn't stupid, maniacal driving notwithstanding—there had been that one stretch where Wendy had timed her for ten miles at an average of 160 mph. Wendy would swear that Del had known which vehicles were going to switch lanes before their drivers did, anticipating and positioning herself with eerie precision. Which was probably why her palms were moist and her pulse was so hard to ignore. Del would come inside and they could bond over a beer while she tried to dig a little deeper into her strange little crime family, and—

"Hey, are you okay?"

Suddenly Wendy found herself staring into Rebecca's concerned face at close range, and it was clearly not a face that she let out very often: *awkward*. "I, uh, I was just thinking," she began, then swallowed. "Come on in."

Her bedsit felt grubby and even tinier than usual with company. "Make yourself at home." She'd turned the bed back into a sofa before she went out, for which she was suddenly grateful. To have invited Rebecca back to slept-in sheets would have been beyond awkward. In truth, she hadn't imagined bringing anyone back here when she'd headed out that morning. It just seemed like a good idea to hitch a ride home, a decent idea to talk to the Deliverator somewhere where she knew they couldn't be overheard, and . . . she was running out of excuses. She popped the fridge door. "Beer?"

"I'm driving," Rebecca deadpanned, holding her hand out.

"Not right at this instant, I hope." Wendy passed her a can. It was the last of a six-pack of Heineken she'd been rationing all week. "Can't offer you any weed, I'm afraid: current employer insists on having a stupid piss-test clause in my contract because they do jobs for the Home Office. Maybe next year." The office was abuzz with rumors that the New Management was going to decriminalize cannabis and opium, the better to raise tax revenue.

Rebecca sighed as she pulled the ring. Her can hissed like an indignant cat. "I wasn't expecting beer *or* grass. Beer's good, though. You wanna make out?" She eyed Wendy with such frank curiosity that her mouth dried up.

"Not on a first date." She opened her own beer and gulped a mouthful of mostly-froth, acrid and sharp. Reconsidered: "Maybe?"

"Is this a date?" Rebecca asked ironically. "Because it started out *really* fucking badly. You need to work on your pick-up technique, girl."

"Yeah well I'm sorry, I—" Wendy was close to babbling— "you were freaking out on me and I thought you were going to run and I wasn't sure how else to find you—" this was a lie, but only a partial one—"and we needed to talk. You, me, your friends. Like I said. But I need you to trust me and I get that you're not going to take me to see them so where does that leave us—"

Rebecca tugged her down to the sofa beside her, and she sprawled, off-balance. "Sit. Drink. Shut the fuck up for five minutes while I think," said the Deliverator, not unkindly.

Wendy sat and drank and STFU'd in hope.

After a minute or so, Rebecca sighed and leaned back, stretching her arm along the back of the sofa behind Wendy's head. "Feeling better now," she admitted. "That drive took more out of me than I expected."

It seemed to call for a response, but Wendy kept it to a laconic "True." She drank another mouthful, suppressed an increasingly urgent need to burp.

"Tell me again why you ain't arresting me."

Wendy glanced at Rebecca sharply, but saw only heavy-lidded amusement staring back at her. "Like I said, my manager ordered me off your case. Somebody paid more for us to drop the investigation than the underwriter was paying us to carry it out. It's how the system works: the company is in business to make money, not uphold the law."

"But you didn't know that when you put the cuffs on me, you were just off-duty." Rebecca grabbed Wendy's wrist, nearly spilling her beer, then leaned across her to grab her other arm. She brought her wrists together—*She's really strong*, Wendy registered—and held them above her head.

"Hey!"

"Let's see how you like it," Rebecca said, then leaned in and kissed her. Wendy squirmed, uncertain where this was going—*trick or treat?*—but she kissed back. Felt Rebecca pressing up against her flank, warm and solid. Eventually, Rebecca pulled back. "What do you want with me?"

"You—" she hesitated, not ready to continue this line of questioning, and shied away from the personal—"I still need to know what was in that box," she said, heart hammering between her ribs. "What the letter was about."

"That's not what I was asking."

Rebecca kissed her again, and this time Wendy whimpered quietly into her mouth.

Oh God, she thought. "Your interrogation technique needs more practice," she whispered, and Rebecca snorted back laughter. "Like this," she added, and now she was the one nibbling at Rebecca's throat.

"The letter." Rebecca moaned softly. "What's so important about it, anyway?"

Wendy stilled. "Four mobbed-up heavies with AKs shoot up a bank, then a bloke with light artillery smears them all over the walls and tries to take out your friends, then *someone else* pays my employer to drop the investigation, and you don't even know what it says?" She retreated from Rebecca. "Has it occurred to you that someone wants whatever's in that letter badly enough to kill for it? And if I could find you, maybe they could find you as well?" *Shit*, she realized with a sudden pang of remorse, *I'm frightening her.* The Deliverator's crew didn't carry weapons; at worst, they hired actors armed with stage props. "I mean, they *might* not try to kill you," she backpedalled awkwardly. "They might just want to invite you back to their place for tea and crumpets and a chance to discuss the works of Søren Kierkegaard—"

"Is that a new band?" Rebecca's brow wrinkled for a moment before she elbowed Wendy in the ribs: "Just kidding." She took a deep breath. "Okay, you got a point."

"Look. Just give me your phone. Uh, and my hands?" Rebecca released her, and handed over a cheap Android. *Probably a burner*, a little corner of Wendy's mind that wasn't quite as irrevocably compromised as the rest noted. She dialed her own phone, waited for it to ring, then disconnected: "Look in your call log, that's my number."

"Uh, okay—"

"Listen." She stared into Rebecca's eyes, unsure whether she was talking to Rebecca, a woman she really fancied, or the mad-eyed Deliverator storming around the M25 motorway at more than two miles a minute in a fiery Porsche: "When you go home to wherever the hell your mates live, tell them I need to see them, right? Their lives are in danger. I'm not going to arrest them. I might try to convince them to come in for a job interview—I'll get a kickback if they hire you—but that's all. You know how to call me, I've shown you where I live, now it's your turn." She squeezed Rebecca's hand as she gave her back her phone. "Call me."

Imp was just about frantic with worry when Del walked in the door.

"Where've you been?" he demanded, casting around behind her. "Why weren't you answering your phone?"

"Was busy." Del dismissed his concerns like lint flicked from her sleeve. "Went for a drive."

"Are you nuts?" Imp closed the door and bolted it behind her, staring. "You went back to the Porsche? Are you trying to get caught?"

"Chillax, I'm down with Wendy."

"Wendy?"

"The rentacop from the bank." Imp began to choke. Del held it for two seconds, then broke into a huge grin. "Gotcha! We ate ice cream, then went for a drive." She kissed her fingertips with scarcely feigned bliss. "Wendy just wanted to see what I could do, so I showed her. Then we went back to her place and made out." She peered at Imp, concerned. "Can you breathe, man? One blink for no, two for yes?"

Imp finally took a shuddering gasp. "Are you *insane*?"

"Nah." Del strolled past him and looked around, then made a beeline for the kitchen. "Any beer?"

Imp stalked after her, more anxious than angry. "Becca, I am *over* you fucking with me—"

"Wendy says some corporation paid her employers to take her off our case. Guess that'd be your sister?" After a second,

Imp nodded reluctantly. "She's not a cop, she says we're cool, she wants to hang out with me, I'm going to say no? I didn't lead her back to us, bro, I'm not an idiot." She reached inside the fridge for a can of Special Brew. "So what's new?"

Imp's shoulders sagged, an armature of tension that had been holding them tense gradually unwinding. "Give me one of those." He wriggled his fingers until Del stuck a chilly can in his hand. "*Sláinte.*" He shuffled back towards the games room. "We were waiting for you to come home before we had a council of war to discuss the options, but Doc and GeeBee are—" he shrugged elaborately—"indisposed. Cheers."

He raised his can ironically and chugged a mouthful, then grimaced. "Awful, simply dreadful. The only thing worse than drinking this horse piss is not drinking it."

Del drank. "Back atcha. What do you mean they're indisposed?" Imp pointed at the ceiling in silence. "Oh. Did they say when they'd be back?"

"Not. A. Clue." Imp collapsed onto the sofa. "But Doc said something about ram-raiding the wardrobe department for props, so I don't think they'll be too long." He fixed Del with a steely stare. "Spill it. Who's Wendy really, and what's her angle?"

"She's a thief-taker. Turns out Hamleys are sore losers, and so are Pennine Bank. She was there to interview the manager when you and Doc walked in, but she's off the case now. Your sister offered more to HiveCo to stop investigating than the insurers were paying. And like I said, she isn't a cop. She doesn't enforce the law."

"Fucksake." Imp face-palmed. "You know all this because she told you while you were making out together? I'm talking hot lesbian cop-on-getaway-driver make-out sex here, am I right? Were handcuffs involved?"

"Essentially yes except for the handcuffs. Well, maybe."

Del froze, then punched the sofa right beside his head. "And fucking stop pushing, you do *not* get the details. We did not end up in bed—"

"—Not this time—"

"—Fuck you, Imp, just fuck off already, okay?"

He raised his hands, then cackled wickedly: "Becca's got a girlfriend! Becca's got a girlfriend!—" He stopped abruptly, shocked sober as it actually sank in. "She was waiting for you."

"Yeah, I *did* say that, didn't I? She wants to talk to us."

"Jesus, Del." Imp grimaced, face contorting in almost physical pain.

"She says her boss is hiring people like us. Some kind of pilot project at HiveCo."

"Are you *insane*?" Imp glared at her. "They'll make you wear a suit and work office hours and piss in a jar—are you trying to grow up or something? One taste of cop quim and you're eager to go down on the Man—"

Del exploded: "Fuck you, Imp, just fucking fuck you!" He expected her to storm out at that point, but she surprised him yet again—this was turning out to be a day for unpleasant surprises from people he thought he knew—and dropped to the sofa instead. "Fuck you," she groused, a final aftershock from the temblor shaking down the walls, "it's not like that!"

"Then tell me," he said with studied insouciance, "what it's like, what it's *really, really* like."

"I'm out of the caper party," she told him. "Shit got too real. We nearly got caught yesterday. Not just Wendy, the asswipes with guns you told me about? And before that, the toy shop. They're paying thief-takers now, turns the heat up under us, know what I mean? Wendy's boss is off our case but—"

"A quarter of a million is what's up."

Her eyes went wide. "Whaa—"

"That's what I went to see sis about. I was going to turn her down, y'know? Because you're right, it's getting danger-ous. Don't wanna play double or quits when the stake is a stainless steel one stuck through the base of my skull. But that was before she pulled HiveCo off our ass. We've got top cover on this, Del, no more thief-takers, no more goons with guns, and a whole lot more money. And she figured out what we need to do, it's just a treasure map—"

The next thing he knew, Del was on top of him with a death grip on his collar, snarling mouth inches away from his nose: "What aren't you fucking telling me, you bastard?"

"The map—" Imp was choking—"the map starts—" Del relaxed her choke hold slightly—"*upstairs*. 'S'not a street map, it's a set of directions. Through the magic door, then down an' out onto the street. The book, the book it leads to is a book of magic spells. Don't have to worry about the men in black any more, but the *book*—"

She let him go and sat down heavily. "Is that all it is to you?" she asked plaintively. "A means to a quarter of a mil-lion quid so you can make your movie? Is that all *we* are to you?"

"No, no—" He shook his head—"no!"

"Get on with you! I shouldn't have fucking come back here, you arsewipe—"

Imp took a deep breath: "Let me tell you about my fam-ily," he said.

"What *is* this?" Game Boy complained, as Doc handed him another dress from the back of the closet.

"Mad props resource." Doc rummaged. "Don't think any of these'd fit Becca, though."

Game Boy looked at the dress critically. Blue with polka dots, 1950s-style full skirt, but the waist—"You're right, it's tiny." The Deliverator had muscles as well as attitude, and was over a hundred and eighty centimeters tall. The dress was the sort of thing his parents would have put him in when he was twelve: they'd have added bows and pigtails and Mary Janes and told him he was adorable. He shuddered, then carried it out of the bedroom and up the corridor towards the growing heap in the drawing room on the way to the stairs. When he came back he asked, "Why are we even bothering? Imp wants cyberpunk."

"Imp wants cyberpunk *now* but just you wait for the next draft of the script," Doc muttered, handing over a cocktail dress. "I think we're done here." They'd already emptied the drawers of unmentionables from the room further down the hall.

"What's the point if none of it fits—"

Doc turned. "One, inspiration. Imp runs on ideas. Two, you don't know, *I* don't know, who Imp's going to hire to act in it, right? Who knows, maybe he's got a petite leading lady on speed dial with his silver tongue—" Game Boy winced and Doc pretended not to see it—"worst case, we can cart it down to a secondhand shop and sell it as vintage. C'mon now, let's drop this lot on the landing, then go check out the Red Route, I've got a good feeling about it."

The Red Route, so named because of the red ochre walls, was a corridor about a third of a kilometer away. Down two flights of stairs, it was illuminated by skylights and gas mantles that hissed softly when Doc held a lighter to them. It had several plain wooden doors leading to bedrooms that clearly hadn't been explored for over a century.

"Look." Doc opened the first door he came to: "An oil lamp!" The brass body of the lamp was dull with age and dust, but the glass chimney and shroud were intact. He picked it up from the dressing table and nearly dropped it. "Hey, it's heavy." He sniffed it suspiciously. "Smells like . . . fish?"

Game Boy gagged. "Oh ick, that's got to be whale oil." Rancid whale oil at that.

Doc put it down gingerly. "Um, all right then. What else have we got?"

"I don't—" Game Boy's forehead wrinkled. "Is this Victorian?"

"Looks that way, but I'm not sure." Doc pulled out a drawer from the dark wooden cabinet. "Wing collars? When did they go out?"

"Check this out." Game Boy was into the wardrobe side of the chest, where a dove gray morning suit hung in pride of place: obviously somebody's long-forgotten Sunday best. "What do you think?" He held it up against his chest, looking past it at the fly-specked mirror: "Think it's about my size?"

Doc pondered. Game Boy was slightly built for a twenty-first-century man, but the suit looked about right. "Try the jacket first," he suggested, then left Game Boy and moved on to the next room. It looked like a lady's boudoir out of the late nineteenth century, though he had no idea which year (or even decade) the dresses came from: it might even be early twentieth, for all he knew. Big hats, floor-sweeping skirts.

He was assembling an armload to cart back for analysis when Game Boy strolled in. "What do you think?" Gee Bee twirled. "Is this dapper or what?"

"Needs a top hat and cane. Doesn't go with your Converse. How does it hang?"

Game Boy shot his cuffs back. "The sleeves are a little long. And the trousers need a belt, but I couldn't find any loops." The trousers in question came halfway up his chest and were falling down.

"That's because they were worn with suspenders and a waistcoat." Doc knew that much. "Okay, you should definitely keep it. You never know, Imp might want us to flash mob a wedding party or cosplay *Downton Abbey*."

"Great!" Game Boy bounced out again to rummage for matching accessories. Doc nibbled the end of his pen, then jotted down some notes about where and what he'd found: metadata for the map of the dream palace they were exploring.

"What period do you think this is from?" Doc yelled down the hall.

"Late nineteenth century, probably 1880s, I think? Do the dresses have bustles?"

Doc scratched his head. "Dunno," he admitted. "What's a bustle?"

"It's a fashion thing: let's just say that from the 1870s to the 1890s, a well-dressed woman would never need to ask 'does my arse look big in that.'" Game Boy came back in, clutching an armful of stuff. Top hat, shirt, waistcoat with a cravat spilling out of one pocket. "Why do I even *know* this stuff? Thanks, Mum, for trying to turn me into a lay-dee." He rolled his eyes, then dumped his loot on the bed before turning to the wardrobe. "Grab that—no, wait, that one—it's big enough it might fit a modern woman—and that, and that. Yeah, and that, and we're done. Let's head back; betcha twenty quid you can't persuade Del to model it for you."

"Think she's back yet? From wherever she went?"

Game Boy froze at the foot of the stairs leading back up to the same level as reality. "Oh *shit,* if the cops caught her and followed her back to the house we could be stuck here—"

Doc dumped his armful of stuff and held out his arms: "Hugs?" The weirdest things could trigger Game Boy, and it looked like he'd just discovered a new one. "Here?" Game Boy grabbed him and burrowed his face against Doc's shoulder, panting. "Slow down." Doc rubbed his back. "Hyperventilating will make it worse. Let me in? I can help." He reached for calm, then *pushed* at Game Boy, hosing down his fiery anxiety with a spray of tranquility.

"Oh God, oh God, oh God . . ." Game Boy's breathing slowly returned to normal. "We're doomed. They'll send me back to my parents, or, or, the door with the air raid sirens, or—"

"There are other ways out," Doc told him. "Different periods, don't you get it? The laundry room on this level has a staircase, too. Other doors leading to other times."

"But look, look—" Game Boy let him go so he could point at the pile of clothes—"don't you know anything about history?" His voice rose, almost to a wail: "History is shit! You can die from an infected hangnail! History is a place where there are no computers, no games, no burgers, no television, no central heating—where they put people like me in lunatic asylums because they don't *understand* or, or—"

"None of that is going to happen to you," Doc said firmly, determined to head off the next panic attack before it could build up a full head of steam and pull out of the station. "We're going downstairs—carefully, just in case—and Imp will shout at us for not being around for a read-through of his revised script, and Del will be bitchy, and—"

"Something is *wrong*," Game Boy insisted weakly. He reached up and pulled his dusty top hat down, concealing his crimson crop. "Something bad is coming, I know it is, don't ask me how."

"C'mon." Doc picked up the bundle of clothes, squished it tight, and offered Game Boy his free hand as he turned back towards the corridor leading to their top floor roost. "If it's coming that means it isn't here *now*, and that's the main thing."

*

When he was a child, Imp—then Jerm—had a family.

There was Imp, who of course the world revolved around: tousle-headed with a devilish dimpled grin for which he'd earned his nickname (before it stretched to encompass the bulky *resario* suffix, before he'd realized what he was in this world to accomplish). Jerm had a dog, a big dumb Alsatian called Nono: it wasn't her real name, but what everybody screamed at her when she did something wrong, which was all the time. Jerm also had a big sister, Evie, who was blonde and curly-haired and just a bit chubby, five years older and conscientious about keeping him out of trouble and wiping his nose when he needed it. Evie *cared*, too much for her own good. She cared when their next door neighbor's cat was hit by a car, she cared for Grandma when they visited her in the home, she cared when Jerm fell out of the apple tree in the garden and hurt his arm (a greenstick fracture, it turned out), and she memorized and cared deeply about everything Mum told her she needed to care about in order to be a good little girl. Evie was eager to please everyone, and Jerm took advantage of this trait at every opportunity, because Jerm was a whiny little shit, and more than a little bit spoiled when he was small.

All that changed later.

Dad was an accountant, dignified in his suit and tie when he left for the office every weekday morning. He wasn't dull, though. He read to Jerm before bed in the evenings, at least until Jerm mastered the skill for himself, and even after that for a while. Dad read through all the childhood classics, from Dr. Seuss to *The Wind in the Willows*, *The Hobbit,* and *Peter and Wendy*, this latter one slightly out of sequence and with certain omissions that Imp only spotted when he read it for himself as an adult. Dad was a voracious consumer of fiction, escaping from reality whenever he could: their house had bookcases the way the other kids at school's parents had cabinets full of video cassettes. Their television was small and dull and didn't have a VCR, and their home computer was the word processing kind, with a green screen and a printer but no games, a leftover from the 1980s. Dad said they couldn't afford to replace it, and indeed they didn't until Jerm needed one for secondary school. Even though Dad was an accountant, they weren't rich.

Partly this was because they lived in a cramped semi near Croydon, with all the drawbacks of London house prices and none of the perks of actually being in the capital. Partly it was because Mum didn't go out to work: she was a homemaker, she said, with an odd, tight-lipped expression when Jerm asked her. She'd been programming minicomputers when she met his father in the late seventies. (Dad had wanted to have at least three kids, Imp later learned. Mum made sure that didn't happen—they'd have been destitute—but later became melancholy, finding her consolation in religion.) One income, two children, London house prices, and Grandma in a nursing home: Dad in a suit and a Ford Granada (later upgraded to a BMW 315), Mum driving a ten-year-old Ford Escort.

Not rich, Imp eventually realized, was not the same thing as *poor*. But he'd grown up in the shadow of wealth. Before the walls of dementia closed in completely and left nothing behind but a terrified wailing shell, Grandma told Evie and Jerm stories about life in the old days. Tales of living in a big town house round the corner from a park with a royal palace in it, tales of the chauffeur and the Daimler and tea at Claridge's, tales of silks and furs and jewels in her box at the opera. Grandma had been an actress in the gone-away days before she met Grandpa, a dashing man about town with an income and expectations, who had an interest in exports, or possibly railways in India.

The reality was somewhat different, marked by a trail of rich folks' tears. Grandpa had been coasting on empty in the wake of family tragedies both personal and financial. Grandpa's two elder siblings had disappeared or died in some scandalous manner that nobody would speak of thereafter. The complicated family trust he'd inherited—set up by his own father, long on Suez Canal bonds and shares in the steam locomotive industry—crashed disastrously in the 1950s. Grandpa's peculiar profession provided less regular income than the Home Office hangman's, for Grandpa was a sorcerer. But magecraft was in eclipse for most of the twentieth century, and Grandma's Russian parentage cost him any chance of employment by the security agency that defended the Kingdom against arcane threats. Grandma had tales of letting the servants go during wartime, but remained silent on the matter of not hiring replacements after the end of hostilities. The death duties levied on Great-grandpa's estate were the last nail in the coffin of the family fortune: by the time Imp's father—Grandpa's sole offspring—stood in line to inherit, the family house had been sold to a hotel baron and Imp's father had reason to be grateful for his aptitude for numbers.

Numbers and magic went together like a horse and carriage, and were in roughly similar demand. The family traded in quaint séances and furtive rituals held in dust-sheeted ballrooms by the initiates of strange religions, rather than the great wreakings and summonings that had once shaken the chancelleries of Europe. Imp's dad had missed out on the strange revival of magic by the secret state, on the gathering momentum of Moore's Law, the systematization and formalization of computation as a sorcerous speciality. Mum might have had an in, but she'd been squeezed out of the increasingly stuffy and male-dominated British software industry in the eighties, too exhausted and pregnant to do aught but let her skills atrophy from disuse. She and Dad shared a certain way of thinking about things, a common fondness for the secret occult power that could be unleashed by way of Newton's fluxions. If they'd met a couple of decades later they might have built a great and terrible magical empire. A couple of centuries earlier they could have brokered their insights for wealth and power at the royal court. But they had the supreme misfortune to be born just too late in the age of rationality to profit from his magic, and just too early to make use of hers.

One rainy half term Tuesday in the February of the year Imp turned twelve, he climbed into the attic in search of distractions. That's when he found the old steamer trunk with Grandpa's initials painted on the lid in faded gold leaf. It had been hidden behind an old coffee table and a stack of suitcases full of Mum's 1970s shoes and dresses. The trunk was locked, but the internet was a thing, and his parents hadn't yet worked out how much mischief a bored Imp with internet access could get up to. FAQs on lock-picking abounded, and it was much more interesting than doing homework: so the desperate curiosity of a bored tween armed with improvised picks and rakes collided with a woefully insecure chest—or rather, a chest warded so that only an heir of the pure bloodline could open it without fatal consequences. Imp was totally ignorant of this, of course. But then again, he *was* the heir in question.

It wasn't his fault that Dad had held off introducing him to the contents and commencing his training in the old ways out of fear that it would distract him from his GCSEs. It wasn't Dad's fault that, after decades of neglect, he'd come to think of magecraft as an eccentric hobby or family tradition, rather than a deadly and puissant art. Nor could Dad be faulted for not realizing that magic was creeping back into the world on the back of proliferating computing devices that attracted the attention of things that thrived on information, so that the arcane arts grew steadily easier and more accessible with every passing year. It wasn't even Dad's fault for hoping that Imp would follow him into a safe and secure career as a chartered accountant, or perhaps an Inland Revenue auditor, and hadn't bothered to explain the family curse to him, or the meaning of the struck-out names on the front page of the family spell book.

But if you leave a loaded handgun lying around the family home, you shouldn't be surprised if a child finds it and pulls the trigger.

By midafternoon, the Bond was pissed off.

If it was galling to be outwitted by a woman, it was infinitely more so to be outfoxed by a dim-witted cycle courier driving a stolen car that was somewhat inferior to the boss's shiny silver Aston Martin. Women, in the Bond's opinion, were only good for fucking and cooking. Yet the car thief with the dreadlocks and attitude had dragged the thief-taker back to the stolen Porsche—which had somehow lost the wheel clamp while they'd been making gooey eyes at one another over ice cream—climbed in, and taken off like the London traffic didn't even exist.

Not being a total idiot, the Bond had stuck a GPS tracker bug behind the front bumper before he trailed the duo to the ice cream kiosk, so he'd been able to tail the thief out to the North Circular before he lost her. He'd jumped a few traffic lights and tripped a whole series of Gatsos along the way, but Rupert's corporate vehicle ownership would cover for him: some hapless minion would be fingered for the speeding tickets and get to exchange his driving license for a commuter rail season pass in return for keeping his job.

But speeding tickets were one thing. What the GPS tracker showed when the getaway driver hit the M25 clockwise was something else entirely: something that could only be described as black magic. The Bond had followed her onto the motorway but after two junctions she was pulling away so fast that continuing the pursuit invited humiliation (not to mention a potentially fatal collision). The Bond swore bitterly and used the next roundabout exit to reverse direction. If he couldn't keep up with her in a chase, he'd just have to ambush her instead.

The Bond tracked the Deliverator as she finished a complete lap of London and then slowed right down, driving back into the beating heart of the capital. But she wasn't coming back to the Borough of Kensington and Chelsea as he'd expected: instead she headed for the trackless squalor of the East End, where no self-respecting billionaire would dream of setting foot.

Well then. Time for Plan B. The Bond opened his briefcase and pulled out a slim notebook computer which he attached to the picocell head unit. It took a few minutes but he narrowed his suspects down to two cellphone IMEIs that came up consistently: one of them had a SIM that resolved to a corporate account owned by HiveCo; both IMEIs had been in tight proximity for the entire duration of the Deliverator's wild ride, and the HiveCo phone had messaged the other one some time after they stopped moving. The Bond opened a map view, then made a call to ask for some additional information. Yes, the Porsche was parked round the corner from the thief-taker's home address. *Well.* The Bond smiled sharkishly and tapped his steering wheel, then settled down for a wait.

The getaway driver didn't stay at the thief-taker's pad for long. The car stayed parked, but the Deliverator's phone slowly meandered towards Liverpool Street via a bus route, before abruptly dropping off the cellphone network. Underground, probably. The phone popped up again at High Street Kensington tube station, then drifted at walking pace towards the park before veering into a side-street leading to—*the fuck?* The Bond thought, confused—*a royal palace? I thought the Queen lived in Buckinghamshire?* He shook his head. Maybe there were more than one palace—*oh.* The cellphone's location plot jumped and the focus narrowed. Obviously there was some signal bounce, and now she was walking along a side-street just to one side of the park.

And then she stopped moving.

Well, well, well. This wasn't what the Bond had been expecting of a petty crook, not at all! But it was extremely suggestive, and begged to be checked out.

The Bond retreated to his hotel room. Over the next two hours he sniffed around the quiet street electronically. He used Shodan to probe for unsecured camera feeds, the cellco tracking databases to isolate stationary phones in the vicinity of his target, and other, less obvious, research tools.

The picture that slowly emerged was decidedly hinky. Kensington Palace Gardens wasn't just any old road: it had the dubious distinction of being the most expensive residential street in the world (unless you counted the Japanese Imperial Palace in Tokyo). The average town house on the street sold for over fifty million pounds and was the property of an offshore investment vehicle, typically a shell company in the Cayman Islands or Dubai owned by a sovereign wealth fund. The Bond thought Rupert de Montfort Bigge was rich; Rupert probably considered himself to be rich; but Rupert could barely afford a tumbledown garden shack on this street.

Bizarrely, none of these billion-dollar residences were inhabited. The entire street was decaying, with rotting roofs, broken windows, and water running down the grand staircases behind cover of their steel security fences and CCTV cameras. These houses were too valuable for mere humans to be permitted to live in them. They were all uninhabited . . . except for the house two down from the end of the street. *That* one had four smartphones sucking signal and a business broadband cable. And when the Bond looked for its security cameras, their feeds had been hacked to relay the view of a different house, three doors along.

After breaking for a late lunch—a Happy Meal: not ideal, but he could grab it and eat in the car—the Bond drove to the nearest halfway normal street to Kensington Palace (defined as one that featured houses inhabited by human beings rather than abstract corporate asset management vehicles) and parked up. He opened his briefcase and unpacked the drone, swapped out camera modules, then programmed in a flight path, being careful to avoid the no-fly zone around the junior royalty clubhouse. Opening the car door, he checked for rubberneckers before releasing the quadrotor. It buzzed away across the rooftops, camera turret swiveling to bear on the target. He checked his phone. Eight minutes later, dead on the nail, the drone returned.

Replaying the footage it sent back confirmed his suspicions. Viewed from above, using the far-infrared camera on the drone, his target stuck out like a sore thumb. Heat radiated through the walls—but the front and back windows were oddly dark, as if there was a layer of cold air trapped just inside them. Other hot spots in the walls suggested running electrical appliances, in stark contrast with the neighboring properties which were dark and derelict. However, it wasn't putting out enough heat to suggest an urban cannabis farm: this was a domicile rather than a factory, albeit a camouflaged one.

Target confirmed, the Bond drove back to his hotel's parking garage and went up to his room for a shower and a brief nap, then began to get his kit ready for an evening out on the town.

"He who controls the past controls the present; he who controls the present controls the future." The Denizen of Number Ten held His cut-crystal goblet of sherry up to catch the light. "I gather from your activities that you agree, Mr. de Montfort Bigge." There was a look in His eyes like black holes in the sky. "Cheers!"

A polite round of applause rose from the other diners as they raised their glasses to the Prime Ministerial toast.

"*Bastard,*" hissed Rupert, freezing the playback. The Prime Minister paused with His glass raised, immaculate in white tie and tails at the Lord Mayor's Banquet—a state occasion in which it was traditional for the head of the government to deliver a speech to the council of the City of London Corporation, essentially the hub of the British financial services industries.

Rupert had been invited to attend. Not being entirely insane he had declined with regrets, citing the winter flu that was doing the rounds. Which was why he was watching the speech from the comfort and privacy of his Jacuzzi in the master suite at Castle Skaro. (The bath, a seven-seater with minibar, mood lighting, high-end home cinema system, and filter/sterilization units, was perfect for entertaining. But sometimes Rupert just wanted to wallow in his own wealth.)

The PM was neither human nor entirely sane, and took a zero tolerance approach to would-be rivals.

Rupe rewound a couple of seconds, then replayed the video at a tenth normal speed. *There.* He backed up and watched the People's Mandate raise a toast to ruination and the death of gods for a third time: *"Wouldn't you agree?"* Glitch. *"Mr. de Montfort Bigge?"* A tiny judder as something or someone, perhaps some enslaved video editing demon, spliced Rupert's name into the outgoing stream with random precision, destined for his eyes only. Similar personalized messages were undoubtedly going out to other movers and shakers, the alienated servants of gods who'd lost the toss when His Dreadful Majesty seized power and instituted the New Management of N'yar Lat-Hotep, the Black Pharaoh Returned.

"Shit," Rupert mumbled as he reached for the coke mirror. *Rumbled.*

Magic was a branch of applied mathematics. Systematized in decades and centuries gone by, it had come a long way from its occult roots. The wild efflorescence of computing technology had brought it crashing back to life, a tsunami of inrushing power pouring chaotically back into the world after decades of drought. Now Elder Gods and ancient horrors were awakening in all quarters. Obscure cults could harness the power of imprecatory prayer to damn their enemies and bring prosperity to their fingertips. Barefoot sorcerers awakened daily in ignorance of the real source of their power, and called themselves superheroes or metahumans—at least until the feeders attracted by the magical computation fizzing in their skulls began to eat their brains. It had all gotten a little out of hand, Rupert conceded—especially once the bastard in Downing Street had gotten the drop on his own patron saint, the Mute Poet.

But when faced with a de facto coup d'état, one must behave with pragmatism and grace, lest one lose one's head. (Quite literally, given the PM's predilection for reaping crania to adorn His glass-and-chromed-steel Tzompantli, the modernized Aztec skull rack He'd erected atop Marble Arch.) Rupert had hoped that his activities might meet with, if not active approval, then at least *tolerance* on the part of the New Management. He'd gone long on the right stocks, shorted others on the back of a handshake and a word of advice from the right lips. Ensured that tithes were paid, in blood as well as money. Tried to look suitably chastened and remorseful for having backed the wrong horse, in other words, meanwhile hoping that his delicate efforts to tip the balance his way would go unnoticed until they bore strange fruit.

"He who controls the past controls the present; he who controls the present controls the future." *Fuck, busted.* Orwell's famous words spoke not just of propaganda; they could have been an explanation of how markets worked, a rationale of Rupert's career, or a history of magic in the modern era. But they meant so much more to Rupert: they spoke of a possible path to survival.

When the New Management came to power, Rupert had pulled in his horns and gone into seclusion for a while to lick his wounds—he hated to come in second, despised being on the losing side—and reflect on lessons learned. And after a while it came to him that the itch he chewed on was caused by an unanswered question: not *Why did He seize power?* But *What stopped Him doing it sooner?*

Magic was getting stronger, true. But magic had been plentiful before. If you gave credence to myths and legend, magic had been everywhere in the Bronze Age, squirting out of the ground like wildcat oil strikes. But in the past couple of centuries there was clear evidence for the rarity of magecraft and the difficulty of executing sorcerous protocols. It was almost as if something had suppressed the metanatural, rendering certain computational processes inaccessible to practitioners of the high arts. It was an impairment that had, ironically, facilitated the ascendancy of the Age of Reason. (If it hadn't happened, Sir Isaac Newton might be better remembered for his alchemical research and his interest in infinitesimals as a tool for confining and constraining devils, rather than his work on optics and gravity.) Perhaps it was the result of some secret agency or power, working behind the scenes to suppress all magical phenomena. Or perhaps it was the Age of Reason itself, the ascendancy of the Newtonian view of the universe as a deterministic chew toy for an omniscient god. Whatever the cause, the end result was clear: magic had become increasingly difficult after the sixteenth century, vanishing almost entirely during the late Victorian age, before making a gradual comeback from the 1940s onwards.

Rupert entertained a bizarre but plausible hypothesis: perhaps the magical drought had come about as a way for the continuum to protect itself from temporal paradoxes—side effects of time travel. Magic gave access to the ghost roads, arcane liminal spaces that linked places and times: to ley lines and paths to other parallel universes, and to the dream palaces of oneiromancer dynasties. But history could only be internally consistent and stable if nobody edited it. Nature abhors a temporal paradox. If magic permitted temporal paradoxes, perhaps magic itself had converged on a local minimum, editing itself out of the historical record until there wasn't enough of it left to alter the past.

Be that as it may. Rupert didn't give a toss what *caused* it. What Rupert wanted to know was how he could *use* it.

Given: some eldritch temporal feedback loop had suppressed magical phenomena on a near-global scale for several centuries until it collapsed in the face of an exponentially burgeoning computational substrate. It seemed likely to Rupert that powerful magical tools had been lost during the drought, rendered about as useful as cellphones in the wake of a disaster that took out the electrical grid they depended on. Similarly, it was possible that even while the drought was in progress, surviving practitioners had continued to create magical tools. Any such artifacts would now be preposterously powerful, supercharged by the wealth of *mana* available on tap. (Powerful enough, perhaps, to alter the past.) But they might well have been destroyed or misplaced during the drought. He'd long been in the habit of collecting useful-looking ritual objects, slapping golden handcuffs on any child of the great magical bloodlines who crossed his path. With the ascent of the New Management he upped his game, putting out feelers to look for any signs of the old and hidden tools of power resurfacing—anything that might contribute to the success of his Great Working. Stumbling across the scion of a family that had once held in their custody a great and terrible concordance—stumbling across her, with her unaware of her ancestors' record—had been a wonderful stroke of luck. All that remained was to enslave her and motivate her to bring it to him.

Rupert snorted up the line of coke his butler had left out for him, then closed his eyes and waited for the sharp edge of his senses to kick in. Overindulging was dangerous, but coming to the attention of His Dark Majesty was even more deadly, and Rupe needed to be on top of his game right now. He killed the Guildhall speech, then pulled up one of his favorite videos: Ms. Starkey on the firing range in the sub-subbasement in London that wasn't on the architectural drawings, working out her resentment on a paper target bearing Rupert's silhouette.

Eve was self-consciously aware of the cameras in her office: she suspected or knew about the ones in her bedroom and bathroom. Her inhibitions made her delightfully easy to torment: whenever she seemed to be losing her edge, Rupert could wind her up again by demanding salacious verbal fellatio. Her barely concealed revulsion kept her keyed up and tense, and whenever she had too much time to spare he found additional tasks to ensure she faced an eighty-hour work week just to keep her head above water. She was already a workaholic; adding sexual frustration turned her into an office demon *and* deprived her of the time to wonder why Rupert had head-hunted her in the first place. Such a happy coincidence that he'd been looking for a new PA just as Eve had been desperate for help with her mother. Who was *clearly* suffering from K syndrome—or, as the public knew it, Metahuman Associated Dementia—which had led Rupert to research her lineage and, on that basis, immediately reel her in and wrap her up as tight as any spider ever wrapped a fly. The rest had all fallen into place: setting up the trail of bread crumbs to lead Eve towards his goal, putting the Bond into position for cleanup afterwards. It was just a shame that Bernard had gotten greedy and tried to turn the fake auction into a *genuine* one. Eve had surprised him by pulling in her estranged brother, but Rupert didn't really care who fell victim to the family curse, as long as the book was legitimately in his possession at the end.

Certainly Rupert went to some lengths to keep his interest in her family and the history of their powers quiet, even though knowing he had such a powerful witch under his dominion turned him on. (Indeed, Rupert found power was the only aphrodisiac that worked worth a damn these days.) He wasn't stupid enough to demand physical, as opposed to verbal, services that might push her into overt rebellion, a rebellion that would force him to fully play his hand. Indeed, Rupert only permitted himself to have physical contact with professionals these days—professionals who he paid to go away afterwards. But he quite enjoyed watching Eve at her most severe in leather and latex, compelled to work his will on some hapless fool who'd made the mistake of crossing him: and he could fantasize about her as he grew stiff. In fact . . . "Bathroom service request," he commanded, holding down the call button on the panel by his cheek. "Send up the skinny blonde English chick, Jeeves, chop-chop that's a good fellow." He listened for a few seconds. "I'm in the tub. Lotioned, lubed, and shaved, I'm going to want it both ways. Jolly good, five minutes."

He let go of the call button with a contented sigh, then reached for his (splash-proof) phone. It occurred to him that he hadn't heard from Eve *or* the Bond for a couple of hours. Which meant his probe of the deadly time-crossed mansion should be well underway by now. Obviously *that*, as well as the PM's unpleasant little surprise, was why he was feeling tense. Well, a brisk session of splashy-splashy and another line of coke should help clear his head.

And then, if they *still* weren't ready to report, he'd have the chopper fly him to Knightsbridge, and he'd take personal control over the retrieval operation.

BACK TO THE
FUTURE

Imp moved around restlessly as he filled Del in on the details of his checkered family history. He had to keep his hands and feet busy or he'd never have the nerve to finish it. Eventually he was done, and by the end of the sorry story he had made multiple printouts of the treasure map and explanatory notes. Rebecca tracked him around the room with a slightly glazed expression. Finally she just said "Fuuu . . ." and trailed off. Then she shook herself and remarked, "I need a smoke."

"Your stash. So. How about it? This evening, do we go after the book?"

Rebecca nodded distractedly as she rummaged in her tin for a roll-up. "So it's, there's a *reason* it's got to be you, yeah, I get that. And the money, and the thing with your sister and your mum, but it's fucking harsh, man, you know?" She always kept a couple of finished joints in her tin, just in case. Now she lit one, sucked in a contemplative lungful, and offered it to Imp. He took it and joined her in silent contemplation for a minute. "Have you told GeeBee and Doc yet?" she asked.

"I don't know if they need to know." He paused. "Was hoping they'd follow your lead."

"No promises." She took the smoldering roll-up back.

"It's entirely up to them. But I get how it's not just about the money for you." She tipped her head back, setting the beads at the end of her dreads clattering. "I want to bring Wendy along on the job."

"No."

"Your sis got HiveCo off our ass. She's not hunting us—"

"I said no!"

"Mellow out, asshole." Del thrust her joint at him. After a moment he took it.

"Why," he said, then puffed furiously. Somebody had once told him that every time you toke, a policeman dies: Imp didn't believe a word of it, but he was all in favor of testing the theory.

"She's made us. That's for one thing. But she let me go. That's for 'nother. She's not a cop. She works security. And she's well hard. *You*—" She poked Imp in the ribs with a bony finger—"are not hard. Doc is not hard. Game Boy is butter. And what you're telling me you want to do, it needs hard."

"Still saying no." But Imp was listening.

"I can't carry you all on my own." She pointed at the treasure map. "I get that you got to start out on the top floor, but the route doesn't end in the house. See that side-door? What do you think *1888* means? This arrow, pointing at Whitechapel. What do you think *that's* about? I'll tell you what it's about: Remember the way the rooms are full of old shit the further you go, that staircase Doc told us about with the air raid sirens?" She tapped the map. "I want Wendy 'coz Wendy is *muscle* an' Whitechapel in 1888 is like no fucking way, man, it's a fucking rookery. Go heavy or don't go."

"But surely they'll greet time travellers like us with flowers!" Imp said, with a tilt of his head so subtle Rebecca

almost thought he was serious for a moment. "Point taken."
He looked pensive. "Afterwards—"

"Your big sis just tripled the fee, din't she? That Dilbert
Wendy works for in his troll-office, bet you he isn't paying
her five hundred a day."

"Oh!" The penny dropped. Unnoticed, the joint guttered
and died in a wisp of smoke. "You think I should hire her."

Del snorted. "Money talks, bullshit walks. Pay her—but
not too much," she advised. "Offer five hundred under the
table, maybe go to two thousand. It's for one day, like? It's
good money. But it's not so much money you'll regret it later
an' try to stiff her."

"You just want me to pay your girlfriend," Imp jabbed,
but the barb was blunt.

Del nodded: "I do, I do." A feral grin split her face. "You
saw what she could do with a bow and arrows? Dontcha
want her on the raid team if the job goes bad?"

"Let me make a phone call," Imp said abruptly. He pulled
his phone out. "Hi, Evie? Yeah, it's me. Got a question. Did
you by any chance pull HiveCo off our back?" He listened for
a bit, then caught Del's eye and nodded minutely. "Thanks,
good to hear." He listened some more. "Yeah, we're talking
it over now. I think it's a goer—wait, *when*? Tonight, really?
You need it by lunchtime tomorrow? Or what?" He turned
pale. "Okay, that's good to know. I'll see what I can do. Hey,
can I bum an extra five thou off you for extra muscle—" He
stopped. "Yes, yes it's the thief-taker. Del says I should hire
her and I thought—" He stared at his phone—"You *what*?"

He hung up and stared at Del.

"What?" asked Del.

"My sister." He shook his head. "She says she'll square it
with HiveCo and get your girl assigned to us." He shook his

head again. "Shoulda expected that from Eve. She takes care of business."

"Why tonight?" asked Del. Her ear twitched at the sound of footsteps descending the main staircase.

"Her boss is coming home and he expects her to hand him the manuscript tomorrow." Imp was clearly trying hard not to roll his eyes. "So it's all hurry up and get it done *right now*."

"Lie down with the man, get up with man-crabs." Del shrugged. "What can you do?"

"Call Wendy," Imp told her. "If you can figure out a way to bring her over without her knowing exactly where we are that'd be good, but don't sweat it: if Eve's hiring, we're covered. Meanwhile, I'm going to talk to the boys."

A light rain was falling when Del met Wendy outside the tube station.

"Hey, Becca." Wendy's grin was contagious. "Didn't expect to hear from you so soon."

"Yeah, well, about that." Del scuffed her boot on the pavement and glared at an officiously busy businessman who was paying too much attention to his phone to think about dodging. "Wanna see the clubhouse? Imp invited you."

"Imp—" Wendy's eyes narrowed. "You know I'm not going to shop you, but if my employers—"

Del took Wendy's arm and threaded it around her elbow. "Taken care of," she said. "Our mystery employer is hiring you as we speak, to help us with a little job tonight."

"I'm going to regret this, aren't I?"

"No—" Del stopped, tugged the other woman closer, and kissed her cheek—"I'll make it up to you."

"I *am* going to regret this." But Wendy followed her lead.

Del gave zero fucks about Imp's fit of the vapors over

showing Wendy where they lived. Yeah, it had been Imp's family's house for generations, but it wasn't now. They were unwelcome squatters who could be evicted or arrested at any moment. Imp needed a reminder before he put down roots.

Del circled around the front of the palace, surreptitiously watching Wendy's face for signs of the disturbing royalty-worship to which so many white English people seemed to be prone—as if purple parasitic mind wasps had laid the eggs of imperial mind-control slavery in their heads, so that perfectly rational people snapped to attention like so many zombies at the first sign of a coat of arms—then led her round the back of the high-walled garden, secretly relieved when the spikey ex-cop passed the test. "What?" asked Wendy.

"Just checking." Del gave her a smile. "C'mon."

"I don't think this can be—what the fuck?"

"Welcome to Neverland."

"No, this can't be right—" Del rattled her front door keys under Wendy's nose. "Wow."

"Used to be in Imp's family," Del told her. "C'mon in."

There was a fancy dress party going on inside the games room, and it was Del's turn to be all *what the fuck, man?* at her crew. As for Wendy, she was having a hard time not catching flies in her mouth.

Imp, who had pulled out his court-appearances suit, was strutting around the room cooing portentous instructions at Doc and Game Boy, with his chest puffed up like a male wood pigeon in mating season. In and of itself this was not entirely unprecedented, but the weird thing was that Game Boy and Doc were going along with it. Game Boy looked particularly dapper in wing collar and top hat; Doc looked like a cadaverously Victorian version of himself.

"What's going on?" asked Wendy.

Doc thrust a laser-printed treasure map at her. "We're going back to the 1880s," he said, as Imp snapped his fingers at Game Boy.

"You'll need outfits," said Imp, pointing at a wheeled rail sagging with Victorian ladies' gowns.

"What the hell?"

"We're going on an adventure," said Imp; "time travel. You need to dress the part." He pulled some papers from his inner pocket and fanned them in front of her. "My sister said she was hiring you via HiveCo—that makes it official, right? But it was Becca's idea really, you'll be doing her a favor, too—"

Wendy narrowed her eyes. "Don't you dare fuck with me," she warned him. "What's this about?" She took the papers and glanced at the top sheet. "This makes no sense—"

"It's a treasure map!" Game Boy said excitedly. "We've been asked to retrieve a lost manuscript from the 1880s. There's a door into history and Imp can handle the book safely but he can't get there and back on his own—"

"*My* story, Game Boy," Imp interrupted with ill-concealed temper. "So you wanted to know what was in that bank deposit box? It was an invitation to bid in an auction. *This*—" he shook his copy of the map at her—"is where our client who won the auction—the client who is hiring you on our behalf right now—wants us to go to pick it up, through the dream roads opening off the top floor of this house, leading back into the shadows of history."

"Time travel." Wendy's eyes crossed. "Fuck me, Gibson'll have an aneurysm. The jurisdictional issues alone—" Imp smirked at her. "You seem to know a lot about this," she said quellingly.

"Long story." Imp looked at her insolently. "In or out?" He shoved a bundle of banknotes at her. They were purple, they were plastic, they bore the face of the New Management beneath a royal crest that had been ancient when Egypt was born. "Just in case whatever the hell HiveCo pays you isn't enough."

Wendy counted the money. "Two thousand." Del could see the gears turning in her mind. "We're not stealing anything?"

"I don't think so," Imp said carefully. "The book was hidden by its owner, misfiled in a private library in 1888. My sis—the winning bidder—bought the location and title to the lost manuscript. That side of things is entirely legal. The library was bombed during the Blitz. Our job is just to go back in time and retrieve it." He twitched slightly.

"Tell me. *Everything*." Wendy gave him a hard stare.

"Why don't you pick something to wear?" He gestured at a screened-off area in front of the windows: "I can explain while you get changed. You, too, Del. When you're both ready—if you still want in—we can go upstairs and get started."

By the pricking in her thumbs and the soreness of her conscience, it slowly came to Eve that she might, conceivably, possibly, however innocently, have fucked up.

Item: Rupert wanted the AW-312.4 concordance. Good enough.

Item: He'd sent the Bond to take care of loose ends, like opposition bidders. Which was standard operating practice.

Item: *Loose ends* could conceivably include anyone below her level who knew about the acquisition. Now, *that* was not so good.

Item: She'd commissioned Jeremy to take care of the retrieval, which was necessary because Jeremy was one of the few people who had the background and training to handle a live codex, and he had an adequate supply of disposable minions to do the potentially fatal bits of the job.

(And now that she came to think about it, was her current employment entirely earned on merit, or could it possibly be due to Rupert's awareness of the existence of her brother and a desire to keep the Impresario on a very long string . . . ? *No, don't go there.* That way lay paranoia and madness.)

But:

Item: It turned out that Jeremy was unaccountably *fond* of his posse of lost boys. Far more so than she'd initially believed, on the basis of the reports filed by the private eye she'd tasked with monitoring him. Conceivably, he might think of them not as disposable extras to burnish the proscenium of his life, but as full actors in their own right: co-stars in his production, so to speak. In which case, he might prove unwilling to expend them as the job required. If they died, would he be angry with her? Indeed, if she didn't take measures to ensure their safety, would he ever talk to her again?

One benefit of working for Rupert was access to specialist services. She'd prudently consulted a very exclusive numismatist that morning. "Hello, darling, it's me again? Rupert needs an assortment of copper and silver coins dated between 1820 and 1885, with a total face value of one guinea. At least six in shillings and another twelve in sixpence, shillings, and half-crowns; the rest is fine in copper . . . Really? You can do that? Perfect! Preferably not polished or cleaned up in any way. Oh, and can you courier it over to me at the front desk within the hour? It's urgent."

The longer she stared at her printout of the treasure map and considered the starting point—the old family manse—the more worried she became. Jerm, the ambitious little shit-weasel, had taken on the job because his eyes were bigger than his stomach and he'd never learned not to attempt to eat anything bigger than his own head. He was out of his depth, and it was her fault. Worse: if he accomplished the mission, Rupert might well take steps to eliminate him because he knew too much. (And because it would further isolate Eve, of course, but that was a given with Rupert.)

After wasting a couple of hours spinning her wheels without achieving anything significant, Eve finally admitted that she could no longer stomach the gnawing sense of dread. By then it was five o'clock. At ground level, in the world outside her hermetically sealed office, the shadows were lengthening towards full dark. She pushed a button on her phone. "Hold all my calls," she ordered. Then she pushed another button. She had to rack her memory to dredge up her latest Gammon's name: "Mister Franke, meet me in the front hall in twenty minutes. Close protection, probably until the early hours of the morning, rough company expected. Dress code is white tie and tails."

Franke was cut from a different cloth to her regular run of Gammons. Eve had gone to great lengths to hire him, some of them extremely questionable. Diverting and editing his resumé so that HR wouldn't notice his professional pedigree was the least of it. She'd had to intercept and edit his criminal background check, to ensure the war crimes indictments and the Interpol Red Notice didn't cause any hang-ups. She'd also leaned on Mandy in Payroll to falsify his pay grade, in order to offer him sufficient incentive to sign on. Franke was considerably pricier than the old Gammon: in fact, he was paid about eight times as much as Eve herself. *On the other hand*, Eve thought, *when you pay peanuts you get monkeys*. So she'd gone out of her way to hire a silverback gorilla who punched in the same weight class as the Bond.

She hung up, removed her headset, and took the lift up to

her bedroom to collect necessities for the expedition. She exchanged her suit for a maxi dress worn under a black woolen coat and broad-brimmed hat, swapped her office heels for a pair of comfortable boots she could run in, and worked her hands into kidskin gloves. Finally she filled her coat pockets: a bag of small glass marbles in one pocket, and a cutthroat razor in the other.

The game's afoot.

She had little difficulty locating Imp. All cellphones in the vicinity of Rupe's residence were monitored, their calls intercepted via an IMSI-catcher. When Imp had visited, the security system took a good sniff at his smartphone, then—because Rupe was an unscrupulous shitheel who gave two-thirteenths of a flying fuck about anyone else's privacy—dropped a tracking bug on it via a corrupt SMS configuration update. Now Eve could stalk Imp on Google Maps, which she used to confirm that right now he was at home.

When she strode into the front hall of Chez Bigge, coat swinging and pocket jingling with thirty pieces of silver from the numismatist, the Gammon was already waiting. "Ma'am." He was in his penguin suit—when Rupe went posh for an evening's party, everybody else suffered in livery for his vanity—and he was packing heat, as usual. He looked like an extra from a steampunk remake of *The Matrix*: his stubby black UMP9 submachine gun was barely concealed by his caped overcoat, and she was fairly sure that was only the most obvious of his weapons.

"You'll need a top hat as well," she told him.

"Yes, ma'am. I'll just be a second." He vanished into the cloakroom then reappeared suitably en-hatted. "Ready ma'am." His expression was professionally incurious.

"We're going to visit my brother and his playmates in

Kensington. Then I'll be taking a trip with them. Walking tour, not driving." She waited impatiently for him to open the front door for her. "Rules of engagement: don't start trouble, but expect it and be prepared to put an end to it." She paused. "My brother and his friends are presumed friendly. Anyone else we encounter is a potential hostile."

"Yes, ma'am."

Franke closed the door and trailed her, imposing in black. The chilly night air was invigorating. Eve fell back a step and took hold of her bodyguard's left arm. "Practice leading me," she said through tight lips. "Understand that this is not an invitation to take liberties."

"Uh, yes, ma'am." A pause. "May I ask why?"

"We'll be visiting a rough neighborhood. Unaccompanied women may be seen as fair game there. If we appear to be together, it will reduce the likelihood of blood being shed." Her smile was as sharp as her razor. "Theirs, not mine."

The Gammon was sufficiently well trained not to comment on their nighttime walk through the quiet affluence of Kensington and Chelsea. Even on the side-streets houses passed hands for tens of millions of pounds and every other parked car was a Range Rover or Mercedes (with a sprinkling of Maseratis and Jaguars to leaven the stodgy mix). She could almost hear his thoughts: *Some rough.*

"This isn't our final destination," she said softly, then led him towards a crossing. "Nor is this."

The houses on the road they entered were bigger and set back behind hedges and fences, with padlocked chains securing their gates and no sign of inhabitation. There were no parked cars and little passing foot traffic. It was a city of the dead in the heart of the capital, a mausoleum occupied by the decaying sarcophagi of the rich and powerful. She felt the ex-soldier's shoulders tensing, noticed the bunch and play of muscles as he scanned their surroundings.

There was a brooding presence at the end of the street. Eve could feel it all the way from the corner, the immanent menace of her family's original sin. It was alive with magic. She doubted the Gammon could sense it; he was alert for more material threats.

Her dog was buried in an unmarked grave in the front garden, a canine gatekeeper's soul pinned before the entrance to Neverland. The first time she'd visited this place she'd been nineteen. Dad had brought her—carrying Nono's ashes in a cardboard box—furtively sneaking under cover of darkness while the last human owners were on holiday. Imp had been too young, Mum already soul-lost to a narrow pursuit of redemption for unspecified sins, and Dad had needed a second set of hands to pass him the chalice while he burned runes into the front lawn using paraquat mixed with canine blood. Nono had been the last of a long line of family Cerberi and Eve still missed that dog, although she'd been old and graying around the muzzle when the cancer took her.

Shaking off childhood memories, Eve approached the front gate. It was chained and padlocked shut, but the lock yielded to her mind's touch with well-oiled ease. It was almost like coming home. She beckoned the Gammon after her, although she didn't expect any problems at the front door. "I'll enter first," she said.

"Yes, ma'am."

Eve took the tarnished brass doorknocker and rapped, hard, three times. The hollow boom brought no response. She waited patiently, then tried again. This time, receiving no answer, she touched the keyhole and extended her will again. All the practice time with the coffee mugs paid off: the cylinder turned and the door creaked open as she pushed. Eve stepped into shadows cast by the moonlight flooding through the window above the door.

"Jeremy?" She called sweetly: "It's your sister Evie! Girls and boys come out to play?" It was a childhood passphrase, as out of place in the darkened lobby as the red dot from the Gammon's laser scope, flickering and dancing the tinkerbell waltz as he probed the treads of the grand staircase.

A glance over her shoulder told her that her bodyguard was perturbed. "Nobody home," she mouthed. Which was a bad sign. Why had Imp decided to tackle the ghost roads to Neverland so early? Her ultimatum hadn't given him much of a choice about doing it tonight but this was precipitous, even by his impulsive and sloppy standards. "I'm going to check these rooms. Rules of engagement apply."

The front room was dark and empty. The back room held humming computers, their screen savers blowing endless fractal Escher prints in a perpetual zoom repeated across a row of monitors. A rail at the back confirmed her suspicions. At first she took it for theatrical supplies—but up close, under the glare of her LED flashlight, the quality of stitching was too high, the fabric too worn. This was the real thing, clothes of historic vintage that had somehow come through to the present day intact and unfaded without conservation. Unless they were the output of a crafter obsessed with the sort of outfits her great-great-great-grandmother might have worn.

"That nails it," she murmured. A box of safety pins spilled half-empty at her feet. A laser printer stood beside the gaming PCs that pulsed softly green as a luminous deep-sea jellyfish. And on the output tray sat a document. One glance at it told her all she needed to know. She looked at the Gammon.

"Yes, ma'am?"

"We're going upstairs," she said.

"Yes, ma'am." A pause just long enough to reveal a blue line in the test strip window: "Is there something I should know?"

Eve thought fast and hard. It was not a stupid question, and Franke was a far cry from the Gammon who'd disgraced himself in the kitchenware shop. "The house we're in used to belong to a family of magicians. Not the Paul Daniels kind, the New Management kind." It was hard to tell by torchlight, but she thought his face paled. "There is a door on the top floor that leads to the ghost roads, paths that lead to other realities and times. The door used to be—*should be*—closed." *Grandpa painted it shut and sealed it with the bound souls of things best unnamed, to lock away the family guilt when he was forced to move out.* "Now it stands open." She could feel no trace of Nono's soul: the canine psychopomp was delinquent, or Daddy's binding had finally dissolved. Perhaps Imp had unwittingly freed her—he'd always had a soft spot for the pooch. She pointed to the map on the printer. "This is a treasure chart leading to a lost artifact. Mr. de Montfort Bigge tasked me with retrieving it. Unfortunately there's a snag. The people I sent after it have already departed, and I need to catch up with them." She reached into her coat pocket and pulled out her own copy of the map, another paper printout. It wasn't safe to trust smartphones or other computing devices in the ghost roads: they were prone to infection by things that didn't belong in this universe.

"Are you up for it?" she asked. It should have been a rhetorical question, but you never knew: Eve was not about to walk the road to Neverland with a submachine-gun-toting bodyguard freaking out behind her.

The Gammon swallowed. "Does the New Management know about this?" he asked.

"The principle of it? Yes, of course," she said impatiently. "But as to the specifics—" she made a show of due consideration—"I'm absolutely certain they will have no objection when I seal the portal after our return." Which was not untruthful, although it omitted so many caveats that it was actively misleading: but Franke knew which way the wind blew, and who signed his paychecks.

He inclined his head. "I'm in," he said. "Just try to remember that I can't protect you against threats I'm unaware of, ma'am. Due warning would be appreciated, if possible."

"Not a problem. I'll explain as we go." Eve returned to the darkened hallway and paused on the first tread, hand on the banister rail: "But first, tell me what you think you know about Whitechapel in the 1880s."

Well, isn't this *a party!*

The Bond watched from the bushes as Ms. Starkey and her heavily-armed muscle knocked on the front door of the abandoned house.

Typical. They'd blundered into his operation just at the worst possible time. He'd arrived on-site right at sunset, all dressed up and ready to dance. Everything he'd need for a night of mayhem and throat-slitting was strapped to his webbing vest. He'd ghosted around the perimeter, checking for concealed alarms, then slithered sideways around the walls, attaching acoustic bugs to the windows. After listening carefully he'd concluded there was nobody in the front, and he'd been scanning the casements with his night-vision scope when the unexpected gate crashers showed up.

There was clearly something wrong with the rooms behind the windows. As he changed angles, the perspective lines on walls and ceiling shifted weirdly, and the back walls showed an uneven pattern of heat traces. Meanwhile, everything in front was cold and chilly. It was like a hunter's blind, built inside the house to conceal the true interior. The placement was all wrong for it to be a sniper's nest—you couldn't even see the street from the front of the building. So perhaps it was a shelter for those being sought, the actual opposite of a hunter's blind? *Very interesting.*

Ms. Starkey knocked on the door a second time, then did something he couldn't see, concealed by her body. The door squealed open and she stepped inside, followed by her bodyguard. The door closed. After a few seconds the heat pattern on the back wall of the front room changed, brightening. *Gotcha*, thought the Bond. A short while later it dimmed. He wished he'd had the time to install surface-penetrating radar; but no matter.

The Bond exfiltrated the garden, donning his trench coat for urban camouflage, and crossed the street to his car. He climbed inside and shut the door, then tapped his headset. "Okay Google, call the boss." He sat up attentively as the satellite phone rang. "Sir."

Rupert was somewhere overseas, or maybe pigging out on blow with a pro domme aboard his private jet. It took him several seconds to reply, and his voice sounded as if it was echoing down a stainless steel drainpipe: "What have you got for me, Mr. Bond?"

The Bond described his findings at Maison Imp, then added, "Ten minutes ago Ms. Starkey entered, with her assigned bodyguard. They went inside and haven't come out. Permission to follow, sir?"

"Granted. Keep to a watching brief for now." Rupert paused. "I'm emailing a route map to you. It's the directions Ms. Starkey and her operators are following. Be aware—" Rupert always adopted a pompous fake-professional manner when he wanted to feel in control of events a long way away—"once you pass through the door on the top floor, you'll be outside the walls of our waking world. The target is hidden inside a dream of late nineteenth-century London. If you can contrive for Ms. Starkey's subcontractors to remain there when she returns with the book that would be ideal. Otherwise we can tie the loose ends up afterwards, what?"

"Sir, watching brief is first priority. Ensure unimpeded return of Ms. Starkey and the book she's collecting, subcontractors optional but can be dealt with later. Is there anything else?"

"Yes: you are to be the last one in and the last one out. If anyone follows you through the gate in either direction, kill them."

"Understood and will comply, sir."

"Jolly good, double-oh seven. Rupert out."

Shaking his head, the Bond levered himself out of his Kevlar bucket seat and went around to open the cramped boot of the supercar. Reaching inside, he opened the gun safe and removed a pair of Glock 18s and loaded them with 33-round extended magazines, then hooked their holsters to his vest.

By the time he'd finished arming up, a quarter of an hour had passed since Eve entered the mansion. That was sufficient, in his judgment. He checked the email that Rupert had sent while he was loading his weapons, rapidly skimmed the high points, and pocketed his ruggedized phone. Then he locked the car and headed for the front door.

Even the best laid plans of elite operators can come to grief on the shoals of what-the-fuck. Rupert's mistake had been to assume that Bernard was an honest broker who'd stay bought and do as he was told. Eve's mistake was to trust her subcontractors—not Imp, but Andrei, who was being paid well to deal with the rival interloper bidder who Rupert's boasting had snagged and Bernard's treachery had invited in. And in the case of the Bond his mistake was to pursue his mission speedily and efficiently, confident in his ability to deal with whatever circumstances threw at him.

Perhaps he should have been more cautious.

As he closed the front door behind him, an unmarked white Transit van slowly cruised along the street. The only visible occupant up front was the driver, but crouched inside the windowless rear were six passengers, all wiry men with close-cropped hair. They wore dark suits of archaic cut, worn with long overcoats and bowler hats.

One of them spoke on the phone, in Russian with a heavy Ukrainian accent. "—Yes, Andrei, is all in hand. What you say? Yes, I see—" He broke off to address the driver through a slot in the plywood front wall of the cargo compartment—"Do you see it? Do you see it?"

"Da." The van slowed, then began to pull in. "Hey, I see Aston Martin. Is area clear?"

"I see it. Andrei, we are on target—we talk more later." The speaker hung up, then looked at his men. "All right, what you wait for? Out! Out! We got a job to do!"

The rear door opened, and the bowler-hatted ex-Spetsnaz crew piled out, suppressed AK-12s at the ready—a modernized, more accurate, more reliable descendant of the venerable AK-47. Despite resembling a heavily armed funeral cortege, they moved speedily into position around the building. Two of them—the leader with the satellite phone, and a demolition specialist—slipped through the gate, leaving the severed ends of the chain behind. The van inched into the driveway leading to the house, then turned and reversed up to the front door. Everyone donned respirator masks and latex gloves, then two of the soldiers disappeared around the back; the others readied compact gas cylinders and ran through the checklist for a forced entry with knockout gas.

They had a kill order for the Bond: shoot on sight. Ms. Starkey's bodyguard would be dealt with similarly. Random squatters could also be disposed of at will. But their employer hadn't quite grasped that Evelyn Starkey was not simply Rupert's sexy blonde piece of fluff but a player in her own right—and this was a fatal mistake.

Shadows gathered.

Alexei Popov from Novosibirsk, the team leader, was a former Spetsnaz sergeant. He'd worked on English soil before, back when he'd been part of a team seconded to the KGB's occult operations directorate. Vassily Panin, the operative in charge, had his head handed to him by the British security services. It spread a pall over everyone's career—those who survived. Now he'd been out of the army for most of a decade. Working on special projects for Andrei was okay. It paid really well, you didn't have to wear a uniform (unless you counted disguises like the ones for tonight's operation), you didn't need to salute every asshole in epaulettes you ran across (unless they were Andrei's shadowy employer: people who didn't kiss his ass tended to disappear), and every so often you got to kill scumbags who had it coming to them.

But this job, this was something else.

"Sound off," he spoke into his throat mike. "Positions, people."

One by one his men confirmed that they were in position, gloves and masks sealed. All good.

"Five seconds. Knockout gas, ready. Okay, two . . . one . . . go!"

Glass shattered in four windows, followed moments later by the screeching hiss of the aerosol bombs his men had thrown inside. They crouched, all holding their breath despite the gas masks. Aerosolized carfentanil was serious shit, an opiate more than a thousand times as potent as heroin. It made a better nerve gas than a painkiller: they'd used it in Grozny, in the Dubrovka theater siege, anywhere there was a hostage situation where they wanted KO gas with an antidote that didn't leave the survivors crippled for life. Alexei clutched a spring-loaded Naltrexone injector tightly in his left hand, counting off his breaths, alert for the first sign of disorientation.

Ten seconds passed, as the hiss from the gas bombs died away. "Sound off," he ordered. When everybody had reported in, he unwound a fraction. "Okay, let's get in there. Go! Go! Go!"

The operatives on door duty hit the lock with a battering ram, shattering the frame and throwing the front door wide open. Two more soldiers rushed past them to cover the interior, flashlight beams skidding across staircase and hallway. Interior doors led to the rooms they'd fumigated: the gas wouldn't linger for long with broken windows and unsealed chimneys.

"Nobody in the back," reported Vassily as Alexei did a quick sweep of the front room. "You're going to want to see this, boss."

The back room was a weird mess. Strange theatrical backdrops blocked off the windows. A huge sofa—almost a double bed—dominated the room, flanked by a rack of clothing and a crazy gaming rig set up with multiple monitors and PCs. Alexei took it in: *Staging area*, he realized. Vassily was pointing at a laser printer. "Get papers."

Alexei peered at the document. It was some kind of flowchart or map diagram, and after puzzling over it for a short time he realized a chunk of it referred to this building. Andrei's intelligence was right: the gate was on the top floor. He keyed his mike again. "Team one, second floor. Team two, third floor. Go!"

The fuse of Imp's family curse was lit the moment Jeremy placed his hand on the cover of the black leatherbound volume. He removed it from the trunk, and opened it to read the flyleaf.

As with a black powder bomb, when the fuse is lit, the powder fizzles furiously, burning down through the pinhole. The bomb is about to detonate, but for a split second nothing appears to happen. A split second: or, in Imp's case, a number of years.

At first he'd mistaken it for an old family bible. Certainly the list of Starkeys and dates, inscribed in copperplate script, suggested a record of births, marriages, and deaths. It was a family dogged by a curse: in every other generation, at least one child's name was struck out. When he turned the page, there was more handwriting, much of it in Latin, some of it in a weird squiggle that hurt his eyes. What English text he could make out appeared to be marginalia and commentary. After a while he realized the squiggles reminded him of a mathematical notation or chemical formulae, or a spiderweb of arrows. (Mind maps were not something he'd encountered yet, and the book predated modern flowchart symbology.) He flicked through pages idly, then came to a cartoonish picture sketched in pencil: stick figures surrounding an inscribed circle with candles burning around its perimeter, and clear references to formulae on the preceding pages.

Finally the penny dropped. *It's a spell book!* he realized excitedly. It wasn't much like the ones in Harry Potter. It looked awfully dry and rather turgid, and he was quite clear on the distinction between the land of *make-believe* and the territory of *is*. But . . . he turned back to the flyleaf and translated: *MDCCCLXIII*, that meant *1863*, the year of Augustus Starkey. "This is really old!" His eyes widened. Below the book he saw a small stack of similar volumes, their covers increasingly fragile and dried-out the further down the pile he looked, nestled beside a black velvet cloth wrapped around a number of tools. Geometer's tools: a protractor and compass sized to hold chalk but made from a dull metal, tarnished black with age. A wooden box of chalks and paper-wrapped crayons. A pair of knives with double-edged blades and stained leather-wrapped handles. Dark blue ridged bottles with corks stoppered with wire and wax. A small wooden letter-writing box, with dried-up inkwells and wooden-handled pens with dipping nibs. And, wrapped in a deep blue velvet cloth with gilt-trimmed tassels, he happened upon something oddly close to spherical—unwrapped, it proved to be a yellow-brown human skull covered with a filigree of intricate graffiti that resembled the notation in the book. "Wow."

Is this some kind of joke? ran through his head, followed rapidly by *No, this isn't funny at all,* and *It'd be too much work*. Mum was too busy and pragmatic, and Dad was too, well, *Dad*, to concoct an enigma like this chest for his amusement. As for Evie, *maybe*, but the skull would totally gross her the ick out. It hinted at black magic, the stench of low-budget Hammer Horror movies on late night TV.

But it had belonged to Grandpa.

Imp carefully repacked everything except the topmost book, or journal, or whatever it was. This he carried downstairs to his bedroom, where he leafed through it for another hour before shelving it between a copy of *Peter and Wendy* (he was reading it for his GCSE practice assignment), and his sister's *The Fellowship of the Ring* (which he had tried to read because of the movie).

Jeremy forgot about the book for a couple days, but that Saturday Evie popped her head around his door and asked, "Have you seen my copy of *Fellowship*?"

"Uh, dunno . . ."

Sharp eyes caught his lie: "So what's this, then?" She stepped inside and her hand went to his bookshelf. "How *could* you forget?" He was still trying to think of an excuse when her fingers slipped sideways and embraced the knobbly black spine. "And what—" She pulled it out. "Hey, where did you get this?"

"I found it in a trunk in the attic. I was just playing," he said defensively.

"Never said you weren't." She opened the book to the fly-leaf. "Oh wow, weird, what was it doing there? Hey, does Mum know about this?"

"Wait!" he said frantically. "It was in Grandpa's box!" Mum was spending altogether too much time on church things these days. Magic books would not be safe in her hands.

"Oh." Evie sounded thoughtful. "So Dad must've . . ." She trailed off, seemingly having reached a decision. "I'm going to show him."

"No! It's mine!"

"It's Dad's," she told him firmly. "You shouldn't take what's not yours, Jerm, it's not right." She marched downstairs with Jeremy hot on her heels, grabbing for the book, which she held out of reach overhead—Evie was tall for a girl, and Imp hadn't hit his growth spurt yet—"*Daaad?*" she hollered.

And so Jerm's light-fingered bibliophiliac ways were brought to book, or at least to the attention of his father, who after a brief moment of alarm seemed minded to be forgiving—as long as Imp learned his lesson. "I was keeping the box until you were both older," said his father. "It's not safe to meddle with that stuff unless you know what you're doing. And you," he glanced at Evie, "thank you for showing me this, but it's not safe to handle. Apparently it likes you, but books like this are usually powered or protected by a ward—a kind of curse—and anyone who's not family will be very unhappy if they accidentally touch it." (This, Imp later learned, was a dark and terrible understatement. Cursed magical texts were nothing to fuck around with.)

"What does it do?" Imp demanded.

"What does . . . ?" Dad was briefly nonplussed: "It's *magic*, son."

"What, you mean like Harry Potter? Or like doing card tricks and pulling rabbits out of hats?"

Dad sighed, so lugubriously that Imp expected an eye roll: "No, stuff like *this*."

Nothing happened for a moment. "Like what?" Evie demanded.

"This," Dad repeated.

Then Evie, who was as level-headed and non-screamy as they came, screamed. And a moment later Imp joined her.

Wendy was skeptical at first, but once Imp explained his reasoning they set to work.

"According to the map we have to go out through a scullery door and cross twelve kilometers of Victorian London to where the manuscript is supposed to be, which is in *this* building. It's the private library of some kind of gentlemen's club, although why it's in Whitechapel is . . . I'm guessing it's where they keep their porn stash? There's a ley line *here* that replaces about nine and a half kilometers of surface streets with two kilometers of, uh—*fairyland*, it says—it runs from a graveyard to an old plague pit, so it's going to be pretty grody, but it's better than a three-hour hike. Hmm. If we find some old money we may be able to squeeze into a couple of hansom cabs, but I'm not sure how much the fare would cost. So let's not count on it: we're walking via the ghost roads."

Imp had taken courses on wardrobe and props in art school because they were as useful to his grand plan as acting and cinematography. Now his expertise with safety pins and fabric shears came in useful. They ended up cannibalizing three or four of the gowns Doc had retrieved to make just two costumes and neither would pass inspection in daylight. But they were bound for a bad part of 1880s London after dark, where the destitute wore rags and the merely poor wore every garment they owned lest they lose the lot if they couldn't find a crib for the night. Hair was the hardest part to disguise. Rebecca's bundled dreads and Wendy's dyke crop would stick out like sore thumbs. But Game Boy produced a battered wig and a pair of mob caps—servants' headgear— and they were good to go.

"You're sure this isn't all an elaborate joke?" Wendy asked Rebecca as they climbed the steps to the third floor. They walked behind Imp, who had his arm around Doc's shoulders as he spun an elaborate yarn about one of his other boyfriends. Game Boy huffed to keep up.

"You just wait, hon." Rebecca grinned at her, then stumbled: "Dammit!" Wendy caught her wrist. "Hem adjustment needed 'ere," Rebecca called up to Imp, "I just tripped: don't wanna break my neck on any stairs if I have to run."

"It's okay to take it up another couple of inches," Doc volunteered. "Working women didn't drag their skirts on the ground back then. Too much sewage in the gutters. That right, Imp?"

"Yes." Imp sounded slightly annoyed to have his exclusive grip on the exposition of social history challenged. "Okay, let's fix this."

They paused to adjust Rebecca's costume, then Game Boy opened the door to Neverland. "Whoa, how does that even fit in here?" asked Wendy.

"It doesn't." Rebecca took her arm and led her into the first passageway, pointing out features to either side. "Look! Bathroom. Bedroom. 'Nother bedroom. Kitchen—"

"Holy crap!"

"Welcome to my family abode," Imp said, ironically.

"You *do* realize you could crash the entire London property market if you opened this up to renters?" Wendy said when they got to the second passageway, home of G Plan furniture and poodle skirts. "Make a fortune on Airbnb."

"The phone signal is crap," Game Boy noted.

Wendy frowned at her mobile. "Shit, you're right. Why?"

"This corridor is stuck in the 1950s. It gets worse the deeper you go," Doc told her. They came to a square interior space with multiple doors on each side. "Which way now, Imp?"

Imp checked his treasure map. "Go left, then ahead two and down three steps to the landing on the right. This way."

Wendy side-eyed Del, who rolled her eyes and shrugged, then very deliberately produced a piece of green chalk. She scrawled an arrow on the wall next to the door they'd just exited. Then the ladies hastened to keep up with the gentlemen of the party, as they forged deeper into history.

The corridors led them inexorably back into the past. Modern styles of wallpaper and paint gave way to older designs that had faded with age. Light fittings held fewer bulbs, and mains sockets became scarce. The familiar rectangular three-pin sockets vanished, replaced by two or three round pins and cloth-wrapped cables trailing from hulking wooden radio-grams and lamps like flower vases wearing bonnets. The furniture became drab and heavily varnished, the woodwork all painted over. When they traversed a kitchen, the range had a coal scuttle. Descending a second flight of stairs and going up a third, they came to a corridor with unlit gas mantles. It was dark until Del produced a Zippo and lit one of the burners. To Wendy's surprise, the lamp shed a brilliant white light.

"The ceramic mantles glow when they get hot," Doc explained. "They're made of thorium oxide, so don't eat any—it's mildly radioactive. And we've gone far enough back in time that they burn town gas, which is mostly carbon monoxide. Never leave a gas lamp turned on and unlit unless you want to die in your sleep."

"Thanks, I'll remember that." Wendy flicked an imaginary lighter's flint, then grimaced as a shower of sparks landed on her knuckle. "Ouch," she mumbled.

They bypassed the library and skirted the drained swimming pool, descended a spiral staircase, then ignored a darkened lift shaft protected by a shuttered grille. Gas lamps became rare and they proceeded by the glow of their phone flashlights. They came to a long corridor lined with pillared arches that descended at an angle, then a claustrophobic rookery of cramped, drunken-angled bedrooms, many of them windowless, with peeling or no paint and rotting cots crammed in edge to edge. The stump of a burned-out candle sat atop an exposed beam. There was another room with bricks and broken planks piled in the corners, strung wall to wall with ropes for the destitute to lean on as they slept upright. Then there was a short ascent to a scullery and cold store, and a final stairwell.

Imp paused at the top for a brief confab with Doc. "Here."

He gave everyone a copy of the map and an old-fashioned box of matches. "If we get separated, you can try and find your own way back."

"What's this for?" asked Wendy, squinting at her matchbox.

"Begging is a crime under the Vagrancy Act. So is sleeping rough. But if you're offering something for sale—even a single match—that's not begging. Also," Doc gave Rebecca a significant look, "if they don't like your face they might try to bust you for soliciting. The match is an out."

Wendy glared at him: "I'd *never*—!" She stopped. "That's grossly unprofessional!"

"Dickensian, even." Imp's face was illuminated from below by his phone which lent it a skull-like visage, deep shadows making pools of his eye sockets. "Let's try not to split up, eh? But if we do, *follow the map* and keep moving. Once you get back to the side-door you're, uh, not *safe* exactly, but you really don't want to get lost on the other side." He licked his lips. "And remember, *this isn't real.* It's a version of the past, but the past was never stable. It can't be stable if time travel is possible. By visiting the past we change things, and it can only stabilize in a state when time travel never happens. Probably something bad happened that prevented this sort of thing, like the way magic mostly stopped working when—" Imp stopped, with a look on his face like he suddenly realized he'd said too much.

Doc took over again. From the moment they'd begun this trek he'd come out of his usual reticent haze to act as their self-appointed guide. "Victorian London was awful. I mean, it was an utterly *shit* place to live, unless you were one of the thousand families—the equivalent of a multimillionaire—"

"—So what's new? I mean old," Del snarked.

"No, really, I mean the air is full of acidic soot particles that condense into choking fogs so thick you can't see three meters past the end of your nose: *pea-soupers*, they called them. The streets are full of horse-crap and dogshit, there's no food hygiene, and a tenth of the population have or are incubating tuberculosis which eventually kills them. Every kind of disease runs rampant. Unaccompanied women are usually prostitutes, so if you get split up you can expect to be propositioned." He nodded at Wendy: she bared her teeth and produced a side-arm baton out of thin air. "Well, maybe not." He looked at Game Boy who stared back, glassy-eyed. "We think of Victorian London as a world capital, but really, it's as dirt-poor as the slums of Mumbai back home. Poorer, maybe. Rich is relative and we're all dressed well enough to be targets for muggers. Let's not go wandering off or splitting up, huh? In fact, let's buddy up: I'm going to keep track of you, Imp, and you, Del. Del, I want you to watch Wendy and Game Boy. Wendy, you can keep an eye on—"

"Let's go," Imp butted in as soon as Doc finished mother-henning them to death with stern injunctions about holding hands and wiping their noses and keeping track of one another. "Time's getting on." He marched to the staircase and started down it, the boards creaking ominously underfoot.

"Hey! I hadn't finished!" Doc squawked after him.

Game Boy looked up at Wendy. "Is this okay?" he asked slowly. "Because—"

"I'm in." Rebecca took Wendy's arm and leaned close. "This is totally wild, right?"

"One question!" Wendy shouted after Imp.

"Yeah?" His voice welled up from the depths of the stairwell like icy water in a cave underground.

"Just what year are we visiting?"

"Didn't I say? Silly me!" He tittered briefly. "We're going to party like it's 1888!"

WHITECHAPEL
NIGHTS

Imp's knowledge of London in the 1880s came from a vacation project Dad had inflicted on him one year around the time he was also studying magecraft. And his father's presentation came to him pre-tested on his elder sister, who had taken a keen interest in the social history of the period.

Eve had studied the map, questioned the wisdom of walking ley lines between plague pits, and googled the tariff of fares for a London hansom cab. It would be about five shillings for a two-person cab, each way.

A sane cabbie probably wouldn't enter Whitechapel at all, and she'd need to switch to a new one after six miles—the mandatory maximum distance for a cab ride, to rest the horses. But she'd paid more attention than Imp to their father's admonitions about the unwisdom of traversing the roads of the dead. Imp was bold, Imp was daring, Imp was (in someone else's frame of reference) reckless. Well, he *might* get to the library before her, but she had every intention of arriving alive, even at night in the year of Leather Apron.

It took no time at all to traverse the maze of corridors and staircases that lurked inside the top-floor closet. Presently Eve found herself facing an unremarkable exterior door. Someone had already come this way: the bolts were drawn back and the lock opened. Glancing around, she saw an arrow chalked on the wall beside the staircase. Good: her brother—or someone in his crew—wasn't completely daft.

"Ma'am?" the Gammon asked uncertainly.

"They came this way and so will we. Come on, there's no time to lose if we're to hail a cab."

They stepped out into night and mist, in an alleyway around the side of the town house. The sickly sweet stench of rotting compost and road apples hung over the damp-slicked flagstones, but it was well swept and clear of obstructions. "With me." She threaded her hand through her escort's elbow and pushed him along the alley. "This could be sticky if we're seen exiting," she murmured. "If we run into a constable—"

"Do you want me to . . . ?"

"No need for that: I'm a scullery maid and you're my beau, we're just stepping out for the evening." She paused just inside the shadowy mouth of the alley. The street outside was brightly illuminated after the darkness of the final maze of rooms in the dream house, and actinic gaslight shimmered in the misty air. At this end of the alley there was a sharp tang of sulfur and wood smoke. "It's not respectable, but a sixpence should suffice." The language of bribery was a universal tongue.

"Yes, ma'am." He glanced either way, then stepped out of the alleyway, adjusting his coat.

A second later Eve followed him. She took his arm again, leaning just inside his personal space: it was a very muscular arm, attached to an absolutely ripped body. *'Tis a pity he's a hunk*, she thought, briefly entertained. She could appreciate a good piece of male ass in the abstract, but she doubted he'd enjoy the kind of games she preferred. "Anyone about?" she murmured. "Left."

"No, ma'am." He turned left and they proceeded along the street. The fog swirled around them, dampening sound and shrouding the buildings to either side in mystery. "What am I looking for?"

"Hazards: drunks, muggers, constables. There may be some overlap. Avoid shooting if possible, it only attracts trouble. What we *want*—" She glanced both ways—"is a cab! Hail it quick!"

The hansom was already occupied and as it passed them she heard a titter of laughter from the passengers crammed on the bench seat, but now the Gammon knew what to look for. "It's tiny," he observed, sounding surprised. "More like a rickshaw than a taxi."

Eve felt a momentary flash of irritation, but let it go. She needed him around for now, and his culture shock was only to be expected. "Horses aren't magic carpets," she pointed out. "It's easier than walking."

"Yes—" He stuck his arm out for another cab, and this time the driver reined in his horse and touched his brim. His face was sallow and lined and the horse was alarmingly bony, but his hansom appeared to be in reasonable condition.

"Where to?"

"Leman Street," Eve announced, and recoiled at the very old-fashioned look the cabbie sent her.

"Oh aye?" He thought for a moment: "That'll be six shillings up front, right enough. And I'm not stoppin' fer anything."

"Six—" Eve suppressed the impulse to sneer at the man. "Very well. Help me up, Peter?"

The Gammon handed her up, then climbed in behind her while she counted out the coins. "Here," she said tartly.

"Let's just see . . ." The driver squinted at his palm. The

coins passed muster, for they disappeared immediately. He cracked his whip past the nag's shoulder. "Trot on!"

The hansom rattled through the streets of poshville— gated Mayfair, tidy Marylebone—before moving into the crowded theaterland between the British Museum and Covent Garden. The streets were busier here, and they got stuck a couple of times between logjams of cabs and throngs of tipsy revellers spilling into the streets. They continued east, the streets gradually becoming cramped and the buildings drabber (aside from a memorable stretch of ostentatious medievalism around St. Paul's Cathedral). They proceeded down Cheapside. The pavements were still crowded but the menfolk were increasingly ragged, and the few loitering women who were visible showed a considerable amount of skin. The still-noisome stench of the Thames merged with the miasma drifting from Spitalfields Market to the north. And now they were clopping and jingling through unlit streets where the foot traffic was fast and furtive, the drunk and homeless lay in the gutter, and occasional wails of pain or pleasure split the thickening fog.

"I'll take ye this far and no further," the cabbie told them, reining in his horse. "Just keep goin' another hundred yards or so, and may God have mercy on *your* soul," he added pointedly to the Gammon, who he evidently held to be a blameless victim of Eve's sinful scheming.

"Thank you very much," the Gammon told him, very formal and sincere. He scanned the street, then stepped down and offered Eve his hand. "If you'd care to come with me, my dear . . ."

Eve waited for the hansom to rattle away then took his arm. With her free hand she reached into her pocket for a bunch of glass marbles. She held them loosely in her cupped palm, but grasped them tightly with her mind's fist. "Next right," she said quietly. "We're entering bandit country. Look sharp."

An eerie howl split the night: perhaps a dog's dying agony or a woman in childbirth. Or maybe it was one of the johns who visited this part of town to slake his carnal appetites, appetites unacceptable in polite society but tolerated in the lawless warrens of London's underbelly.

They passed a pub. The door was crudely hammered together, lacking window panes. It hung ajar and as they passed Eve saw an interior scene lit by flickering candlelight that would have given Hieronymus Bosch nightmares. Bodies with legs outstretched on the bare floor, their backs propped up against the wall as they suckled on bottles of gin. The bar was a couple of planks propped atop damaged beer casks, the proprietor a brawny thug pouring pints into battered tin cups. In the refuse-littered alleyway outside a woman hitched her skirts up beneath a drunk, while an infant crawled in the slops by their ankles.

The Gammon's head was swiveling in all directions. "What are you thinking?" Eve demanded.

"I'm thinking I haven't seen anything this lively since that one time I was on close protection duty and my principal's girlfriend insisted on going clubbing in Pattaya right after the USS *Nimitz* came into port." He moved his right hand closer to his machine pistol. "It took four of us to get her to safety, and the master chief needed rabies shots." His shoulders tensed as footsteps approached. "Let me handle this, ma'am."

A shadowy figure emerged from the mist. "'Ello there," he said, touching a fine-gloved finger to his hat. "What 'ave we here?" The accent was fake (he dropped his h's inconsistently), his boots were finely polished, and his coat unpatched. "That's a fine bit of totty you've got there, sir! 'Ow much do you want for 'er?"

Eve froze her face to hold back her killing smile. The marbles in her left hand vibrated, growing warm with anticipation. But curiosity stilled her lethal impulse: How would her escort handle things?

"She's not for sale," the Gammon said tersely.

"Aw, say it's not so? I've got half a guinea to change your mind! You could go 'ome and enjoy yourself an' leave the business end to me."

Half a guinea? That's far *too much.* Eve twitched. Her marbles grew almost too hot to hold.

"No." The Gammon's head turned almost imperceptibly, checking to confirm that the importunate pimp wasn't the distraction in an ambush. "Go away."

"Nah, I *don't* fink that's gonna happen—"

He was wrong. Things happened extremely fast:

Eve's would-be purchaser brought his left hand out from behind his back and stabbed at the Gammon. He was holding a folding Parisian Apache gun—one-third revolver and one-third stiletto, with a knuckle-duster for a grip.

The Gammon stepped into the blow, embraced his assailant, and held him tightly against the anti-stab vest he wore under his waistcoat while he brought the muzzle of his UMP9 up under the pimp's chin.

Eve had other worries. She whirled and opened her left hand, huffing with effort as she flung her will at the marbles. There was no betraying bang of gunpowder and no whip-crack as they broke the sound barrier—she wasn't *that* strong—but a rippling hiss as the glass bullets drilled holes in the mist, and, almost simultaneously, thudded into flesh.

Eve was reaching for another handful of glass beads even as she heard a bubbling moan and a body falling; footsteps fading into the mist told her that their third assailant was out of the picture. She finished her pirouette, to see the Gammon had marched their attacker back against the wall and pinned his wrists to the crumbling brickwork.

"What part of *no* didn't you understand?" the Gammon asked mildly. The pimp gobbled incoherently. He sighed. "Never mind." He pulled the trigger and Eve winced at the bang. Contrary to movie folklore, suppressors didn't actually silence guns—they just rendered them less deafening. *At least he had the sense to select single-shot,* she thought. "We should get a move on," he commented as if nothing untoward had happened. His gaze tracked past her and came to rest on the other body in the alley. "Looks like you didn't need me after all." He sounded affronted.

"Nonsense, a lone woman on her own in a place like this would just attract more trouble." Eve kicked the Apache aside, then checked her bodyguard for damage. "Button your coat, he slashed your stabby to ribbons and I left my sewing kit a hundred and thirty years in the future." She took his arm. "Now let's be off before their friends come to steal their clothes."

The Gammon shook his head as they hurried deeper into the byways of Whitechapel. "Just as long as you pay for my rabies shots when we get home, ma'am."

They were halfway to Whitechapel when Doc started on the Ripper lore; to everyone's surprise it was Game Boy, not Wendy or Rebecca, who punched him first.

But before that happened they found their way onto the ghost roads.

The graveyard was tiny and ancient, tucked behind a church near Pembroke Square. Nobody had been buried in it since the eighteenth century. By their own time it had long since been redeveloped and turned into a commercial property let.

The mist swirled thick behind the lich-gate and the air tasted of muddy river silt, of things left buried and now long forgotten, so ancient that even the ghosts of the mourners' grandchildren had faded. Imp led them between headstones and family memorials to a grove of beech trees that clustered like stately pallbearers around a forbiddingly gated crypt. He checked his papers in the glow of a cheap penlight: "It's here but we need to spring the lock—" He frowned. "Shit. Can anybody pick—"

Wendy rolled her eyes. "Leave it to me." She crouched. "Torch." She held out her hand for his penlight, then shone it in the keyhole. "Hah." She touched the lock, and an age-blackened key shimmered into existence. It turned easily, then vanished as she pulled the gate open: dust to dust, ashes to ashes. "What now?"

"Eh, well." Imp looked abashed, as if he'd just been caught with his fly at half-mast. "Follow me? Oh, remember not to eat or drink anything you find in here or you won't be able to leave. And the natives aren't friendly."

Doc said, "Crosscheck your buddies?" Then he nudged Imp. "Is the eating or drinking thing for real?"

"I don't know, Dad might have been gaslighting me—I was only fourteen—but do you really want to find out? Are you feeling lucky?"

"Babes in the fucking woods," Wendy murmured disgustedly.

Rebecca looked at her sharply, then took her hand. "Stick with me, I can always find my way to wherever I'm going."

Wendy gently tugged her hand free. "Where we're going I might need both hands for fighting."

"Stop it stop it stop it!" Game Boy quietly shouted, his

voice breaking in a quiet shriek: "I can't stand this shit!" He darted ahead and ran down the steps leading into the crypt before anyone could stop him.

"Welp," said Doc, diving after him: and that was that.

Lit by smartphone flashlights, the crypt was a disappointment. Stone walls, stone floors, thick stone shelves fifty centimeters apart. Some of them bore crumbling wooden boxes, while others were covered in leaf mold and rat droppings. But as they moved deeper, the shelves disappeared, the walls narrowing to a stone tunnel that forced Doc and Imp to lower their heads. Then the tunnel roof disappeared, leaving lichen-crusted flagstones underfoot that formed the paving of a sunken lane surrounded by mossy hedge-topped banks that rose out of sight.

The lane was almost as dark as the tomb itself. Moonlight wasn't filtering this far down. It felt as ancient as the first stone-age settlements up the river on whose banks the Romans would later build the trading camp of Londinium. A couple of times Wendy thought she saw a faint flicker like swamp light; and her ears kept straining to catch a faint, malignant titter that seemed to hover just beneath the threshold of hearing, masked by the clatter of five pairs of boots beating on stone.

After thirty seconds or twenty minutes (it was hard to tell) Del complained: "This is creeping me out. Does anyone else feel like you're taking seven steps forward every time you lift your feet?"

"That's a feature, not a bug," said Imp. "We're on a ley line, remember?"

"Just stick close and we'll be fine," Wendy reassured her.

"Not necessarily." Doc sounded indecently smug about something.

"What makes you say that?"

"We're doing okay for *now*," he said, "but wait until we get to Whitechapel."

"Don't wanna know," said Game Boy. He sounded tense but Doc missed the warning signs and mansplained regardless:

"The year is 1888. Whitechapel hasn't been cleared yet: in fact, it's one of the last remaining rookeries, ancient slums that grew up after the great fire of 1666. Originally they were properly built houses but there were no planning regulations back then. Slumlords built in the backyards and gardens and added stories until the buildings were close to collapse, roofed over alleyways and turned it into an impenetrable maze. There were no police in the modern sense of the word until the 1820s—"

"—Until the twenty-ninth of September 1829, to be precise," Wendy interrupted.

Doc continued, oblivious: "So the rookeries were lawless and dangerous. By 1888 Whitechapel had survived mid-Victorian attempts to clean up and redevelop the other rookeries, and it was notorious for prostitution and drink. Also illegal gambling clubs and opium dens, but the prostitution was out in the open. About six percent of the women of late Victorian London worked as prostitutes—80,000 of them at any time—many of them in brothels, but a lot of streetwalkers, too, some as young as thirteen, the age of consent in those days. Which means—"

Rebecca cleared her throat. "Anyone tries to lay a hand on me, he's going to *suffer*," she announced.

"You'll get us all in trouble if you start a fight," Doc blundered on. "Just keep close and most of the low life will avoid us, is what I'm saying—if we look like a mixed group who know where we're going—"

"Crapsack London is crap, sucks to be female." Wendy put a warning edge in her voice. Game Boy's shoulders were as tense as clocksprings. "We got the message, wise guy."

"—But really, you don't want to wander off. Because it's 1888, and Jack's on the prowl—"

That was as far as he got when Game Boy spun round and punched him.

Game Boy wasn't aiming to hurt, but a fist in Doc's stomach when he wasn't expecting it shoved all the air out of his lungs and left him doubled over. "Stop it!" Game Boy shouted. He stopped dead, looking at Doc and Imp with wide eyes. "I can't stand this shit. I just want it to be over."

"What did I say?" Doc whimpered.

Imp took him by the shoulders and led him gently aside. "I think you just triggered the person who was forced to spend his first fourteen years as a girl." Imp glanced at the others, taking in Rebecca's furious scowl and Wendy's impassive face, which might as well have had *keep digging, son* tattooed on it. "Count yourself lucky Boy snapped first: Del and her friend aren't far behind."

"But what did I—"

"Listen." Imp leaned his forehead against Doc's and stared into his eyes. "*Everybody knows*, Doc. Everybody knows as much as they can stomach about Jack the Ripper, and they won't thank you for telling them anything they don't already know, because they don't *want* to know the stomach-churning details. They especially don't want to know the unvarnished truth. They know where we're going, son, and they're scared and angry and handling it really well. Now take a deep breath and apologize. And *you* stick close to *them*. Got it?"

Wendy and Del and Game Boy were pretending not to listen. Now Game Boy nodded at Imp, a silent *thank you*.

"Um. I'm sorry, people? I really didn't mean to—"

"It's all right." Wendy smiled at him too brightly, spun round raising her hands, and unleashed half a dozen arrows in as many heartbeats. Her bow howled, a gut-throbbing brown note that cried death: the arrows flickered and faded as they pierced the mist behind them.

Doc paled. "I'm *really* sorry," he wrung his hands.

"I doubt it, but that's okay," said Wendy. "Just don't do it again, or you really *will* be sorry." The bow vanished back to wherever it had come from.

The silence gathered thickly around them for a few seconds, broken only by a faint giggle like glass windchimes tinkling in the breeze.

"Did anybody else hear that?" asked Game Boy.

"Guys." Imp side-eyed the sunken road in either direction. "We shouldn't hang around here, it's not safe." He cleared his throat and gave Wendy a significant look. "Also, don't shoot unless you mean to kill? It pisses them off."

And all at once they were marching again, hurrying, almost running, really, desperate to get out from between the clutching embankments to either side; desperate to reach the end of the ghost road leading into a dream of London in the darkness.

The Bond made reasonable time.

The idea of being eaten by magical horrors with too many teeth for the crime of stepping on a ley line did not appeal to him, nor did the risk of running into Eve's minions. So he decided to make his own way, and outpace them in the bargain. He had certain advantages. For one thing he'd grown up in the rural Midwest before he enlisted, with horses and traps as well as tractors and crop sprayers. For another thing he knew London, and the layout of the main streets hadn't changed so very much between the nineteenth century and his own era. And finally, he was a solidly built gentleman wearing a small arsenal. Nobody rational would want to mess with him.

It was late evening when the Bond stepped out into the mist, and there weren't many people about. It took him almost half an hour to flag down a hansom cab. He had no coin, but he paid for the loan of the cab with the most valuable currency of all: he spared its owner's life. (A syringeful of flunitrazepam ensured the cabbie would spend the night comatose in the park.)

The cab-horse was in poor shape, but the Bond wasn't overly concerned so long as it didn't go lame before he reached his destination. Wearing the cabbie's cape and hat he blended in with the London traffic, and he drew the curtains closed around the passenger seat to obscure its lack of an occupant. He made good time until he reached White Church Lane where he abandoned the cab, hitching the horse to a railing outside an ostler's yard on the edge of the slum.

As a precaution he'd halted in the relative safety of Aldgate to review the treasure map. Now he stepped down from the cab, stretched his legs—he'd been sitting on the hard bench seat for three hours—and marched determinedly into the darkness and stink. He carefully avoided eye contact with the youths loitering on the street corners, the hookers sending come-hither looks from the sidewalk by an alley. There was a curious familiarity to the street life. Fashions and architecture aside, it could have been the wrong side of the tracks in half a dozen cities back home. The shape of the past left an eerie imprint on the present, and one slum was much like another.

The Bond made his way through the warren of crooked

alleyways and rubbish-strewn backyards. Nobody was rash enough to try and mug him. Beggars and whores were thin on the ground at this time of night. The few who were still working were plying their trade on better-travelled byways. He passed a few red-lit doorways, the classier ones guarded by toughs with stout sticks, and every street seemed to have a pub or two—identifiable by the drunks passed out in the gutter outside—before it gradually came to him that he'd lost locational awareness.

The narrow streets were twisty and unadorned by signage. In the mist it was hard to tell whether he'd passed three alleyways or four, or whether the last one had simply been the gaping maw of a derelict building. He could wander in this maze for hours, or until some enterprising shitlord assembled a gang of jackals to take down the disoriented lion. He frowned. It looked like he was going to have to recruit a native guide.

The cabbie whose ride he'd borrowed had carried a purse full of change. It was mostly copper, but there were some silver coins as well. The Bond didn't know much about the weird-ass money here—some strange shit to do with pennies and shillings, tarnished copper coins with a weird number of edges, he couldn't even figure how many groats made change for a tangerine let alone how many guineas there were in a florin—but a taxi fare was a taxi fare. If the cabbie had been out all day, then the purse was probably most of a day's takings, which gave him a handle on what four silver crowns, a few shillings and sixpenny bits, and a bunch of coppers translated to in terms of wages.

So the Bond stopped at the next pub he came to and went inside.

For a Whitechapel dive bar it was reasonably well lit and clean: a couple of soot-stained gas mantles were lit, there was sawdust on the floorboards, and there were stools for the drinkers to sit on and trestles for them to prop their pints and their heads on. It wasn't very busy, which struck the Bond as odd. The clientele was exclusively male, and apparently preoccupied with drinking themselves into oblivion.

The Bond approached the bar and produced a small silver coin, a sixpence. "I'm looking for—" he began.

The bartender slapped a tin mug full of villainously dark beer on the counter in front of him, grabbed the coin, and bit it. "Aye," he said, "that's good for two more, like. Unless ye be wanting change?"

"Keep it." The Bond raised the mug, took an injudicious swig, and choked it down: spitting might cause offense. It definitely tasted as if something had died in it. "I'm looking for a guide."

"Oh aye, out for a night on the tiles are we, sir?" The barman managed to sound disapproving, conspiratorial, and lascivious in the same sentence.

"Not exactly." The Bond gave him a hard stare. "I'm looking for a club that's around here, a gentleman's club called the Piers Gaveston Fellowship—they have a reading room—"

It wasn't clear exactly who moved first. The Bond was always alert, and unconscious reflexes set his arms in motion before the other guy did more than tense. He'd barely begun to raise the cosh from under the bar when the Bond grabbed his wrist with his left hand, and twisted. The barman cursed as he dropped the stick, then whimpered faintly as he saw what the Bond held in his other hand.

"How about we calm down?" said the Bond, smiling: "You wouldn't want my finger to slip, would you?"

The bartender stared down the muzzle of the Glock 18 and swallowed. "We din't want none of that kind in 'ere," he said. "No trouble, like." He swallowed again. "Folks is just jumpy."

"I didn't say I was a member of the club," said the Bond, smiling fixedly: "I just want somebody to show me where it is."

"Eh, let's not be hasty, like? I can mebbe find you someone, for some ready? Don't want no trouble 'ere." His gaze drifted sideways. The Bond sidestepped abruptly and allowed the would-be white knight to see the pistol. Inebriated courage gave way to sudden sobriety. "Alf," implored the barman, "Alf! Don't—" Alf was already backing away, his hands raised and a rictus of fear on his face.

"'E's the Ripper," Alf moaned, "'e's Leather Apron 'isself come to butcher us all!"

The Bond's smile froze over. "Don't be stupid, the Ripper doesn't shoot people." He raised his pistol and thumbed the selector to single-shot. "Go stand by the bar."

"*Noooo*—" The other denizens of the bar were either slithering towards the door or sitting very still in whatever shadows they could find.

If vinegar doesn't work, try honey . . . "Who wants to earn a silver crown?" asked the Bond. A shiny coin appeared between the fingers of his left hand.

"'E wants someone to take 'im to the molly-lord's club 'ouse!"

One of the lowlifes struggled to his feet. "I kin do't," he slurred. At first the Bond thought he was drunk, but then he noticed one side of his face sagging, the same side as his limp.

"A crown when you get me there," the Bond promised. Expression hardening, he added, "Don't even think about crossing me."

"Ned would never," began the barkeep, then thought better of it.

"Gissa sixpence now?" whined Ned. He clutched a cloth cap so ingrained with dirt that its brim was shiny.

"A crown when we get there," repeated the Bond. He

made the pistol vanish, but allowed Ned and the bartender a glimpse of his tactical webbing and holsters. "Let's go."

Ned picked up his tin cup and chugged it frantically, dribbling when he put it back down. "Foller me," he said, burping as he shuffled towards the door.

The Bond followed, keeping the bartender in view until he was out the door. It wasn't until he was alone in the mist with the shuffling Ned that it occurred to him to wonder just what the Piers Gaveston Fellowship had done to render themselves so peculiarly unpopular.

Alexei had a problem: none of their phones were working properly.

"Come on," he muttered, hitting the button to bring up the secure connection to Andrei back at Head Office for the umpteenth time. His phone flashed a loading animation at him, then crashed back to the home screen with a strangled squawk and a message about a connection timeout. "Who made this fucking junk!"

They'd gotten up to the top floor with no sign of company, found the odd door where no door should be that the map indicated was the start of their route. Vassily and Igor had thrown the windows wide open at front and back, and after Alexei's KO gas detector had shown a solid green LED for three minutes they'd taken off their respirator masks. The targets were clearly somewhere ahead, so Alexei made an executive decision to pursue.

But by the time they'd gone along one corridor, then through an odd windowless hallway, along another passage, and down some stairs to a library, Alexei was seriously done with this Escher architecture shit. And the loss of signal was no joke.

"Can anyone get any signal in here? Because my phone's fucked," he announced.

"Sorry, boss . . ." Boris shook his head. "No signal here either."

"*Anyone* with signal?" No hands went up. "Well fuck." Alexei pocketed his phone and took stock. "Close up." He noted the chalk marks scrawled by the door they'd come through. "We're on their trail. Yevgeny, Igor, take point. Boris, eyes on our six. Everyone on the map? Everybody clear we're on node seven—any disagrees? No, good, let's move out."

They flitted through the confusing maze of corridors and stairs like ghosts, touching nothing and making as little noise as possible. They were hampered slightly by the need to check every room they passed for ambushes, to seek the most minute clues that the man they pursued might have left as to his path. But they went fast and hard, for they'd trained since their earliest time as teenage conscripts in how to storm occupied buildings and leave the silence of a graveyard behind them. However they were a team, and so they were slower than one reckless assassin intent on getting to his destination ahead of a concerned executive assistant and her bodyguard: who in turn was trying to outpace a clown-car raid team of junior supervillains led by a theatrical impresario. By the time they came to the outside door leading to the misty streets of another version of old London town, the moon had set. Their quarry was already half a city ahead of them. And the tinkle of glockenspiel mirth stalking them grew ever-louder in the mist.

Even though she was still soft and untempered in those days, Eve wasn't a screamer. Nor was Imp. But when Dad spread his arms wide and took on the physiognomy of a mummified corpse with blazing blue orbs of fire in his eye sockets, both his children were ever-so-slightly freaked out.

"Magic," Dad explained, "is real. And if you don't know what you're doing it will kill you, just like grabbing a live high-tension cable." He sounded so matter-of-fact, standing there in his chinos and polo shirt as the green wormy threads writhed hypnotically in his eye sockets. "In case you were wondering this is an illusion, but a practical one: it's a preconstruction of what I'll look like in two hundred years' time." The litchfather rubbed his bony hands as if they were cold. "Dead, in other words. Like you'd be if you tried to handle the family spell book and weren't of the blood descended, so that the ward recognized you. This is your first lesson: don't touch the book, or let anyone else touch it, unless I'm present. And especially don't try to use it until I've taught you how to do so without turning yourself into this—" he pointed at his gaping mandible—"in the here-and-now. Because there are no comebacks from death."

He made a strange gesture with his left hand then beamed at them as if he'd just accomplished a fine party trick, entirely himself again.

"That includes your mother," he added. "She has—had— her own kind of magic, but it isn't ours."

So that was how magecraft came into Imp's life: Sunday morning sessions with Dad and Evie while Mum went to church (for the social, she said at first).

Magic, it turned out, was complicated, and involved quite a lot of equations in something like a cross between Boolean algebra and Aramaic graffiti. There was more than one way of doing magic, and more than one kind of effect it could produce, but their family was best at one particular speciality—oneiromancy, with a sideline in chronomancy. (Other stuff like mind control, telekinesis, and setting Marjorie Blake's hair on fire when she had her big brother's gang beat up Imp for trying to grope her in year four,[1] were far less reliable.)

Oneiromancy was the magic of dreams, which according to Dad weren't just the brain's glial system flushing out crap and resetting itself while fixing memories of the previous day. They were fragmentary ghost memories of other versions of reality, other timelines that had diverged from the one the dreamer inhabited. Dad taught them how to assemble a memory palace to store their dreams, and later to use it as an aide-mémoire for spells—the algorithms that produced effects in the dream palace. He taught them the dangers of attracting mindless feeders and mindful malevolent demons, how never to conduct even a minor working without first constructing a safety grid to hold hostile entities at bay, to always wear a ward (a compact defensive charm) in case of occult attack. He taught them about ley lines and ghost roads and the affinity of anonymous spaces for one another—closures, he called them—how you could use hotel passageways as a shortcut to buildings on the other side of the world, if you could avoid being eaten by the things that lurked in the emptiness behind the walls of the world. He taught them that history was formed from the collapse of a tottering Jenga-pile of paradoxes that edited each other into a neutral, anodyne paste of nobody assassinating their own

1 Lessons were Learned, the hard way, by everyone. In Imp's case the lessons were: (a) don't be a groper, and (b) burning hair smells *terrible*. Also (c) don't whine to your big sister, lest she punish you harshly before forcing you to apologize to your victim.

grandparents because time travel was never quite discovered in time for them—

Meanwhile, Imp's regular schoolwork suffered, even though his memorization techniques and his facility with maths were amazing. He had the most peculiar lucid dreams: his school had an art department and still taught the subject to GCSE and AS level, but he was asked to drop it. (One of his teachers took a funny turn after inviting Imp's class to try their hand at drawing something based on M.C. Escher's tessellations: she was still signed off sick at the end of term.) This, paradoxically, pushed Imp towards other, related subjects. His ability to memorize his lines for a school theatrical production was prodigious, his performance at English was good, and he was outstanding in mathematics. But he seemed uninterested in IT skills and business studies (to Mum's despair) and goofed off in science class.

As for Evie, she was studying hard for her A-levels with next year's university selection round in mind. Dad wanted her to study Accountancy; Mum leaned towards Law. In the event, she split the difference, getting into a former redbrick university to dutifully study Business and Economics, her ticket to the paperwork entitling her to get into job interviews.

There were special lessons, taught one-on-one by Dad, as they grew older. Dad would sometimes take Evie out for an afternoon or evening of what he called *special training*: it was all very mysterious and Evie refused to tell Imp about it, beyond a terse "When you're older." It had to be carried out at an undisclosed location that was difficult to get into. In his imagination, Imp built up a college of mages who ran open day sessions for amateur sorcerers, or maybe a crypt in a graveyard that had to be broken into after dark. Dad didn't help by dropping occasional hints about Grandpa and his ancestors—the all-important bloodline—and the old family home. Apparently six (or more) generations of oneiromancers had lived in the big house and used it as their occult laboratory, trafficking with the inhabitants of dreams and building new imaginary rooms whenever they added a new spell to their growing inventory. When they'd been forced to sell the manse to cover death duties, they'd lost a lot of mysterious-but-unspecified stuff. Hence the memory palace. If it was encoded in your head, it would take more than a house fire or bankruptcy proceedings to take it away from you—nothing short of a death in the family could cost you knowledge.

So things continued until Imp was eighteen. Evie had graduated the year before and was working as a management trainee at a large financial consultancy, hoping to get onto their promotion fast-track. (Evie was, as usual, eager to please.) Meanwhile, Imp was . . . not *off course*, exactly, but the course he'd chosen did not meet with his parents' full approval. Imp was applying to art schools with the goal of pursuing a career in media production. Mum and Dad weren't exactly *opposed* to it, but they didn't understand what it involved, or how it could possibly work. He could quote figures about the creative sector's financial output and the demand for video editing professionals and scriptwriting opportunities in the gaming industry until he turned blue in the face, but they still didn't understand why he couldn't try for law school, then take the Bar Vocational Course and get pupillage. He was a bird trying to explain air to fish, a fox cub raised among wolves.

And that's how things stood until the catastrophic Sunday when Imp learned about the family curse.

"This isn't like *Assassin's Creed Syndicate at all*," complained Game Boy.

"Yeah, because your PlayStation games stink like raw sewage," Wendy snarked. They paused at the darkened maw of an unlit street where buildings clumped like rotting teeth in the mouth of a blind drunk. "Where *is* everybody?"

"Don't know." Del turned in place, checking the tunnel they'd just exited. It looked as if it had once been a night soil alley, and backing onto it were the privies of actual houses with yards. Now it was almost roofed-over in places, the sky blocked out by overhanging rickety balconies to either side, and it was awash with ankle-deep filth so vile it stunned the nose like a fist to the face. Something twitched and scuttled close to one wall, half-submerged in ordure: a rat, perhaps, or the world's biggest cockroach. "Staying out of this crap, I'm guessing."

"No, I mean—" Wendy gestured past Imp and Doc, who were poking around a doorway further down the alley, possibly because it was all they could see by the light of Doc's flashlight—"isn't this place supposed to be densely populated? Sleeping twenty to a room, stacked up like timber?" Mist swirled just beyond the reach of Doc's light, deadening all sound but a steady *plop plop plop* of filth dripping onto bricks streaked white with saltpeter.

"It's nothing but a dream," Imp said loudly.

"But the kind of dream that kills," Doc cautioned. "Don't ever lose sight of that."

"A *dream*?" Game Boy was outraged.

"It was my family's speciality," Imp said defensively. "Oneiromancers, able to enter the past through dreams. Or maybe dreams of the past—of other pasts that never happened, or that happened and got trampled over by time travellers."

"The fuck are we doing here, then?" demanded Del. "What's it a dream *of*?"

"It's a dream of the version of 1888 where the book we're looking for was misfiled and lost, rather than our 1888, where the book went back into a closed library collection and got bombed to fuck during the Blitz. And maybe if we find the book and take it home with us this stops being a dream, and the version of history where the book was correctly-filed-and-then-bombed, *that* turns into the dream."

"Fucking time travel," complained Doc. "Makes my head hurt."

"But the people—" Wendy repeated.

"It's a dream. Dreams attract resonant stuff that doesn't happen in the real world." Doc coughed significantly. "The lasses who'd be working are hiding or sticking to well-lit streets, this is poor pickings for beggars, everybody's abed, and the police are looking to protect the money, not the likes of people who live here. So we're anomalous—"

"Hey, everybody," Game Boy broke in, "what's this?" He'd found the one door in the alley that wasn't stove-in or hanging drunkenly askew. Now he stood in front of it, peering at a chiselled engraving in a stone plate to one side. "What's that name again, Purse Galveston something?"

"We're looking for the reading room of the Piers Gaveston Fellowship," Imp announced. "Named after King Edward II's catamite. There was a notorious Oxford drinking club in the eighties—nineteen eighties, that is—who took his name. They were basically an upper-class BDSM orgy club. This bunch is somewhat older." He did a double-take. "Hey, is this—"

"Yep." Game Boy looked smug until he clocked the lack of a doorknob. Indeed, the door was most formidably shut, a barrier of blackened oak studded with iron rivet-heads, with only a keyhole by way of an entry point. A very *old*-looking keyhole, clearly not fronting for a modern cylinder lock or anything easy to extract or pick. "How do we get in?"

"We knock," Wendy said. She flexed her hand and a baton appeared: "Open up in the name of the law!" she called as she pounded on the door.

"Uh, honey—" Del caught her eye, shook her head, looking amused—"when did they first take women in the filth, anyway?"

Wendy swore, then glanced back down the route they'd come. Nobody stirred in the mist, but: *Whitechapel*. The police had swarmed the area after the bodies began to turn up, conducting house-to-house searches and interviewing hundreds of suspects. There'd been vigilantes, the Whitechapel Vigilance Committee, harassing strangers and stalking butchers, surgeons, and anyone else with cause to carry sharp knives for work. "Dammit," she muttered, "criminal damage it is, then."

Wendy made her baton disappear. In its place, a steel battering ram coagulated out of the mist. It was heavy, and an ice-cold sweat broke out on her forehead as she pulled it into existence. Wendy's power of illusion had its limits. Her pulse hammered and a chittering sounded in her ears, like a million hungry mandibles chewing at the edge of her sanity. "He-help me," she tried to say, sagging under the weight of the steel cylinder.

Del grabbed two of the handles. "I've got it," she said. "Together?" Wendy nodded wordlessly, concentrating on staying conscious and lining the head of the cylinder up on the unseen lock behind the keyhole. "Okay, in three, two, one . . ."

CRASH.

The impact jarred all the way up to Wendy's shoulders. Del voiced a muffled grunt of pain. "Shit!" The door held, although it had buckled around the keyhole. "What the hell?"

"Try again," Wendy gasped. "I can't hold it together much longer."

"Let me guide it?" Game Boy stepped in close and laid his hands over Wendy's wrists. "Now—"

CRASH. Something gave way and with a shriek of tearing metal the door swung inwards, away from the strike plate. The lock mechanism clattered to the tiled floor within. "Hey, what if there's someone in—"

"Allow me?" Imp stepped across the threshold, grinning as he pushed his shirt cuffs back. "Some light would help—no, I really don't think there's anybody home."

Wendy let go of the battering ram and it vanished instantly. The pressure on her skull subsided more slowly. "Breaking, and now *entering*." She steeled herself for the inevitable sense of wrongdoing as she followed Imp into the entrance hall. "Is anybody home?" she called, feeling slightly fatuous after the tumult of smashing in the front door.

Game Boy followed her. "I hope we're in time—" he began, just as Imp turned his flashlight up to full brightness and lit up the roof—"Oh *shit*."

Eve was fretful because an unpleasant sense of déjà vu had stolen up on her as she realized what she was doing: once again pursuing a male family member through empty night-time streets towards an illicit destination, hoping she'd be in time to save him from the consequences of actions she'd unwittingly set in motion.

"It *should* be here," she muttered grimly, checking the map for the umpteenth time. Under her breath: "Dammit, Jeremy!"

The alleyways and yards of Whitechapel grew danker and more noisome the further away from the main roads they went. Eve hadn't seen any open doors and red-shaded lamps for a while, nor constables or costermongers; not even tattered match-selling beggar children. If she had to guess the time she'd have said it was past midnight. While the fog still swirled, a chilly drizzle had begun to fall.

"Any ideas, ma'am?" Even the Gammon, Franke, was showing signs of unease.

"We're looking for an alleyway off Dutfield's Yard by Berner Street, not far from Whitechapel Road—" Eve stopped, realizing she was talking to herself, a habit she despised in others. "Unmarked sturdy door faced with rivets and a sign saying Piers Gaveston Fellow—"

"Like this one?" The Gammon froze, then stepped warily aside. He brushed back his coat and reached for his UMP9.

"Bingo." Eve's shoulders heaved as she saw what he'd found. A door that stood ajar, blackened timbers punched in around the lock. "Dammit, we're late."

"Ma'am, if you're going in I suggest—"

Eve levitated a fistful of glass marbles and smiled at him. He shut his mouth with an audible click. "Stand guard. Nobody enters. Clear?"

"Yes, ma'am." She crossed the threshold, feeling a prickly chill run up her spine as her sight dimmed for an instant. "I'll cover the approaches from inside."

"You do that." She entered the hallway, then paused to listen. There were doors inset with panes of glass at the end of the hall, but there was also a staircase spiraling up into the gloom. *Offices*, she thought. *Where are the offices? Up or down?*

She pushed through the darkened door, then pulled out her flashlight. Parquet floor, a wood-panelled wall with a transom and inset window, more doors. One of them stood ajar, affording a glimpse of white tiles and a familiar whiff of bleach. There was a gilt title above the small window: RE-TURNS. An itchy sense of unease told her that either there was no librarian on duty, or if there was, she really didn't want to meet him.

Upstairs, she decided. She darted back to the staircase. "Going up," she quietly called to the Gammon. He didn't stir from his position behind the door, submachine gun held ready and eyes vigilantly focussed on the alleyway.

Dammit, Imp. She skidded on the landing halfway up—her boots filthy, probably ruined by the icy muck splashed halfway up her ankles—then caught herself on the banister rail, a knobbly yellowed ivory thing that reminded her of the artistic style of H.R. Giger. Finally she reached the top step and paused, reconsidering. *If it's Imp's gang we're good, but if it's somebody else*—a handful of marbles lacked a certain something in the deterrence department, however lethal they might actually be. She slowed, wishing she'd taken the Apache gun or borrowed the Gammon's spare pistol. Not that she needed a firearm if she wanted to poke holes in people: but folks tended to stop and listen when you pointed a gun at them. And right now Eve was all about making people stop and listen, rather than performing highly inadvisable summoning rituals in a liminal space haunted by the ghost of Leather Apron.

The landing at the top of the stairs had smaller doors to either side, but directly ahead of her a big pair of double doors with glass windows promised something more. A dim radiance flickered behind them. She switched off her flashlight, then approached, lurking in the darkness, listening.

"—*Hell* designed this place? It's creeping me—" A woman's voice.

"Naah, it's just ossuary kitsch." Eve took a deep breath of relief: the speaker was Imp. He continued, "If you want to see the real thing, you need to visit the Sedlec Ossuary in the Czech Republic: it's got a *great* website. I reckon these are just plaster replicas, there's no way you could get your hands on that many skeletons in London without somebody noticing—"

What? Eve blinked. She glanced up at the shadowy lintel above the door, at the chandelier dangling from the shadows above the stairwell. Emboldened by knowing it was her brother's crew on the other side of the door, she flicked her flashlight at it. No, it wasn't an H.R. Giger homage, not in the late nineteenth century: the graceful chandelier was festooned with chains of human vertebrae, lamp-holders set in bouquets of skulls, braced by arms of . . . well, arms. Eve switched the flashlight off. *Creepy but not dangerous*, she decided, and pushed the double doors open.

"Imp?" she called: "It's me! We need to talk."

The library was made of bones.

Imp cringed as he looked up at the room's vaulted ceiling, arching two stories above his head. Cornices and ornamental moldings of femurs and skulls; roof beams exposed like the rib cage of a dead giant, chandeliers of . . . bones, more bones, bones atop bones, everywhere *bones*.

The wooden bookcases seemed to be safe at first glance—once living, now dead, bone becomes brittle and ceases to be a decent structural material—but they were fretted with a veneer of sliced fingerbones and surmounted by a display of maxillaries and mandibles. And the closer he got to them, the more realistic they looked.

"Guys, I don't think these are fakes." Doc's whisper was a loud library-hushed voice. "What *is* this place?"

"A club library." Imp scuffed his shoe on the black-and-white tiled floor, leaving a dark trail. "Shit." He looked around, counting bookcases. "We must be looking at two or three hundred shelf-meters of books on this level alone." There was a narrow walkway around the waist of the room, reached by a cast-iron spiral staircase in each corner of the library. It provided access to the higher shelves, for the room was walled in books to a height of perhaps five meters. Above the uppermost shelf a row of oval windows like so many eye sockets kept vigil over the outside world.

Doc was already poking at one of the shelves. He pulled out a leatherbound volume and opened it. "Hey. Engravings? Engravings of—" He did a double-take. "Interesting, I didn't know it was legal to print this kind of stuff back then."

"What kind of—" Game Boy crowded him—"porn? Hey, it's hot man-on-man love." He looked worried. "I think."

"What was this place again?" Wendy asked.

"If I had to guess, going by the books I'd say it's the private collection of a rich dude sex club." Imp peered at the nearest bookcase, then slid a slim volume out. "Mm, Catullus, but not as we know him. *Heh.* I mean, the Victorians were really uptight in public about morality, but *in private*—"

"The bones," Game Boy reminded him.

Imp shrugged. "Death and sex, two big taboos that taste great together."

Game Boy winced.

"So this is club dead sex." Del sounded annoyed. "You want me to search all this necroporn, bro? What's the title of the book, anyway?"

"It, uh, doesn't have a title," Imp admitted. "It's something with the catchy title of AW-312.4 which may or may not be a handwritten concordance of the true *Necronomicon*, and it was produced by an Archbishop Rodriguez, about whom surprisingly little is known. There might or might not be a Vatican Index Librorum Prohibitorum stamp on the flyleaf. And it's rumored to be bound in the archbishop's skin so it's going to look a bit weird—oh, and don't, *really don't*, try to read it—"

He stopped. Del was backed up all the way against a bookcase, staring at him wide-eyed. "What?" he asked: "Did you think Eve would pay us a quarter of a million to retrieve it if it was just a simple matter of waltzing in and picking a book off the shelf?"

"No, but—"

"Imp?" He startled, then spun round and aimed his flashlight at the doorway. "It's me! We need to talk."

Caught square in the beam, his sister raised one hand to shield her eyes.

"Who's—" Wendy raised her bow and arrow and began to draw—"this—" as Eve raised her other hand and began to open it, a palmful of glass spheres catching the light—

"Stand down, everybody chill! This is my sister, the one who's paying us! Eve, what the fuck?" Imp's heart tried to climb out through his throat.

"You haven't taken the book yet?" Eve demanded anxiously.

"No, we only just got here—"

"Great! I mean stop, wait. The book—"

"It's cursed, isn't it?" Imp guessed.

Eve nodded vigorously. "Yes! But that's not why I'm here. When I told you there wasn't any chance of pursuit I think I spoke too soon." She turned round. "This place—I wasn't expecting the decor, I must say—I came to say you can expect unfriendly company if you hang around too long. And there's a problem with the curse on the book, too."

"Unfriendly company." Game Boy stepped out of the shadows and walked up to Eve. His attempt at an intimidating approach foundered on the fact that she was taller than he. "What kind of unfriendly? Like those nutters from the bank? Or is it some other kind of asshole?"

"My boss likes to big himself up in front of his friends. The snatch squad at the bank is just one possibility—they're dead, but there are worse people out there. I brought a bodyguard—he's covering the front door—but we don't have much time." She looked at Rebecca. "You can find things, right? Can you locate it, *please*? Don't touch it—just go to wherever it is on the shelves and point to it?"

"I'm not a fucking dowsing rod," Del grumbled. "Say I can find it. What then? You're just going to take it and not pay us for our work?"

Eve shook her head. "No! It's not like that. I *can't* take it. It's protected by an anti-theft ward—if you try to steal it, it kills you."

"Well that's just *peachy*." Game Boy pouted. "You were going to tell us about this when?"

"Oh, it's perfectly safe to handle if somebody else has triggered the curse and you took it from their still-smoking body." Eve paused. "Or if they sold it to you."

"You bought it, didn't you?" Imp walked towards her. "*Didn't* you?"

"I *think* so. I may have screwed up that side of things," Eve admitted. "It's unclear."

"What's unclear?"

"It was up for auction: obvs, right? But it's not clear that the person auctioning the location of the manuscript actually owned what they were selling, that's the thing. Also, ancient death spells and intellectual property law don't always play nice together. I, uh, my boss has a standard procedure he has me follow in cases of handling blackmail and extortion. We pay the ransom, then once we've destroyed the threat I repossess the payment from the blackmailer's bank account. Via a Transnistrian mafiya underwriter—"

This time it was Wendy who interrupted: "The Russian mafiya has *underwriters*?"

"*Transnistrian*, please, and yes, criminal business models are inherently expensive because they have to pay for their own guard labor—there are no tax overheads, but no police protection for carrying out business, either—so of course they evolved parallel structures for risk management, mostly by embedding the risk in a concrete slab and dumping it in the harbor—anyway. At what stage does the book consider itself to have been legitimately acquired? And by whom? Is it safe for you to handle it, as my employee? What about as an independent freelance contractor not subject to the HMRC IR35 regulations? Am I an acceptable proxy for Bigge Enterprises, a Scottish Limited Liability Partnership domiciled in the Channel Islands, in the view of a particularly dim-witted nineteenth-century death spell attached to a codex bound in human skin by a mad inquisitor? It's like digital rights management magic, only worse."

She took a deep breath and turned to Imp: "Anyway, it's *probably* safe for either of us to take it off the shelf and look at it, as long as we don't try to read past the flyleaf or remove it from the library. We've got a degree of immunity to cursed spell books, at least the ordinary kind. But if we try to make a withdrawal—bang."

"Huh." Del strolled over to the far wall and ran her fingertip along a shelf. "Prove it." She half-turned and smiled proudly at Eve, baring her teeth.

"Crap," Eve muttered under her breath. "That's it? That's the lost concordance?"

Rebecca's fingertip rested on a dusty shelf of bone, almost touching the cracked spine of a volume bound in a stiff, almost golden-hued leather quite at odds with the volumes to either side of it (which had the boring uniformity of a bound run of law gazettes or dirty magazines). "I think this is it. Mind you, it could be a compilation of tax records from the Duchy of Cornwall in 1688—how would I know? I'm not taking it."

"Sis—" Imp took her shoulder—"you don't have to. It's your boss's problem, isn't it? If there's some risk it's going to do that . . . don't do it if you don't have to, is what I'm saying?"

"Oh, but I *do* have to. Because how else do you think I'm going to get back at the bastard?"

She grinned like a skull as she reached for the book, and for a moment of frozen panic Imp sensed that the book grinned back.

CHARNEL LIBRARY

The last normal day of Eve's life began much like any other Sunday: she slept in an hour later than on a regular workday, then travelled by tube and overground to her parents' house.

After graduation she had moved in with her then-boyfriend for a few months, but they'd split up under the pressure of sixty-hour work weeks and sharing a bedsit-sized flat while in their first training-wheels relationship. (Also, their sex life had been lacking a certain something—which she only discovered later.) She'd moved out again, into a room in an HMO shared with three other millennial girls all straining for a grip on the bottom rung of corporate serfdom: a baby solicitor, a freshly minted hospital doctor who only ever came home to snore, and a junior marketing manager. Still, it was better than going back to her old bedroom in the wilderness beyond Heathrow, even though her digs were just as far from the office and cost her a thousand a month more than her parents' spare bedroom.

By turning up around noon, Evie ensured that Mum would already be out. Her church-going had gone from mildly serious to moderately alarming over the past five years, as she drifted from a wooly mainstream C of E congregation towards a hardcore evangelical import from the USA. If Evie turned up too early Mum would try to get her to come along. She hated to say no, but something about the eight-hour-long audience participation services with the meals and the singing and the readings from their weird apocrypha—*The Apocalypse of St. Enoch the Divine*?—resonated in all the wrong ways with her magic. She'd been to one service and sneaked out halfway through after throwing up in the ladies'—just the memory of it left her distinctly nauseous.

The combination of religious faith and actual ritual power made Evie deeply uneasy. It was as bad as if her mum was a habitual drunk-driver, so she reacted by pretending to herself that it wasn't happening. And the easiest way to make that work was to avoid any reminder of it.

That lunchtime she found Dad in his den (really a windowless closet off the side of the living room, which he'd fitted out with shelves, a comfy chair, and a fold-down desk bolted to the wall), wearing his threadbare sorcerer's robe over jogging pants and a gray sweatshirt with a coffee stain on the front. "Hey, Daddy." She leaned forward to kiss his bald spot. "How's life treating you?"

Her father sighed uneasily then smiled for her. He picked up the leatherbound journal he'd been writing in and closed it then stood up, a trifle creakily. "I'll make tea," he said. With his back turned, he added, "I'm worried about your mother."

Oh crap. Evie dutifully tensed up, even though—she hated to admit this even in the privacy of her own head—Mum was increasingly alien to her these days, her eyes coming alive with enthusiasm only when she tried to overshare her faith with someone who made the mistake of asking how she was. Evie followed Dad out to the kitchen. "Is it her church habit again?"

Dad shoved the jug kettle under the tap and filled it. White noise washed out conversation for a few moments. He closed the lid, placed it back on its base, and turned it on in silence, lost in thought as he prepared the teapot and measured out the correct quantity of his precious breakfast tea leaves. It was a calming ritual he carried out every day, for as long as she could remember. Now his hands were shaking. "It's cancer," he finally said. "Cancer *and* church. One or the other I think I could handle."

Evie felt a momentary sense of unreality, the instant in which, stepping off a curb, one sees the oncoming dump truck: the instant in which one is committed to that fatal footfall, toes caught in mid-stride and unable to avoid the disaster, but aware of rushing towards one. "What kind of cancer?" she heard her voice ask.

The kettle came to a rolling boil and switched off. Dad filled the teapot before continuing. "Bowel cancer," he said, calmly enough. "She was too embarrassed to talk about the spotting. Her GP noticed something wrong during her health MoT and referred her for screening."

"Oh crap—sorry." Dad normally didn't like it when his little girl swore, but either he didn't notice or he chose to ignore it this once.

"Her pastor told her to ignore the doctors and trust in the Lord," Dad added, as calmly as if he were discussing the weather. "She doesn't like the idea of chemo, Evie. I've had enough of this church. I intend to take them down. Will you help?"

And there it was, the moment of impact, and she found herself nodding and going along. "Sure. Which one are they, anyway? I mean, is she still with the Promise, uh, the—"

"The Golden Promise *Ministries*, yes. Bunch of gold-digging prosperity gospel charlatans." Dad's tone was even, but there was a quietly venomous undernote to his voice that his daughter could barely recognize. "Evie, I'm not going to let my wife die just to line the pockets of a high-rolling American preacher in a ten-thousand-pound suit. She was sane before he got his claws into her. She'll thank us once she's back in her right mind and the cancer's in remission."

Evie's tongue froze to the roof of her mouth. "She won't consent," she said carefully. "Have you got medical power of attorney?"

"No." Her father looked grim. "Never thought we'd need it, and now it's too late. It's much harder if the subject refuses consent."

"So you're going to do it without her willing . . ."

For a moment Dad was distraught. "Do you think I want to? Do you think I shouldn't? They've planted something in her head, Evie, and it's *growing*, there's less of her with every week that goes by."

She blinked at him. "You mean, they *literally* planted something in her? Like what, one of the lesser daemones?"

"Yes, *exactly* that. You can see it in her mouth when she eats—she's avoiding the dentist, did you know that?" He spoke harshly. "It's eating her soul, and I intend to kill it."

"That's—" Her breath caught. "She's definitely possessed?"

Her father stood stiffly, as if his knees ached. Of a sudden Evie realized that he was, in fact, old: or at least middle-aged, which from a twenty-three-year-old perspective was the same thing. Hair thinning and graying to ashy silver, belly sagging over the waistband of the jeans he wore on his day off, a reminder that he'd met her mother after a rock concert in 1980. "Come with me," he said.

Evie trailed him upstairs to what had once been her bedroom. It had been repurposed at some point in the last few months, her own detritus boxed up and stripped out, Mum's hand clearly at work. A dressing table had been installed in place of her desk, bearing a small and obscenely personal shrine. Gilt-framed photographs of a smiling toothy preacher man surrounded a stainless steel cross big enough to crucify her childhood Barbie; a Bible rested before it, oddly disproportionate.

"What the heck?" Evie asked her father, backing up against the wall to which she'd once taped posters of Take That.

"Look." Dad picked up the Bible and riffled the pages, turning to the New Testament—no, turning *past* the New Testament. "Look at the apocrypha in this thing. Try to read them."

Evie took the book with nerveless fingers. "I don't think I can." A dizzying sense of wrongness swept over her. It was open at a title page: *The Final Codex*.

"Then let me show you. Here." Her father flipped forward. "The Apocalypse of St. Enoch the Divine, does that ring any bells? No? Good, because it shouldn't." He frowned at her. "It's a summoning ritual, Evie, one that purports to bring about the return of the Christ-child. Only that's tosh and nonsense, every initiate knows he isn't sleeping under some damned pyramid on a dead moon—" He stopped and cleared his throat—"still, it summons *something*. Opens a door that should have been welded shut and buried under a tectonic subduction zone eons ago," he said bitterly. "It's hers. She sleeps in here, now. Her Church forbids non-reproductive sexual activity of any kind—or even contact with the opposite sex—and she's post-menopause."

"Dad." Evie winced. "*Too much information.*"

"I want to save her." He looked haggard.

Evie bit her lower lip. "How?"

"We need an exorcism to get rid of that goddamned tongue-leech. Which means I need rather more *mana* than I've got to hand here . . . I'm going to have to consecrate the tools in a place of power where the family Lares can hear me. Which means going back to the manse again. Are you with me?"

"Shit." She winced again. "Sorry, Dad . . . yes, I'll come and spot for you. When do you want to do it?"

Her father glanced at his wristwatch. "Now is as good a time as any, don't you think? Jeremy's staying with his loser friends—" a curl of the lip emphasized Dad's opinion of art students in general and Imp's choice in flatmates in particular—"so at least he's out of the way. Your mother won't be home until after seven, and it's nearly noon. If we're discreet we can be there and back and get everything prepared in time for tea. I'll slip her something to make her dozy and we can perform the rite in our—I mean my—bedroom."

There were so many holes in Dad's plan that Evie ached every day thereafter, whenever she thought about the horrible risk they'd taken in the name of her mother's sanity. Yet at the time it all seemed reasonable and sensible. They'd taken the course of least resistance. Mum would thank them afterwards, wouldn't she? Never mind that Dad knew, going in, that it would take more power than he could normally channel. Never mind that Dad intended to petition the family Lares—the domain-specific micro-deities with whom his ancestors had made a blood pact—to grant him that power. Never mind that it came at the price of the inter-generational curse that had struck out so many names in the family spell book. Never mind that the curse was why her grandfather had nailed shut the doors and buried guardians at all four quarters of the grounds, then fled the house he'd grown up in. Never mind that power always came at a cost, and the price of the family bloodline was paid in blood by every second generation.

Never mind that the price was too high, and that Dad wasn't the one who'd pay it. Mum was in desperate danger, her very soul in peril of mutilation by feeders from beyond the walls of the world: and ever-dutiful Evie had always been more eager to oblige than was prudent.

Under the New Management, everybody knew that magic was real, and that occult beasties generally found muggles tasty with ketchup. What Rupert had overlooked was the possibility that an overly autonomous agent with an overly realistic fear of magic might eschew magical transit shortcuts entirely, in favor of something he understood.

The Bond knew better than to set foot on a faerie path alone, without so much as a cold iron horseshoe or a bag of salt about his person—at least, not unless his life was already in danger. Consequently, his hansom-hijacking hijinks set his arrival time back behind the team of Transnistrian insurance loss adjusters. But it also meant that they didn't overtake him before reaching the misty warrens of Whitechapel.

(This was not entirely the Bond's fault. Rupert was leery about employing minions with a working grasp of magic. He only used them if he had a noose around their throat, and that in turn necessitated a degree of micromanagement: cameras in every corner of their offices, accommodation in a secure dormitory attic, escorted at all times by a bodyguard assigned by the Bigge Organization. That sort of thing.)

But wherever the blame might lie, going off the map— even briefly—had cost the Bond his lead, and picking up a local guide had cost him even more time.

"It's in 'ere," said Ned, pointing at a dark backstreet opening off the yard they stood in. The yard was fitfully illuminated by a gas lamp bolted to the back wall of an unusually well-kept house. (Its ground-floor windows were all bricked up: presumably it was the home of someone who chose to live in Whitechapel and could afford the lighting as a deterrent against burglars.) Ned spat: the mist hereabouts was so thick that it swallowed his expectoration before it hit the cobblestones. "Not gunn' any further. Pay me."

The Bond produced a coin and held it just out of reach. "Why not?" he asked.

"Them Piss-Gavey boys will fuck you up." Ned's idio-lect warped towards modernity when he swore: or perhaps scatology was less prone to updating than other linguistic elements.

"How." The Bond paused. "What do they do?"

"Issa molly house, but it ain't like the others. Lads who go in ter try their luck fer a shilling, e'en if they come out again they're nivver right in the head." Ned spat behind him. "'S not right. 'S'not fucking right. What they do in there—"

The Bond flipped Ned the coin, a silver sixpence, and he dived to grab it. The Bond was pretty sure that a molly house was a gay brothel. Well, they could keep their fucking hands off *him*. Assuming it *was* a knocking shop, of course—it was called a reading room, and he was here for a book, so fuck, a library in a molly house would do. "You can piss off now," he told Ned, giving him a hard stare. Ned tugged his cap down, shoved the coin in his cheek, then staggered away up a narrow yard beside the building with the lamp. The Bond allowed him to go: his silence wasn't worth the price of a bullet. But a few seconds later there was a muffled thud and a sound that the Bond recognized as a body falling on pavement. Then a metallic chink and a clatter of something bouncing off the bricks.

The Bond bolted sideways and flung himself around a cor-ner, drawing one of his pistols. He crouched and crab-walked away from the yard, keeping his head down. A couple sec-onds passed, then the gut-shaking crack of a fragmentation grenade reverberated from the walls. Ears ringing, the Bond barely heard the ping of shrapnel hitting the opposite wall. He loped back to the entrance, raised his gun and braced his wrist, careful to keep one eye closed. As he covered the alley Ned had chosen, a shadow emerged from the mist, and he squeezed the trigger.

A Glock 18 outwardly resembles a regular Glock 17 semi-automatic pistol—except that it was developed specially for the elite Austrian EKO Cobra counter-terrorist unit. It's capable of burst and fully automatic fire at 1200 rounds per minute, making it one of the smallest submachine guns on the market.

The Bond wasn't one to spray and pray: he aimed and squeezed the trigger repeatedly, three-round bursts that set the mist swirling beneath the shattered streetlamp. A scream, cut off sharply, told him he'd hit someone. Whether it was Ned or his assailant was impossible to tell. He ducked back into the alley and darted back down it as hastily as he dared, relying for night vision on the eye he'd screwed shut against his muzzle flash. He counted as he ran. He'd fired three bursts, giving him twenty-four rounds left. He reached for a spare magazine with his free hand. Both his guns had the extended, 33-round magazine, but his accuracy shooting left-handed would be compromised and he could swap magazines faster than he could swap guns.

As he neared the corner of the building the harsh crack of a modern Kalashnikov sent him diving for the ground. He was up against professionals; he'd tried to outflank them from behind the building and they'd done exactly the same thing. But it was suppressive fire—they hadn't seen him, of that he was sure. Which meant they were ahead of him and trying to cover their entry—

As he lay on his back aiming his gun towards the corner of the building, someone opened up on full auto. But they were firing away from him. *Interesting.* The Bond's lips drew back in a feral rictus. He rolled over and scrambled to his knees just as a different gun started firing, single shots, much louder, like a shotgun. So two factions were shooting at each other now? *This is going to be fun*, he thought, reloading his pistol, then reaching under his coat for a concussion grenade as he stealthily approached the end of the alley.

Half deafened by the gunfire-induced tinnitus ringing in his ears, the Bond missed a tinkling as of malevolent glass windchimes, following him up the alleyway.

Alexei was having a really bad night.

First they'd missed the asshole assassin even though they'd run through the building like Satan's laxative. He was almost certainly ahead of them—he might be the kind of bastard to hide in a closet long enough to shoot them in the back, but he wasn't a coward and Alexei's back was still intact, so their target had to be in the lead. The banging open door on the darkness and mist proved it conclusively. So Alexei was on edge as he and his team followed the directions to the ley line route from the graveyard. Although they *did* cheat slightly; the instructions took no account of the utility of night-vision goggles on a moonless night as they flitted along the fog-bound sunken road into London's past.

"Fuck this dogshit haze," Yuri complained when they slowed for a regular breather, an hour down the lane. "No telling when you're going to trip on a tree root or run into a low branch if you keep pushing it."

"Tough." Alexei grunted. "Have deadline, no time to waste." Although it was true. On a good night in the woods his guys were ghosts, moving silently through ground cover. But something was wrong tonight. Alexei had caught a thin branch like a horsewhip across the face. Then Igor had nearly broken his leg on a hidden pothole, and Yevgeny had sprained his ankle on one of the lurking, hostile tree roots Yuri was rabbiting on about. It was almost like the road didn't want them here. And that fucking glassy laugh he could swear he kept hearing—it had to be a hallucination, didn't it? Maybe his mask seal hadn't been as tight as he thought and he'd caught a whiff of happy gas. The impulse to turn and hose down the road behind him with steel-jacketed disinfectant was strong—but not quite strong enough to break fire discipline. Alexei was a professional, and so were his guys, and nobody was about to start shooting at shadows. Yet.

The plague pit at the end of the sunken trail was something special, and no mistake. His crew went through it with hackles raised and guns twitching outward, covering each other with eyes wide open as Alexei whacked on the locked mausoleum gate with the butt of his gun until it unfroze and opened with a screech like the waking dead. He hustled out onto the sidewalk—pavement, the Brits called it—and tried to breathe a sigh of relief, but relief wouldn't come: not now, not here, not with tentacles of mist coiling lasciviously around his ankles.

"Have you reconsidered decision to apply for a career as insurance loss adjuster?" Yevgeny asked mordantly. "Maybe should have pick something safe instead? Like test pilot for zero-zero ejector seat?"

They pressed on into the dank, narrow streets of Whitechapel, sticking close together with guns held close, stocks folded for concealment beneath their overcoats. They only passed a handful of locals, and one group clustered outside a bar who grunted a challenge at them. "Are with Vigilance Committee!" Alexei glared at them and twitched his coat aside far enough to reveal a gun barrel. They backed down.

The mist grew thicker as the alleyways and backstreets grew darker and narrower. Alexei was half-tempted to go off-map and start blasting holes through the rotten brickwork and decaying wooden doors to either side, to punch a demolition tunnel through the obstacle course of urban architecture lying between them and the decadent nobles' reading room. But no: their supply of pyros was strictly limited to whatever Yuri and Igor had packed in their leather satchels (typically a kilo of C4 and a brace of flash-bangs), and there was no telling what kind of unwanted attention they might attract if they started blowing shit up. This was London in 1888, but not the London the history books described. This was a London born of the folkloric horror myths that future London told about its past. A London in which magic had never guttered and died, a London liminal and unstable in its absolute form, crumbling away in the yellowish pea-souper smog clouds that pervaded the frayed edges of reality.

Whenever Alexei glanced over his shoulder he had the most disturbing feeling that the street behind him was not the one he'd just walked down but a hasty substitute, swapped in from some eldritch continuum of crapsack dipshittery stalked by the ghosts of maniacal serial killers and adorable Dickensian street urchins; where every barber's shop was owned by a grinning slasher with a meat pie sideline, and every bedroom window offered a glimpse into the life of a soiled dove waiting for her Leather Apron lover. This was not the real Whitechapel of 1888 but the Whitechapel of the clichéd collective unconscious: pencilled, drawn, and inked from the scripts that London told about itself.

"Fuck this shit up its left nostril—" Igor began to complain, then emitted a strange, burbling gurgle. A moment later there was a thud of a body falling.

Alexei spun in place, flipping his AK-12 up and out as he scanned for threats. Around him the other five—no, four now—did likewise. Yevgeny dropped to his knees over a mound in the mist while Yuri and Boris took up positions. "He's a goner," Yevgeny reported after only a couple of seconds. "Both carotid arteries severed. Very clean work."

Alexei swore some more in the privacy of his head: a howl of pure rage and frustration directed at the night and mist around them. "Boris, get his satchel and piece. Guys, follow me. Shoot anything that moves."

They strode through the alleyway shoulder to shoulder. It wasn't far if the map was telling the truth. Silvery giggles like shattered window glass echoed faintly from above, behind, and the sewer grates below, taunting: but Alexei and his crew held their itchy trigger fingers for now. If Tinkerbell wanted to fuck around with the Transnistrian loss-adjusters, she was about to find her life insurance renewal premium had just gone to infinity. But they were too professional to light up the street without a target.

They had a mission to accomplish. And the reading room was just around the next corner.

"Bring me my sedan chair, minion," Rupert announced: "Failing that, ready my helicopter. Flight plan for Barclays London Heliport." He paused momentarily to think. Ms. Starkey would know what to do, but this understudy . . . "Have the Bentley waiting for me when I get there," he added, "and prepare my suite at HQ. You—" he addressed the naked woman lying on his bed—"see yourself out, there's a good girl." She snivelled something in response, but his attention was already directed elsewhere.

In principle it was possible to have his pilot set down in Kensington Park, within walking distance of HQ—but the police tended to frown on it. Something about babysitting for the royals living at the palace next door, and stopping random joggers from getting sucked into the pedestrian cuisinart or tail rotor or whatever the technical term for it was.

By the time all the red tape was sorted out it'd be faster to set down at the heliport in Battersea and drive, just like any other prole. He'd tried to get planning permission for a helipad on the roof a few years ago but got knocked back. (Maybe it was time to ask Ms. Starkey to revisit the application process again, when she got back to work? Perhaps a bigger donation next time, or better blackmail material. That sort of thing usually did the trick.)

Rupert ended the call and sighed heavily. "You just *can't* get the staff these days," he announced as he began to button his shirt.

Eve was out of the loop (and most interestingly so, having left HQ in the company of a bodyguard Rupert didn't remember authorizing her to hire). This was unusual enough that the Security Desk had discreetly paged him. The Bond was also incommunicado despite having been ordered to report in frequently. Rupe had hoped that a brisk BJ would clear the free-floating anxiety that was fogging his usual analytical brilliance, but in a moment of post-orgasmic clarity he realized that the only thing that would exorcise his personal demons would be the certain knowledge that his chess pieces were still on the board, in play, and on his side.

Hence the helicopter ride.

Cocooned in the Versace-designed luxury cabin of his AgustaWestland AW109E Power Elite, Rupert hunched over his BlackBerry in a black humor. He *needed* that book, he realized, not like a market acquisition or a hostile takeover or a pretty blonde whore, but like the next hit of heroin, or maybe a life raft after his yacht foundered. This need was no mere desire, it was a matter of raw animal survival. The more he thought about it, the more the Prime Minister's subliminally encoded message in the Mansion House speech freaked him out. The PM was a benign horror, but a horror nonetheless, and not one inclined to shower mercy on the worshippers of his rivals.

Rupert

His vision doubled: his head struck the restraint behind his seat as his jaw clamped shut. An icy sweat drenched the small of his back.

Rupert

The voice inside his head was louder than thunder and softer than a silk noose around his throat.

He tugged his headset off hastily. The thunder of the rotors overhead was a whisper on the breeze compared to the call he answered. "Master?" he said aloud, before he remembered to verbalize inwardly. "My Lord?"

The Book of Dead Names calls to me, Rupert. What have you achieved?

Rupert squeezed his eyes shut, a gut-loosening fear churning his stomach contents like wavecrests before an onrushing storm. The Mute Poet seldom spoke quite so clearly, and *never* tried to micromanage his priesthood. Perhaps that's why it had been the PM's faction who achieved the first-mover advantage, executing their adroit takeover of the government before any of the rival faith communities—the Red Skull Society, the Cult of the Mute Poet, the Chelsea Flower Show—got their shit sufficiently together to immanentize even a minor eschatological reality excursion. The PM was, unlike most of the other long-absent Gods, forward-looking to the point of almost integrating into human society: he reputedly *knew how to use email*, which put him light years ahead of Tony Blair. But the Poet had been speaking to Rupert for a couple of years, his demands becoming increasingly urgent and specific. And now this. It was a breakthrough, indicative of the Poet's awakening into this realm. Previously it took a successful rite of unholy communion to get a peep out of him, using the larynx and auditory nerves of a freshly sacrificed victim as a hotline. A megaphone blast delivered straight into Rupert's head was new, and also betokened an unaccustomed sense of urgency on the part of a weakly god-like entity whose clock ticks were measured in millennia.

"I have my best people working on obtaining it, My Lord. I expect results very soon."

Rupert reached for the cocktail cabinet, which was currently stocked with bottles of Fijian spring water and Goldschläger (the latter because everything palatable in this month's load-out had already been quaffed, and the valet service hadn't restocked the chopper yet). He twisted the lid off a water bottle and gulped from it, wetting his bone-dry mouth.

"Rivals attempted to intervene, but I put a stop to that," he added. "However, the Prime Minister . . ."

The Black Pharaoh is of no concern. Time is fleeting. The next suitable conjunction for the Rite of Embodiment begins in less than two months. There will be another opportunity a lunar year hence, but the Path of Flowery Death is opening right now and Xipe Totec stirs.

"I *hate* those Aztec fuckers," Rupert complained before he realized he'd spoken aloud. Mortified, he ground his teeth together. The Mute Poet was kind-hearted and enlightened compared to the followers of the Red Skull cult, appropriated and imported into Europe in the sixteenth century by Spanish occult treasure hunters returning from Mesoamerica. If the reign of the Black Pharaoh was bad enough, the return of the Flayed God would be . . . well, it would *not* go well for the Mute Poet Fan Club in general and Rupert de Montfort Bigge in particular, given his role as Lord High Adept of the Inner Chamber.

Your devotion is recognized. Bend every sinew to the recovery of my liturgy, bring it to me immediately and without delay, and I will smile upon you. Otherwise . . . not.

And Rupert was suddenly alone in his skull again.

It was not quite one o'clock in the afternoon when Evie and her father crossed the park and stood across the quiet street from the chained-shut gates of the ancestral family manse.

Later she would have plenty of time to regret her lack of foresight. But she'd been coming here with Dad since she was sixteen, not every month but often enough that breaking into someone else's locked-up property had come to feel almost routine. Indeed, over the past two years Dad had roped in Imp from time to time, saying he was old enough to walk the boundaries and reinforce the wards, doing his bit to help lock down the family wyrd. But today there was no Imp. It was just her and Dad on a little-travelled street. Which simply meant there were fewer bodies to share the guilt.

Dad had shown Evie that the trick to breaking and entering was to hide in plain sight. They approached the chained-up gate openly, carrying clipboards and wearing high-visibility work vests. Dad pretended to open the padlock with a key, but he'd charmed the lock long ago so that it would open at a touch for any who bore their blood. He swung the gate wide open, and Evie strolled in and stared up at the house while he made a show of closing and relocking it. Dad triggered another spell macro that blinded the CCTV to their presence. Then he began his rounds, pacing the perimeter of the overgrown garden, pushing through the knee-high grass and the wildly overgrown hedge to check on the bones and ribbons and the skeins of silver wire fine as cobwebs that bore the charge of stored magic, or *mana*, that deflected curiosity and dampened desire in anyone who crossed the threshold of the grounds.

Eleven pottery urns were buried in two rows, flanking the path leading to the front door. For generations their family had grown up with dogs: their loyal pets lived on in a tenuous afterlife, penning in the Lares that haunted their humans. Eve had helped Dad bury Nono here about four years ago, the most recent (and the last) arrival in the canine cemetery. The security company who patrolled these buildings had long since stopped trying to bring dog patrols round: the mutts went bugfuck, whining and trying to bolt. As for Evie, she felt a sad and tremulous comfort, as of a wooly presence leaning an imaginary shoulder against her hip, shaking at the specific frequency of a dog wagging its tail. There'd be no new additions. Not unless Evie or Imp started families of their own and brought puppies home to play with a new generation of Starkeys. And that couldn't be allowed to happen.

"Let's do it round the back," Dad proposed after they finished walking the perimeter. "Keep watch while I set up."

Evie nodded, and stared at the boarded-up windows at the back of the house. The high stone wall between the garden and the park was capped with broken bottle glass embedded in cement to keep trespassers out. Just inside the wall, trees that had barely been saplings when Grandpa sold the manse had matured, growing up warped from the weight of the walls. They spread their branches above Dad's workspace, a flattened square of grass where he'd spread a tartan rug weighted down with the paraphernalia of his trade: a small brass bell, an athame, his latest notebook—a continuation of the family spell book—and a skull. Eventually he opened his day pack and lifted out a lunchbox and a stainless steel flask, the ritual offerings of food and wine for the Lares. Rather than scribing a pentacle or summoning circle as he would on a hard surface, he laid it out carefully using skeins of braided silk cord. Then, with Evie anchoring one corner of the ritual space, he took up his own position and began the opening propitiation.

The rite was familiar and her part came easily to Evie. It was the first thing they did, every time—an offering of food and drink and a symbolic re-establishment of the ties that bound the Lares to the Starkey family. There was no set time or season for it, nor any significant sacrifice or purification ritual required. It was more like watering a plant or feeding the family dog than actual magic. This time, however, Dad followed it with a more alarming rider. "Lend me your *mana*," he politely requested, "to aid us, your family, in our time of need." He raised the skull and turned in place, presenting it to the four quarters, and Evie could swear that faint green striations glowed in the recesses of its eye sockets. "Lend me your blood, your bone, your sinew, your spirit: your blood to live, your bone to strengthen, your sinew to bind, your spirit to drive the hungry ghosts from the soul of my wife." For a moment Evie felt a tightening in her scalp and a buzzing tingle in her fingertips, almost as if she had been brought before the regard of something ancient and unsleeping. Then it passed, and her father bowed his head. "Thank you," said Dad, and he returned the skull to the crimson velvet bag it lived in. "And so, the contract is sustained." Evie's skin crawled as if someone had cast a handful of soil across the mouth of her future grave.

Dad was uncharacteristically quiet on the way home. Usually these rituals put him in a cheerful mood. As often as not he'd stop in a pub for a pint by way of unwinding. Evie found these refreshment stops useful, because he relaxed enough to explain what they had just done, both the superficialities (which as often as not she already understood) and the deeper significance. But this time Dad headed straight for the tube station, lips drawn tight and crow's feet deepening around his eyes.

"Dad, what was that at the end about sustaining the contract?" she asked as they turned the corner onto their street. A fine rain had started, tickling her face and the backs of her hands. "Is there something I should—"

"You needn't worry about it." Dad shut her down casually, irritating her: as with most parents, he sometimes forgot that his offspring were adults and reverted to treating her like a six-year-old. He wasn't totally oblivious—there was no *pretty little head* to talk down to here—but Evie knew a snow job when she heard one, and the tension in his jaw was obvious. "It's nothing important."

"The only contract with the Lares I'm aware of is the one that requires—" she swallowed—"you know what? I *don't* want to know."

Her father drew a deep breath as he unlocked the front door. "That's right, *you* don't want to know," he admitted sadly. "It'll make sense afterwards. Not to your detriment," he added hastily. "I wouldn't lay *that* on you."

"Fucksake, Dad," she said, not unkindly. She hadn't asked to be born under the family curse, any more than one might ask to be born with a genetic disease or a high risk of hereditary breast cancer. But at least the curse came with side benefits—unlike the ailments, if you could call an ability to harness the power of dreams a benefit when it could so easily slide sideways into nightmare.

"Just remember not to call me Abraham," he snarked. Then the gloom cloud dropped again. "I'd never do that to one of my kids. Although Jeremy *has* tempted me a time or two."

The nature of the family's relationship with their Lares was contractual: in every second generation the family would provide the Lares with a sacrifice, and in return the Lares would provide the family with the power to walk through dreams and warp dreams into reality.

When Great-great-great-to-the-*nth*-gramps had signed in blood on the dotted line, it had probably seemed like a superb bargain to a sociopathic pre-Victorian paterfamilias. Life was cheap in those days and the family had grown rich and powerful trading in powerful artifacts, visiting other realms. As recently as 1900, one in five infants died before the age of five: a century earlier, it had been closer to two in five. What was another child's life cut short in sorrow and pain, if it was the price of safety and prosperity for their siblings and nieces and nephews? Great-great-grandma had birthed twelve babes, of which eight survived to adulthood. Great-grandpa was one of the survivors. *Group selection* was the term for it in evolutionary biology: sacrificing a life to enhance the survival prospects of one's kin.

But the drought of magic had coincided with the onset of the demographic transition, the birthrate plummeting even as the survival rate among infants rocketed, and the sacrificial pact grew onerous. One infant among many was few: one among few amounted to many. Grandpa's sacrificed sibling, his name struck through in the family spell book, had been the last, for Grandpa had only the one brother, and had been guilt-stricken thereafter. Dad was an only child. Evie and Imp were two, and Dad had declined to ritually slit either of their throats, although Mum's melancholia—

"Dad, did Mum ever try to—" Her mouth dried up as he led her into the bedroom and pushed the bed to one side, revealing a pre-scribed containment circle.

"Yes," he said, after staring at his feet in silence for almost a minute. "We'd hoped that the contract might be fulfilled if, if—"

"—An early termination?"

"—Was not acceptable to the Lares." He nodded slowly, caught up in decades-old grief. "The contract specified it had to be a natural born child. She *tried*, Evie, she did it to protect you both. It didn't work."

"There must be another way around it, surely?"

"Not that we could find." He sighed. "Magic's easier now, though. It may not be necessary any more. Or there might be new possibilities. Cloning, maybe. Something with stem cells. Who knows?" He draped a cloth across the bedside table and then laid the skull upon it, an improvised altar for a scratch-built ritual exorcism. "It'll only become an issue if you or Jeremy want to have children."

"I'd dissolve the contract with the Lares first," she warned him. "Walk away from the power."

"Yes, well, you wouldn't be the first to try to do that. Unfortunately life has a way of making liars of us, for all our good intentions." He carefully scribed a trail of sea salt around the circle. "Our ancestor didn't have the foresight to add a termination clause, so it runs in perpetuity. There's a write-up in volume four and a commentary in volume nine of the annals. The price of forfeiture tends to be the life of the contracted party. In fact, the whole goddamn binding is a trade of power for death. The whole point of the sacrifice is to deflect the death onto someone else, rather than the adept's own head."

Life sucked but it sucked less than the alternative, Evie would freely admit. Also, the way magic was becoming easier these days gave her a prickly premonition. It wasn't just that she was gaining experience, becoming more proficient. Something fundamental was shifting in the world, and in the long term it would be to their benefit. Maybe they wouldn't need the grotesque pact with the Lares for much longer.

Maybe she and Imp would acquire sufficient power in their own right that they'd be able to break free of it. The future beckoned, offering hope for the kind of prosperity their family hadn't known since Great-granddad's days.

Presently all was in position. Dad checked his watch. "Your mother should be home in an hour or so. We should cook tea, Evie. You can say you did it as a treat? She'll like it if she thinks you're learning to look after yourself."

"Huh." Evie sniffed, mildly offended: "Just because you don't want to, Dad!" But she headed for the kitchen all the same, calling, "Why don't you make yourself useful and lay the table?" over her shoulder.

"I'll do that." Her father shuffled through into the dining room and began assembling place mats and cutlery. "Your mother will feel sleepy after supper and want to go and have a lie-down," he called.

"Do I want to know?" Evie asked. "Where do you even get roofies, anyway?"

"I'd *never* do that to Jenny!" His offense was tangible. "As long as she sits in her usual place she'll find it hard to keep her eyes open."

"Ah, volume six, section three?" She mentally patted herself on the back as she raided the freezer for Sunday's ready meal and then set to work peeling spuds and preparing fresh vegetables to go with it. Gravy would come last.

"That would be your great-grandfather's memorandum on sleep disorders and their treatment, yes. It was a regular money-spinner before modern tranquilizers came along."

"Got it." Evie pulled out the roasting pan, turned on the oven, and got the rosemary, sea salt, and olive oil ready. The saucepan full of potatoes was already simmering. She drained them and readied them for roasting as her father scribed a soporific ward on the underside of her mother's chair.

Finally, with the food in the oven and the good silverware set out (and a bottle of burgundy uncorked to breathe), she followed Dad upstairs to lay out the trappings of the exorcism grid under the bed Mum slept in these days: bell, handcast clay vessel, ritually purified stopper, the skull in which the Lares' flame rode, like a kitsch prop from a sixties horror B-movie—

And then the front door lock unlatched, and nothing more stood between Evie and the end of her childhood.

A burst of automatic gunfire from the lobby at the front of the building rattled Imp's teeth in his head. "Get down!" shouted Wendy, who ignored her own advice and darted for the spiral staircase up to the mezzanine gangway. Eve crouched, cradling the leatherbound volume in her arms. Glass marbles floated around her head, catching the gaslight like a shattered halo. Game Boy squeaked and dived behind the librarian's desk at the front of the room.

A moment later there was another burst of gunfire—Imp couldn't tell who was shooting slower pistol bullets and who was spraying assault rifle rounds, but the two shooters were audibly different. A body fell backwards through the doors at the front of the reading room, then rolled sideways to a seated position and put three rounds through the door at waist height. The shots reverberated, deafening in the confined space. "Get the table!" shouted the new arrival. "Barricade!"

"Do it," snapped Eve. To the prone gunman: "Are you hit?"

Del tipped the table at the front of the room over on its side, and shoved it towards the doorway. A moment later Game Boy shot out from behind the front desk, grabbed a table leg, and did something odd that somehow levered it up on one edge, so that the table top was vertical right behind the doors.

"Not hit," the gunman gasped. He wore immaculate formal evening attire and had somehow kept his hat on through the firefight, but his white gloves were stained gray with gun oil and he stank of burned powder. He pulled a magazine from inside his cloak and reloaded his submachine gun. "Sitrep, ma'am?"

"Who's out—" *Boom.* Eve winced as the room was shaken by a concussive blast. A thin shower of plaster dust rattled from the front cornice.

"Looks like they brought a grenade launcher, ma'am. Sorry." The Gammon didn't look sorry; he looked cold-bloodedly professional as he rolled to his feet and rapidly took stock. "You, you, and you—" he pointed at Game Boy, Imp, and Doc—"if you want to live, start moving furniture *fast*. We've got maybe three minutes, then they'll force entry through the windows—"

The hiss and thud of an arrow met the crash of breaking glass and a climactic scream, dwindling: "No they won't," Wendy called down.

"Who the fuck are *they*?" Imp asked, finally getting a grip. He glared at the Gammon. "And who the fuck are *you*?"

"He's with me." Eve rested a hand on Imp's shoulder. "Listen," she told the Gammon, "we need to make sure whoever's out there gets this book, then we need to follow them—not too close—and retrieve it when they die."

The Gammon stared at her, hard. "Why can't you just swipe it?" he asked. "It's not as if there's a librarian on duty. Ma'am."

Eve smiled tightly. "It's cursed. If you take it out of the library that would be stealing and you'd die, sweetie. Unauthorized withdrawals are *not* permitted."

Suddenly the Gammon's eyes narrowed. "So it's a weapon."

"A weapon?" Game Boy squeaked.

"We need to make an exit," Imp announced. "Me and Doc, and—Wendy—we have to go first. You and Evie need to make it look like we're retreating. Del and Game Boy, can you guys hide? Or, I dunno, play dead?"

Del kicked off first: "You have *got* to be fucking—"

"—Bad guys shoot their way in, find dead bodies and a book while Eve and—"

"—Sergeant Franke—"

"—Retreat under cover. Bad guys take the book and GTFO. Game Boy, you follow them until they drop dead, then you're merely picking the book up and handing it to Del. Doc and I will make sure nobody looks at you, and we're outta here. Plausible?"

"I love it when a plan comes together," Franke quoted, deadpan.

Boom. Another shower of plaster dust. Imp's ears were ringing, almost loudly enough to drown out the hoarse shrieking from outside.

"How many are there?" Eve demanded as a protracted burst of gunfire rattled what was left of the window glass.

Franke froze, looking thoughtful: "Too many—and that's not an AK." He flicked on a flashlight clamped to his gun and lit up the back wall of the library. There was a discreet door beside the spiral staircase at the far end of the catwalk. "Go there. Go now! Go! Go! Go!"

"Do as he says, kids, unless you want to play with our new friends," Eve announced. She walked towards the middle of the room and carefully positioned the book on the floor, facedown. "I renounce custody," she declared formally. "Whatever you do, don't touch it now: it's armed—metaphorically, at least."

"Fuck it, this is a *very bad plan*," Game Boy complained quietly. He headed towards the back of the library, where a series of bays jutted into the room, and disappeared between two upright bookcases.

There was a crash from beyond the front doors and the table wobbled. Wendy briefly popped her head up to check out a window, then ducked down again; she picked up her skirts and raced down the spiral staircase. "'Ware grenades!" she warned.

Imp grabbed the handle of the small door at the back of the library and twisted. "It's locked!"

"Shift." Wendy pushed him aside. "In or out?" she asked over her shoulder.

"Out," said the Gammon, raising his gun to cover the front entrance from behind a trolley laden with unsorted volumes waiting to be reshelved.

"Good call." Wendy's hands were suddenly filled with a battering ram. "A hand here?"

"What do I do?" Doc took the weight of the rear of the ram.

"Count of three: one . . . two . . . three . . . go!" Together they swung the ram at the doorknob. The door splintered around the lock as it crashed open, revealing an unlit staircase leading down past shelves of supplies.

Imp directed: "Into the basement, everyone except Game Boy and Del. Remember the book won't kill anyone unless they take it without permission. We'll wait near the exit and follow the trail of bodies."

"Fucksake," grated Del, melting into the shadows near the spiral staircase. A moment later Game Boy emerged and lay prone atop one of the bookcases, face to the wall. In the torchlit twilight he resembled a decorative molding. Del followed him, taking up a symmetrical position on the other side of the room.

"Good luck to you, too," Eve said coolly. Del flipped her off as Imp and Doc trotted down the stairs. There was another crash from the other end of the room and the table lurched inward as their assailants tried to ram the front doors. Eve glanced at Franke: "Remember, we need to make it look good, but at least one of them has to survive."

"You know it's risky, ma'am?"

"Don't talk to me about risk: I've been living on borrowed time ever since he was born." She jerked her chin at the cellar door, where Imp had just vanished into the shadows.

Franke focussed on the table blocking the entrance. "Here they come," he breathed, switching from flashlight to laser sight. A red firefly danced across the underside of the table. "In three, two—" Glass shattered high above them; gaslight caught the tumble of two canisters to the middle of the floor. "Grenades!" snapped the Gammon. "Get out!"

He squeezed off a short burst at the back of the door just as the front doors crashed inwards and the two canisters hit the tiles. "Cover!" he shouted. Eve's halo of glass marbles shimmered and erupted towards the doorway as the Gammon fired three more rounds and darted back into the basement stairwell. Eve was close on his heels: she pushed the damaged door shut behind them moments before a brilliant light and concussion lit up the room and the gunmen stormed in.

ACQUISITIONS AND TAKEOVERS

I am not paid enough for this shit, the Bond thought disgustedly, as fog swirled around his ankles. He bent over the body at his feet, probed with two fingers above the stiff blue collar. The unconscious constable's pulse held steady. *Fuck*. He reached down with his other hand, grabbed the man's chin, and yanked hard until he felt the cervical vertebrae grind. In the distance, wooden rattles clattered like knucklebones in a graveyard crypt, converging on the Whitechapel rookery.

The cop had nearly iced him, and it would have been entirely his own fault that he'd fallen to an amateur. He'd been so busy reloading and focussing on the headbangers with the full auto kit that he'd nearly missed the double-barrelled shotgun sneaking up behind him. Loss of situational awareness was a perennial problem, and—he froze, alerted by the sound of a different caliber of automatic weapon opening up.

Well, fuck this for a game of toy soldiers. Stalking Miss Starkey's clown crew was one thing. Taking on a goon squad with AKs was another. Throwing feral Victorian cops toting shotguns on their home turf into the mix was something else again—and now some joker was lighting up the night with a machine pistol. *Nope, this mission's a bust.* Four groups stalking each other in the fog: *What is this, a fucking Pe-*

ter Pan pantomime? All it needed was a crocodile scuttling around with a ticking bomb in its stomach, leatherbound death on four legs. It didn't matter how good you were; if enough bullets were flying, you could catch one in the neck purely at random. This was shaping up to be a total shit-show, and the Bond was acutely aware that he was hanging his ass out here without backup.

Oh well. Someone else could get their hands wet collecting the consignment. They'd have to come back to the house if they wanted to get home, and when they did, he'd be waiting for them.

The Bond kept his back to the wall as he stole away from the firefight at the front of the reading room. There was a crash of breaking glass as something whizzed out through a skylight and disappeared into the night: they were fighting inside the building now. Another hiss, and someone screamed above his head, then fell off the building and hit the cobblestones with a meaty thud. A grenade exploded round the front, the blast muffled by the mist. It sounded like a pitched battle.

An alleyway over, a corner turned, and the screams and percussion ebbed as if they were a distant memory of another world. But the wooden rattles were still audible, coming closer. The mist parted briefly, affording the Bond a glimpse of two burly figures in police helmets and capes. Unfortunately, it also gave them a glimpse of him. "Stop in the name of the law!" shouted one of the constables. "'E's the Ripper!" shrieked an unseen woman. The Bond winced and dived into the next street as the clatter of a policeman's rattle echoed off the walls behind him.

The gunfire and explosions cut off abruptly as he rounded the corner, crossed a backyard (carefully skirting a noisome midden), and turned onto White Church Lane. He drew his coat tight, concealing his webbing vest and twin Glock 18s. Boots on cobblestones behind him, hurrying: "Stop, I say!"

Fuck. The smog, a classic yellow-tinged pea-souper that smelled of burning coal and sulfur, was getting thicker. The Bond hurried towards the hitching rail where he'd left the stolen cab. Entirely predictably, it was gone: not just the horse and hire-trap, but the hitching rail too. He squinted into the murk, eyes watering as he searched for what he knew to be there. There'd been a pub, and there still was, but the signboard was . . . was it the same one? Navigating by pubs in the late Victorian East End of London was like navigating by fire hydrants in Manhattan. As he looked around, the Bond gradually realized that he was on the wrong street: he'd lost situational awareness again and taken a wrong turn, become lost inside Whitechapel.

The Bond was not a neophyte navigator. He'd hiked through mapless jungles in Central America and trackless mountains in Afghanistan. He wasn't a slave to satnav and GPS, like so many contemporary civilians: he'd been orienteering since he was old enough to tie his own bootlaces. But navigating Whitechapel in 1888 was another matter. The whole point of a rookery was that it was unmappable, with seventeenth-century streets crossing medieval routes cleared by the Great Fire of London that subsequently got filled in and fractally overgrown. People lived in a rookery because they could afford no better or they didn't want to be findable. A surveyor who ventured inside without a police escort would likely wake up several miles away with a splitting headache, minus his charts, instruments, wallet, and clothing—if he ever woke up. And this version of Whitechapel was just *wrong*, like the dream of an architect delirious on absinthe, specifying angles that didn't add up properly.

Another police rattle clattered behind him and the Bond

took off into the mist and night again, furious and hunted as he searched for something, anything, he recognized and could orient on: a church, a pub, a hitching rail.

Behind him, the silvery chatter of windchimes in the fog tinkled louder.

"That was lovely, dear," said her mother, lining up her knife and fork to bisect her empty plate neatly. She covered her mouth, trying and failing to suppress a yawn. "I'll just . . . I think I need a lie-down."

"You go right ahead," her father said indulgently. "Evie and I will do the washing up."

Mum was *really* out of it. She hadn't been herself for months, but this was by far the worst she'd been in Evie's presence. When she came home she didn't ask Evie why she hadn't come to church with her, or how her flatmates were, or . . . anything, really. She just smiled vaguely, recited grace, and ate her food, swaying tiredly in her chair. Her body was sitting at the table but her mind was elsewhere. Evie had never been any good at aura work, but even she could tell there was something wrong. It wasn't a zombie-like absence; it was somehow Stepfordian to Evie's mind. It was as if her mother's soul was a candle wick that had been pinched between finger and thumb so that the flame was out, only a burning ember at the tip bespeaking the possibility of reillumination. *I hope Dad knows what he's doing*, she told herself.

Mum yawned again, this time without covering her mouth. Her eyelids were closing, lifting slightly then falling again. She made no move to stand up, but the swaying was growing more pronounced.

"Evie, would you mind helping your mother upstairs?" Dad asked. "Otherwise I think she'll fall asleep at the table."

"Yes." Evie stood, and helped her mother up from the chair. Mum mumbled something that might have been a gargled *Thanks*, then shuffled towards the stairs, her head nodding. Evie got her up to the landing and into the bedroom, terrified that she might face-plant on the carpet at any step. Finally, they were there. "Why don't you lie down, Mum?" she suggested.

"Yes, I'll just . . ." Her mother sat on the edge of the bed, then slowly toppled backwards until she sprawled crosswise atop the covers. A moment later she began to snore.

Evie removed her mother's shoes, then tried to turn the sleeping woman. Mum turned out to be unexpectedly heavy. "Dad? Dad!"

Heavy thudding on the stairs. "What is it, Evie?"

"A hand, here? She's totally zonked. I can't move her."

"Let me." Dad slid his arms beneath his sleeping wife and gently took her weight while Evie swung her legs up on the bed. *"Oww."* He straightened up and rubbed the small of his back, breathing heavily. His brows wrinkled as he stared at the sleeping woman, as if she was a puzzle he couldn't solve.

"Dad." Evie found herself holding his hand. "It's going to be all right."

"No, no it isn't." For a moment he sounded distraught.

"But Dad—"

Her father leaned over her mother's head. "Attend," he told Evie, slipping into the didactic, professorial manner he adopted for her lessons in magecraft. "Your mother is infected." Using his thumbs at the sides of her jaw, he gently levered her mother's mouth open. "Observe."

Evie only just made it to the toilet. She never again ate a Sunday roast.

When she finished, she rinsed out her mouth in the sink, and lingered in front of the bathroom mirror staring at her face, seeing half her mother's features reflected back at her. Her hands were trembling, not with fear or anger, but with a less familiar emotion: hatred.

She joined her father. "What the *fuck* is that *thing*?" she snarled, wiping her runny nose on the back of her sleeve. She pointed past her mother's sagging lips, at the silvery articulated shield nestling in her lower jaw like an armored parody of a normal tongue: "How did it get in there?" She reached for it, but Dad caught her hand.

"There is a species of deep sea isopod, *Cymothoa exigua*, that is called the tongue-eating louse. It crawls into a fish's mouth and attaches itself to the tongue. It's a vampire—it severs the blood vessels supplying the tongue, which falls off, and then it attaches itself, drinking the fish's blood and becoming its new tongue." Her father swallowed. "This is a relative. It's what that church she goes to uses in place of a communion wafer."

"But it's *eating* her *soul*—" Evie lost it and went straight back to the bathroom. It was a couple of minutes before she could speak again. *"Fuck."*

"Why doesn't somebody stop them?" she demanded, when she could face the bedroom again.

"How?" Her father shrugged, and for a few seconds the entire weight of the world was mirrored in his expression of despair. "They're too powerful, Evie. They've got the government wrapped around their little finger—their head preacher man is best mates with the Prime Minister. They've got thousands of communicants who've taken the host, like your— like Jenny." He swallowed. "If you take them on, they'll steamroller you. Put you on a plane to Colorado Springs and make you one of them. Evie, we're small fry. We can't—"

"*You* can't." Her eyes burned with rage. "I'll find a way, Dad, *that* I promise you." She picked up her mother's hand.

"That I promise *her*. This is evil, and I'm not going to stand for it. Whatever it takes—I'll do it." Her back straightened.

"You can help me right now by checking my circle and lighting the candles, love." While they'd been talking, dusk had fallen and the bedroom had dimmed to twilight. "We can discuss what you might be able to do—*might*—about the Golden Promise Ministries some other time. Assuming they fail to raise their sleeper," he added in an undertone. "If they succeed, we're all fucked."

And without further ado they began their half-assed and foredoomed attempt to exorcise her mother.

The style of invocation her family used was long on preparation and props but short on chanting. Dad had already diagrammed the precise integration of forces he wanted to produce on an expanse of paper tucked under the bed. It was a simple exclusionary ward, to force out anything non-human—and by *human*, he'd been careful to include in his definition the human microbiome, and endosymbionts like mitochondria. (As his ancestors had discovered the hard way, failing to do so had varied and drastic consequences ranging from explosive diarrhea to sudden death.) What it boiled down to was an occult vermifuge. The Lares' *mana* or stored power, bottled up in the inscribed skull like an osseous Leyden jar, would surge through the grid and burn out anything that didn't belong inside it. Simple, powerful, foolproof.

Dad was already breathing heavily and sweating as they started. "Are you feeling okay?" Evie asked.

He nodded tensely. "I'll be fine." His brow wrinkled in concentration as he chanted instructions to the reined entities in the skull, invoking the long-ago pact his family had made with them.

Mum lay on her back, mouth slightly agape, snoring softly as Dad chanted. Evie echoed Dad's invocation, but something felt wrong even though the ritual objects were all beginning to glow softly with the radiance that bespoke an operational summoning. She felt oddly hollow. And Dad seemed to notice it, too: his voice rose, his ritual commands growing emphatic.

Evie licked dry lips. *This isn't working*, she thought. *Why isn't it working?*

The bell sitting on the floor at her feet, at the end of the bed, chimed softly, and she startled.

"In the name of our ancient agreement I command thee to—"

"*A sacrifice has not been made,*" tinkled the bell, and somehow Evie understood *exactly* what it was saying, what the Lares were conveying through the medium of metal. It was a language not English, but something much older that plugged straight into Broca's area in her frontal lobe, generating speech in a form she could understand. "*Broken dependency. Backtracking. Failed to initialize compact. Make sacrifice or die.*"

"What—" Alarmed, Evie tried to step away from the circle, but her legs refused to obey her.

Dad looked up at her in horror. "Evie!"

"—Does it mean?" she heard herself asking.

"Oh god. Oh god. Oh god. The curse."

Of course, Evie realized distantly, Mum refused to have any more kids because she couldn't bear to let Dad sacrifice one of them—*as if Dad would ever do that to me or Jerm*—Her father was no psychopath, nor even an abused and damaged teenager like Grandpa with his endless guilt over what was behind the painted-over door on the top floor of the house he couldn't bear to live in any longer—

"*Make sacrifice or die,*" demanded the Lares.

—One must die in every two generations, that the pact with the Lares be renewed: and now Eve found herself staring into her father's eyes as his pupils blew out, darkening in the twilight—

"Can we abort?" she asked.

Her father shook his head. "Not at this stage, no . . ." He swallowed as he stared at her. "I'm sorry, Evie: be strong for me," he said, raising the athame, the ceremonial knife. Then, before she could stop him, he said, *"Take me instead."*

Alexei and his crew stormed the library. There were defenders: at least one with a submachine gun, and a joker with a bow. They fucked up Boris but good. He was up on the roof with Yuri, scoping out the interior and positioning to drop stun grenades inside, when he took an arrow to the knee and fell off the roof. They were all wearing ballistic vests, but arrows were much slower and heavier than bullets and he lost his balance and fell. *Fuck.* The occupants retreated and Alexei's crew wasted vital minutes checking the offices in the back and upstairs, making sure nobody was sneaking around behind them, before they discovered the targets had barricaded the fucking doors with an oak table or something. At which point Alexei saw red. The forced entry went smoothly but when they rammed the table out of the way they were too late: a door at the other end was already closing, and although Yevgeny wasted half a magazine on it, there was no likelihood of a kill. With his team at half strength—Yevgeny was limping badly and Igor and Boris were dead—he wasn't about to go clearing ratholes.

Get the fucking book. Get the hell back to the mansion. Shoot anyone who gets in the way. Get home and bring the house down behind you. Simple. Right?

"*Fuck,*" he hissed, sweeping the catwalk under the upper shelves with his flashlight as Yevgeny and Yuri methodically took the lower galleries and the librarian's counter.

"Is fucking *library*. How the fuck we meant to find right book?" complained Yuri. He poked his gun barrel at a stack of unshelved books at the front desk, dislodging them.

"Index cards. *Stop* that. If it is a mess, search will take ten times longer."

"Index cards—" Yuri processed—"in English?"

Alexei forced himself not to clout his subordinate. Yuri was not the sharpest hammer in the toolbox. "Yes, Yuri, in English." Except according to Intel, the book had been deliberately misfiled. *Fuck*.

Their forced entry hadn't exactly left the library in pristine condition. There were cracks in the plasterwork and dust everywhere. Broken glass and books on the floor, tumbled higgledy-piggledy in the gloom. Gas lamps hissed but barely beat back the darkness. No blood, dammit, and Alexei wanted to see blood *badly*, wanted it with an urgent and righteous anger. Because fuck this job, fuck these English assholes with their smug magical mojo, fuck this shithole version of London—he hadn't seen this much poverty since the time he'd been posted to the favelas outside Rio—*fuck*. All this shit for one goddamn book?

He shone his flashlight towards the door at the far end of the room. Broken lock, clear signs of a hurried exit. Books strewn around the path of the defenders' stampede. *They wouldn't be so stupid*—he told himself, even as he strolled towards the big leatherbound tome that someone had dropped facedown on the floor in their hurry to escape the flashbangs. *Well, maybe*. He grinned humorlessly and reached for the magic compass doohicky on a cord that hung around his shirt collar. It twisted in his grip and tugged straight at the book on the floor. "Hey, Yuri, is your lucky day," he called softly as he edged towards it, every sense on full alert for trickery, "or is maybe an IED." Because if *he* was mounting a staged withdrawal he sure as fuck wouldn't leave his target lying on the floor—but he might yank the cover off and use it as bait for a trap.

But the charm-fetish-thing still tugged towards it. Which meant it was full of magical go-juice. *Well.* Maybe it was a trap, but—Alexei bent towards it. There was nothing to be seen: no wires, no pads, no infrared beams visible in his night-vision scope. "Yuri. Does this look clean to you?"

Yuri joined him in his inspection. "Sure, boss. What, you think they drop it while run away?"

"Why, yes, Yuri." Alexei straightened up. "That's what I think." He forced himself to relax and shake the tension out of his neck and shoulders, even though his heart was still hammering and he was on a hair-trigger in case the asshole with the submachine gun popped up again.

"Then why we not—" Yuri bent towards the book—"take book and go home?"

He straightened up, cradling the book across his body as he looked at Alexei expectantly.

Alexei gave him a hard stare, then nodded to himself. "Yes, Yuri, why not," he breathed. Raising his voice: "Yevgeny? Target acquired! Going home! Last one to the bar is buying!"

He turned and strode back through the ruined front doors of the reading room, into the lobby, and then into the Whitechapel night. Behind him, Yevgeny and Yuri followed.

His ears still ringing from the flash-bangs, he didn't hear the glockenspiel tinkling that followed them out of the library.

Game Boy waited for the angry bowler-hatted Russians with the very big guns to leave, counted to fifty, then sat up. He clutched his head and suppressed a moan of pain as he blinked furiously, trying to flush away the purple and green afterimages. He'd had his head turned to the wall when the flash-bangs detonated, but the wall in front of his face was painted ivory and the flashgun aftermath was taking its time to fade.

"*Fuck*," he whispered, frightened to move: even breathing seemed like a dangerously risky activity. But his sixth sense twitched, prodding him. He needed to make a speed run and start *nownownow* or it'd be *toolatetoolatetoolate*—and through the muffled buzzing in his ears he heard nothing else, no footsteps or grumpy Slavic tongues. He rolled over and looked down on a scene of devastation by gaslight. Books and broken glass strewn everywhere, furniture smashed or pushed aside. Across the galley from his niche he saw shadows stir. "Becca?"

"Shh." The whites of Del's eyes were startling in the darkness. Her drab gown was draped unevenly about her, like a fallen curtain or a pile of dirty laundry.

"They've gone and I'm on my way." He straightened up and dropped lightly from his hiding place. Del followed, a rustling fall of cloth across the shadowed floor. "They went out the front door. You go out the back and meet me round the side."

Game Boy nerved himself to move. He pulled his top hat tight around the crown of his head, shot his shirt cuffs (then thought better of it, and tugged his gray coat sleeves down over their bright white shine), and cleared his throat. *Bad men with big guns.* Well yes, but he'd done it a million times before in games, done it for reals as well—stolen a letter right out of Becca's new girlfriend's grasp, ducked and weaved between security guards—*but bullets.* Game Boy swallowed. Then he ghosted out through the drunkenly askew front doors, feeling the familiar prickle of knowing where to put his feet, where to lean his back, nudging at the back of his skull with a hungry, chattery feeling like insects chewing on his tension.

It was still night out there, and a sea of mist rose nearly to his kneecaps, swirling in the dim overcast from a million streetlights diffusing through the smog. The air was acrid, choking, and cold. *Leftleftleft* said his scalp, driving him with a sense of unease. *Catchup.* He heard boots clattering on cobblestones ahead, then a low chatter. Polish or—he supposed this was Russian—sounded odd to his ears, the phonemes unfamiliar and nasal with rolling Rs.

He heard an abrupt strangled wail cut eerily short. It broke through the ringing in his ears and his talent screamed *divefortheground*. Game Boy dropped face-first to the pavement, choking on the sweet-sick stench of raw sewage nearby, just before an arpeggio of eardrum-pounding automatic gunfire cut the night apart just above his head. He wasn't the target, though. The target was a tinkling, chilling laugh of tinkerbell windchimes ringing in the steel breeze, voicing a wild, malignant glee that made his skin crawl. He'd heard it before, back in Imp's mansion, and thought nothing of it. But it had followed them through the maze of memories of times past, growing more terrifying with every passing era: the Lares, the household gods bound to Imp's family by their curse.

"Fuckfuckfuck," Game Boy babbled under his breath, frightened half out of his wits even though the angry shouting gunmen hadn't spotted him. Someone else had caught their attention, but not their fire. Only one of them was shouting now, clearly issuing orders to the others. Bright spotlight beams lashed out, visible like searchlights in the foggy air as they crisscrossed the alleyway with lethal blades. Game Boy threw himself sideways, out of the path of deadly light. He heard metallic clicking and barked orders as the gunmen swapped out their magazines. One of them crouched over another, who had fallen, bubbling bloody froth that ran black in the tenebrous gaslamp glow. Something was stalking them.

Game Boy waited until their flashlight beams shone away from him, then scuttled for cover against the nearest wall. There he waited and watched, shivering from tension.

The one who had fallen did not move again, and now there were two. The one who had been on the receiving end of the other's orders bent and picked up something rectangular—the book, Game Boy realized. And now his power was shouting *GoGoGo!* in the back of his head again, so Game Boy was off—racing away from them in the opposite direction, half-skipping and shuffling to break up the rhythm of his stride, until a prickling in his scalp told him to duck into a doorway and push. The door, slimy and rotten beneath his fingers, swung inwards into darkness.

Game Boy skipped along a narrow passageway in total darkness, walls close enough to touch without stretching his arms, and bounced over more than one body—sleeping or dead, he couldn't tell—then into a room where he dropped and rolled to avoid clotheslining himself on a horizontal rope against which sleeping derelicts leaned. Another rope, another roofed-over yard, rats scuttling for cover.

A silent voice sang glassy-toned in his ears: *"Jack be nimble, Jack be quick, Jack duck under the razor's flick"*—and then there was another door, an alley with flagstones slippery with noisome muck, a rotting gate, and another narrow street carpeted in unnatural mist. He tiptoed to the next corner and turned, to see two retreating backs half-shrouded by the smog, their bowler-hatted heads twitching side to side. His talent had taken him on a shortcut through a doss-house just as the thugs with the book began a sweep of the alley for threats. If he'd been in sight—

Game Boy darted after them, sure-footed with the practiced buzz of a speed run through a well-known level. Only his lack of health potions and power-ups held him back; that, and the sick knowledge that he'd never played this game before in his life, and might not live to do so again if he took a step wrong. *Jack be nimble*, this is the Ripper's vestibule, *only I'm not a—*

A gurgling scream and a hand up-flung in the coiling fog-banks of the past: this Ripper targeted men as well as women, hard or soft made no difference. Game Boy dropped again, shivering with fear, as the last man standing from the goon squad screamed imprecations into the night then punctuated his rant with a squeezed trigger, blasting gunpowder shadows that strobed across the weeping brick walls on either side.

It takes about a minute, a quietly rational corner of his mind narrated: a minute from taking the book without permission to being struck down. *The curse isn't instantaneous.* Assuming the stalker in the mist was actually the curse finding its way to the target, and not something else, some metaphysical epiphenomenon of this fever dream of Whitechapel made real. Not Leather Apron, not Spring-heeled Jack, but the tangible effect of a curse applied to a physical object. Game Boy breathed deeply of the foul air, suppressing his coughs until the gunman wound down from his screaming jag and ran off into the night, heading in the direction of the plague pit and ley line. *He totally lost it*, Game Boy marvelled. *Not so easy to be a hard man when you're on your own among aliens, is it?*

Game Boy crept across the alley to where the book thief had fallen. It was mercifully dark, shrouding the dead man's face in shadows and hiding the frightfulness that had been inflicted on his body. He'd dropped the book a few paces away, and Game Boy nearly tripped when his toe struck the spine. *Bingo*.

He raised his face towards the fuming chimneys and the clouds above and whispered, "Deliverator? I've got a package for you."

Something rustled behind him: he jumped and spun round just in time to see the end of a rope drop to the pavement. A couple of seconds later a body dropped from the gutter above, stockinged feet gripping the rope as Del abseiled down from the rooftop. She unhooked her sling, shook down her hitched-up skirts, and stepped away from the wall as another body joined her. Game Boy's jaw fell. "*Mountaineering gear?* Where did you get *that*?"

"Remember the Boy Scout motto?" Wendy said ironically. She let go of the ropes and harnesses: a moment later they thinned into vapor, merging with the mist.

"We took to the rooftops 'coz that seemed safest, what with all the shooting," Del explained. "Where's the book, then?"

"Oh, wait." Game Boy took a deep breath, then bent down. "Hello, book," he said, laying hands on the leather cover: it felt greasy and slightly warm, and his mouth tasted like he'd just licked the contacts of a nine-volt battery. "I am picking you up because you seem to be lost, and I'm sure you need help finding your way back to your rightful owner." It seemed *very important* to get these words exactly right. "I want to help return you to where you belong. It's not right to leave books lying around on the streets in the rain. Del—" Game Boy swallowed—"here is a book. It does not belong to me but I want to help it go where it needs to be, to where it rightly belongs. I'm *sure*—" his mouth was abruptly dry—"it won't hurt someone who is trying to *put it right*. Would you accept it from me now? It needs to go home."

The devil was in the details: if the curse was activated

by illegitimate acts of possession, Game Boy might have triggered it (or not), but by passing it voluntarily to another before the curse could fully power up, he was simultaneously insulating Del from it and removing himself from its crosshairs. Or so he hoped. Promising to take it to where it belonged was just a belt-and-braces precaution. He didn't want to be on the receiving end of a razor-blade smile just because an insane eighteenth-century inquisitor hadn't anticipated modern offshore financial vehicles in his ritual magic's definition of ownership.

"Got it," said Del. She opened the carpetbag she carried and slid the book carefully inside. "Follow me, I know exactly where we're going."

"To meet up with Imp and Doc?" asked Game Boy.

Del nodded. "Then we're taking the ley line."

"About time, too," said Wendy, glancing around. "This place is getting to me." A gibbering howl of sorrow and heart-stricken loss spiraled into the night, and the clappers of police rattles buzzed like huge, slow-moving hornets in the mist. "I can't wait to get home."

Del stalked up the alley beside Wendy, Game Boy scurrying along to take up the rear. Behind them, a slow tinkle of windchimes sounded, slow and doubtful. And then they went elsewhere.

"We've dropped the ball," Eve announced, "I need to get home ahead of the rush. Which presents us with a bit of a problem."

"Hmm," said the Gammon, staring up the high street. They'd made their way out of the slum and onto a relatively well-lit road near Spitalfields. "We could take another cab . . . ?"

"Not fast enough. We could take the ley line route instead,

but we'd be behind them and on foot and we need to get ahead."

A man on a bicycle—a recognizably modern safety bicycle with a chain drive, not a penny-farthing—pedalled slowly past, and Eve smiled, delighted. *But of course, we're at the right end of the 1880s*, she thought.

The last decades of the nineteenth century had been a time of massive change and innovation, with new inventions coming thick and fast, upending the old order. Telephones, steam turbines, electricity, an endless litany of change: gas fires, electric timers, cylinder phonograph music players, movie cameras.

The modern safety bicycle was just another of the innovations of the 1880s, albeit one of the most visible. It landed in the middle of the decade with a bang, like a Victorian harbinger of the iPhone. They were suddenly everywhere, the first form of cheap mass transportation to emerge and a must-have personal accessory for the modern generation. Unlike the earlier penny-farthing, safety bicycles didn't require gymnastics to mount and dismount—and they were available to women, who took to them with alacrity.

By 1892 they'd killed the older two-wheeler stone dead. And they were the answer to Eve's dilemma.

"Mr. Franke? Get us bicycles."

"Yes, ma'am."

The Bond hid among piles of skeletons wrapped in stiff and rotten shrouds like too-old spiderwebs. While he lurked, he brooded: and as he brooded, he checked his sole remaining pistol.

They're not late yet, he told himself. The indefinite *they* applied equally to Imp's motley crew and the assclown Transnistrians (whom he had every intention of teaching a short, sharp lesson in fire discipline), or even the chilly ice maiden Miss Starkey. It was only a matter of time before somebody brought him the book, and when they did he'd be ready.

He'd made it to the plague pit highlighted on the map, swallowed his misgivings, and tackled the sunken road at a ground-eating jog. Time moved strangely in this space, and he wasn't sure how long he'd been there—but whatever, he'd not run into anyone along the way and it was pretty clear that neither the Lost Boys nor Miss Starkey were up to the sort of brutal wilderness forced-march he'd cut his teeth on in BUD/S land warfare school. (The mafiya guys were another matter, but he was pretty sure they had run into something— *someone*—heavily armed. They wouldn't be coming at him without prior attrition.)

The ley line thoroughly spooked him. That bell-like mocking laughter—he'd lit up the sunken path with his guns, bullets thundering into the mist. It hadn't worked, and he'd expended half his remaining ammunition along the way. He'd also lost his second Glock 18. He'd put it down while he prepped a reload magazine, and when he reached to pick it up again the tree roots fought him for it, gnarly tubers coiling around the grip and the barrel until he released it and fled, swearing up a silent blue streak inside his skull.

So now here he was, holed up in a graveyard charnel house at the homeward end of the ley line, all tooled up and waiting for a partner to dance with—

Voices. Echoing up the tunnel that led from the rusty gate onto the sunken road. "I tell you, we're nearly home. See? The floor, here? We're nearly back to the garden gate."

"I barely care." A squeaky voice. "My feet are killing me. Like, I've got blisters on my blisters."

"You can have a footbath when we get home, dearie."

A man, somewhat effeminate in the Bond's disdainful opinion. "Keep moving. You're sure you haven't seen any sign of Eve?" He sounded worried: *Interesting*. Possibilities fanned out in the Bond's mind, a flowchart of goal-directed options from theft and murder to hostage-taking and torture.

"Could she have gotten ahead of us?" asked Squeaky-Voice.

"Anything's possible, I suppose," said another, deeper male voice, roughened from smoking (or the damnable coal smog back in dream-time London town), "but I doubt it." *And so do I*, gloated the Bond.

"Fucksake, let's just get this over with," groused a different woman. One of the lesbos from the cafe in the park, the Bond figured.

They were nearly in range, so he stepped out from the charnel room and raised his gun. "Good evening." He smiled, the moonlight inking his eye sockets with shadow and turning his teeth the color of old ivory.

The short, squeaky-voiced guy screamed and clutched the arm of one of the other overgrown kids. They were barely out of their teens: sucked to be them. The girls stood shoulder to shoulder. The black one clutched a carpetbag against her chest, her chin aggressively tucked down as she glared at him: her special friend looked like she might be more of a problem from her posture—*Some martial arts training there*, the Bond thought—but was focussed on his gun. *Good*.

"You are going to give me the book," he explained patiently. "Otherwise you will all die, and I will take it from you anyway."

"How do we know you won't kill us?"

The Bond resisted the impulse to roll his eyes: "Because I don't fucking need to. Have you any idea how hard it is to find 9mm Parabellum in London these days?" (The answer: *extremely* hard, unless you had an end-user certificate and a licensed arms dealer at your beck and call who could have it shipped to your boss's private island base and flown in on his VIP helicopter.) "Give me the book and I'll let you live. I'll shut the gate behind me when I go. You're not stupid so you'll sit tight and give me a fifteen-minute head start before you follow me because if I ever see you again I will kill you. Clear?"

He snapped his fingers. "Do. It. *Now*."

"Give him the book," said Squeaky-Voice, his tone dismal.

"Fuck." The black woman sounded totally disgusted as she held up the carpetbag. "Really?"

"*Do it,*" hissed her girlfriend.

"Stop!" the Bond said tensely. "Put the bag down and open it. *Slowly*. Show me." This was when they'd try something if they were stupid.

She put the bag down and then opened the top. One of the boys slowly reached for a pocket. "Flashlight," he said.

"Very, very, slowly." The Bond smiled again and the boy shook in his boots as he carefully removed a phone and tapped its screen.

The interior of the bag lit up, revealing a leatherbound volume.

"Kick it towards me," said the Bond. "Now I want you to go back that way, all the way down the tunnel to the sunken road—" their impresario-ringleader startled, as if he hadn't realized the Bond had known about it, how stupid was he?— "behind the gate. And then you wait fifteen minutes. Remember that. You got a stopwatch on that thing? Fifteen minutes, or maybe I shoot you. Do you understand?"

The Impresario nodded. "Worst game of hide and seek *ever*," said the squeaky-voiced boy.

"You got it. Now piss off. Damn meddling kids."

They backed away, looking bereft. Lost, maybe. Sucked to be them, utterly incapable of fighting back in a real man's world. The Bond grabbed the bag with his free hand and hastily retreated to the crypt entrance. He holstered his gun, then shut and locked the cast-iron gate. Next, he pulled out a small double-barrelled syringe of quick-setting epoxy resin and squirted it into the keyhole. It'd be set hard in two or three minutes, although it'd take a day to cure to full strength. But that didn't matter. It'd stop them picking the lock, and he'd hear the noise if they somehow smashed the gate while he was still in the vicinity. Once he was home, well, he had a couple of kilos of C4 in the boot of the Aston Martin: more than enough to drop the entire rotten Georgian town house on their heads before they found their way back from Neverland.

Whistling tunelessly to himself, the Bond jogged through misty streets towards the Starkey family mansion, and the portal back to the real world.

"Fuck. Fuck. Fuck."

"Shut it, Game Boy, I'm *trying* to think here."

Game Boy rounded on Imp. "Since when are you in charge any more? You got us into this mess! Why didn't you roll him? Or you, Doc—"

"I tried." Doc massaged his temples. "My head hurts. He had a ward—"

"He also had a *great big gun,* and in case you hadn't noticed there are no save points in real life," Imp scolded Game Boy.

"I shouldn't worry, though," Wendy chipped in. "He'll be dead soon enough."

"Why—"

"Oh." Game Boy smiled. "Oh. *Oh!*"

"Yes, *oh* indeed." Del smiled back at him. It was not a friendly smile. "He's fucked. That guy's a dead man walking, he just doesn't know it yet."

"*If* Eve's right about the curse," Imp pointed out. "And *if* her boss didn't send him as insurance, did that occur to you? And we need to get moving. I've got a bad feeling about this place. Like the wallpaper is falling off and there's something rotten underneath."

"Sit tight," Wendy told him. "It's only been a minute and he can murder the lot of us if we run into him before, the, the curse hits." She took a deep breath. "Did you see the size of the magazine on that thing? I'm pretty certain it's a Glock—the Met use them—but the fully automatic version. While we're bunched up in here . . ."

She punched her left hand forward and flourished her fancy compound bow in front of Del: "I'm not feeling *that* lucky, thank you very much." The bow vanished. "Anyway, assault with a deadly weapon is not my cup of tea and I'm not feeling much love for a self-defense plea in mitigation, so let's maybe wait another twelve minutes before we try to get ourselves killed?"

Game Boy spoke up again: "I'm not sure we can hang on that long." He shivered. "You know that thing when you're on a trap run through a kill zone and the ceiling's coming down right behind you and it's a trade-off between movement speed and hit points? I'm getting that feeling. *That* one. We're on a timer and we don't have fifteen minutes."

"You're saying we're fucked," said Doc.

"Yeah, and *you*—" Game Boy rounded on him—"this isn't helping." He deflated.

Imp focussed on Game Boy. "You're *absolutely sure* we've got to move right now?"

Game Boy nodded.

"Okay, I've got this." Wendy shoved her way to the front of the queue and marched straight up the stairs to the gate at the front of the crypt. "Torch." Del passed her a flashlight and she summoned up the same skeleton key she'd used before. "Huh. Shit. It's not going in properly, it's—*fuck*! He jammed the lock!"

The key morphed frantically in her hand, expanding into a pry-bar and then a flat surface she could use for leverage. But the lock was well and truly jammed. "Fuck." Wendy froze, then looked over her shoulder. "We're going to need to break it, but if he's waiting outside he'll hear—"

Del laid a calming hand on her shoulder. "Peace! There will be no battering here. Listen, can you make a stepladder?"

"Yes, but—" Wendy gestured at the staircase—"it might slip—"

"Not if you hook it over the top of the gate."

Game Boy was positively frantic, hopping up and down on his toes: "Do it! Do it! Do it! The bad things are coming!"

Wendy made Del's ladder appear, while Imp gaped, his usual pose of detachment abandoned for the time being. She stood aside as Del scrambled up the ladder and dropped to the graveyard dirt on the other side of the gate. "Game Boy? You go next." Wendy gripped one side of the ladder. "If I let go it'll fade," she said tensely. "Go on, *go*, I can't hold it for long, it's too heavy."

The Lost Boys scrambled over the gate and dropped—or in Doc's case slithered—down the bars on the other side. Finally Wendy scrambled up and over. Del caught her, cushioning her fall. "That was wicked!"

"Thank me when we're home," Wendy gasped.

"Come *on*." Game Boy scurried towards the lich-gate, paused, then scuttled forward some more. "It's safe," he called quietly. "The big bad is behind us, not in front."

"Big bad?" asked Doc.

"Tink—Tinkerbell," Imp stuttered, on the edge of losing his shit completely. He'd heard the glassy chimes of malevolence ringing through the streets of a London that never was, the voice of the Lares in their true form, kept out of the real world by the psychopomp pets interred in the grounds of the mansion. Propitiated by the blood of Starkeys, generation after generation, maintaining custody over the family's dream-buried treasures. He'd never truly *believed*, until now, whatever Eve said: and believing, he felt no desire to clap.

Together they traced their route back to the door to the real world. The mist swirled thickly now, forming bizarre illusory sculptures that climbed hip-high in places, dulling sounds and making it impossible to see more than a hundred meters in any direction. "Walls are coming down," Imp repeated. He peered at the mist between his legs. "Does anyone else see this?"

"See what?" Doc took the bait.

"Mermaids and pirate ships," he murmured, "the set dressing for the ultimate pantomime—"

"We can't stay here." Doc took his arm and tugged. "It's not safe."

Imp didn't move. "Scared now. Don't wanna leave. You can't make me."

"Yes I can." Doc wrapped his arms around Imp. "You're not staying. They're illusions for kids, Jerm, it's trying to trap you."

Imp fell silent as Del and Wendy followed Game Boy through the side-door, even though it was alarmingly ajar. If Game Boy's gamer sixth sense said it was safe to proceed, then the bad man with the gun wouldn't be waiting on the other side.

"Dude," said Doc. "We can't wait."

"But the book—"

"Forget the spell book, that asshole's going to get what he deserves from the curse—"

"—No, I mean the *other* book, the one I need to be inside—" Ticking crocodiles and flying infants and a shadowless boy with the burned-out corpses of stars in his eyes—

"You can't live here," said Doc, then gently kissed him. After a couple of seconds, Imp relaxed in his embrace and kissed him back, hugging him tight. Finally they separated for air. "You've got to grow up sooner or later," Doc told his lover.

Imp took a deep breath of Neverland. "I never wanted that."

"Come on. Come with me, or your sister wins."

Imp scowled. "It isn't like that, we're not *rivals*." Neither for human sacrifice, nor the favor of their father.

"Prove it, then."

The mist rose chest-high now, extruding tentacles filled with hypnagogic images that swirled almost to their heads. Some were fantastic, others were scarily plausible; but either way, they sucked the eye in and demanded the attention of the beholder. Elves and dragons danced a deadly waltz across high moorlands, around a castle on a mountain at the center of a perfectly circular lake that had once been a giant city beneath the shattered moon. Then all were swept aside to make room for a merry row of gibbeted felons, dangling like the Devil's Christmas baubles along a Regent Street where carol singers chanted praise before the throne of the All-Highest, the Dread Lord of Downing Street—

"This is amazing," Imp whispered. "All the dreams of films unmade: I could be Fritz Lang—" He shook his head.

"What do you think your sister saw in the mists here?" Doc challenged him: "Come on, tell me!"

"Eve . . . she lost her *I*; she'll have seen nothing." Imp smiled crookedly, or maybe it was meant to be a grimace. "Evie would have been another matter."

"I have no idea what you're talking about and I'm scared now." Doc relaxed his grip, now that Imp was at least responding to stimuli. "Come on, let's go home."

Imp sighed, then set one reluctant foot in front of the other. "I'll never get a source of raw material like this again," he complained.

"Save it for later."

The mist rose head-high and obscured almost everything now, but a faint rectangular glow limned the outline of the doorway. "Come on." Doc tugged Imp's hand. "Nearly there!"

"Nearly where?" Imp's voice sounded so dreary.

"Nearly home. Just another step." Imp wasn't moving. Doc tugged, but Imp's feet were planted. He turned and grabbed Imp's arm in both hands and heaved him forward, feeling a faint sucking resistance as his shoes slithered free of the dream pavement and they crossed the threshold into a lobby lit by the cheery yellow glow of a low-power incandescent bulb and the welcoming cries of their friends.

"What took you so long?" demanded Game Boy as Del slammed the door behind them. "What happened?"

"He froze up," Doc told them.

Imp rubbed his forehead with one hand while he leaned against the door. "I feel drained," he complained. Then he looked down, and shuffled nervously aside, searching for something on the floor.

"What is it—" Doc began, just as Imp said, "Has anyone seen my shadow?"

But answer came there none.

The Bond had a smug. But of course, to his way of thinking he had good reason for it.

Despite the pileup of hunting parties outside the Neverland reading room, he had the book. The black dyke chick had given it to him fair and square and her crew of deviants and shoplifters hadn't even tried to stop her. No surprise: they didn't have enough guts to house a tapeworm between the lot of them. The men were faggots or trannies, the women were ugly bitches, and he was . . . well, he was going to be a lot richer once he figured out how to extract Miss Starkey's collection bonus from her bank account and fence the goods, which would be a lot easier once the numb cunt was dead.

He hurried through the nodes of the treasure map with bag in hand. Somewhere off in another room the wind-chimes were jangling—somebody had probably left a window open—but it wouldn't matter for much longer. Not once he set the charges and brought the house down.

He was feeling the burn now. He'd walked several miles around Whitechapel, managed to avoid getting sucked into a firefight—there was always an insane adrenaline crash afterwards—then pushed through the crash and jogged several more miles up that spooky sunken road. He hadn't brought any protein bars or hydration, not having expected what he'd found on the top floor of the haunted mansion. He was probably dehydrated by now, and he wasn't as young as he used to be. As he faced the seventh flight of stairs (three up, then two down, not to mention a whole bunch of corridors and a ring around the roses) he thought, *Why not take the elevator?* After all there was a lift just two corridors and a receiving room away from his current location, and he'd seen the other elevator doors on the top floor. It was the brass wire slam-door kind that had been current in the late nineteenth century, but dammit, why not? It'd save a couple of miles of this shit, and the Bond was all in favor of doing that right now.

The Bond stole along the passage to the elevator lobby. But as he came close, who should he find but Miss Starkey and her bodyguard, already waiting for the lift car as if it was no big deal? How the bitch had gotten ahead of him was a question for another time. Right now, his biggest problem was the Gammon with the submachine gun who was covering her six. He was alert and doing his job properly, which is to say he'd clearly swept the lobby seconds ago and was now drawing a bead on the darkened elevator shaft beyond the shuttered gate. Miss Starkey was looking the same way, her back turned to the Bond. The whine of ancient machinery covered the Bond's final step, although something—possibly a shadow, or his presence disturbing the air flow—made the Gammon whirl towards him and aim just a fraction of a second too late. A tight cluster of red-rimmed holes flowered around the bridge of his nose and he dropped like a sack of potatoes, his gun clattering to the floor.

"Freeze!" barked the Bond. Miss Starkey froze in the act of turning. "Hands on top of your head, fingers laced!" She complied. "Kick it away! Now! Do it or I shoot! Face the wall!" The sinister windchimes chuckled their appreciation of his performance.

The lift finally put in an appearance, sliding glacially down to halt behind the gate.

The Bond licked his lips. "Open the lift gates," he ordered her.

Miss Starkey stiffened, then shrugged, drawing attention to her arms, her hands—

"One hand only," he warned. "Then back on top of your

head." He had zero intention of giving her the slightest opportunity to make a dive for her bodyguard's gun, now resting on the carpet halfway across the lobby.

Beside her feet, a pool of blood was spreading. Miss Starkey stepped delicately around it to reach for the outer gate. It clattered as it retracted. She drew the inner gate back as well, revealing a wood-panelled room, as cozy as a coffin sized for two.

"Go inside and face the wall," said the Bond, already stiffening with anticipation. This was not quite how he'd envisaged the trapped-in-a-lift-with-Miss-Starkey scene playing out—her dressed like a Victorian widow and himself returning from a mission exhausted and sweaty—but it was close enough. "Move!" he growled, stepping over the dead meat. He had a headache: best to get this over with.

Miss Starkey finally spoke. "Did you get the book?" She sounded mildly curious, as if she was asking about the weather or the latest test series. Her lack of fear was irritating.

"Shut up, bitch." He held his gun to the back of her head as he dropped the bag on the floor of the lift and drew the outer gate shut with his now-free hand. Then he reached for the inner gate. "I got it. We're nearly done here. No witnesses, like M said."

"Who's M?" she asked.

"The boss, Rupe—" He gritted his teeth furiously against the rapidly worsening pounding in his skull—"shut up! Only speak when I tell you to! Do you understand?" She shrugged again. He winced as he glanced at the brass control panel, then pushed the topmost button—black Bakelite with no label. "Going up." The lift began to rise.

"Do you want money?" she asked tonelessly, ignoring his earlier order. "Whatever he's paying you, I can pay more."

"Turn round." She slowly turned to face him, her expression botox-blank. Miss Starkey didn't have resting bitch face; she didn't have resting *anything* face. She'd have revealed more of her thoughts to him if he emptied his magazine into her perfect turquoise eyes. She was, however, beautiful. Beautiful like a priceless Ming vase or a very expensive supercar, one outside his price range. The kind of beauty that made him want to hurt her, to bring her down to the level of his own inner ugly, to make her feel something of the ache that gripped him right now, everywhere from his head to the soles of his feet. He shivered. This wasn't normal; this was the vestibule to the land where dreams come true.

"Kneel," he demanded.

She knelt. "What do you think you're doing?" she asked.

"Anything I fucking feel like. Tell me, how much is the book worth? Really?"

"How much is anything unique worth?" She might have shrugged. "How much is your life worth?"

"More than yours." He held his gun to her forehead one-handed, his cock springing rigid with excitement. "Yes: I know about the curse."

"Why do you think it hasn't killed you?"

"I made them give me the book," he gloated, willing his hand not to shake. He was sweating: it was unaccountably cold in the lift car. "Any final words?"

"Mm, yes. Did I ever make you a cup of coffee?" She looked up at him with a quizzical smile on her face.

"No, why—" He felt *really* sick. "The book. It's worth . . . worth . . ." *I'm burning up*, he realized. A fever out of nowhere, sweeping over him like one of the sudden death diseases of childhood that swept through Victorian London leaving black crepe and tiny headstones in its wake. "Shit."

"I didn't ever make you coffee," Miss Starkey said, "so you missed out on my special demonstration. Pity, that."

The wall of the lift rippled in front of his vision, and began to fog. The pain behind his eyes was excruciating. He tried to squeeze the trigger, but his hand wasn't working properly. In fact, nothing was working properly. The Bond leaned against the back wall of the lift, breathing hard.

"Wha . . ."

"A mug of coffee contains about half a liter of water," Miss Starkey calmly explained. "I can bring it to a near-boil in about a minute. A human skull contains about two liters of stuff that can be approximated to greasy water. I can raise its temperature by ten degrees Celsius in about fifteen seconds. That's enough to denature proteins, such as neurotransmitter receptors, like soft-boiling an egg—"

But the Bond wasn't listening any more. His feet drummed a tetanic tattoo on the elevator car floor. He'd bitten his tongue badly, a bloody froth trickling from his lips.

Eve winced. "Damn it," she complained softly.

Finally, the lift arrived at the top floor.

Eve rose and took a couple of deep breaths, clearing her mind. Then she leaned over the bag and addressed it politely in a dead language no human tongue had evolved to utter: "By the life I claimed on your behalf, the next one is yours also." She opened the lift gates, stepped out, and closed the gates again. With ghostly mental fingers she reached through the lift gates and pushed the button to send the car back to the ground floor. With a somewhat greater psychic exertion, she ripped out the wires behind the call button. Then she made her way back towards the real world.

Behind her, shadows lengthened in the lift as it descended towards Neverland. Inside it, the carpetbag sat in lonely splendor on a floor restored to pristine condition, all evidence of the Bond's presence banished like a dream. Within the bag, the leatherbound book throbbed gently as a dead man's pulse, waxing plump and powerful.

Imp and his crew knew better than to touch the book. Which, to Eve's way of thinking, was a very good thing indeed. She knew better, too: custody of the tome had already cost her family far too much. They'd bled for it ever since the late nineteenth century, when an ancestor had acquired it and foolishly followed one of the rituals it described, trading baby lives for Lares to protect his family and heirs in perpetuity. As long as it slumbered in Neverland it couldn't do too much more harm—but now that it had come to the attention of Rupert and his friends, it fell to Eve to cover it up again.

Sacrifices had to be made, starting with the Bond.

Eve had always been of the opinion that when life handed you lemons, you should make lemonade.

Rupert dabbed at his forehead with his monogrammed silk kerchief, then paused on the landing to wheeze. *Damn these stairs*, he thought irritably as he reached for his asthma inhaler.

Eve had popped out of the office with her alarmingly overpriced bodyguard a few hours ago, then she'd completely dropped off the map, as Rupert had discovered on arrival at London HQ. However, Tech Support had a tracker on her smartphone, and Rupert held the other end of its high-tech leash. It had led him here, to a decaying shitpile on Kensington Palace Gardens. It was an investment property, currently overrun by squatters and suchlike riffraff. According to the Tech Support database one of the squatters was a Person of Interest—Eve's younger brother.

Rupert had brought bodyguards along. They made short work of the gate, and he stalked through the overgrown debris-strewn drive to find a stove-in front door and shattered windows. *Disgusting*, he thought. *What on Earth is she doing* here? The only clue he could see was parked just around the corner—his Aston Martin. Obviously the Bond had come here, then Eve had followed him for some reason of her own . . .

"Sir, I'd recommend that we check the building for squatters before you enter?" one of his guards advised.

Rupert smiled tightly and shook his head. "I'll be perfectly fine," he told the man. "You fellows can stand guard outside. I don't expect I'll run into any trouble." At least, not into any kind of trouble that might pose a threat to a High Priest of the Mute Poet. Rings of power dug into the fleshy skin at the base of his fingers, and he wore a ward under his shirt collar. His waistcoat lining was spun from the silk of a venomous spider, embroidered with fell runes and a powerful grid to absorb incoming imprecatory energies. It would take more than merely human malice (or bullets) to wound him.

He'd entered with flashlight in hand, only to find chaos. Tables overturned, paper strewn everywhere, a lingering sickly stench. One of his rings pulsed luminous blue. *Poison*, he realized, startled, then commanded the ring to decontaminate the entire building. *What kind of squatter throws poisonous substances around his own digs?* Curious and curiouser.

Of course he'd brought along a copy of the rather odd diagram Eve had printed before she nipped round to visit her brother. Looking at the diagram, it made more sense now. It was a map of sorts, and it started out *right here*. In fact, now he thought about it, this must be the document Eve had tried to buy at auction. He chuckled quietly. So the lost concordance to the *Book of Dead Names* had been in her family's custody all along, but she hadn't known? Such irony!

It would be interesting to hear what Eve had to say for herself before he dropped the hammer on her.

By the time he made it to the top floor Rupert was breathing stertorously and sweating like a pig. His opinion of Eve's brother, low to start with, was now at rock bottom. How could anyone stand to live in such a shithole? Obviously he was an even worse wastrel than the reports had indicated, back when he had a PI looking into Eve's background.

But now Rupert found something promising: a door, wedged ajar where no door should be—a door between two rooms, and it was the source of the occult power he'd felt flowing through the building like effluent from an overflowing sewer. *Well then*.

Rupert strode forward into the corridor behind the impossible door. He'd read of such interstitial spaces: he knew the hazards. This one was long-term stable—it had to be, anchored as it was by the Starkey family's magical pact (never call it a curse, for it brought such wonders into the world). Eve had undoubtedly come this way. So in all probability had the Bond.

He had just arrived at a curious sight—a dead hedge maze in a glass-walled penthouse, a roof garden or conservatory of sorts dotted with markers like graveyard headstones—when he heard footsteps. A door at the other side of the conservatory opened and a familiar figure stepped onto the path through the skeletal bushes. He drew himself up. "Miss Starkey!" he called, smiling widely. "Good to see you at last! Have you found the book?"

She gave no sign of hearing him, but as she drew closer he registered that something was not quite right. Her gait was tired and her eyes dull. She wore a coat over a long dress that dragged on the footpath, its hem filthy and soaked in mud or some other noisome liquid.

"Miss Starkey!" he called again, peremptory. "Pay attention!"

Eve finally looked up. Her lips moved soundlessly, as if she was mumbling something. Rupert tensed and readied his rings of power, swollen with *mana* and charged with the blood of innocents. To confront an oneiromancer in the dream palace of her family, where every room represented an inherited spell, was dangerous even for him, even though his control over her was unassailable.

"Where. Is. It?" he demanded, enunciating each word clearly and distinctly.

"What?" She shook her head and saw him, as if for the first time. "What? Mr. de Montfort Bigge? What are you doing here?"

"It's been eight hours, Miss Starkey! You've been gone from the office since yesterday afternoon. Did you find the book?"

She looked down—not at his feet, as he expected, but at one of the stones protruding from the maze. "Oh yeah, he's here." She rested a hand companionably on top of the stone before engaging with him: "Do you know what this is?" she asked.

"Do I care?" he asked, not unironically.

"Life . . . can be defined as the set of natural processes that copy information into the future. Power comes from the destruction of information, by computational or other means, you know." She patted the headstone. "Our power—yours, mine—comes from death, doesn't it? The *Book of Dead Names*, the so-called *Necronomicon*. Or the bodies in the sub-subbasement, the altar in the chapel in Castle Skaro." She shrugged: "They all tap into the same source of energy." She patted the headstone again, looking thoughtful. "Only the personal cost varies."

"Where is the book?" Rupert repeated, a hint of steel creeping into his voice.

"My family is at least honest: the pact we made requires us to sacrifice our own, and we hurt and we bleed and we remember them." *Now* she smiled at him, an expression quite fey with derangement. "These are the graves of my ancestors' brothers and sisters, did you know that? They're all buried in here. *This* one is Grandpa's younger brother. Imp would have been buried here, too, if Grandpa hadn't broken and Dad hadn't chickened out. He paid for it with his life, and all I got for it was a doubly incontinent nursing home bed-blocker with no tongue."

"Fuck your mother!" Rupert burst out, exasperated. "Where is my *book*?" he demanded, taking a step towards her.

"Fuck *you*, Rupert, I *quit*!" She sent him a glare that by rights ought to have reduced half of London to cinders.

"You're overwrought," he snapped. He could escalate, he realized, but then he'd have to reveal his true degree of control over her, and she'd react unpredictably. "We'll talk about this in the office—"

"You can get the book yourself." She straightened up. "It's in the elevator, which is stuck on the ground floor. Give me the map, I'll mark it for you." She snapped her fingers at him. "Come on, I don't have all day to wait around—"

Rupert handed her the map, and a pencil. "I understand you're very upset," he oozed, "but I'm sure if you sleep on it you'll feel a lot better. And really, you can't quit." She scribbled illegibly in the margin and drew an arrow on the map, pointing to the alleged location of the elevator. "Go home, take tomorrow off, and we'll pretend we never had this conversation—"

"Enough." She shoved the map back at Rupert, and pointed to the arrow. "Go through that doorway—we're in this room, here—and down the hall, then keep on the map until you get to the lift. It's stuck on the ground floor, the call button up here burned out. There's a carpetbag in the lift, and the book's inside it. I verified it: it's the real deal."

"You had it and you left it there?" Rupert said with palpable astonishment.

"Believe me, it would have been *very* unwise of me to have carried it further!" she said sharply. "You can go get it yourself if you want it so badly. Like I said, I quit: I no longer work for you."

"You can't quit," he repeated, "but we will continue this conversation in the office, the day after tomorrow." He strode off in the direction she'd indicated.

Eve turned away from him and departed, unwinding the trail through the labyrinth of dreams, leaving the family graveyard in peace.

A few minutes later, Imp, Doc, Del, Game Boy, and Wendy walked in, checked their bearings on the map, and exited through the same doorway as Eve.

Far below the dead conservatory, malign windchimes played their Tinkerbell theme again as Rupert opened the gates of the elevator and reached for the spell book lurking in the shadows, sleek and vicious with anticipation, waiting to feed again on dreams of death and avarice.

A week later, Imp returned to Bigge HQ to visit his sister in her office.

The Lost Boys had spent six days tidying up after they got home. The scene that had greeted them on their return was dismaying. Broken glass everywhere, overturned or slashed furniture, someone had trampled the Christmas present Imp had so carefully wrapped for Game Boy, and the kitchen sink contents had achieved sapience and were threatening to sue for full human rights. There was only one thing for it: they did the best they could with the front door, then bedded down on the top floor, Imp and Doc in one bedroom, Wendy and Del in the other, and Game Boy in the bathroom.

The morning after they won the war for Neverland, Imp had set them to work tidying, scrubbing, cleaning, and fitting new glass in the broken window panes. Four days later the house was spick and span, everyone had their own bedroom back (although Del seemed to be spending most of her time round at Wendy's flat), and the door to Neverland was nailed shut and boarded over, with a second coat of paint drying.

Then Imp received a text message—a very headmistressy SEE ME—and of course he had to go and find out how Eve had fared with her boss.

This time, he didn't dress to impress. What you see is what you get, and in Imp Eve was going to get what he wanted to grow up to be, which was to say, an aspiring director of artistically challenging long-form visual media, starting with the movie he intended to make: *Dead Lies Dreaming*.

When he got to the front door of Bigge HQ and rang the bell, he discovered that there had been a few changes.

"Mr. Starkey, sir? Please come in and have a seat! Would you like some tea or coffee? Your sister will see you shortly—" The receptionist fawned on him and the imperious butler was perfectly polite, as long as Imp ignored the apprehensive sidelong glances that implied he feared Imp might have him flogged for insolence. Which, quite honestly, wasn't Imp's kink, any more than the conventionally pretty blonde receptionist who kept pushing her chest up at him. (For the time being, Imp had decided, his type consisted of Doc, and

Doc alone—at least until he got bored with the lack of variety and decided he was poly again.)

After accepting a cup of very fine tea—just to shut the poor woman up and stop her fussing—Imp settled down to wait. He didn't have to cool his heels for long. "Jeremy!" His sister smiled warmly as she stepped out of a corridor leading back into the town house, an expression which (judging by the butler's double-take) was most unusual. "Long time no see!" she added, unironically air-kissing him as she led him into a gigantic and luxuriously appointed executive lair.

"This isn't your office," Imp said, sounding stupid even to his own ears. There was nothing for it: he doubled down on the oropharyngeal toe-massage. "Moving up in the world, baby?" He propped his hip against the desk and grinned crookedly at her.

Eve shut the door, stalked around the desk, and flopped bonelessly into a classic Evil Overlord chair that was probably worth more than the house they'd grown up in. "Welcome to my world," she said, with a careless wave at the bay window overlooking a neatly manicured garden that went on and on and *on*, looking out over some of the most expensive real estate in the world.

"Wait, what—" Imp's brain finally caught up—"you got a promotion?"

"What can I say?" She shrugged: "Dead man's shoes." She smiled a pixie grin that Imp hadn't thought he'd see again, not since the day their father died.

"Wait, your boss . . ."

"He was so eager he went to get the book himself." She frowned slightly. "You didn't run into him upstairs, did you?"

"No! What happened?"

"I told him I quit, and he could get it his own damn self."
She glanced around. "Obviously I worded it very carefully.
And did it in precisely that order."

"Wait, you—"

"I resigned, then I told him where he could find the book."
The fey grin came out to play again. "He never came back.
I'm pretty sure the curse got him: if not, he wandered off into
Neverland and didn't make it out."

"Damn." Imp rubbed his forehead, frowning. "How? I
mean, he bought it, didn't he? Isn't he its legitimate owner
now? Shouldn't it have recognized him?"

"You might think that, but the book doesn't necessarily
agree." She smiled to herself, a knowing expression that made
Imp's blood chill momentarily. "Rupert was the chief executive of de Montfort Bigge Holdings, you see, an investment
vehicle domiciled in Skaro for tax purposes, private equity
with a specialty in highly unprofitable global subsidiaries—
subsidiaries that forwarded their profits to Rupert's beneficial
trust via a double Irish with a Dutch sandwich, or whatever
wheeze the rocket scientists in accounting have replaced the
Double Irish Jammy Tax Dodge with this week, to stay one
jump ahead of the legal loopholes the authorities keep trying
to close on us. And sure, he told me to acquire the book for
him. And yes, I did that. But I didn't pay for it using money
in one of Rupert's personal accounts, or even a company he
owned a majority share of.

"Instead, I used Rupert's funds to buy a house. And then
I remortgaged it. It's a very valuable property, apparently—
it's on Kensington Palace Gardens, don't you know? I think
you can guess the address. Anyway, it gave me a line on the
twenty-five million and change I needed in order to preempt
the auction, plus a bridging loan and a few other odds and
ends I needed. This all went through a management company

I set up, and by the way your name is on the deeds along with mine. Which means the purchase of the book used money coming directly from an offshore financial entity that you and I jointly own, which owes Rupert the twenty-five mil but what the hey, he's not about to come and collect it any time soon."

Imp flapped his jaw. "What. The. Fuck?"

"Dad was right, you know: accountancy really *is* magic," his sister told him. "Only I figured that out too late," she added quietly.

"The curse affected anyone who took the book and didn't own it. But we owned—we own—the family house again? So the curse couldn't affect you or me, or someone acting under our instructions, but your boss . . . oh dear fucking me." He rocked back and forth, thinking furiously.

"I'm pretty sure Rupert learned about the book a few years ago, when he hired me. But it took him ages to find the map Grandpa left lying around, and even longer to set me up to go fetch. He told me to buy the book for him. But he didn't say *how* I was to buy the book for him, and I was very careful indeed not to give him any authority to collect the book on my behalf."

"Which is why you resigned first, before you told him where you'd left it." He looked at her, eyes glittering. "What now?"

"You go back to the house you co-own and check your bank balance," she said. "I paid the finder's fee we agreed, in full. The solicitors should be getting in touch soon. When they do, forward me their email?"

"But, but . . ."

"I'm putting you on salary," she announced. "You'll be listed as a janitor, working at, oh, a certain property I mentioned buying earlier: duties to include any housework necessary to keep it in order, the money isn't great but it includes on-site accommodation for yourself and up to four designated friends and family? You should have plenty of time left over for making movies on the side. But your principal job—which will *not* be written down anywhere—is to keep that fucking door shut. And don't, whatever you do, breed. Are we square?"

Imp stood. "This isn't fair!"

"Jerm." She walked around the desk until she was close enough to reach out and touch his nose: "*Life* isn't fair. If life was fair the family curse would come with an escape clause, Dad wouldn't have died for you, Mum wouldn't be in a care home, and your elder sister would probably have babies instead of control of a multi-billion-pound hedge fund." She looked thoughtful. "Although the hedge fund is a *really good* consolation prize, come to think of it."

A pair of cut crystal tumblers filled themselves from the decanter on the sideboard and floated across to her. She took one and passed it to Imp. "Here's to family," she proposed, and they raised their glasses to their parents, and the brothers and sisters and children they would never have.

(THE END—for now)

extras

orbitbooks.net

about the author

Charles Stross is a full-time science fiction writer and resident of Edinburgh, Scotland. The author of seven Hugo-nominated novels and winner of the 2005, 2010 and 2014 Hugo Awards for best novella ('The Concrete Jungle', 'Palimpsest' and 'Equoid'), Stross's works have been translated into over twelve languages.

Like many writers, Stross has had a variety of careers, occupations and job-shaped catastrophes in the past, from pharmacist (he quit after the second police stake-out) to first code monkey on the team of a successful dot-com start-up (with brilliant timing he tried to change employer just as the bubble burst). Along the way he collected degrees in Pharmacy and Computer Science, making him the world's first officially qualified cyberpunk writer (just as cyberpunk died).

In 2013, he was Creative in Residence at the UK-wide Centre for Creativity, Regulation, Enterprise and Technology, researching the business models and regulation of industries such as music, film, TV, computer games and publishing.

Find out more about Charles Stross and other Orbit authors by registering for the free monthly newsletter at orbitbooks.net.

if you enjoyed
DEAD LIES DREAMING

look out for

INK & SIGIL

by

Kevin Hearne

Al MacBharrais is both blessed and cursed. He is blessed with an extraordinary white moustache, an appreciation for craft cocktails — and a most unique magical talent. He can cast spells with magically enchanted ink and he uses his gifts to protect our world from rogue minions of various pantheons, especially the Fae.

But he is also cursed. Anyone who hears his voice will begin to feel an inexplicable hatred for Al, so he can only communicate through the written word or speech apps. And his apprentices keep dying in peculiar freak accidents. As his personal life crumbles around him, he devotes his life to his work, all the while trying to crack the secret of his curse.

But when his latest apprentice, Gordie, turns up dead in his Glasgow flat, Al discovers evidence that Gordie was living a secret life of crime. Now Al is forced to play detective — while avoiding actual detectives who are wondering why death seems to always follow Al. Investigating his apprentice's death will take him through Scotland's magical underworld, and he'll need the help of a mischievous hobgoblin if he's to survive.

CHAPTER 1

Scones Should Come with a Warning

Deid apprentices tend to tarnish a man's reputation after a while. I'm beginning to wonder when mine will be beyond repair.

Fergus was crushed by a poorly tossed caber at the Highland Games.

Abigail's parachute didn't open when she went skydiving.

Beatrice was an amateur mycologist and swallowed poison mushrooms.

Ramsey was run over by American tourists driving on the wrong bloody side of the road.

Nigel went to Toronto on holiday and got his skull cracked by a hockey puck.

Alice was stabbed in a spot of bother with some football hooligans.

And now Gordie, who was supposed to be my lucky number seven, choked to death on a scone this morning. It had raisins in it, so that was bloody daft, as raisins are ill-omened abominations and he should have known better. Regardless of their ingredients, one should never eat a scone alone. Poor wee man.

None of their deaths was my fault, and they were completely unrelated to their training in my discipline, so that's in my favor, at least. But still. People are starting to wonder if I'm capable of training a successor.

I'm starting to wonder too. And I'd like to have a successor soon, as I'm past sixty and rather wishing I could spend my time on sunny beaches, or in sunny gardens, or indeed anyplace where I might see the sun more often.

Scotland is not known for its sunshine. The Highlands get two hundred sixty days of rain per year. But it's no fun for people in other countries to think of us as perpetually drenched, so I believe the popular imagination has painted us with kilts and bagpipes and unfortunate cuisine.

The muscle-bound constable standing outside Gordie's flat in Maryhill and doing a fair job of blocking the entrance held up a hand as I moved to step around him and reach for the door. He was in no mood to give me a polite redirection. "The fuck ye daein', bampot? Away an' shite," he said.

"Ram it up yer farter, Constable. Inspector knows I'm comin', so get out ma way."

Oh, yes, and colorful language. Scotland's reputation for that is well deserved.

My cane is in fact a weapon that a person of my age is allowed to carry around openly, but I pretended to lean on it as I pulled out my "official ID" and flashed it at him. It was not a badge or anything truly official but rather a piece of goatskin parchment on which I had written three sigils with carefully prepared inks. Any one of them alone would probably work, but in combination they were practically guaranteed to hack the brain through the ocular nerve and get me my way. Most people are susceptible to manipulation through visual media—ask anyone in advertising. Sigils take advantage of this collective vulnerability far more potently.

The first one, Sigil of Porous Mind, was the most important, as it leached away the target's certainties and priorities and made them open to suggestion. It also made it difficult for the target to remember anything that happened in the next few minutes. The next one, Sigil of Certain Authority, applied to me, granting my personage whatever importance the constable's mind would plausibly accept. The third, Sigil of Quick Compliance, should goad him to agree to almost any reasonable order I gave next and make him feel good about it, giving him a hit of dopamine.

"Let me pass," I said.

"Right ye are, sir," he said, and smartly stepped to the side. There was plenty of room for me to enter now without contact and no need to say anything more. But he'd been a tad rude and I believed it deserved a proportional response, so I shouldered past him and muttered, "I pumpt yer gran." He flashed a glare at me but said nothing, and then I was in the flat.

The inspector inside did not, in fact, know I was coming. She was middle-aged and looked a bit tired when she swung around at my entrance, but she was a good deal more polite than the constable. She had decided to let her hair go grey instead of dying it, and I liked her immediately for the decision.

"Hello. Who are you, then?"

There was a forensics tech of indeterminate gender taking digital pictures and ignoring both of us, an actual camera pressed to their face instead of a phone or a tablet extended toward the victim. I deployed the official ID once more and gestured at the body of poor Gordie, blue in the face and sprawled on his kitchen floor. Years of training, his hopes and mine, all spread out and lifeless. "Tell me what ye know about the man's death."

The inspector blinked rapidly as the sigils did their work and then replied, "Neighbor in the flat downstairs called it in because the victim fell pretty heavily and pounded on the floor—or the neighbor's ceiling—a few times before dying. A choking accident, as far as we can tell, unless the tox screen comes back and tells us there was something wrong with the scone."

"Of course there was something wrong," I said, looking at the half-eaten remainder sitting on a small saucer. "It had raisins in it. Anything else of note?"

She pointed toward the hallway. "Two bedrooms, but he lived alone. One bedroom is full of fountain pens and inks. Never seen the like. Bit of a nutter."

"Right. That's why I'm here. I need to send that stuff in for testing n' that."

The inspector's features clouded with confusion. "He didnae drink any of it."

"No, no. This is part of a different investigation. We've been watching him for a while."

"We? I'm sorry, I didnae catch your name."

"Aloysius MacBharrais. Ye can call me Al."

"Thanks. And you're investigating his inks?"

"Aye. Toxic chemicals. Illegal compounds. That sort of rubbish."

"On ye go, then. I didnae like that room. Felt strange in there."

That idle comment was a huge warning. Gordie must have

had some active and unsecured sigils inside. And all his inks—painstakingly, laboriously crafted with rare ingredients and latent magical power—had to be removed. The last thing the world needed was some constable accidentally doodling his way to a Sigil of Unchained Destruction. I'd secure them and preserve them for later analysis, keeping the successful decoctions and viable ingredients, and destroying the rest.

I turned without another word and went to the hallway. There were three doors, one presumably being the loo. Layout suggested that was the first door on my left, so I went to the second and cautiously cracked it open. It was his bedroom, and there was a desk as well with a small collection of pens, inks, and papers—all for normal correspondence. I snatched a sheet of stationery and selected an Aurora 88 pen from my coat pocket. It was presently filled with a rust-colored ink using cinnabar for the pigment and a varnish infused with ground pearls, fish glue, and the vitreous jelly of owl eyes. I drew a small circle first to direct the effect at myself, then carefully but quickly outlined the shapes of the Sigil of Warded Sight, which looked like a red eye, barred and banded over with simple knotwork. Once completed, the sigil activated and my sight changed to black and white, all color receptors dormant. It was the most basic defense against unsecured sigils: I could not be affected by them until this one wore off—or until I destroyed it myself. It had saved me too many injuries to count.

Putting the pen away and hefting my cane defensively, I kept the sigil in my left hand and crossed the hall to open the door to Gordie's study. A waft of foul, funky air immediately punched me in the nose, and I wondered why the inspector hadn't said anything about it before. It smelled like a sweaty scrotum. Or maybe ten of them.

"Gah," I said, and coughed a couple of times to clear my lungs. I heard titters coming from the kitchen and realized the inspector had left out that fact on purpose. No wonder she'd told me to have at it. Her politeness had been a ruse to draw me to an olfactory ambush.

But I'd been wise to guard my vision. Gordie had far more than a few sigils lying around. The room was full of them, warding against this and that. The walls were lined with raw wooden workbenches and chairs, and cubbyholes full of labeled inks and ingredients glinted on the left. The main bench for ink preparation was opposite the door, and it was stained with pigments and oils and binders and held stoppered bottles of yet more inks. There was also a labeled rack of fountain pens and trays of paper and cards for sigils, along with sealing wax, a melting spoon, and a box of matches. Several cards pasted on the wall above the workbench had recognizable sigils on them for selective sight and attention that should make me— or anyone else who entered—completely ignore what was on the right side of the room. That's why the detective inspector had felt so uncomfortable. She felt something was going on in there and most likely saw it, but the sigils wouldn't let her mind process it. My warded sight made the sigils ineffective, so I had no difficulty seeing that there was a hobgoblin grunting and straining to work his way out of a cage placed on top of the workbench. That was a sight I never thought I'd see.

Different from pure goblins and more mischievous than outright malevolent, hobgoblins were extraordinarily difficult to capture as a rule, since they could teleport short distances and were agile creatures as well, with impressive vertical leaps aided by their thick thighs. This one was trying to reach one of several sigils placed around his cage on little metal stands, like draught-beer lists placed on pub tables. His long, hairy-knuckled fingers waggled as he stretched for the sigil nearest him. If he could reach one of them and tear it up, he might have a way out, since the sigils were more of a prison for him than the actual cage was. He froze when he saw me staring at him, openmouthed.

"Wot?" he said.

I closed the door behind me. "What are ye *daein'* here?"

"I'm in a cage, in't I? Ye must be the cream of Scottish intelligence. Cannae be anywhere else if I'm no free, ya fuckin' genius. But at least ye can see an' hear me. The bird who was here before couldnae."

"I mean why does he have ye caged?" The fellow didn't appear to be an unusual hobgoblin worthy of capture or study; he was short and hairy, square-jawed, his face adorned with a fleshy nose and eyebrows like untrimmed hedgerows.

"He's a right evil bastard, that's why. Or was. He's deid, in't he? How'd he die?"

"Raisin scone."

"So it was suicide, then."

"Naw, it was an accident."

"He didn't *accidentally* eat a raisin scone, now, did he? So it was suicide."

I shrugged, conceding the point. "Who are you?"

"I'm the happy hob ye're gonnay set free now. Unless ye're like him."

"I'm no like him. I'm alive, to begin with. Answer ma questions truthfully and no more dodges. Who are ye and why did Gordie imprison ye here?"

"Said he was gonnay sell me. He's a trafficker in Fae folk, so he is. Or was."

"Nonsense." I stamped my cane on the floor. "Tell me the truth!"

The hobgoblin stood as straight as he could in his cage—he was only about two feet tall—and placed his right hand over his heart, deploying the phrase that the Fae always used when they were swearing the truth or asserting reality. "I tell ye three times, man. He's got a buyer. I'm s'posed tae be delivered tonight. And I'm no the first he's sold. There was a pixie in here a couple of days ago, didnae stay long." He pointed to a slightly smaller, empty cage sitting next to his.

This information was more of a shock to me than Gordie's death. I'd had apprentices die on me before, but none of them had used their knowledge of sigils to traffic in the Fae. Carrying away the inks and pens of my old apprentices had always been a sad affair, because they'd been pure souls who wanted to do good in the world. This situation suggested that Gordie hadn't been such a soul. Trafficking Fae? I didn't know such traffic existed.

"But ... we're s'posed tae boot the likes o' ye back to the Fae planes whenever ye show up here."

"*We*, did ye say? Oh, so ye *are* like him. Just with a twee dandy mustache, all waxy and twisted."

I squinted at him, considering how to respond. Hobgoblins tend not to take well to naked aggression, but they have that pubescent sense of humor young boys have, which I can deploy rapidly when occasion demands. "It's no twee," I said. "It's luxuriant and fullbodied, like yer maw."

The hobgoblin cackled at that, and I noted that his teeth were abnormally bright and straight. It wasn't a glamour, because my sight was still warded. He'd had some work done. Since when did hobgoblins pay for cosmetic dental work?

And his clothing was notable too. I couldn't identify colors in black-and-white vision, but he wore a paisley waistcoat with a watch chain leading to the pocket, but no shirt underneath it. There was a triskele tattooed on his right shoulder, the sort I've seen associated with Druids. Black jeans and chunky black boots. Maybe he was an unusual hobgoblin after all. His eyes glittered with amusement.

"Come on, then, ol' man. Let us out."

"I will. But ye still have no told me yer name."

"For wot? Are ye gonnay send me flowers for the Yule?"

"I need to bind ye to leave this place safely."

"But then ye can bind me for anythin' else ye want in the future. I'm no letting ye have that power. Ma current situation has made me a wee bit distrustful."

"Well, I don't want tae set a hobgoblin loose in a room fulla binding inks. Do ye know who's s'posed to be buyin' ye? Or for why?"

The hobgoblin shook his head. "I don't. But yer lad Gordie had some papers over there he liked to shuffle around an' murmur over. The bird had a look an' said they were nonsense, but maybe they're no to an ol' man. Ye look like ye went tae school back when yer hair wasn't white as lilies."

I moved to the workbench and scanned the papers I saw there. Gordie had been preparing sigils for later use, but there was no helpful explanation of his business dealings. The hobgoblin might be making this all up, and I hoped he was, because otherwise Gordie *had* been an evil bastard and I'd been a consummate fool. But the fact was, Gordie had done some impressive sigil work in this room. Work that should have been impossible for him. There were sigils I hadn't taught him yet—like the Sigil of Iron Gall—which meant he'd also crafted inks for which I hadn't taught him the recipes. He'd obviously been keeping some secrets, which didn't bother me, because apprentices are supposed to do that. What bothered me was that someone was teaching him behind my back.

"I think I know who ye are," the hobgoblin said. "There's s'posed tae be a Scottish sigil agent with a waxed mustache. Are ye called MacVarnish or sumhin like that?"

"MacBharrais."

"Ah, that's it. Heard ye were sharp. But if ye had that wanker Gordie tossin' around behind ye, maybe ye're no, eh, pal?"

Maybe not. On a scrap pad where Gordie had scrawled lines in different inks to make sure the flow was good before drawing sigils, he had written: *Renfrew Ferry, 8 pm.*

"Ye said ye were s'posed tae be delivered tonight? Was it at eight?"

I got no response except a grunt and the sound of torn paper. I turned to see a triumphant hobgoblin freeing himself from the cage, one of the sigils that dampened his magic having been destroyed. He couldn't have reached it physically—I saw him fail as I entered—so he must have managed to exert some magical pull on it to bring it to his fingers. That was precisely the sort of thing that should have been impossible with multiple copies of it around him. The only explanation was that their potency must have waned significantly, the magic all leached from the ink, and with Gordie dead and obviously not paying attention, it was little wonder.

Cackling and flashing those white teeth at me, the hobgoblin leapt off the table and made for the door. I was out of position and woefully slow; there was no time to even break the seal on a prepared Sigil of Agile Grace.

"Laters, MacVarnish!" he said, and bolted out the door. A thud and screams followed shortly thereafter, and there was a shouted "I'm glad yer deid!" before a shocked silence settled in the kitchen. I emerged from the room, far too late, to see the inspector and the tech on the ground, holding their noses. The hobgoblin had leapt up and punched them for the fun of it, and Gordie's body now lay twisted in a much different position, having recently been kicked. I could still see his face, though, a look of frozen surprise that this was his end, that his brown hair was mussed and he had a few days' stubble on his neck and jaw, blue eyes widened in horror that he would be literally be caught dead wearing his Ewok pajamas.

"What in the name of fuck?" the inspector cried. "What was that just now, a pink leprechaun?" She'd had no difficulty seeing the blighter once he'd exited Gordie's room. I'd not seen the hobgoblin's skin color with my vision limited, so I filed that information away for future reference. Her eyes lit upon me and anger flared in them as she rose from the floor. The constable from outside burst into the room, also holding his nose. I needed them out of there right away, because Gordie's entire flat had to be scoured for clues. The official ID came out before they could lay into me and I gave them what for.

"Clear this flat now! Leave immediately and return tomorrow. That's an order. Go! Work on sumhin else!"

They scarpered off under the sway of the sigils and would probably return sooner rather than later when they remembered someone had punched them and they wanted answers. I needed to get answers of my own before then; Gordie had caught me napping, but I was fully awake now.